Diane Armstrong is an award-winning author whose novel *Nocturne* won the Society of Women Writers' Biennial Fiction Award in 2009. Diane was born in Poland and arrived in Australia in 1948. At the age of seven she decided to become a writer. All Diane's books have been bestsellers, and have been shortlisted for major literary awards. She has been published in Europe, Israel and the United States. Diane lives in Sydney.

By the same author

Mosaic: A Chronicle of Five Generations
The Voyage of their Life
Winter Journey
Nocturne

DIANE ARMSTRONG

FOURTH ESTATE • *London, New York, Sydney* and *Auckland*

Fourth Estate
An imprint of HarperCollins*Publishers*, Australia

HarperCollins*Publishers*
Australia • Brazil • Canada • France • Germany • Holland • India
Italy • Japan • Mexico • New Zealand • Poland • Spain • Sweden
Switzerland • United Kingdom • United States of America

HarperCollins acknowledges the Traditional Custodians
of the lands upon which we live and work, and pays respect
to Elders past and present.

First published in Australia in 2011
by HarperCollins*Publishers* Australia Pty Limited
ABN 36 009 913 517
harpercollins.com.au

HarperCollins*Publishers*
Macken House, 39/40 Mayor Street Upper
Dublin 1, D01 C9W8, Ireland

A catalogue record for this book is available from the National Library of Australia

ISBN 978 0 7322 9090 0 (paperback)

Cover design by Darren Holt, HarperCollins Design Studio
Cover images: children by Kurt Hutton/ Getty Images; all other images by shutterstock.com
Author photograph by Keith Arnold
Typeset in Sabon LT Std 12/20pt by Letter Spaced

For Michael

Chapter 1

As soon as Hania heard the explosion she looked at her mother's face and knew that the fragile calm of their home had been shattered.

Eda Kotowicz sprang towards her and clutched her arm. 'They're shooting!' she cried, her eyes wide with terror.

She pushed Hania past the table heaped with woollen jackets and skirts waiting to be hemmed, and they stumbled to the back of the house where a stained bathtub stood between the mangle and the copper laundry tub.

'Quick, get down,' Eda panted. 'They'll be here any minute.'

Hania crouched behind the rusting tub, her fingers scraping against the rough surface as she squirmed to free herself from her mother's grip.

She tried to speak but her mother clamped a hand over her mouth and whispered, 'For God's sake, don't make a sound.'

As the frightening staccato noise continued, they heard someone banging on their front door. Her mother's body grew rigid and her eyes became black pinpoints of alarm.

'I won't let them get you,' she mouthed.

They heard people running and shouting, but the thumping on the door didn't let up, and above the din they heard a girl's voice calling out, 'Hanny, come out and see the fireworks.'

Hania pulled away from her mother and ran down the hallway, almost tripping on the worn cotton runner in her haste to open the front door. Beverley, her friend from across the road, was jumping from one foot to the other, and flicking her fine fair hair from her eyes.

'Hurry up, Hanny. You'll miss all the fun!'

Hania liked Beverley's version of her name. Hanny sounded affectionate and made her feel less foreign.

Beverley was pulling her arm. 'Come on, it's Cracker Night, and we've still got loads of Roman candles and double bungers left.'

Hania stood on the narrow verandah of their Bondi Junction semi under the curved iron roof, and stared at the bonfire blazing in the middle of the road. So that was what the teacher had meant by Empire Day, and why the boys in the street had spent the afternoon collecting bits of wood and fallen branches and piling them up on the edge of the pavement.

She hardly recognised Wattle Street. Night had fallen quickly, and the sky was the colour of the dried ink inside the inkwell on her desk at school. The crackling flames leaping towards the starlit sky, and the flash of the fireworks lighting up the faces of the children as they darted around, gave this ordinary backstreet an air of mystery. It was like watching a magic show: nothing was as it seemed, and anything could happen.

'Hey, youse kids, hurry up with them branches.'

Hania looked around and saw their neighbour, Pop Wilson, throwing bits of wood onto the fire. Straightening up with a groan, he wiped the sweat dripping down his knobbly nose. His face, which was always red, now resembled a ripe tomato about to burst.

Behind him, Beverley's father, Bill Noble, snapped a branch across his knee and threw it onto the fire while small boys raced around it, whooping and yelling. They hurled their tom thumbs on the ground and ran for their lives when they heard the bang. A safe distance from the flames the girls let off Catherine wheels and Roman candles; the little kids waved sparklers, their eyes round with wonder at the arabesques of light.

Hania gazed at the lively scene around the bonfire, and ached with envy. They were all so light-hearted and carefree, even the parents, and their lives were so uncomplicated.

Once, she had felt like that too. That was back in Poland, when she had lived with people she loved. Every Sunday they would take her to church where the priest used to say that the Jews had crucified Our Lord.

She had been happy there until the day a strange woman suddenly appeared, thin, bony and angry like a witch in a fairytale. Hania was eight, and by then she'd spent almost six years with the Majewskis, whom she called Mamusia and Tatuś, and whom she regarded as her parents. She shrank from the strange woman's embrace, and she clung to Mamusia's hand when the woman started crying and shouting. Without raising her voice, Mamusia said that they'd risked their life to look after Hania and they'd die before they let her go.

To Hania's relief the woman went away, but the following day, when her foster parents were out, she reappeared. 'You have to come with me, I'm your mother, and I love you. You're not Catholic, you're Jewish, you're my child,' she kept saying.

Hania felt sick. She didn't believe any of the shocking things this woman was telling her, but the woman dragged her away and took her to Warsaw. She never saw her foster parents again.

Even though four years had passed, every night before she fell asleep, Hania wished she could hear her foster mother's soothing voice again and feel her gentle hand stroking her hair.

Her reverie was broken by her mother's shrill voice. 'Come inside!' Eda shouted. 'Look at those stupid people, lighting fires and setting off explosions. It's dangerous. Come inside at once!'

Hania sighed and looked around, reddening with embarrassment because their neighbours, Mrs Browning and Miss McNulty, were standing nearby, listening to her mother's angry foreign words.

Verna Browning, who was leaning against her picket fence, gave Hania a sympathetic smile. Although she couldn't understand what Mrs Kotowicz had said, she could hear the anger in her voice, and she felt sorry for her daughter who was obviously not allowed to join in the fun.

'What a shame,' she said in a low voice to her next-door neighbour. 'She'd probably like to come outside like the other kids.'

Maude McNulty tightened her lips and smoothed down the crossover apron she wore over her grey woollen dress.

'These people don't fit in,' she said. 'The government's making a big mistake bringing them out here with their strange ways. Oil and water don't mix. Australia for the Australians, that's what I say.'

'But Our Lord says we should love our neighbour,' Verna said.

'Charity begins at home,' Maude McNulty rejoined. 'Anyway, some of these foreigners aren't even Christians. They're changing our country, and not for the better.'

Verna pushed a strand of white hair from her plump face and murmured something vague that stopped short of assent. If only Alf was still alive. He always knew what was right, while she could never make up her mind about these matters. It was true that a lot of foreigners had settled in Bondi Junction in the past couple of years. In their street alone, apart from Hanny and her highly strung mother with the unpronounceable surname, there was that strange European fellow across the road. And another foreign family had moved in a couple of weeks ago, a couple with a pretty daughter, who kept to themselves.

She looked up and saw the newcomers standing inside their gate. She waved and the wife gave a timid smile, but the man just bowed and looked away, as stiff as a clockwork toy.

Whenever she went shopping in the Junction these days, Verna heard foreign voices, and they always sounded as though they were arguing. And these peculiar shops were springing up, called 'delicatessens', which sold smelly cheeses and dark bread speckled with funny seeds. But at the same time she felt sorry for these people. It must be terrible to leave your home and country and start again in a place where you couldn't even speak the language.

She turned to Maude McNulty. 'Mr Calwell says we need migrants,' she said.

'That's all very well, but he doesn't have to live next door to them,' her neighbour retorted. 'I wouldn't be surprised if they were Communists. Once you could understand what everyone was saying but nowadays they're all jabbering in their own lingo on the trams and buses, loud as you like. No manners. They should all go back where they came from if they don't want to learn English.'

She lowered her voice and moved closer. 'And I don't believe they're so poor, either. Only yesterday there was an article in the *Daily Standard* saying they were buying up all the flats.'

That gave Verna the opportunity to change the subject to something closer to her heart. 'Ted's got a job on the *Daily Standard*,' she said proudly. 'He's not a cadet any more. He's wanted to be a journalist ever since he was a nipper, and now he's done it.'

Maude McNulty nodded and turned her attention back to the fireworks. 'Empire Day isn't what it used to be,' she mused as more rockets and Roman candles flashed in the darkness. 'In my day we had wonderful pageants and parades, and the ships in Port Jackson were lit up like Christmas trees. Even the ice carts and potato stalls had Union Jacks on them. Every year thousands of us children would form a giant Union Jack in Centennial Park. Did I ever tell you about the time I headed the procession dressed as Britannia, in a helmet and shield and a long white frock?'

Verna Browning nodded absently. She'd heard this Empire Day story every year on 24 May since she'd moved to Wattle Street as a bride twenty-five years before. Despite its name, there were no wattle trees on the street even then, only the same low hedges and the frangipani trees whose trunks twisted towards the sun and scattered their creamy flowers on the footpath.

Back then all the homes were semis, snuggled up against each other like stitches cast too tightly on knitting needles, and all the neighbours knew each other. These days blocks of flats were springing up all over the place, and some of the large homes were being turned into boarding houses. The Aussies still left their front doors open all day so the kids could run in and out, but with all the foreigners flooding in, things were changing fast.

Verna looked up, and in the window across the road she saw a man's pale face. As she watched, the light was switched off. A few moments later a shadowy figure emerged from the gate and disappeared into the night.

Maude McNulty, whose rapier gaze never missed anything, nudged her. 'Did you see that?' she whispered in a conspiratorial tone. 'It's the mystery man. He's like a ghost. Never talks to anyone. I'd like to be a fly on the wall and see what he's doing in there, with all that tapping and hammering. Must be up to something.'

Verna didn't like gossiping, but she couldn't deny that there was something odd about the man. He walked without seeming to move, never looked you in the eye and, although he'd moved in several months before, she had never heard his voice. As far as she knew, he'd never spoken to anyone in the street.

She noticed Hanny, the little foreign girl next door, watching the fireworks from inside her gate. 'Come outside, love,' Verna called. 'You'll get a better view.'

But Hania shook her head so vehemently that her thick brown plaits bounced against her white school blouse.

'I'm all right, thank you, Mrs Browning,' she said in her foreign accent, and Verna marvelled that after such a short time in Australia Hanny could already speak English.

'You can call me Aunty Verna,' she said. 'The other kids do.'

* * *

Hania had noticed that all the children on Wattle Street called the adults 'aunty' and 'uncle'. They all had real aunts and uncles, too, as well as cousins, grandparents and godparents. After their visits, the kids would come out into the street and show off their new socks, hankies or Little Golden Books. Hania liked calling the neighbours aunty and uncle, but when her mother had heard her addressing Beverley's father as Uncle Bill, she'd worked herself up into a rage. 'He's not your uncle! Your aunts and uncles are dead and don't you forget it. These people are total strangers.'

Hania was turning to go back inside when the boy across the street, the freckled kid they all called Meggsie, jumped over her fence. His nose was smeared with ashes from the bonfire, and his hair, which was the colour of boiled pumpkin, stuck out from the top of his head like a cockscomb.

'Here y'are,' he said, handing her a sparkler which sizzled with tiny stars. 'Wave it around. Don't be scared. It won't hurt you.'

As she stretched out her arm to take it, she felt her mother's hand grip her shoulder. 'How many times have I told you to come inside?' she shouted. 'Shut the door and get in now!'

'I'll stick it in the fence so you can see it from inside,' Meggsie called out.

Hania went into her room, slammed the door and listened for her mother's footsteps, half expecting her to burst in and shout at her again, but the house was quiet. She was probably hemming the clothes she'd brought home from the factory. Tiptoeing to her bookshelf, she took down her Polish edition of *Alice in Wonderland* and poked her finger inside the brown-paper cover until she felt a tiny object wrapped in tissue paper. She unwrapped it, and took out a small gold cross. Stroking it lovingly, she knelt beside her bed and, exulting in her defiance, put her hands together and prayed to Jesus to restore her to her foster parents.

Chapter 2

The bonfire was still crackling and sparks were flying into the night sky when Emil Bronstein slipped out of his house that evening. From the way the two women across the road were watching him, he sensed they'd been talking about him; pulling his hat low over his narrow face, he continued walking.

With its small brim and the dark green feather in the grosgrain band, Emil's hat broadcast its European origin in defiant contrast to the understated wide-brimmed fedoras worn by Australian men. It was the jaunty style he'd always worn before the war, and he'd bought it just before boarding the ship, without realising that it didn't suit his state of mind or his new country.

The pungent smell of cordite and the smoke rising from the bonfire made his chest constrict until his breath came in short gasps. A black cat with a heart-shaped white spot on its chest shot across the road in front of him, terrified by the bunger one of the boys had just hurled to the ground. The children were still running around, yelling and letting off crackers, while their mothers shouted at them to be careful and not to go too close to the fire. Emil hunched his shoulders and, quickening his pace, left the noise and smoke behind.

At the end of Wattle Street, past the corner shop with its posters for Kinkara Tea, Craven 'A' cigarettes, Vincents APC Powders and Dr McKenzie's Menthoids, Emil turned into Barton Street. The spacious two-storey homes with their wrought-iron balconies contrasted with the labourers' semis in Wattle Street, but Emil didn't pay them much attention. He walked rapidly without knowing where he was going, driven by a need to keep moving. High above him the night sky glittered with a million stars whose icy beauty reinforced his solitary existence and the indifference of the universe.

In Glenayr Avenue the elaborate façade of Kings Cinema was hung with gaudy posters advertising the coming attractions. Emil stopped and stared at the face on the poster which had been pasted so carelessly onto the wall that the face was pleated with tiny creases. The man whose compelling gaze seemed to pierce the poster wore a shiny top hat, a scarlet cape and a neatly trimmed black beard. Behind him a woman seemed to float in the air, and on one side a girl spilling out of a tight sequined dress was pointing a pistol at the magician. In thick black letters the notice announced that in a month's time, Morris the Magnificent would electrify the audience with his death-defying bullet act.

As he gazed at the poster, Emil could feel his fingers moving as though of their own volition. He imagined they were spinning dozens of billiard balls at a time, making bouquets of flowers appear and disappear, sawing a woman clean in half. He saw the audience's eyes widened in amazement, and heard their gasps of terror.

He shook himself violently to dispel this memory of a world which, at the whim of an evil wizard, had disintegrated into a heap of ashes.

He made a strange sound, which might have been a groan or a sob, and forced his attention back to the advertisement. Even in this remote corner of the world, performers were emulating the feats of the great magicians in the never-ending quest to surprise their audiences and enjoy the hollow triumph of eliciting gasps of wonder and amazement. For that moment of suspended disbelief, that victory of illusion over reality, they were prepared to risk their reputations and even their lives.

'Never again,' he muttered as he pulled the rough collar of his coat higher against the wind that blew up from the beach.

He walked on, past blocks of red-brick flats, until he found himself facing the famous curve of pale sand, photos of which he'd seen in travel books back in Germany. He sank onto a wooden bench, breathing in the sharp, salt smell of the sea, and listening to the crash of the waves as they hit the shore. A scruffy dog ran around a nearby lamppost, raised its leg and a moment later left a dark stain at its base. A couple strolled past, their arms around each other, whispering and laughing.

Alone in the darkness of the May night with the relentless boom of the waves in his ears, he didn't know how long he sat contemplating the immensity of the ocean. With the taste of salt on his lips and the dull roar of the rollers resounding in his head, he walked away from the beach but, lost in his thoughts, he didn't notice the kerb and tripped. When he looked down, he saw that the sole of his right shoe had come away from the upper. He cursed under his breath. These were the only shoes he had.

By the time he hobbled back to Wattle Street, the bonfire had gone out, but the smell of smoke and cordite still hung in the air. Some of the adults were talking in low voices by their front gates and stamping their feet against the cold.

'I reckon it's been a good Cracker Night, don't you?'

Startled, he turned in the direction of the voice. It was Kath, the woman next door. She was watching her son, the red-headed boy they called Meggsie, whose face was smudged with soot. He was running around helping the men clean up the street, picking up the paper wrappers ripped from the fireworks, gathering bits of wood and scooping the ashes into a dustpan.

Emil could see that she would have liked to chat, but he gave her a curt nod and looked down at his shoes.

'It's gone cold now,' she said, and pulled the woollen cardigan closer around her full breasts. 'I'm just waiting for Meggsie. The others are already in bed. At least they'd better be!'

He was still looking down, and she followed his gaze.

'Your shoe! What a shame. Hang on a minute and I'll go inside and get you some Kromite. That's how I fix the boys' shoes.'

Emil knew that Kath was bringing up four sons on her own, and that she worked as a barmaid in one of the pubs in Bondi

Junction, but whether she was widowed or divorced he had no idea. He didn't want to know, didn't want to become involved with these people. He made a noncommittal sound and started moving towards his gate, but she was already hurrying out with a flat piece of black rubber and a tube of adhesive. She handed it to him and explained how to repair the sole.

'Don't forget to give it time to stick down,' she called, but he'd already disappeared inside.

Men were a strange lot, that was for sure, Kath mused as she leaned against her fence and watched Meggsie rushing around. But there was something about this foreign bloke that aroused her interest. He was like a ghost doomed to roam the world searching in vain for a warm corner to rest.

She was used to silent men. Her father had hardly uttered a word for years. That was during the Depression, after he'd lost his job and they were evicted from their house. Her throat still closed up whenever she remembered sitting on the pavement beside their rolled-up mattresses and bundles of pillows and blankets, like a mob of gypsies. Her baby sister screamed and her little brothers kept nagging that they were hungry and tired, but she was too shocked to speak, terrified in case any of the girls from her class saw her and found out that they'd been thrown out for not paying the rent.

All the stuffing went out of her father after that. He grew increasingly demoralised by having to join the long queue at Circular Quay every week for their food coupons, then trudging over to Central Railway to collect the rations and walking all the way home again because he couldn't afford the tram fare. He'd started pilfering from the metal box under the bed where her mother kept the shillings she'd so carefully saved, and spent them at the pub.

Her grandmother had taken the six of them in, although she was on a widow's pension herself and lived in two rooms over a shop in Randwick. But her hospitality came at a bitter price: a diet of bread and dripping, and a never-ending litany of complaints about no-hopers bludging off others. Kath's mother took in washing and ironing from the mansions on the hill to earn a few coins and railed at Kath's father night after night. After a year or so she started coughing, a dry, rasping cough that left her gasping and exhausted.

'He knows how to make babies but not how to look after them,' Kath's acid-tongued grandmother used to mutter, flashing Kath's father dirty looks. But Kath loved her dad. He scoured the neighbourhood for things more affluent neighbours had discarded, and sometimes brought little presents home for them. She still remembered her joy when he gave her the music box with the spinning ballerina, which she'd kept to this day.

He cobbled together a billycart for the boys out of bits of wood and some old pram wheels. At night, his tongue loosened by the drink, he'd tell fanciful stories about Irish leprechauns, Scottish hobgoblins and Celtic wizards and he'd call her his *mavourneen.* She had no idea what it meant but it made her feel special.

When her father died, the doctor said it was heart trouble, and her grandmother said it was the drink, but Kath knew he drank because he despised himself for being weak and useless. By then her mother had started coughing up blood, and a year later she was dead.

'You'd better come in now,' Kath called to Meggsie. 'You know you've got to be up early.' The boy was up at five every morning to do his paper round, and the few bob he brought home came in handy. She knew the other women in the street looked down on her for being a barmaid, but if she had a job they approved of, like standing all day in a neat black frock at Attwaters department store, selling yards of ribbon and bias binding, she wouldn't earn enough to feed and clothe her boys.

Anyway, she didn't care what the old biddies in the street thought. But what did hurt was the way her gran kept muttering that 'the apple doesn't fall far from the tree'. It wasn't just that she worked in a pub. Ever since she'd married Jack, Gran had never missed an opportunity to have a dig at her, because she'd committed the unforgiveable sin of marrying a Protestant.

Becoming a barmaid had not been a career choice but a solution of last resort. She'd been good at school, proud of her neat copperplate handwriting on the slate, and the columns of sums that always added up. Her teacher had said she should go to secretarial college, but her education ended at thirteen when her mother died and she'd had to leave school to help

Gran look after the younger kids. She met Jack when she was sixteen, and by then she couldn't wait to escape from the misery of life with her grandmother.

Ten years later Jack shot through, and she was left with no money, no training, and four kids to look after, so drawing beer was the best job she could get. The tips weren't bad, especially after Mick Kelly, one of the regulars, started calling her Rita.

'Hey, cop a load of this sheila!' he shouted soon after she started work behind the counter. 'Rita Hayworth's pouring our beer!' The others craned forward, saw the thick auburn hair parted on the side and falling in waves down to her shoulders, the hourglass figure, and the look that warned them not to get fresh, and the nickname stuck.

But even with tips, it was a struggle to put food on the table for four boys who were always hungry, and to find twenty-five shillings for rent every Monday. Cyril Aldred, the publican, had often hinted that nothing would make him happier than to give her a raise, if only she were more friendly. He wanted her to stay back some evenings after six, when the pub closed, but she figured her best bet was to treat his suggestions as a joke. 'Now what would Mrs Aldred say about that?' she'd quip, but instead of cooling his ardour, her flippant remarks had the opposite effect, and she noticed that lately he was finding more opportunities to corner her in the cellar or behind the stairs.

A clanking sound roused her from her reverie and she

smiled as she watched Meggsie help Bill Noble drag a rubbish tin into the middle of the road. He was laughing as if it was the best fun he'd ever had. That kid was halfway there and back again, she chuckled to herself. But he had his serious side too, and sometimes she forgot he was only twelve and talked to him as though he were an adult, confiding in him about her worries.

'Come on, love,' she said. 'Come inside, I'll make you some Milo.'

'I won't be long, Mum,' he called. 'I'm just going to help Uncle Bill take the bin out the back.'

She nodded and went inside. She sat down at the small kitchen table and took out the lined exercise book in which she kept a tally of every penny she spent, alarmed at the speed with which the money melted away, even though she economised as much as she could. From her grandmother she'd learned to make bubble-and-squeak from leftover potatoes and vegetables, and she knew dozens of ways to cook mince.

That was one good thing about her job. Blokes were always coming into the pub with stuff they reckoned had fallen off a truck. Spuds were still scarce, but they often managed to get hold of a pound or two for her, and sometimes they brought in a chook as well. They sidled in, and by the way they winked and gestured, she knew they'd brought in something 'on the QT', as they called it.

Only the week before, Mr Aldred had held out a ring, which he said was an emerald. 'It's for you,' he whispered, pushing his face against her cheek so she could smell his beery breath. 'It matches your eyes.'

'Now where would I wear that?' she had said lightly, pushing past him to avoid his puckered mouth, which was always moist at the corners like the slimy trails that snails leave behind.

The blokes hadn't been in with chooks for a while, and it was time for the rabbit-o to come around to Wattle Street again. Rabbits were much cheaper than chooks, and the man always skinned them on the doorstep, but she couldn't bring herself to eat them, though the boys had no such qualms. She turned her attention back to her exercise book and made a shopping list.

Her boys were growing fast, and not in chronological order. Alan was already taller than his older brothers. She darned their socks until there was more darn than sock, and mended the holes in their shoes with Kromite, but Ray had outgrown his and she wondered where she'd find the money to buy new ones.

Kath dozed off with her head on the exercise book, the pencil still in her hand. She dreamed that she was buying Ray's shoes at Gardiner's shoe store when a policeman grabbed her. 'You're under arrest because those shoes fell off a truck,' he shouted. She tried to tell him she couldn't go to jail because she had four kids to look after, but he pushed her into the back of the paddy wagon and slammed the door behind her. She woke with a start, relieved that it wasn't the paddy wagon but her front door closing behind Meggsie, who'd just come home.

Chapter 3

Ted Browning tightened his grip on the leather strap as the tram swung around the corner of Elizabeth Street, past the mannequins decked out in woollen suits and coats with big padded shoulders in the plate-glass windows of David Jones department store. Suddenly the tram lurched to a halt, narrowly missing a 1948 Austin that had tried to overtake it, and Ted almost dropped the *Daily Commercial News and Shipping List* with its notification of migrant ships arriving in Sydney. He'd circled the SS *Napoli* which had left Genoa seven weeks before and docked at Circular Quay that morning, bringing another six hundred migrants from Europe.

The tram rattled towards the Quay, and the conductor walked along the running board, calling, 'Fez pliz' in his nasal voice. As the passengers handed him their threepences or fourpences, he bent down to tear the tickets from his scuffed leather pouch and the metal badge on his cap glinted in the morning light.

Ted slid into a vacant seat and felt in the pocket of his jacket to make sure his shorthand notebook was still there. For the tenth time he went over the questions he wanted to ask the new arrivals, to avoid another tirade from his boss.

'Your last story was shit, and if you file another one like it I'll push it up your arse and make you eat your words,' Gus Thornton had roared the previous week, and from the smirks of the other reporters in the newsroom, he knew they'd heard every word. Gus made no secret of his contempt for young reporters whom he described as untrained, unintelligent and unemployable.

Although his dream of becoming a reporter on Sydney's most popular daily tabloid had come true, Ted had a sneaking suspicion that he'd gone after the wrong job. Not even in the American pulp novels he liked reading did editors behave like dictators, caring only about sensation and circulation. And since the *Daily Standard* had now outsold every other paper in the city, its editor had become an absolute monarch.

'Are you sure you want to work on that paper?' his mother had asked the night before, pointing at the sensational headline above a photo of a girl flaunting her large breasts in a low-cut blouse.

Ted shrugged. 'People want to be entertained as well as informed, you know.'

His mother didn't reply because just then an unpleasant odour wafted in from next door. She sniffed. 'Is that garlic?' she murmured, wrinkling her nose. 'Our foreign neighbour — I can never pronounce her name — seems to use an awful lot of it.'

Despite Gus's intimidating manner, Ted loved the adrenalin rush of working on this paper. He didn't expect his mother to understand the lure of being right in the centre of exciting events, of being part of an exclusive group of people the public admired and despised at the same time. He wanted to reveal facts that crooks, standover men and politicians wanted to conceal, and to write articles that exposed crime and corruption. And you could do that working on a tabloid as well as on a broadsheet.

As the tram swung around towards the Quay, the office buildings and department stores that cast long shadows and blocked the light from the narrow city streets were replaced by an expanse of grey water which splashed against the harbour wall, spraying foam onto the pathway. Wooden ferries painted green and yellow squatted at the jetties, and in the distance the triangular white sails of small yachts bobbed in the waves, framed by the great iron arch of the 'Coathanger'. Although it was sixteen years since the bridge across the harbour had been completed, whenever Ted saw it he remembered how, as a small boy, he'd watched the two parts of that arch coming together in slow motion until they finally met.

He jumped off the tram at Circular Quay. An unshaven man in baggy trousers held up with string threw something into a rubbish bin, missed, and seagulls screeched as they swooped down on the remains of his greasy potato scallops.

A gust of wind from the harbour blew off his grey felt hat and ruffled his light brown hair, which fell across his forehead. As he pushed his hair back with his hand, he wished the barber would get rid of the kink that made him look like a schoolboy even though he was twenty-two. He chased the hat along the waterfront, rammed it on his head, and hurried on.

Past the pier, three old men sat on the seawall, empty buckets beside them, reeling in trails of slimy seaweed.

'There's a young bloke in a hurry,' one of them said, tossing a cigarette butt into the water. 'Slow down, son,' he called to Ted. 'Time always catches up with you in the end.'

'I'm hurrying so it can't catch me,' Ted retorted, and heard the men laughing. 'Cheeky bugger,' one of them called out.

He found the SS *Napoli* moored near Bennelong Point. It was a grey hulk with rust stains showing through a sloppy paint job. Probably another of those cargo ships that had been hastily converted to carry human cargo: displaced Europeans. Looking up, Ted saw passengers wandering around the deck or leaning over the rail, looking anxiously for familiar faces on the wharf below. He was relieved he'd got there in time, before they disembarked.

'Where do you think you're going?' one of the wharf officials barked, blocking his path. 'Can't you read? No unauthorised persons allowed.'

Ted was on the point of explaining why he had come when he changed his mind. They mightn't be keen on reporters snooping around.

'It's all right,' he said, flashing a confident smile. He held up his press card in front of the man's face and whipped it away before he had time to read it. 'I'm a security officer. Where's Captain Karamanlis?'

The man looked uncertain and glanced around for someone in authority to check Ted's credentials, but there was no one in sight. He shrugged and waved him on. 'Ask one of the officers when you get on board,' he said. 'That's if you can get those dagoes to understand anything you say.'

Ted ran up the gangplank and slipped into the lounge to mingle with the passengers before any of the officers noticed him. The room had the sour smell of mould, overcooked vegetables, and stale sweat, and the air was charged with tension. The passengers were impatient to disembark but some problem on the wharf had delayed the unloading of the luggage. Children chased each other around the deck, shouting, and adults made ineffectual attempts to control them while their eyes darted towards the portholes to see if anything was happening.

Some passengers were pacing around, taking nervous puffs of their cigarettes and talking excitedly, while others were staring anxiously at the Quay and the tangle of crooked streets rising from it as they tried to read their future in the red-tiled roofs of their new country.

Ted was bewildered by the babble of voices, all speaking different languages. This was what the Tower of Babel must have been like, he thought, and made a note to include that observation in his article. He went over to a group of passengers who were sitting on bright green leather chairs in a corner of the lounge. Taking his notebook and pencil from the inside pocket of his tweed jacket, he cleared his throat, smiled brightly and introduced himself.

'I'd like to tell Australians about your impressions of the voyage,' he said. 'What it was like?'

Most of them stared blankly at him or shook their heads to indicate that they didn't understand, but a small blonde in a little head-hugging hat pushed forward.

'There are many Communists on this ship,' she said in a ringing voice, her sharp features contorted with fury. 'It is very shocking. I come from Lithuania to get away from them and they are here with us. Every day they sing the "Internationale". In Russian!'

A stooped man behind her spoke up. 'And I can tell you another thing about this ship,' he said. 'Too many Jew Communists.'

Now that these two had broken the ice, others began to air similar grievances. Some came from countries Ted couldn't place on the map, like Latvia, Lithuania, Ukraine and Estonia. A tall, thin man planted himself in front of him. 'Those are bad peoples. They should not be allowed here. You will see, this is Fifth Column. They come to spread Communism and destroy Australian government.'

Ted's heart was racing. Communists coming here by the boatload! Gus Thornton wanted a sensational story and he would give him one. Ever since the war had ended three years ago, the Reds had overrun much of Europe. Some people said that one war had ended and another had begun. Everyone was on the alert, watching for signs of Commies trying to worm their way into power. Especially now that Mr Chifley had won the election, and they had a Labor government supported by trade unions which, as everyone knew, were riddled with Commies.

Gus often said that Eisenhower shouldn't have pulled out in 1945 but should have gone on and fought the Bolsheviks, to stop them taking over most of Europe. 'The next war will be between us and the Soviets,' he predicted whenever they heard about Communist repression in eastern Europe. Although Ted, like most people, was suspicious of the Reds and their agenda, he wondered if people were going overboard with this Communist hysteria.

Only a few weeks before, he'd been sent to interview an Australian pianist who had refused to play 'God Save the King' at the beginning of her recitals in the Town Hall. 'Make sure you get her to admit she's a fucking Commie, or at the very least a fellow traveller,' Gus had ranted. But she'd looked at Ted with bewildered eyes and told him that she had performed all over the world, and nowhere else had she been expected to play the national anthem at her concerts.

Within a few minutes he was besieged by people complaining about Communists on board. Some of them mentioned Jew Communists, which to Ted seemed a contradiction in terms. From what he'd always heard, Jews owned gold and property — not the kind of people who'd be Communists.

The comments were becoming repetitive, and apart from accusations about Russian songs, no one had any proof. He needed to find people with a different point of view.

Out on the stern deck, a small group of passengers sat huddled around a pile of battered valises.

'You look for Communists? Here?' A woman with short curly hair looked at Ted in amazement. 'Nazis you should look for!'

He thought he had misheard. 'Nazis? On this ship?'

She was nodding so energetically that the curls sprang out and bounced around her face. 'Moshe, come and tell this gentleman what people we had on this ship.'

A slightly built young man glanced around and motioned for Ted to follow him inside. 'You want to hear about Nazis? Come with me.'

'Just a minute,' Ted broke in. 'I don't get it. You said Nazis. But we're not allowing any Germans into Australia unless they've been cleared by immigration, so how can there be Nazis?'

Moshe gave a derisive laugh and said something to his companions. Turning back to Ted, he said, 'Not German Nazis. Nazi helpers in Lithuania, Hungary, Ukraine and Croatia.'

Ted felt he was getting out of his depth. This didn't make any sense. The only Nazis he'd ever heard of were Germans. Moshe looked Jewish, so maybe he was paranoid, as Gus used to say. Ted knew that Gus had no time for Jews. 'Fucking troublemakers,' he called them. 'Money-grubbers. Always complaining of being persecuted.'

Moshe walked over to a fellow with a shock of fair hair who was sitting on a worn case tied with string. 'Hey, Peter, he wants to know about Nazis,' he said, pointing to Ted.

Peter nodded. 'At my table in dining room, mens from Lithuania, they talking to Ukrainian mens in German, so I understand. They say they in militia, they shoot Jews in Kaunas. They say, too many Jews on ship, why we did not kill them all? Also man from Ukraine say his group kill Jews in sandhills near Lwów.'

Ted felt dazed. All these extraordinary stories and strange place-names. Could he believe these people? Their intensity was certainly compelling. He'd never heard of those militias and had no idea that they'd collaborated with the Nazis. Surely men who'd done things like that wouldn't be allowed into Australia? This was far more complicated than he'd expected. He'd have to talk to someone from the Immigration Department and check it out.

Back in the office, he knocked on Gus Thornton's door, eager to tell him what he'd heard.

The editor was enthroned on his raised dais, surrounded by a fug of cigarette smoke. With his mountainous body dressed in a 1930s American gangster-style suit with wide stripes, big padded shoulders and a red polka-dot bow tie, Gus Thornton reminded Ted of an underworld character from a Dick Tracy comic. He listened to Ted with narrowed eyes, puffing on the thin black Sobranie in his gold cigarette-holder.

'Bloody waste of time,' he roared when Ted had finished. 'Just rumour and hearsay. Can't trust anything these people tell you. They all hate each other.'

Then he shrugged. 'Go with the "Red Menace arriving on migrant ships" story. Three hundred words, no more. Write a lead that will grab the readers by the balls, and keep it snappy. I don't want a fucking novel.'

'But what about the Nazis?'

'What about them?' Gus shouted. 'If you want to write a story about the kikes, find out how come they arrive here with enough dough to buy blocks of flats before they have time to say Ikey Solomon.'

Ted took a deep breath. Trying to keep his voice steady, he asked, 'If I find proof, can I run the story about the Nazis?'

His editor's reply could be heard at the other end of the building, but it wasn't fit to be repeated in polite company.

Chapter 4

Verna Browning was hanging Ted's white shirts on the line, but her mind had wandered back to her wedding day twenty-five years before. She had been close to thirty by then, already on the plump side, and she'd been resigned to staying on the shelf, when one of the English girls in the office had introduced her to her brother. 'He's a bit on the quiet side,' she'd said, as though apologising, but Verna liked the lanky bloke with the slow Somerset accent who only spoke when he had something to say. She knew from the moment they met that this was a man she could rely on. He was solid. Alf wasn't given to compliments but he told her that he liked her because she wasn't empty-headed like other girls he'd known. And he liked the way she listened when he talked. A few weeks later he asked her to marry him.

Verna was daydreaming about her wedding day when Maude McNulty poked her head over the loose palings of the wooden fence which separated their backyards.

'Did you know that some new reffos moved into the house on the corner yesterday?' she said. 'A young couple they were. Their suitcase was held together with a bit of rope. I wonder where this lot came from.'

Verna took the wooden peg from her mouth and continued hanging out the washing. Maude McNulty never missed a thing. 'That woman should join the police force,' Ted often said. 'She'd catch more crooks than most of the cops I come across.'

'There are four reffos living in that place already,' Maude McNulty was saying. 'How come they're allowed to let so many rooms?'

Verna shrugged. 'That's what boarding houses are for, I suppose.' She took another shirt from the wicker basket, shook it several times to loosen the creases, surveyed it and decided that next time she'd add more Reckitt's blue to the rinse water.

'It's not right,' her neighbour persisted. 'There should be a law against it. This isn't India. Anyway, they're taking up all the rooms and flats. No wonder the boys coming home from the war can't find anywhere to live.'

Verna put another peg in her mouth and nodded. It was true. Just the other day she'd got talking to a young woman who told her that she and her husband had to live with his parents because they couldn't find a place of their own and they couldn't afford key money for a flat. Every day she read angry letters in the paper from people who blamed the government and the migrants for the housing shortage, and the *Women's Weekly* was full of articles advising women how to deal tactfully with the mothers-in-law they were living with.

She didn't think the migrants could be blamed for all the housing problems, though, and, tired of the complaints, she turned back to the clothes line, hoping that her neighbour would take the hint. From the corner of her eye she saw Maude McNulty was still there, her sharp eyes darting all over the yard.

'The Johnsons are clever, letting out all those rooms, I'll give them that,' the old woman said. 'With this flood of reffos, I reckon they'll soon make enough to retire.'

Picking up the empty basket, Verna retreated inside, letting the door close behind her more loudly than she'd intended. She wondered what had turned her neighbour into such a misery, and what Maude McNulty had been like in her youth, although she couldn't imagine her ever being young.

She sniffed as she passed the mountain of newspapers piled up in one corner of the passageway that ran between her semi and the one Hanny and her mother were renting. Ted bought every newspaper and magazine and insisted on keeping them all, though when he'd get round to reading them, heaven only knew. Moisture had rotted the tattered edges, and from the musty smell that rose from the yellowed papers, she suspected that the neighbourhood cats had sprayed them to claim their territory. Exasperated, she decided to get rid of the papers once and for all.

The houses on her side of Wattle Street backed onto a narrow lane where the rubbish bins were kept, and she was stuffing the papers into her bin when a woman appeared at the other end of the lane, looking rather lost. Verna had never seen her before, and she wondered if this was the one who had just moved in.

'How're you going, love, all right?' she called out.

The woman seemed to be looking at the rubbish bin.

'The garbo's coming tomorrow,' Verna said and, seeing the woman's puzzled expression, mimicked tipping the rubbish out. 'Tomorrow morning,' she said.

'Ah, tomorrow,' the woman repeated in a foreign accent.

Verna walked down the alleyway towards her, picking her way among the long grasses and the vines of morning glory draped over the fences. In spring, nasturtiums sprang up in the grass, exuding their strange metallic scent, and in summer the grass was sprinkled with the yolk-coloured weeds the kids called wet-the-beds. When honeysuckle climbed on the vines, they'd pull off the scented flowers and suck the nectar from their stems. Every afternoon after school, the lane resounded with the noise of children playing in the paddock on the other side, but in the mornings the lane was quiet.

Verna was panting by the time she reached the newcomer. 'Anything you want to know, just ask me, okay? I'm Mrs Browning. I live down there,' she said, and pointed. 'Number seventeen.'

The woman nodded and said something that Verna didn't catch. Perhaps her name, which sounded something like Sal or Sally. She was about twenty-five, Verna thought, tall and pleasant-looking, with curly brown hair pulled back from her wide forehead and rolled up at the back. She had a wistful expression. She probably missed her homeland and the people she'd left behind. But at least she had a husband, according to what Maude McNulty had said.

Verna sighed. Her married life had come to a sudden end with an artillery barrage in Tobruk. Alf had been under no obligation to enlist in the army at his age, but she hadn't been able to stop him. 'Have to do my bit for the Old Country,' was what he'd said. It still made her angry to think of it. She admired his patriotism, but she felt angry. For him, for herself, and for Ted. What a waste of a good man.

She would have liked to talk to the New Australian woman, to tell her that she understood how hard it was to adjust to a new way of life, but the woman had already gone back inside the house.

Sala Wajs sank onto the lumpy mattress and looked around at the room they were renting for a guinea a week. In the entrance hall she could smell the sweetish odour of mice, and the greasy smell of rancid lamb fat wafted from the door that led to the landlady's place at the end of the hall. In their room, the bedding smelled of stale sweat. Tattered blinds that wouldn't keep out the light or give any privacy hung from the small window. On the beige wall, where the paper was peeling away at the joins, someone had hung a fly-spotted photograph of a caravan of camels walking into the brilliant sunset of an Arabian night. Dejected as she was, Sala couldn't help smiling at such an incongruous scene in this dismal place.

Their suitcase stood on the torn lino floor, between the bed and the dressing table with its tarnished mirror, still locked and tied with rope. Sala wondered if she'd ever have the energy to unpack. The woman she'd just met in the lane seemed kind, with her soft white hair and plump face, but she hadn't understood much of what she'd said. What was that strange word — *garbo*? At first she'd thought she meant the film star, but then she'd said something about tomorrow.

In between frequent bouts of seasickness on their seemingly endless voyage, Sala had tried to learn some English, but she'd never come across the word *garbo*. Curious, she pulled out the English-Polish dictionary from her large leather holdall, but after a few moments she slammed it shut. The word didn't exist.

Everything had happened so fast since they'd arrived in Sydney three weeks ago. With their ready smiles, Australians seemed quite ingenuous, almost childlike. Even strangers she passed in the street smiled and said, 'How are you?', but they never waited for a reply. As far as she was concerned, the best thing about Australia was that it was at the other end of the world. From what she'd read, she'd expected something exotic, so she had been surprised to find trams rattling through the city, and not a kangaroo, snake or horse buggy in sight.

She looked disconsolately around the room. Szymon had grabbed the first place they could afford, and with his typical ebullience he had enthused about its advantages, taking no notice of her comments about the dreary decor and horrible smells. Close to Bondi Junction and the shops, only ten minutes from Bondi Beach, and just around the corner from the tramline, he'd said, and he'd handed over the first week's rent without waiting to see if she agreed.

She had set her heart on the spacious, airy flat they'd seen in Bondi Road, where the sun streamed in through the balcony that reminded her of home, but the landlord had wanted two hundred pounds key money before letting them move in. 'Don't worry, Sala,' Szymon had said with the bravado that she had once found so comforting, 'one day I'll buy you the whole block. But for now, this will do us.' And without waiting to unpack he'd rammed his hat on his dark wavy hair and shot out to look for work.

With arms that seemed to weigh more than her whole body, Sala started unpacking. There wasn't much. She'd been told that the climate in Australia was hot, but apart from the cotton dress she was wearing, the only light clothes she'd brought were a printed skirt and two blouses made from parachute silk, which was so popular in Poland after the war. She laid them on the bed beside the navy shantung suit still wrapped in tissue paper.

Szymon had bought it for her in Marseilles just before they boarded the ship. When they'd seen it in the window of a boutique, she hadn't even wanted to try it on. They couldn't afford it, she'd argued, and anyway, it was too sophisticated with its New Look peplum jacket and long pencil skirt, but he'd insisted, and, worn down by his enthusiasm, she'd tried it on. Standing awkwardly in the centre of the shop, she looked in the mirror and saw a woman in an outfit that didn't suit her, but from the way Szymon's eyes lit up when he looked at her, she'd realised that he was seeing something totally different. She was still protesting that it was far too expensive while the saleswoman wrapped it up in swathes of tissue paper. It was the most stylish outfit she had ever owned, but now she knew she should have stood her ground and bought something lighter and less formal.

Sala had spent much of the time on board ship lying on her bunk in the airless cabin she shared with fifteen other women, or pretending to sleep on one of the stained canvas deckchairs. She'd told Szymon she felt seasick, but it hadn't only been the smell of sump oil, vomit and the heaving of the ship that had made her feel ill. It had been the sinking feeling in her stomach, the growing conviction that she should never have married this man who was her opposite in every way. It was strange that the qualities that had attracted her in the beginning irritated her so much now, but she knew why she had needed him. She had felt desperate for someone strong to cling to after the war, when all that remained of her past life were aching memories and bitter regrets.

Sala pulled up the torn Holland blind and looked outside. The windows of the other houses had their curtains and blinds drawn, shielding their inhabitants from the light, and from the unwelcome glances of passers-by. But although the windows were covered, some of the front doors were wide open. Funny people, she thought. It was all right to walk in, but not to look in. Streets in European cities bustled with people walking, talking, shopping and meeting friends in cafés. Everyone lived in apartment blocks, but here people seemed to live lonely lives in separate houses on empty streets.

The sudden rumbling of a cart and the clip-clop of hooves on the road broke the silence. A middle-aged man whose baggy shorts revealed surprisingly muscular legs was hoisting a large block of ice from the cart and onto the large leather cape draped around his shoulders. Bending under the weight, he ran towards a semi several doors away. Curious to see what he was doing, Sala went outside.

He saw her on his way back to the cart and stopped running. 'Need some ice for the ice chest, missus?'

She shook her head.

'Lots of people are getting them electric Silent Knights, but I reckon the good old ice chests do the job. Still, you can't stop progress, can you?'

She heard a harsh sound like a jackhammer and looked around but she couldn't see anyone.

He laughed at her puzzled expression. 'That's a kookaburra making that racket.'

'Kookaburra,' she repeated slowly.

'It's a bird, love. Some people think they're laughing at us and they might be right. Just got here, did ya? Don't worry, you'll soon learn the ropes.'

She was still trying to figure out where the ropes were when he called out, 'Cheerio', picked up the reins, gave a low whistle and the Clydesdale trotted around the corner out of sight.

Sala went back inside, her spirits a little lighter after her encounter with the ice man. She hung out Szymon's well-cut serge jacket with the big lapels, laid out his trousers, which he always kept under the mattress to keep their creases, and placed the tan shoes with the white caps in the dark wardrobe whose doors creaked but didn't close. She looked at her watch and wondered whether he'd get the job he'd gone for that morning.

About two years before the war, an Australian businessman called Max Furstenberg had visited the textile factory where Szymon worked in Łód-z˙. Mr Furstenberg had travelled to the textile centre of Poland to learn how the factory operated because he planned to open a similar one in Sydney. The factory owner had asked Szymon to show the visitor around, and at the end of the visit Max had said, 'If you ever come to Australia, I'll give you a job.' Szymon had laughed at the idea of going to Australia, but he'd never forgotten the offer.

'Don't forget that was eleven years ago,' Sala had pointed out that morning. 'How do you know he'll still remember you?'

But Szymon had had no doubt that the offer would still be open.

She envied his energy and optimism. Unlike Szymon, she had no idea what kind of work she'd do here. She had been fourteen in 1939 and she'd assumed that she'd become a doctor, like her parents, but by the time the war finally ended, she had no parents, no sisters, no home and no future. With everyone gone, earning a living had been the last thing on her mind. Why go on living, that was the question. And now, three years later, she still hadn't found the answer.

Too restless to stay in the room with her dark thoughts, Sala wandered outside again. She was studying the geometric arrangement of the small mosaic tiles on the verandah when she heard a woman's rapid footsteps coming down the street, and saw a head poking above a pile of coats and jackets. As the woman hurried past, a cherry-red jacket slipped from her grasp and fell onto the road.

Sala ran out, picked it up and caught up with her, but as she held out the jacket, a check skirt slipped off the pile.

'*Cholera psia krew!*' the woman muttered.

Hearing the Polish swearwords, Sala burst out laughing. 'So you're Polish too!' she said.

Eda Kotowicz was struggling to get a firm grip on her unwieldy bundle. 'They usually pick the clothes up from my place, but the driver was sick today so they asked me to take them to the workshop in the Junction. I'll never agree to do that again,' she said.

On an impulse, Sala said, 'Give me some of those things. I'll help you carry them.'

As they set off side by side, they chattered in Polish, delighted to have found each other.

'I'll tell you what,' Eda said. 'After we drop off the clothes, I'll show you the delicatessen where you can get rye bread, salami and cottage cheese. All the other shops sell white bread that tastes like cardboard, and cheese that tastes like soap. But I can't find unsalted butter anywhere.'

Near the corner, they came to a man with a big belly bulging under his white singlet. He was clipping his hedge with shears. Fascinated, Sala stopped to watch the deft way he neatened the edges until not a single leaf protruded above the rest, as though he'd used a ruler.

He looked up and wiped his red face. 'Lovely day today, ladies,' he said. 'How are yez?' and without waiting for a reply, he resumed trimming his hedge.

Eda gave a short laugh. 'That's Australia. People here are like children. Last week they lit a huge fire in the middle of the road and let off fireworks for hours. I got a terrible fright, and as usual my daughter thought I was being hysterical.'

She sighed, and Sala shot her an inquiring glance, but Eda quickly changed the subject.

'I don't think I'll ever understand Australians,' she said. 'They're totally different from us.'

Sala thought about her white-haired neighbour, the ice man, and the man with the shears. Maybe being different wasn't such a bad thing.

Chapter 5

The Art Deco façades of the redbrick mansions in this part of Kings Cross gave no indication of the type of tenants who lived inside, Ted thought as he walked down Macleay Street. Once the homes of solid, established families, they'd been converted into apartments and now housed bohemian types who believed in free love, and callgirls who offered love for sale. There were rumours that behind these locked doors, satanic rituals, sex orgies and perversions involving whips, masks and chains took place. Ted had heard that the participants included artists, musicians and politicians, but as he entered the stately vestibule with its wood-panelled walls and outsized Grecian-style urn on an oak table, he wondered if the rumours were true.

As he stepped into the wrought-iron lift cage and pressed the button for the second floor, he was already composing the lead of what would be his first crime story. He'd stumbled on the case by chance. Gus Thornton had sent him to the police station in Darlinghurst to collect some facts and figures about youth crime, which was one of Gus's obsessions.

Only that week a seventeen-year-old farmhand had bludgeoned a farmer and his wife to death with a hammer on a property near Parramatta; when questioned by police, the lad was quoted as saying, 'I dunno why I done it. They was good to me an' that. I just saw the hammer and somethink come over me.'

That had set Gus off on one of his tirades about the loss of Christian values, the breakdown of law and order, the lack of discipline in the home and the growth of illiteracy.

Speaking about the case, an Anglican minister had been quoted as saying, 'This murder is the product of our violent age which has turned its back upon God.'

Although Gus had little time for God's self-appointed interpreters, he had no qualms about exploiting violence to sell newspapers, and he sent Ted to gather statistics for a series he planned to run about the dissolute youth of today.

The police station was located around the corner from the neo-Grecian columns of the Central Criminal Court in Taylor Square, just down the road from the old sandstone building that had once housed Darlinghurst Gaol and its gallows, although no hangings had taken place there for the past forty-one years. As he passed the imposing arched entrance, Ted wished he could have interviewed the hangman to find out what it felt like to pull the lever that plunged someone into eternal blackness.

As he walked along the quiet street, he almost tripped over a toothless wino sprawled in a doorway, mumbling to his empty bottle. There was no one else around, and nothing to suggest that not so long ago this old inner-city suburb with its rundown terrace houses had been part of 'Razorhurst',

Sydney's notorious crime district which was controlled by pimps, madams and razor-wielding thugs. But on this bright May morning it looked as innocent as a criminal spruced up for his day in court.

A block further on, Ted ran up the three stone steps leading into the Darlinghurst Police Station. Inside, the slow-moving sergeant hitched his trousers up over his belly and gave Ted a look that said he had more important things to do than talk to rookie reporters. Then, hitching up his trousers again, he bent over his newspaper to study the race form.

Pinned to the wooden noticeboard on the wall were so many notices about unsolved cases of rape and murder that they overlapped one another. Obviously more policemen were needed to deal with crime. Only the other day a woman near Wattle Street had received a cheque for two guineas from the police department for catching two burglars as they were breaking into her neighbour's house.

As Ted waited, the black bakelite telephone on the counter started to ring. Pretending to concentrate on the posters, Ted inched closer to listen, and from the sergeant's comments he gathered that a woman had been shot in Kings Cross. The sergeant scribbled something on a notepad, tore off the slip of paper and disappeared out the back. Glancing around to make sure no one was looking, Ted pocketed the top sheet and hurried from the station.

Out in the street he'd scanned the sergeant's imprint and made out the address. Kings Cross was only a couple of tram stops away, and with a bit of luck he'd get there before the other reporters got to hear about the shooting.

The door to the flat was slightly ajar. He pushed it open and stood in a dimly lit corridor whose walls were covered in silver paper splashed with large roses. He got as far as the doorway leading to the lounge room when a burly detective barred his way.

Holding up his CIB warrant card, the detective barked, 'I'm Detective Sergeant Jim Mitchell from Darlinghurst Police Station. Who the bloody hell are you?'

The detective had the shoulders of a footballer and the belligerent expression of a bouncer in a strip club. Even the cigarette stuck to his lower lip looked menacing.

Ted introduced himself and showed his press card.

The detective's bloated face seemed to swell above his collar as he shouted, 'Clear off before I throw you out! This is a crime scene!'

'Oh, come on, give me a break, this is my first job,' Ted pleaded. 'I'll get the sack if I don't get the story. Go on, tell me something about the victim and I'll write such a glowing story about you that they'll make you commissioner.'

Just then Mitchell caught sight of his offsider emerging from the adjoining room. 'Solved the crime, have you?' he barked.

'It was probably her last visitor,' the young constable stammered. 'There were two teacups, and there's some tea in the pot.'

'Thanks, Sherlock,' Mitchell sneered. 'I'd never have worked that one out.'

While the detective was needling his colleague, Ted peered into the next room and was intrigued by its atmosphere of claustrophobic intimacy. He supposed that this was what they called a love nest. The plush winged armchairs facing the long couch, the heavy velvet drapes caught with tasselled cords, and the crimson wallpaper embossed with gold fleur-de-lis. The paintings on the walls showed women in lascivious poses that made Ted blush, though he couldn't help sneaking glances at them.

Then the breath got stuck in his throat. The dead woman looked as though she was about to pour tea from the silver pot on the table, except for the bright red stain on her white silk blouse and the way her head was slumped on her chest. There was blood on her hair, which fell forward over her face, part of which had been shot away. In her small right hand she still held a cigarette. On the table stood two empty cups with fluted gilt edges and sprays of country roses on the porcelain. The fine china was the only personal touch in the whole flat, and it touched him.

He jumped when he heard the detective shouting, 'You still here? Fuck off before I throw you down the bloody stairs!'

Ted couldn't get the case of the murdered callgirl out of his mind, and two days later he returned to the building. Glancing around to make sure that Detective Sergeant Mitchell wasn't around, he rang the bell of the adjoining flat.

The woman who opened the door wore a lacy black negligee which emphasised her pasty complexion. Ted guessed she was on the wrong side of thirty, maybe even older. Her fluffy hair looked blonde, but when she pushed it back from her face he saw the roots, like the black lining of a yellow coat.

'Not bloody cops again!' she groaned.

Ted held up his press card. 'I'm a reporter. I just want to ask you a few questions,' he said quickly. 'Off the record, if you like.'

'Okay, but don't quote me, love,' the woman slurred, drawing the flimsy negligee around her flabby shoulders. 'Scarlett had lots of visitors. That was her name. Scarlett O'Halloran. Lovely girl she was. Didn't drink or swear.'

'Any idea who might have killed her?'

She shrugged. 'Haven't got a clue, with all the clients she had. Day and night they came, all different ones.'

She tried to light her cigarette, but her fingers shook so much she had trouble getting the lighter to spark.

'Want a whiskey, love?' she asked, pouring herself a big slug from a cut-glass decanter. 'I know you reporters like your grog.'

She eyed him up and down, and gave a girlish giggle.

'You're a good-looker, with those broad shoulders and baby-blue eyes. Why don't you take your jacket off and let Doris make you comfortable?'

Ted's face flamed with embarrassment as he declined her offer.

Doris didn't tell him much. She'd been asleep after a heavy night and hadn't woken up until she heard the shot.

'Made me jump, that did,' she said. 'At first I thought it was one of them double bungers they let off on Cracker Night, but then I remembered that was a few nights ago. You lose track of time in this kind of work.' She gave him that sly look again. 'Anyway, that's when I got up and knocked on her door, but she didn't answer so I went in. Poor Scarlett. I'll never forget that sight as long as I live.'

'How did you get in?' he asked.

'We always had each other's keys. Just in case.'

Her eyes slid appreciatively from the blue tie that matched his eyes, to the sharp crease in his trousers. 'You look like one of them blokes in the ads for men's suits,' she said. 'Sure you don't want to slip off that jacket and let me help you relax?'

He shook his head. 'How long had Scarlett been living here?'

Doris shrugged. 'She was here when I came, that'd be three years ago now, but I dunno how long she was here before that.'

'Did you know where she came from, or anything about her life before ...' He tried to think of a delicate way of saying 'before she became a prostitute'. 'Before she came here?'

'Nah. We never talked about that. No point. This is where we ended up, and that was that.'

He was at the front door when she began to cry with loud wheezy sobs. 'The bastard! I hope they catch him and string him up. A lovely girl she was. Who would have wanted her dead?'

Ted was wondering that himself as he walked down Macleay Street. It was one of those golden late-May mornings. The sky was a cloudless duck-egg blue, and it seemed as though winter had forgotten to arrive. The soft southern light lit up the feathery foliage of the gum trees and dappled the pavements. He could never understand why migrants complained that Australian trees were colourless. They just didn't know how to look.

He was walking past the California Café when a sign in the window caught his eye. *Apple pies with pure cream.* Most days his lunch consisted of a devon-and-pickle sandwich brought to work in a brown paper bag which he smoothed out, folded and took home again because paper was still scarce. But today he'd shot out without his sandwich, and the sign in the café window reminded him that it was lunchtime. Beneath the sign, printed in big capitals, were the words: FILLED WITH CREAM FROM OUR OWN COWS.

Intrigued, he pushed the door open. Although the war had ended three years ago, fresh cream was still rationed. The proprietor bustled around serving the customers, many of whom seemed to be foreigners, judging by the conversations.

'What's the story about the cream?' Ted asked when the owner came to take his order.

'You wouldn't believe it,' the man said, wiping his hands on his white apron. 'You'd think it was still bloody wartime with all these food restrictions and rationing. The inspector came around a few weeks ago and wanted to fine me for breaking the law because we're only allowed to use cream for butter and cheese. So I had to get a lawyer and go to court to prove that the cream I whipped for the pies came from my own cows. And then I had to produce receipts to show I'd bought them!'

Ted made a note to pass on this bizarre bit of local news to the roundsman who wrote the *Life's Like That* column. He ordered the apple pie and, feeling daring, ordered Vienna coffee instead of tea. He took a pack of Capstans from his pocket and lit up, listening to the four men in the banquette behind him as they shouted and interrupted one another. Ted wondered why New Australians were so impatient and loud. Although he couldn't understand what they were saying, there was one word they kept repeating. It sounded like *Bonnagilla*. Perhaps it was the name of a town in their homeland, or a girl's name.

His thoughts drifted to the gorgeous girl who'd recently moved into Wattle Street with her parents. He'd only seen her once but he couldn't get her out of his mind. Tall and slender as a shaft of sunlight, with hair so pale that it was almost white, she had the most delicate features he'd ever seen. Ted was daydreaming about her as he got up to leave the café, but the men at the next table were still arguing about Bonnagilla.

Chapter 6

Sitting in his cubicle in the smoke-filled newsroom, Ted yanked the sheet of paper from his typewriter, screwed it into a tight ball and tossed it into the wastepaper basket, which was already overflowing. He'd paid for the typewriter from the measly three pounds a week he'd earned as a cadet, but now he punched the keys with the desperation of a boxer fighting a losing match. Shifting in his chair, he read what he'd written. He could already hear Gus calling it a crock of shit, and for once he agreed. He'd managed to write the lead for the story about the callgirl's murder in Kings Cross, but after that his mind had gone as blank as the paper he'd been feeding into the machine, and even Gus's threat that he'd ram the typewriter up his arse if he didn't file the story by three o'clock hadn't got him going.

He was disappointed that Gus hadn't been impressed by the speed with which he'd shot into the murdered girl's flat, or by what he'd found out from the woman next door. 'Bloody useless!' Gus had shouted. 'No suspects, a neighbour with amnesia, and a victim with a phony name. Another Pyjama Girl, doomed to remain unidentified for years. And where are the statistics on teenage crime you were supposed to get?'

The staccato of typewriters all over the newsroom, and the occasional burst of raucous laughter, made it impossible to concentrate. Joe Black was describing an incident at the Journalists' Club the night before. Joe's drunken antics were legendary, and in addition to his drinking, he was a compulsive gambler. Ted could never decide whether to believe him or not.

'You know that poker machine they've got there?' Joe was saying. 'Well, it kept swallowing all my tokens, and I got so mad I grabbed a sausage roll, stuffed it into the bloody machine and yelled, "You've got it all now, so you may as well have my dinner too!" And now I'm banned from the club!'

Ted was laughing as he turned back to his story, but when he reread what he'd written he felt sick. His copy was as wooden as his desk. It was about as exciting as a shopping list. And that's what it was, he realised. A list. It didn't have any heart. Adrenalin rushing now, he threaded in a fresh sheet of paper and began to type, and this time his fingers flew over the keyboard. He was writing about two dainty teacups, a cold pot of tea and an unlit cigarette in a dead callgirl's hand.

'What's this long-winded crap you've churned out?' Gus roared when he read Ted's copy an hour later. 'Are you reporting on a crime or writing a novel?'

Ted took a deep breath. 'I didn't think we needed all the gruesome details. Anyway, the story was more touching with the personal details.'

Gus was eyeing him with his ferocious stare. 'Let me tell you something. People like being shocked. The more lurid it is, the more it terrifies them and the better they like it. If they want to be touched, they read the *Women's Weekly*.'

He looked distastefully at the copy in his hand. 'We're almost on deadline, so hurry up and take out the guff. And next time don't be so fucking sentimental. And let the facts speak for themselves. Our readers aren't all cretins.'

After he'd rewritten the article, Ted sat back and reread his notes from the SS *Napoli*. Letting Communists into Australia would be bad enough, but the thought of Nazis sneaking in was even more shocking. His father had died at Tobruk fighting the Krauts, and letting Nazis and their collaborators settle here would be a betrayal of what he'd fought and died for.

On his way home on the tram that evening, Ted remembered sitting in the Star Cinema on Bronte Road at the end of the war, his mouth dry as sand as he watched the Cinesound newsreel showing thousands of skeletons heaped on top of wheelbarrows and being tossed into a mass grave at a concentration camp in Germany. He remembered feeling as though someone had plunged a fist into his stomach. 'That's what your father fought and died for,' his mother had whispered. 'To put an end to that.'

His father had never been a talkative man, but before setting off to fight he'd sat Ted down and explained why he had enlisted, as if he'd known that this would be the last time they'd talk. In his slow Somerset accent he'd said, 'You have to stand up for what's right, son, no matter how hard it may be. If people like you and me don't, then the bad ones will win, and we wouldn't want to live in a world like that, now would we?'

Alf Browning was an uneducated man who'd probably gleaned his philosophy of life from scoutmasters and Boys' Own annuals. But although Ted had scoffed at those naive sentiments while his father was alive, he was surprised how often he still heard his voice in his head, sometimes with a hint of reproach. His father was the most honest person he'd ever come across, and deep down he suspected he wasn't half the man his father had been.

The man sitting beside him on the Bondi Junction tram got off, leaving his copy of the *Sydney Morning Herald* on the seat, and Ted picked it up as they rattled across the city. It was ten past five; the shops, department stores and offices had just closed, and the tram was filling up with office girls, sales assistants and secretaries on their way home from work. Ted stood up to give his seat to a stout woman who gave off a cloying smell of cheap scent. 'Thanks,' she said, flopping into the seat. 'Good to take the weight off my feet after standing all day selling ruddy gloves.'

Scanning the paper as the tram lurched along, he read that Sir Laurence Olivier and his wife Vivien Leigh were about to tour Australia. They were going to appear in *The School for Scandal* at the Tivoli Theatre. If only he could afford to buy tickets. He still hadn't figured out a way of getting to know the New Australian girl, but having tickets for the Tivoli show would give him the perfect excuse to knock on her door and ask her out. He could already imagine her lovely face lighting up at the prospect of seeing the famous couple in real life. But by the time he'd paid his mother board and bought tram and bus fares, there wasn't enough left over for theatre tickets.

Turning the page, he read that the United Nations had approved the formation of the new state of Israel, and that Cardinal Mindszenty had been arrested by the Communist government in Hungary. A long report discussed the plight of three English women who were imprisoned in Moscow where their husbands had diplomatic posts.

As he read on, the contrast between this serious broadsheet and the racy tabloid he worked for, with its emphasis on short articles, large photos and sensational reporting, made him squirm. Perhaps his mother was right and he should have aimed higher, but it was hard for a young reporter to get his first break, and he'd jumped at the chance of working for the best-selling paper in town. Perhaps one day, when he was more experienced, he'd get a job on the *Herald*, but for now the *Standard* would be a good training ground.

An article on page three of the paper caught his attention and he struggled to hold onto the strap and turn the page without knocking the feather off the hat of the woman standing in front of him. Headed MORE MIGRANTS HEADING FOR OUR SHORES, the article included quotes from Mr Redvers Morrison, a former security officer with the immigration department who had served his term in the field and was now returning home to a desk job. He had apparently just returned from Germany where thousands of displaced people from all over Europe were applying to emigrate to Australia.

Moving carefully to avoid the feather, Ted managed to extricate his notebook from his pocket and jot down the name. Ever since his visit to the SS *Napoli* the previous week, he'd been curious about the screening process for migrants, and it looked as though Redvers Morrison would be the ideal person to put him in the picture.

Several days later, after numerous unanswered telephone calls and a succession of excuses designed to fob him off, Ted managed to arrange an interview with Redvers Morrison. To allay any anxiety the department might have about his real motives, he'd been careful to point out that his aim was to describe the situation in the displaced persons camps to his readers so that they'd appreciate the immense difficulties the immigration officers faced, and be reassured that only the best types of refugees were admitted. He felt no compunction about being so devious. Deception was a necessary tool to ferret out the truth from people determined to conceal it.

As it turned out, his ploy had worked. Perhaps Redvers Morrison had convinced his superiors that this was exactly the kind of article they needed to make their policies more acceptable to the readers of a newspaper whose attitude to Mr Calwell's immigration program was negative, to say the least.

Walking along Bridge Street, past bank buildings and office blocks that cut out the sun, Ted whistled a bouncy pop tune under his breath. '"A you're adorable, B you're so beautiful …"' A pretty blonde walking in the opposite direction gave him a knowing smile, but Ted hardly noticed her. As usual, he was thinking about the New Australian girl. He'd walked past her place many times hoping to catch sight of her again, and to strike up a conversation, but she was never there.

As soon as he was ushered into Redvers Morrison's spacious office and faced the suave-looking man with silver hair and neatly trimmed moustache sitting behind a cedar desk his confidence waned. Mr Morrison didn't look like a man who'd let his guard down and reveal anything that might bring the government's policies into disrepute.

Ted listened to his rambling and evasive replies and scribbled down all the clichés, platitudes and bureaucratic jargon in shorthand, without challenging them or raising any controversial issues. When he gauged that the time was right, he asked which countries the migrants were coming from.

Resting his elbows on the edge of the desk, Redvers Morrison steepled his fingertips. 'Poland, Hungary, Latvia, Lithuania, Estonia, Yugoslavia, Italy, Greece, you name it.'

'Do you speak any of their languages?'

'Languages?' he repeated. 'A bit of school French. *La plume de ma tante,* that sort of thing.'

'And what about the other security officers. Do they speak any other languages?'

Redvers Morrison frowned. 'I wouldn't know. But how is this relevant to your article?'

'Well, I'm wondering how you interview people if you can't speak to them.'

'We have interpreters.'

'But how can you tell if they're translating accurately?'

Mr Morrison was drumming his fingers on the cedar desk. 'Look here, what are you getting at? We do whatever's necessary to make sure the wrong people don't slip through the net. And in case you're worried about Communists getting in, let me assure you that we have some reliable people in the DP camps who fled from the Communists and are only too happy to help us to identify them.'

Ted looked thoughtful. He recalled the Lithuanian woman on the SS *Napoli* whose face was contorted with fury when she talked about the Communists on board.

'So these people are helping you to spot the Communists,' he said slowly. 'And who's reporting on the Nazis?'

'We don't admit any Nazis.' Redvers Morrison looked pointedly at his watch. 'I'm afraid you'll have to excuse me,' he said. 'I have an appointment.'

While Ted waited for the tram back to the office, he tried to sort out what he'd been told. Somewhere behind all that verbiage lay the truth and he wondered whether he'd have the skill to unravel it. Perhaps he should have taken Gus Thornton's advice and stuck to youth violence.

Chapter 7

Hania was sitting at the table, picking at the beef goulash on her plate, when the smell of grilled lamb wafted in from outside and made her mouth water.

'Can we have lamb chops for dinner one night?'

Eda Kotowicz shuddered. 'You want I should cook lamb chops? Isn't it enough we have to smell them every night?'

'Well, can I have dinner at Beverley's one night then? Aunty Muriel said I could.'

Taking her mother's silent shrug as consent, Hania decided to push her luck. Ever since her mother had befriended Mrs Wajs from the boarding house on the corner, she had become more approachable, but even so, Hania knew she had to tread warily.

Her mouth full of goulash, she said, 'Beverley asked me to come to her Sunday school picnic. Can I?'

Eda frowned. 'A Sunday school picnic? With the church?'

'It's nothing to do with the church,' Hania said quickly. 'It's a picnic at the beach, that's all.'

'That's what you think,' her mother retorted. 'The picnic is just an excuse. They want to convert you. Listen to me.

I know people. Remember how those people in Poland tried to turn you into a Catholic?'

Hania pushed away her plate and fiddled with the edge of the tablecloth. Her mother would never understand. Every Sunday she had looked forward to the solemn ritual of the Mass. Sitting with her foster parents, she breathed in the spicy smell of the incense and the waxy scent of the flickering candles, and listened to the altar boys in their white lace surplices singing like angels in heaven. When she gazed at the statues of Jesus and Mary, they looked back at her as if they could see inside her heart, and the little gold cross her foster mother had placed around her neck made her feel safe.

She looked helplessly at her mother. 'Why can't you understand? This isn't Poland, it's Australia. Beverley's parents know I'm Jewish and they don't care. They're not trying to convert me, they just want to include me.' She was shouting now. 'There'll be races and games, and all the kids in the street will be there, but I suppose I'll have to stay home and miss all the fun like on Cracker Night. It's not fair!'

'You think they don't care you're Jewish but as soon as there's trouble, they'll call you a dirty Jew and say you killed Jesus,' her mother shouted back.

'There'll only be trouble if you make it,' Hania yelled, storming out of the kitchen and slamming the door. In her bedroom she took the cross from her drawer and, clutching it in her hand, threw herself onto the bed. 'I don't care what you say, I'm going to the picnic,' she sobbed.

* * *

On Sunday morning Eda Kotowicz was sitting on the sagging couch beside a pile of coats and jackets, finishing off the buttonholes and hemming the skirts, when Hania came out of her room, buttoning her coat. Snapping off a thread with her teeth, Eda looked up. 'Where do you think you're going?'

'To Tina's,' Hania said.

She knew her mother wouldn't object because Tina's Greek parents were even more strict than she was, and hardly ever let her go out. After school and on weekends, Tina wiped down the marbled red-and-white laminex tables, or served behind the counter of their milk bar in Oxford Street. The only time she went to a Saturday matinee was when she fibbed that she was going to Hania's place. Beneath Tina's bright smile Hania recognised a simmering resentment, and she knew that she and Tina both suffered from restrictions imposed by migrant parents in a way their Australian classmates could never understand.

'Make sure you're home by three,' Eda said. 'These skirts have to be ready by tomorrow morning, so I need you to sweep the floor and hang out the washing while I'm finishing them off. And watch how you cross the road.'

Hania ran out of the house and ducked into Beverley's house. Aunty Muriel was already wrapping sandwiches in greaseproof paper and placing chocolate crackles in biscuit tins, while Beverley and her little sister Daisy were crunching the cocoa-covered rice bubbles that had spilled onto the table.

Finally all the food was in a wicker basket, covered by a white doily with a crocheted edge, and the women and children set off towards the tram stop, chattering excitedly. Hania kept glancing behind her to make sure her mother wasn't on the verandah, and she didn't breathe out until they'd turned the corner.

By the time they spread everything out on the grass facing Bronte Beach, the fathers had already picked up a full milk churn from the Dairy Farmers depot in Spring Street. While some were pouring milk into mugs, others were mixing bright green cordial in iron buckets. The children were clamouring for food, but the mothers insisted on spreading neat gingham cloths over the tartan rugs before starting the picnic.

'Now close your eyes and bow your heads. We're all going to say grace together,' Uncle Bill said.

Hania looked around to see what he meant. The others all closed their eyes, except two small boys who were nudging each other and giggling behind their hands, until their mother noticed and gave them a clip on the ear.

'God is great, God is good, let us thank Him for our food,' they chorused. A moment later, dozens of hands were reaching for the sandwiches.

'They're like a swarm of locusts,' Verna Browning laughed.

'Come on, Hanny, don't be shy, take one,' Aunty Muriel said. 'If you wait too long, they'll all be gone. The way this lot are diving into them, you'd think they'd just come out of one of those camps like the Jews in the newsreels.' She stopped abruptly when Verna nudged her and inclined her head towards Hania. Remembering her mother's warning, Hania held her breath, but Aunty Muriel didn't say anything else as she held out the plate of sandwiches.

The bread was cut into dainty triangles and neatly filled with egg and lettuce, Kraft cheese spread, Vegemite or devon and pickle, so different from the thick hunks of rye bread her mother made with strong-smelling salami and garlic-flavoured pickled cucumber. As she bit into a triangle with Vegemite, she felt the white bread smooth against the roof of her mouth. As soon as the sandwiches were gone, the children grabbed chocolate crackles, hundreds and thousands sandwiches, iced buns and slices of sponge cake filled with jam and whipped cream.

When no one could eat any more, the games started. The fathers rolled up their shirtsleeves and rounded up the kids with their good-natured grumbling. They sorted the children into groups according to their age, and while one of the fathers stood at the starting line blowing a whistle, two held a rope across the finishing line.

Hania giggled while Uncle Bill tied her right leg to Beverley's left. Hobbling across the lawn together, trying to keep in step to avoid tripping, they touched the tape first and collapsed on the grass shrieking with laughter. After that, they went in the sack race, and the egg-and-spoon race, and when the races were over, Uncle Bill suspended apples on lengths of string tied to the thick branch of a pine tree. Then he tied the children's hands behind their backs and told them to eat the apples, which were bobbing and swaying in the breeze. Meggsie was the first to finish his apple, but some of the smaller kids complained that it wasn't fair because he was taller.

The fathers threw themselves into organising the games as though they were state championships, while the mothers stood on the sidelines, cheering and clapping the winners, and Hania again found herself envying these children their playful parents. No matter how hard she tried, she couldn't recall anything about her own a father whom she'd last seen when she was two and a half years old. She knew that he'd been taken to a labour camp at the beginning of the war and had never come back, but her attempts to find out more from her mother had been fruitless. Just once her mother had confided with a sorrowful look, 'Your father adored you. I never saw a man so besotted with a child.' Hania had repeated those words to herself like a magical incantation, as though they might have the power to evoke some memory of her father.

Talking about him upset her mother too much. It was another forbidden subject that Hania had learned to avoid, but at times like this she wondered whether he would have understood her, and whether he would have been as fun-loving and affectionate as Beverley's dad.

When the games were over, the girls brought out their skipping ropes and chanted 'Bluebells, cockle shells, eevie ivy over,' as they skipped, while the boys tore around the lawn with bats and balls, playing cricket.

Hania was sitting on the grass beside Beverley when Meggsie ran towards her, swinging an empty thermos in one hand and clutching sixpence in the other. 'My mum wants me to go across the road to the tearoom to get hot water for the tea,' he said. 'Want to come?'

He was hopping from foot to foot, and he spoke so fast that the saliva sprayed through the gap in his front teeth.

He was a funny boy, Hania thought, with his skinny legs, freckled face and the carroty hair which stood up at the back of his head like a porcupine. She was about to shake her head when she remembered he'd given her a sparkler on Cracker Night.

On the way to the tearoom, she asked, 'Why do they call you Meggsie?'

He looked at her in astonishment. 'After Ginger Meggs, silly. You know, the kid with red hair in the Sunday comics.'

As they waited for their hot water, she remembered hearing some of the boys at school calling him other names, too, and a couple of times she'd seen him fighting in the playground with boys bigger than himself. Beverley had told her that the other boys often teased him because his mum was a barmaid, and that's when he lost his temper and punched them.

Hania would have liked to ask him about that, and to tell him that she thought those boys were nasty, but she was too shy to raise a subject that might upset him, and they walked back to the beach without speaking.

While the adults were sipping their tea, Beverley took hold of Hania's hands and pulled her up. 'Come on,' she said. 'Let's go over to the sandhills.'

Meggsie sprang up. 'Last one there is a rotten egg!'

Exhilarated at having the hills to themselves, the three of them made whooping noises and pranced around in a circle, mimicking the Red Indians they'd seen in the cowboy flicks at the Saturday matinees.

'Race you to the top!' Meggsie shouted. The girls panted as they clambered behind him, clutching clumps of spinifex to stop their bare feet from sinking into the warm, soft sand. By the time they reached the top, they were out of breath.

They weren't alone. Sitting with his back to them, leaning into a hollow, his legs stretched out in front of him, was a man. Beside him lay a small olive-green hat with a feather sticking out of the narrow brim.

'It's the weird man that lives next door to you,' Beverley said to Meggsie in an excited whisper. She caught Hania's arm. 'What's he doing?'

They craned forward. The man was moving his hands so fast that their eyes couldn't keep up with their speed. It looked as though things were being twirled and tossed, not by human hands but by some machine.

'You'd think he had dozens of balls up in the air, but I can't see anything,' Hania whispered, while the others watched, too mesmerised to speak.

Just then, he turned around. He stared at the children with an unblinking expression of such intensity that they bolted down the sandhills as though the devil was after them with a pitchfork.

Back at the beach, they flopped onto the grass, confused by what they'd seen.

'He's creepy,' Beverley said. 'My mum reckons he's always hammering and banging at night, and never talks to anyone.'

She turned to Meggsie. 'You live next door, why don't you watch and see what he does? I reckon he's up to something, and the police are probably after him. If we find out what he's up to, maybe we'll all get a reward.'

Meggsie nodded. 'I'll watch him. It'll be our secret. We won't tell anyone. Cross your heart and hope to die.'

Hania went home feeling elated. This was like the stories in her favourite magazine, *The School Friend*. Every Monday after school she and Tina rushed to the newsagent's and spent the afternoon reading exciting stories about schoolgirls who solved mysteries and brought criminals to justice, and wishing that they could find a mystery to solve. Well now she'd found one. And she wasn't alone any more. She was part of a secret society.

Chapter 8

Kath sat on the rug shielding her eyes against the sun as she watched Meggsie running down the sandhill ahead of Beverley and Hanny. Despite his sunny nature, she knew that his life at school wasn't easy. He often came home with bruises and although he never admitted it, she knew that some of the boys made fun of him because she was a barmaid and his father had shot through. She scolded him for fighting but she was glad he wasn't a sissy. A boy growing up without a father had to learn to stand up for himself.

The younger boys were playing cricket and she heard Alan shouting, 'You dropped it, you mug!' Ray tackled him and they were both on the grass, punching and kicking.

She usually regarded their fights as normal skylarking, but sometimes she wondered if Gran was right and they were growing up wild. 'Those boys need a firm hand. You want to send them to a Catholic school before it's too late,' she'd said accusingly. 'You've made a mess of your life but don't make the kids suffer for your mistakes.' In a more conciliatory tone, she'd added, 'If you send them to St Joseph's, they probably won't charge you, seeing as how you haven't got a husband.'

The idea of asking for charity, especially from the Church, made Kath's blood boil. There was no way she was going to send her boys to a Catholic school, even if they paid her. The last time she'd been inside a Catholic church was a few months after Meggsie was born. That was twelve years ago, and she'd sworn never to go back.

She had wanted him baptised in the Catholic Church, but Jack wouldn't have a bar of it. He always listened to 2CH, the Protestant station that broadcast anti-Catholic propaganda, and whenever she heard it, she switched the dial to 2SM, which threatened non-Catholics with hellfire. Jack was adamant his son wasn't going to be a little tyke and, sick of the arguments, she finally gave in. To her grandmother's horror, and the disapproval of her sister who had married a Catholic, Meggsie was baptised in the Church of England. She named him Kevin after her father, which upset her grandmother even more as she'd wanted him named Francis after the saint.

Meggsie was only a few weeks old when two nuns came to the house and told her off for not baptising her baby in the Catholic Church. A week later, the priest arrived.

'You've committed a mortal sin, and because of you, your child is doomed to live in perpetual limbo,' he thundered, pointing an accusing finger at her. He was an old man with a craggy face and white hair that seemed to stand on end as he spoke, and she felt she'd been cursed by a Biblical prophet.

Shaken by his words, Kath took the baby to St Xavier's to

be christened, but the priest refused to perform the ceremony because the child had already been baptised elsewhere. He told her she was a disgrace to the Catholic Church, which would no longer have anything to do with her. She'd run out of the church clutching the baby and sobbing in humiliation and fury. That's when she'd vowed never to return, and she had kept her promise.

In the eight years Kath and Jack were together, they had four children. Jack never wanted so many kids, but although she'd turned her back on the Church, Kath couldn't bring herself to use birth control. One day when she was pregnant again and still changing nappies, a neighbour told her she'd seen Jack at the races with another woman. They fought constantly after that and their arguments sometimes ended with her screaming at him, and him lashing out and giving her a swollen lip or a black eye. The following day he was always contrite and brought her flowers, and she tried to hide the bruises from the kids. With four boys under six to look after, she felt she had no choice but to stay with him.

Gran had been right about Jack, but Kath was determined not to allow history to repeat itself. She wasn't going to land on her grandmother's doorstep as her parents had done. Too proud to ask for help and too humiliated to reveal her situation to anyone, she concentrated on looking after the boys while she racked her brains for a way out. But one day Jack took the decision out of her hands. He said he was fed up with her, the kids' screaming, the chaos and the never-ending bills. He'd been gone a month before she could bring herself to tell her grandmother that her husband had deserted her.

With a sigh, Kath looked around to see what the boys were up to. Alan and Ray had stopped fighting and were weaving among the picnickers, kicking a ball, while Pete, her youngest, was sitting near Verna, contentedly stuffing another piece of passionfruit sponge into his mouth. She lay back on the grass under a cloudless sky, the sun warm on her eyelids and the light breeze rustling the leaves overhead.

Chapter 9

Ted was sitting at his desk in the newsroom, doodling. All around him, typewriters clattered, doors slammed and chairs scraped against the wooden floor. Every few moments Don Fraser, the sportswriter, let out a curse, and then, seeing the stiffened back of the reporter who wrote the women's pages, he apologised for swearing in front of a lady, which provoked loud belly laughs from the men.

Don turned around and saw Ted hunched over his typewriter. 'You're a bloody conchie!' he called out.

Ted shrugged. The old hacks did as little work as they could get away with, and ridiculed the young reporters for being too keen.

Another week had passed, and he was supposed to be writing the story about teenage crime, but his heart wasn't in it. He couldn't get the immigrants and the murdered callgirl out of his mind, but he hadn't had any luck following up either story. No one had been charged with the murder, and his calls to Detective Sergeant Mitchell had gone unanswered.

Just then a message boy ran through the newsroom looking for him. Gus wanted him in his office immediately.

Guiltily Ted grabbed his sheaf of papers about juvenile crime to show that he was on the case.

'Off to see God, are you? Hope it's not bloody Judgement Day,' Don joked as Ted rushed out of the newsroom. 'Don't forget the first commandment — I am the Lord thy editor and thou shalt have no other gods before me!'

Gus's mountainous figure was silhouetted in a nimbus of light from the late-afternoon sun pouring in through the window. Ted stifled an urge to laugh at this bellicose Buddha with the cigarette-holder stuck in the corner of his mouth. Gus stubbed his Sobranie Black Russian into the marble ashtray before acknowledging Ted's presence.

Poking his index finger at a letter on his desk, he said, 'It's for you. Seems this bloke read your story about the migrant ship last week. Reckons he can tell you something,'

'Does he say what?'

Gus ignored the question. Leaning forward, he jabbed his finger at Ted. 'Listen. Anyone who volunteers to give you inside information, or expose somebody, you can be bloody sure they've got an agenda, and if you don't find out what their agenda is, they'll use you like a ten-bob whore.'

He pushed another black Sobranie into his cigarette-holder, lit it with his monogrammed lighter and, with an imperious gesture, waved Ted away.

Written in exemplary copperplate handwriting on quality notepaper, the letter was signed *Mr George Addison*.

I hope I'm not being presumptuous, Mr Addison wrote,
*but I was encouraged to contact you after reading your
excellent interview with the passengers of the SS* Napoli
in the Daily Standard, *a paper I must admit I rarely
read unless someone leaves it on the tram.*

*Until a month ago, I taught English at Bonegilla, a
migrant camp near Albury.*

Ted read on with growing interest. Bonegilla. So that was
what the New Australians had been discussing so heatedly
at the California Café. But after the promising opening, Mr
Addison meandered for two pages. He listed his qualifications,
explained why he'd applied for the job, and went on to
enumerate the difficulties of teaching English to people from
so many different countries and of such varying levels of
education. Finally he came to the point.

*It came to my attention on a number of occasions
that there were irregularities in the running of the
camp and I have good reason to believe that among
the migrants there are individuals who should never
have been allowed to enter this country. I started to
make inquiries about the screening of migrants, and I
am convinced that it was my attempt to uncover the
truth and to expose these undesirables that led to the
termination of my contract.*

Mr Addison indicated that if Ted was interested in pursuing the matter, he'd be willing to divulge more information to him in person. Ted put down the letter and reached for the telephone. The man who answered had a reedy voice, and a pompous way of speaking that reminded Ted of his Latin teacher at Sydney Boys' High who always wore a graduation gown draped around his shoulders like a toga. They arranged to meet at Cahill's restaurant in Castlereagh Street the following day.

On his way home that evening Ted hoped that Mr Addison wouldn't turn out to be an old crank who saw conspiracies everywhere. But if he had some evidence to show that illegal immigrants were infiltrating Australia, Gus would have to agree that the story was worth pursuing. He could already envisage the headline — REDS UNDER OUR BEDS — with his by-line underneath.

The tram was even more crowded than usual with workers returning home from town, mostly men in grey suits with large lapels and baggy trousers, and women in hats and gloves. Undeterred by the cramped space, some women were knitting, and their needles clicked incessantly. Hanging onto the leather strap, Ted glanced to the right, and his heart stopped. Standing on the other side of the compartment was the girl who was rarely out of his thoughts. She was looking the other way, and he watched her with an enraptured gaze. She had the kind of European complexion he'd only read about: porcelain-fine skin that had never been touched by the sun. Her flaxen hair was caught back from her heart-shaped face with small clips; it made her look like a schoolgirl, but even under her coat he could see that there was nothing girlish about her figure.

She flicked her hair back from her face and he saw that the tips of her ears protruded through her hair, like a pixie's. Ted swallowed. He knew he would want to keep looking at this girl for the rest of his life.

At that moment she turned and saw him, and he felt his face burning, because he knew that his infatuation was written on his face.

'We are like sardines, no?' she laughed, and her cheeks dimpled. She regarded him for a moment. 'I think so you live near me.'

He elbowed past two men to get closer to her. 'I'm Ted Browning,' he said and for some reason he suddenly felt the need to clear his throat. 'We live in the same street. Funny we've never met, isn't it?'

She laughed her rippling laugh again, and he felt he was levitating, like the woman on the magician's poster outside Kings Theatre.

'My name is Lilija Olmanis.'

He tried not to stare at her. 'Lilija?' he repeated. He'd never heard such a beautiful name.

She nodded. 'Latvian for Lily.'

'And what's the Latvian for my name? Tedmanis?'

She laughed as though he'd made the wittiest comment she'd ever heard, and he laughed too, and neither of them noticed that the other passengers were looking at them and smiling indulgently.

'Have you been hiding?' he teased. 'I've been trying to catch sight of you for weeks.'

Two parallel lines appeared between her eyebrows. 'Catch? What is that?'

Just then the tram jolted and he caught her as she tottered towards him.

'Like that,' he said, and they both laughed again.

'I am happy you catch me,' she said, and he was enchanted by the blush that coloured her cheeks.

Engrossed with each other, they almost missed their stop in Oxford Street, and they laughed as they jumped out of the tram. As they walked towards Wattle Street together, Ted slackened his pace to make the walk last longer. She was eighteen, she told him, and wanted to be a nurse.

He looked at her delicate wrists and ankles. 'You're too dainty to be a nurse. You should be a film star,' he blurted, and wanted to kick himself for sounding so unsophisticated.

They were almost at the corner of Wattle Street; time was running out. He had to think of something to detain her.

'Do you like ballet?' he asked.

She nodded, and her hair bounced on her slender shoulders.

'They're showing *The Red Shoes* at the Prince Edward. Would you like to see it?' He held his breath and waited.

She stopped walking, looked down and didn't say anything

for what felt like a very long time. When she looked up, she looked troubled.

'My father don't — doesn't like for me to go out,' she stammered.

'It's only to the movies,' he cut in. 'It won't be a late night. We could meet in town, see the film and come straight home. Would you like me to ask him?'

She shook her head.

'But you're not a child, he can't keep you locked away.' Ted was surprised at his own persistence.

'Maybe for you I am adult, but for Father I am still child. No boyfriends,' she said.

'What about your mother? What does she say?'

Lilija shrugged. 'She say what he say. Always.'

They were already in Wattle Street, and with an anxious look in the direction of her house, she hurried away.

That evening, after Ted had finished the grilled lamb chops, peas and mashed potatoes his mother placed in front of him, he thought about his conversation with Lilija with a growing sense of frustration. There had to be some way of making a date with her.

The Andrews Sisters had just finished belting out 'Rum and Coca-Cola' on 2GB, and Al Jolson was singing his mother's favourite song, a sentimental ditty called 'When You Were Sweet Sixteen'. Verna was singing along with him in her clear soprano voice.

'Mum, is Nola Wilson still nursing?'

Verna Browning wiped her soapy hands on her apron. 'I have no idea. I remember her poor mother telling me that Nola had started nursing at Sydney Hospital, but I don't know what she did after that.'

'I could ask Pop Wilson,' he said.

His mother shot him a sharp look. 'What's all this about, love? Is it to do with your work?'

He smiled, amused at the way his mother always assumed he was working on a story.

She was still looking at him, waiting for an explanation.

'I was talking to … you know, that girl up the street,' he said, trying to sound casual. 'She wants to do nursing, so I thought Nola might be able to give her a few tips.'

'And give you a good excuse to see her again. What's her name?'

'Lilija,' he murmured, revelling in the pleasure of rolling her name on his tongue. He turned away so she wouldn't see him blushing. He couldn't hide anything from his mother.

'I don't know that I'd mention it to Pop,' Verna said slowly.

It was a fair while since Nola had started nursing. At least eight years, Verna calculated. Maybe more. A lively girl, she was; good-looking too, with that glossy chestnut hair and nice figure. She hadn't seen Nola for years. When the war had started, Violet Wilson had said Nola had become a WAAC and had sailed to the Old Country on a troopship, but she had never mentioned her again after that. Maybe the girl had stayed in England.

Verna sighed, thinking of poor Violet who had dropped dead from a heart attack five years before. Now that Ted had brought it up, she realised that she hadn't heard Pop mention Nola for years. She wondered if they'd lost touch, but if they had, and that caused him heartache, he never said, and she never asked, even though they'd had been neighbours for over twenty years. People were entitled to keep their lives private, although she did notice that the number of wine bottles Pop lined up on his front porch for the bottle-o seemed to be growing.

'I wouldn't mention Nola,' Verna said again.

She scanned her son's face and read his thoughts. 'Don't worry, love, I'm sure the New Australian lass will get all the information she needs from the hospital when she applies for the job.'

She smiled at him. 'And I'm sure you'll come up with some other way of getting to know her.'

That was the end of the conversation because it was time for her favourite serial. Pulling her winged armchair closer to the Kosy heater, she turned the dial on the large walnut console to tune in to *When a Girl Marries*, and picked up her knitting bag.

She was knitting Ted a striped sleeveless vest but every few minutes she put down her knitting and thought about the private lives and hidden heartaches behind closed doors.

Chapter 10

As soon as Szymon came in and hung up his hat and coat, Sala placed a loaf of rye bread and a plate of cottage cheese in front of him and made a helpless gesture in the direction of the food.

'I couldn't get near the stove today with all the other women fighting over it,' she said. 'The kitchen here is awful. It smells of rancid grease. It's probably never been cleaned. It makes me feel sick.'

He put his arm around her. 'Bread and cheese is fine with me. But are you sure you're not feeling sick for some other reason?'

She shrank from him and sat down at the table. 'I feel sick because the kitchen is disgusting,' she said pointedly. She knew what was on his mind.

'I was hoping you were pregnant,' he said as he sat down beside her.

She raised her voice. 'How can you even think of having a baby in a place like this? Look at us. How could we provide for a child when we don't have anything?'

'Don't worry, Salcia.' He used the affectionate form of her name whenever he tried to talk her round. She knew that his favourite sister had been called Salcia, and he loved using the name. 'You'll see, in time we'll have everything.'

She knew he got that optimism from his father, the rabbi. That was another major difference between them. She'd grown up in a secular, urban family in Łódż, whereas he was one of nine children of a rabbi in a small town. Whenever food was scarce, or the children needed shoes, his mother would wring her hands in despair, but his father would say it was an insult to God to lose hope, because God would always provide.

Sala stopped spreading the cottage cheese on her bread and looked up. 'I suppose you still think God will provide,' she said bitterly. 'Just like He's provided everything else in our lives.'

Szymon shook his head. 'You have to have faith in the future, and the future means children.'

Now that there was no hope of avoiding the subject, she ploughed on. 'I don't know how you can think of bringing children into a world like this.'

'It's the only world we have,' he replied. 'And isn't that what Hitler wanted, that we should all die out? You want to help him? Can't you see that not having children means he's won?'

Sala turned away, shaking with anger, and stood to clear the plates. In all their arguments Szymon was like a steam train gathering speed downhill. But this was one argument he wasn't going to win. For once, she wasn't going to be browbeaten. No children.

She stole a glance at him. He was raking his hands through his thick dark hair as he sat hunched over his English–Polish dictionary. With his thick black eyebrows that arched above his deep-set eyes, he would have been handsome if his nose hadn't been flattened by a German rifle butt.

Watching him she felt the confusion that was poisoning their relationship. She admired his strength and optimism, but at the same time she resisted it.

The saucepan of water came to the boil on their small primus stove, and as she sipped the black tea and sucked a cube of sugar, the steam rose from the glass and her mind wandered off into another room, another glass of black tea, and another man.

Forcing herself back to the present, she peered over Szymon's shoulder. 'What are you looking up?'

He pushed the wooden chair away from the table and leaned back. 'I'm trying to find a word the foreman used. When I asked him to tell me what it meant, they all laughed. They're always making fun of me, and I want to make sure it doesn't happen again.' His eyes flashed with anger. 'You know how humiliated I was the day I went to see Max Furstenberg about the job.'

Sala nodded. She remembered his resentment when he'd told her about the disdainful way the secretary had looked him up and down, from his brown shoes with the white toecaps, to the jacket he wore draped over his shoulders, European-style.

'You want to see the boss?' she had asked. 'Do you have an appointment?'

He frowned, and she rephrased the question. 'Does Mr Furstenberg know you are coming?'

'I try to make appointment from Poland but line is busy, so I come in person,' he'd said, but from her blank look he'd realised that his sarcasm was lost on her.

'This isn't how we do things here,' she'd said coolly.

'I been in concentration camps six years,' he'd exploded, 'and they do things different there too! So now you tell how you do it here, please.'

Shocked at his outburst, she'd risen hastily from her desk and asked him to wait. A few moments later, Max Furstenberg had appeared. He'd taken one look at Szymon and slapped him on the back. 'Szymon Wajs! Funny thing, I always knew you'd turn up!'

But when Mr Furstenberg had taken him into the factory to show him the knitting machines and introduced him as an expert from Poland, the foreman had scowled at the boss's new protégé. Szymon had arrived early on his first day, eager to get started, but whenever he'd asked the foreman to explain something, he hadn't been able to understand the answer because the man spoke with a broad accent, and his thin lips hardly moved when he talked. Finally, he had raised his voice, and that's when the foreman had said the word Szymon couldn't catch, even though he'd repeated it several times during the day. From his tone, and the laughter of the other men on the factory floor, Szymon had realised he was the butt of a joke, and the sooner he figured out what it meant, the sooner they'd stop making fun of him.

'It sounded like *fakov* or maybe *farkov* but it's not there.' He looked up from his dictionary. 'There was another word he used — *skab* — but I can't find that either.'

'Try *s-c-a-b*,' suggested Sala. She'd spent the long weeks on board the ship studying English, while Szymon had passed the time playing poker, and she had some idea about the vagaries of the spelling.

'I've got it!' he exclaimed. '*Dry skin that's formed when a wound or sore heals.*'

He slammed the dictionary shut and swore. '*Cholera psia krew!* This dictionary is useless.'

'They must be Australian words, that's why they're not in there,' Sala suggested.

'What do you mean, "Australian"?' he shouted. 'What are they, Hottentots from Timbuktu? Don't they speak English here, with their King, their flag, and their Empire Day?'

It was useless trying to talk to him when he was in this mood but his bad moods never lasted, so she opened her English grammar book and waited until he'd calmed down.

He slurped his tea and put down the empty glass. Taking her hand he said, 'Salcia, now that we're getting settled, I'd like to light candles on Shabbas.'

She set her mouth in a straight line. In her own family, being Jewish had meant little more than festive dinners at

Passover and Rosh Hashana. On Yom Kippur her mother was the only one who had fasted, and she'd done it out of respect for her own parents and for tradition, not for any religious reason. They never lit candles on Friday nights.

'Settled?' she repeated. 'Just look at this room.'

'Settled enough to light candles,' he said.

'You know I'm not religious. I don't believe in any of that stuff.'

He moved closer to her and looked into her face. 'Do it for me, Salcia. It means a lot to me.'

There were tears in his eyes and she knew he was thinking of the Friday nights at home with his parents, brothers and sisters who were no longer alive. She nodded. If candles and blessings would help to fill his emptiness, she would do it. If only there was something that could fill her own void.

He put his arms around her and drew her down onto his lap. 'I'm earning six pounds a week at the moment, but Mr Furstenberg said that in time he'll make me foreman, and then I'll get a raise. You'll see, Salcia, I'll buy you that block of flats you liked in Bondi Road. Or perhaps like the one where Fela and Lutek live.'

She couldn't help smiling at the grandiose ambitions of this man who had only arrived a few weeks ago and was a factory worker on the basic wage, but from the expression on his face, she knew he was serious.

* * *

When they'd arrived in Sydney, his cousin Fela, who had sent them their landing permit, was waiting for them on the wharf.

As soon as she saw Szymon she threw her arms around him, and then stepped back and screamed. 'What happened to you? You used to be so handsome!'

His hand flew to his misshapen nose. 'There's been a war, or haven't you heard?'

Fela had migrated to Australia in 1938 with her husband Lutek who had foreseen the looming tragedy in Europe and had talked her into leaving. By migrating when they did, they'd escaped the fate of most of the Polish Jews and arrived in Sydney at a time when manufacturing businesses were thriving. Lutek had started up a handbag factory and by 1948 he'd made enough money to buy a spacious apartment with a balcony in Bellevue Hill.

'The Australians call it Bellejew Hill,' Fela said as they drove Sala and Szymon from the ship in their new Holden. Sala didn't understand the joke, but she was too engrossed looking out of the car window at the leafy avenues and impressive homes to take any notice of what was being said.

Inside the flat, Sala stood in the hall transfixed. It was as though time had rolled backwards. She might have been standing in her parents' home before the war, in a world of Persian rugs, walnut sideboards and porcelain figurines. She had forgotten that before the war people had taken their belongings with them, because they'd still had possessions to bring.

They'd been at Fela and Lutek's place for about a week when at dinner one evening the conversation turned to life in Sydney during the war.

'You know, we suffered here too,' Fela said in an aggrieved tone. 'We had blackouts and we had to cover the windows and put covers over the car headlights, and there was barbed wire all along Bondi Beach. And there was rationing. We couldn't get butter for love or money. Did you know that Japanese submarines came into Sydney Harbour? They even fired a few shells. It was terrifying. We were staying in a flat in Bondi at the time, and one of the shells fell just outside our place. You should have seen the hole it made in the pavement!'

Sala and Szymon exchanged glances but said nothing.

Things came to a head when Sala spilled some borsch on the tablecloth. Leaping to her feet, Fela screamed, 'That tablecloth came from my mother's house!' She scurried back and forth, feverishly removing all the plates and dishes from the table, refusing to allow anyone to help as she scrubbed the cloth with soap, muttering that the beetroot stain would never come out, and her tablecloth was ruined.

Sala went into their bedroom and sat on the bed, white with anger and barely able to speak when Szymon came in to see what was wrong. 'Your cousin's crying about a tablecloth and she thinks that not having butter is a tragedy, while we —' She stopped, too choked to say any more. 'I'd rather sleep on a park bench than live here with them.'

The following day they'd rented the room in Wattle Street.

'There's a telephone in the hall. I should ring Fela and let her know how we're going,' Szymon said.

Sala bristled. 'Tell her I'm going to commit suicide because I've got a ladder in my stocking.'

'Don't be like that, Salcia. You can't expect them to understand what we went through. They mean well.'

'They're ignorant and insensitive,' she snapped. 'You talk to them. I've got to figure out what kind of job I'm going to get.'

She knew he was right about one thing: you couldn't expect anyone to understand. And there was no way you could talk about it. If you went into details, people would stare at you with horror or pity or, worse, disbelief. But you couldn't blame them. There were times when even she couldn't believe what she'd gone through. But glossing over things would mean trivialising the enormity of it all. Tragedy couldn't be explained. It had to be endured.

If it hadn't been for Ernst Hauptmann, she wouldn't have survived. At the thought of his heavy footsteps on the wooden floorboards above the musty cellar, her heart started racing. She had to think about something else.

'I'm going to see about getting a job tomorrow.' She spoke loudly to drown out her memories.

Szymon smiled and patted her shoulder. 'I'm glad you're starting to settle down.'

Chapter 11

Ted paced outside the entrance of the Prince Edward Theatre, pulling up the sleeve of his overcoat every few seconds to check the time. Every now and again he glanced across the road at the men in dinner suits and the women in floaty evening dresses as they mounted the steps of the Hotel Australia.

A small crowd had already gathered on the footpath to gawk at the Sydney celebrities arriving for the ball being held in honour of Laurence Olivier and Vivien Leigh. As the chauffeur-driven Daimler of the guests of honour pulled up noiselessly outside the hotel, Ted craned forward, but all he saw was a shimmer of a white fox-fur stole, a gleam of pearls, and the back view of a man who was shorter and stockier than he'd expected. Then the Oliviers disappeared inside and the crowd dispersed, murmuring breathlessly about the famous couple.

Ted fumbled in his coat pocket for a Capstan, lit up, took a few puffs, then threw the cigarette in the gutter and resumed his pacing. He decided to wait another five minutes, and then five more. He should have known it was too good to be true when, after two weeks of pleading, Lilija had finally agreed to meet him. Now that she'd started nursing at the hospital, they met on the Bondi tram after work whenever her shifts allowed, and he had made the most of the opportunity to persuade her to go out with him. Now he wondered whether it was the amused glances of the passengers who had heard his entreaties the previous evening that had induced her to agree to a date she had no intention of keeping. There was no point hanging around any longer because she wasn't going to show up. What a fool he'd been, thinking she'd come.

Then he looked up and there she was, running towards him, out of breath, with her fair hair streaming behind her, shining in the streetlights.

'I thought you weren't coming,' he blurted before he could stop himself.

'Matron was angry. She doesn't — didn't allow us to go,' Lilija said, taking his arm.

As they walked towards the entrance, he noticed that people turned to look at her as they passed, and he held her hand more tightly. Looking at her, he had the peculiar feeling that his heart had suddenly grown too large for his chest.

They passed the liveried commissionaire and entered the cinema, which advertised itself as *Sydney's Theatre Beautiful*, and he smiled as he watched her gazing at the marble walls, plush royal-blue and gold carpet, and the massive fountain with its concealed lights at the base of the curved marble staircases leading to the dress circle.

'It's like a palace,' Lilija said in a hushed voice.

As a Chinese gong struck five times to indicate that the show was about to begin, they moved towards the gilded doors of the stalls, and a tall usherette in a crisp burgundy uniform showed them to their seats. Lilija looked up at the crystal chandelier suspended from the dome, the marble statues decorating the sides of the auditorium, and the two tiers of seats in the gilded dress circle. The lights dimmed and she caught Ted's arm and pointed. Something was emerging from under the floor, and as they watched, an organ appeared, with a blonde woman in a satin evening gown seated at the keyboard.

'That's Noreen Hennessy,' Ted whispered. 'She plays every night before the film starts.'

Noreen Hennessy flashed a megawatt smile at the audience, bent forward and, in a voice that always made Ted think of treacle, announced, 'My song for you this session is a medley from the new Broadway musical *Kiss Me Kate* by Mr Cole Porter.'

As the theatre filled with the rippling sound of the Wurlitzer organ, and the patrons tapped their feet in time to the catchy tunes, Ted glanced at Lilija. She looked like Alice in Wonderland and, unable to wipe the delighted grin off his face, he supposed he looked like the Cheshire Cat. As soon as the medley was over, Noreen Hennessy inclined her blonde head to acknowledge the applause, and the organ slid slowly beneath the floor.

A moment later a shiver of anticipation ran through the audience when a fanfare introduced the Movietone newsreel.

As usual, most of the items concerned the growing menace of Communism and, in his urgent tone and plum-in-the-mouth accent, the narrator announced that a state of emergency had been proclaimed in Malaya as a result of the murder of some rubber planters by Communist guerrillas. In Czechoslovakia the Communist Party had tightened its grip on the country, and in Germany the Berlin Blockade had just begun. There were two other items as well. Footage from London showed the King and Queen gazing adoringly at Princess Elizabeth's newborn baby boy. This was followed by a report about the Middle East. Arab armies of six nations had declared war on the newly established State of Israel.

During the interval between the newsreel and the main feature, Ted started to ask Lilija something, but the film credits were already rolling so he opened the box of Fantales he'd bought before the show and they settled into their wide plush seats to watch *The Red Shoes*.

Ted thought the story might prove too difficult for Lilija to follow, with its complicated plot-within-a-plot about a ballerina forced to choose between her love of dancing and her love for a man, a situation which paralleled her role in the ballet, but whenever he stole a glance at her, she seemed absorbed in the movie. During the love scene, he reached over to take her hand, and brushed against something small and hard under her woollen skirt.

He realised it was part of the suspender that fastened her stocking, and when he visualised what the suspender belt covered, and thought how close he'd come to touching her warm thigh, he felt a rush of excitement and hurriedly placed the packet of Fantales across his lap so that she wouldn't see the embarrassing bulge.

When the film came to its tragic end and the ballerina lay dead on the railway tracks, Lilija sobbed so much that he had to wait for her to calm down before they could leave the theatre.

As they made their way through the throng towards the tram stop, Ted remembered what he'd meant to ask her. 'How come your father changed his mind about letting you go on a date?'

She looked down and fiddled with her gloves. 'He doesn't know. I tell him I stay in hospital for evening shift.'

He put his arm around her shoulders and pressed her against him. 'You little fibber!'

'I don't want him to be angry, but also, I want to go with you.'

As the tram clattered in the dark, Lilija pressed her face to the window, looking out at the empty streets. 'In Riga,' she said, 'peoples go out at night. They walk, meet friends in clubs and cafés. Here, no. Why?'

It had never occurred to Ted to question this before. Perhaps it had something to do with the fact that the pubs closed at six. Or because Australians were homebodies who lacked the spark that the French described as *joie de vivre*.

'It's the English temperament, yes?' she said.

'We're not English, we're Australians.'

'Not same?' she asked.

'Not same,' he laughed, and helped her off the tram. Above them a crescent moon cast its pale light over her hair which was the colour of starlight.

Stopping under a street lamp, he bent down to kiss her lips, brushing them lightly at first, and he felt her smooth cheek against his, cool as marble in the evening air. But when he kissed her more passionately, she pulled away and looked around.

'Don't people kiss in Riga?' he teased. 'Or are you afraid your father will find out?'

She didn't reply straightaway and he saw that she was struggling for words. 'My father is good man, clever man,' she said after a while, and he realised that she resented his implied criticism. 'In our country he is hero, but here he is nothing. So much bad things in his life. I don't want to make more.'

As they walked slowly towards Wattle Street, she told him that their life in Riga had changed when the Russians invaded in 1939 and deported hundreds of thousands of Latvians to Siberia. She and her mother had fled to the countryside, where her grandparents had an orchard. She swam in the stream that flowed through their land and picked peaches and apricots from the trees. But when the Germans came, her father went into the army. She rarely saw him until the war was almost over, and the Red Army was about to enter Latvia. That's when they escaped to Germany to avoid being deported and killed.

History had never been Ted's strong point, and recent Baltic history was totally beyond him, but the stories he'd heard from the Baltic migrants on the SS *Napoli* aroused his curiosity. 'Why did they deport all those people? What for?'

She sounded exasperated at his ignorance and naivety. 'For nothing. For having a business or a farm. For not wanting Communism. Communists are thieves and murderers.'

As she spat the words out, her features hardened and her eyes blazed with anger, and he felt he was looking at a stranger. More questions were gnawing at him, but he didn't want to make her more agitated and he wished he hadn't started this conversation — it had ruined his hopes for a romantic end to the evening.

He took her hand. 'Did you like *The Red Shoes*?'

'I like, but too sad. In my life, things good, then bad. Now, with you, is very good, so I am afraid.'

He looked at her face and knew that he wanted to spend the rest of his life making her happy. The feeling was so intense that it felt like an electric current shooting through his body.

She said goodbye at his front gate and insisted on walking to her place alone. He crept forward and waited until he heard the front door close behind her, then tiptoed into his house so as not to wake his mother.

That night he dreamed that he was back in the Kings Cross flat again, but this time the dead girl had been shot through the heart, and he recognised her face. It was Lilija.

Chapter 12

Sala got off the tram in Bayswater Road, looked around and checked the address she'd jotted down on a slip of paper. She crossed William Street, and when she saw two fire trucks parked outside the old brick fire station, she knew she was heading in the right direction.

As she walked down Victoria Street towards the Maccabean Hall, she passed narrow terrace houses that seemed to be stuck together, connected by a continuous row of black wrought-iron balconies. Too small to sit on, they were decorative, but as useless as a lace collar on a dress.

She thought back to the balcony of her parents' home in Łódż, where she used to stand and watch the people in the street below, hoping to catch a glimpse of the boy she liked. On autumn evenings a light breeze would swirl beech and chestnut leaves around the pavement. The entrance to their home was flanked by massive statues that supported the balcony. As a small girl she had often wondered what would happen if those statues got tired of holding up the building and suddenly let go. Now she knew. She sighed. Nostalgia was like water, and you had to keep your mind watertight or memories would seep into the smallest crevice and flood it with helpless longing.

Past the big hospital she checked the address again and found the Maccabean Hall a block away, in a tired-looking building of liver-coloured brick, slightly recessed from the road. Pushing the brass handle on the door, she entered the foyer and waited until the caretaker directed her to the door marked *Jewish Welfare Society*.

Inside a dimly lit room, several women sat tapping away at typewriters. When she asked for the social worker, someone pointed to a desk in the far corner where a middle-aged woman with glasses stretched out her hand with a welcoming smile and introduced herself as Franka Feldman. To Sala's relief, she was Polish.

'I've been in Sydney for eighteen months now and I know how hard it is when you first get here,' Franka said, pulling up a chair for Sala. She leaned forward with an encouraging smile. 'Now, how can I help you?'

Reassured by her kind expression and straightforward manner, Sala said, 'I need a job but I don't know what work I could do. I haven't got any qualifications or experience. Unless you call surviving the war "experience".'

Franka nodded. 'That's the kind of experience we often come across in here. Pity it's not marketable,' she said. 'Tell me, what kind of work would you like to do?'

'In Poland I wanted to study medicine, but the war put an end to that idea.'

'There are various courses that would enable you to study and work part-time. Would you like to be a medical technician, for instance?'

Sala shrugged. 'I don't really know. Besides, how will I understand what the lecturers are saying?'

'My husband is much older than you and he's studying medicine again. I can assure you that when he started a year ago, his English was probably no better than yours,' Franka said. 'It depends how determined you are.'

'And what kind of work could I do while I was doing the course?'

Franka studied her for a few moments. 'Can you clean?' she asked.

Sala frowned, and Franka added, 'I mean, can you wash floors, polish furniture, that kind of thing?'

'I suppose so.'

'As it happens, one of our cleaners has just left, and we need someone in the mornings from six till eight. If you're interested, I can arrange for you to start tomorrow. You won't earn very much, but you'll have most of the day to yourself.'

She was already flicking the pages of a thick prospectus that listed courses being offered at Sydney University and at various technical institutions. 'Here we are,' she said. 'There's a course in medical pathology that you could do part-time. But you'll have to wait until next year to start.'

Sala walked away from the Maccabean Hall with a light step. It was the personal connection with Franka Feldman that buoyed her spirits even more than the relief of having a plan of action. She was comforted by Franka's motherly manner, and for the first time since coming to Sydney she felt she'd met someone whose advice she could trust.

She didn't have long to wait for the Bondi tram, which she recognised by the red circle inside a white square in the front. When she slid into her seat, she wondered what her job would be like, and what Szymon would think about it.

Back in Wattle Street, she passed the postman who shrilled his whistle each time he pushed mail into the letterboxes.

Verna Browning was standing at her front gate. 'Hello, love. Have a good day?' she asked, but before Sala could get the words together to reply, her neighbour had disappeared inside. A few doors further on, a tall thin man with a stern face took a letter from his box. He bowed stiffly when she passed, and turned away.

As soon as she heard Szymon's key turn in the door that evening, she ran to greet him.

'You look happy tonight, Salcia,' he said. 'What did you do today?'

'I've decided to enroll in a course and become a medical technician. And I've got a job.'

He hugged her. 'That's my Salcia. No wonder you're pleased with yourself.'

But when she explained what she'd be doing, he scowled. 'My wife a cleaner? For this we came to a new country? I don't earn enough for you, so you have to clean other people's dirt?'

She felt crushed. 'It's not dirty work. I went to the Jewish Welfare Society this morning to see about work and —'

Szymon broke in. 'You went there, after the reception I got?'

A few days after they'd arrived in Sydney, Szymon had taken his cousin's advice and gone to the Jewish Welfare Society to find out about conditions in Sydney.

'They treated me like an ignorant peasant, as if I didn't know how to behave in civilised society,' he fumed. 'Remember that sheet of instructions I got? You should, you translated it for me.'

She did remember. It advised newcomers not to speak foreign languages in the street or on the trams, to keep their voices down, not to congregate around Kings Cross and Bondi, and not to wear long overcoats or carry flat leather portfolios.

'Szymon, calm down,' she said. 'The social worker I saw was very helpful, and the cleaning job will give me time to study. Now come and sit down. I've made schnitzel for dinner.'

'I'm not hungry,' he said. He sat down heavily on the bed with his back to her and unrolled a copy of the *Daily Standard*, which he bought every evening. Even though he couldn't understand much of it, he usually figured out what the articles were about from the headlines and the photographs.

She could see that his pride was hurt but she wasn't going

to give in. 'Szymon, this is the first time since we left Poland that I've made a decision about my life. It's the first time I've felt hopeful about the future. Don't spoil it.'

'Hopeful because you're going to wash floors for a few shillings a day? That makes you happy?'

'Don't you understand that I need to earn some money and study something I'm interested in?' she retorted. 'Anyway, that's what I'm going to do.'

'Do what you like! I don't know why you got married if you're going to do whatever you like. You should have stayed with your bloody *Volksdeutsch*.'

'I wish I had!' she retorted.

'Well it's not too late,' he shouted, and walked out, slamming the door behind him.

Sala flung herself on the bed and sobbed. Their arguments always ended this way. There were things she hadn't told him about Ernst Hauptmann, and never would, but at times like this she wished she'd never mentioned him at all.

It was a cold night and she had pulled the blankets and bedspread over herself in bed when she heard the door open. By the way Szymon tiptoed across the room and placed his shoes gently on the floor so as not to wake her, she knew the fight was over.

'Salcia,' he whispered, putting his arms around her. 'I'm sorry. You know me, I shoot my mouth off.'

Before she had turned towards him, his hot hands were already moving underneath her flannel nightdress, searching for the secret places that made her arch her back and raise her hips towards him. But, for her, making love was a source of solace rather than ecstasy. She kept her eyes closed and tried to block out the memory of footsteps treading on the wooden floor and the squeak of the hinge that opened the trapdoor.

While Szymon was spreading plum jam over his rye bread the next morning, he said, 'Salcia, this is a wonderful country. Did you know there was a Jewish governor-general here in the 1930s? And I'll tell you another thing. The Prime Minister, Mr Chifley, used to be an engine driver. It's unbelievable. An engine driver who becomes a prime minister. This is the real socialist utopia.'

Sala couldn't help smiling. Szymon was as thrilled as a schoolboy who has just found out that his sporting idol has moved in next door.

'No one here cares whether you're educated, rich or famous, as long as you're a good bloke,' he said.

'As long as you're not a bloody foreigner,' Sala said. She'd been reading the letters column in the newspapers, with their frequent complaints about migrants. And there was that old woman who lived next door to Mrs Browning. Whenever Sala walked past her, she could feel the hostility. Sometimes the old woman glared and muttered under her breath while her black cat rubbed against her stick-like legs. All the old witch needed was a broom.

But, as usual, Szymon saw things differently. 'You can't expect them to like us. We are different. They're not used to us yet, but they will be.'

'It's strange, isn't it,' she mused. 'A huge country with hardly any people, an empty centre, and no history.'

'That's exactly why I love it,' Szymon said. 'A country without a past but with a big future.' He put his arm around her. 'Listen, Salcia, we're going to have a good life here, better than we've ever had.'

'Especially when you buy me that block of flats you promised.' She was teasing, but he didn't smile.

'Just you wait and see,' he said. 'And I won't need your two pounds a week for a deposit.'

It was cold and dark when Sala rose next morning, and as she pulled on her beige sweater over the green-and-white check skirt, her fingers were so numb with the cold that she could hardly do up the buttons of her woollen jacket. She regretted having agreed to take the job, especially when she stood shivering at the tram stop half an hour later, her teeth chattering and her hands like blocks of ice.

'Pretty cold today,' the conductor said as he tore off her ticket. 'Off to work, are you?'

She nodded miserably and pulled the lapels of the jacket closer around her.

'Cheer up, love. It'll get better,' he said and continued on his way past the almost empty compartments calling, 'Fez pliz.'

'It'll get better,' she repeated several times, copying his inflections, and by the time she reached the Jewish Welfare Society she felt more cheerful.

She was met in the entrance hall by a dumpy woman with shifty eyes.

'So you finally got 'ere, did ya? We get goin' at six.'

Sala looked at her watch. It was ten past. 'The tram,' she stammered.

'Never mind the excuses,' the other woman cut in. 'Tomorrow, be 'ere at six. I'm Beryl.'

She opened the closet where the mop, wringer pails, brooms and dusters were kept and banged tins, jars and bottles around. Sala didn't know what any of them were for, and Beryl gabbled so fast that she couldn't figure out what Oxydol, Johnson's cream wax, Spic and Span, Bon Ami and Brillo were supposed to do.

'Just follow me and watch,' Beryl snapped, and proceeded to rush from room to room, dusting, polishing and mopping at a speed that left Sala bewildered.

'Bloody foreigners,' Beryl muttered. 'You'd think at least they'd learn the lingo.'

'Lingo?' Sala asked, but with an exasperated gesture the woman marched ahead and she had to run to catch up with her.

Sala had no idea why the woman was so antagonistic, and couldn't wait for her shift to end so she could get away.

She was hurrying towards the front door when she almost collided with Franka Feldman.

'How did you go?' she asked and, seeing the answer in Sala's face, she added, 'Beryl's not a bad soul. You'll see, her bark is worse than her bite.'

Sala made a noncommittal reply and hurried out of the building. It was a little warmer now, and as she walked towards the tram stop she took her hands out of her pockets, undid the top button of her jacket and filled her lungs with cool, fresh air. The windows and roofs of the Austins and Vauxhalls parked along the road were dripping with condensation. Drops of moisture were hanging off the spear-shaped leaves of the eucalypts, and the edges of the wrought-iron balconies were gleaming in the morning sun.

As she sat down on the bench to wait for the tram the Australian woman sitting beside her asked where she came from. She nodded sympathetically when Sala told her, and said, 'It must be so hard coming to a new country.'

Sala's tram squealed to a stop, and as she hurried towards it the woman called out, 'Good luck to you.'

Touched by the stranger's unexpected kindness, Sala felt tears spring to her eyes.

Chapter 13

The night was damp and chilly, and Eda Kotowicz rubbed her cold-stiffened fingers in front of the kerosene heater. In the weak light of the single-bulb lamp, she began hemming a skirt, but as she pushed the needle into the thick woollen fabric, she saw neither thread nor cloth. Only yesterday her new friend Sala had said that Australia was a nation without a past, but Eda felt she had enough past to fill up the whole country.

As she turned the garment around and continued to hem, woven into the material she saw the phantom faces of those who had vanished into pillars of greenish smoke, faces that stared at her so reproachfully she had to look away.

Her grandmother, who always found a piece of chocolate for her; her grandfather, who told her wonderful stories about dybbuks and golems; the parents she'd never appreciated; the gentle husband she hadn't loved enough; the little boy … Her hands trembled and she stared into space.

It would have been a relief to cry, but there was a band of steel tightening her chest and locking her emotions. Except for anger, which seeped through the veins and burned through the flesh. Sometimes she felt that this band was all that held her together, and if it ever loosened she would spill out of her skin.

Before coming to Sydney, she'd believed that a new country would mean a new beginning, but as she threaded the needle again and snapped off the cotton with her teeth, she reflected on her mistake. She'd left Poland because it didn't feel like home any more. It had become a vast cemetery, with all her loved ones buried in its soil. But she'd had another reason for wanting to migrate to the other side of the world: consumed by jealousy and fear, she'd wanted to make sure that the Majewskis would never get their clutches into Hania again.

As she picked up another skirt and began to hem, she reflected that she didn't belong here either, and probably never would. Her dream of starting a new life in Australia with a daughter who loved her seemed more improbable with every passing day.

She heard shouting outside and went out onto the verandah. It was only three boys kicking a ball, and calling out to one another. Hania and two other girls were playing hopscotch on the pavement.

As soon as they finished their game, Hania ran over to her mother. 'We're going to play in the paddock now, okay?'

'What about your homework?'

Hania pulled a face. 'I haven't got much. I'll do it later,' she said, and before her mother could argue, she ran off with the others. With a sigh, Eda turned back to her sewing. The gap between them seemed to be widening, and she despaired whether they would ever understand each other.

In the afternoons after school, the vacant lot behind the lane became a playground for the children of Wattle Street. Overgrown with weeds and long grass, its uneven ground became the scene of rounders, cops and robbers or princesses and pirates, but their favourite game was acting out the movie they'd seen at the Star or the Coronet the previous Saturday afternoon.

'Let's do *Little Women*,' Beverley said, and added quickly, 'I bags be Meg.'

That started an argument because all the girls wanted to be Meg, but when Kay, a skinny girl with buck teeth and lank hair, wanted to be Amy, Beverley objected. 'Hanny should be Amy, because she's the prettiest,' she said.

The role of Beth, who dies early in the story, was given to Beverley's little sister, who always tagged along behind them.

When the girls' roles were settled, they argued over who should be Jo's suitor. When Kay suggested her older brother, Beverley shouted her down and suggested Ricky who lived around the corner.

'He's a show-off,' Kay protested. 'He always mucks up.'

Hania suggested Meggsie, and blushed bright red.

The other boys hooted and made derisive noises as Meggsie reluctantly left off being Biggles and stopped shooting down

Messerschmitts to take part in the soppy story the girls were acting out.

'Hubba, hubba! Make sure you get to kiss your girlfriend!' Ricky yelled, pointing at Hania.

The girls couldn't remember what happened first, Meg's marriage, Beth's death or the publication of Jo's book, and while they were arguing about it Meggsie sneaked back to his mates, who let him be the Prisoner of Zenda and proceeded to whip him with a bunch of tall grasses they'd tied together.

After the games were over, Hania was sitting on the grass weaving clover and dandelions into a garland when Meggsie planted himself in front of her.

'I know where there's a haunted house,' he said. 'Want to see it?'

Her heart started thumping. 'Is it far away?'

'Nah.'

She knew her mother wouldn't let her go but, emboldened by the success of her deceit at the Sunday school picnic, she decided not to ask. Her mother would think she was still playing in the paddock.

They ran towards Oxford Street and when the Bondi tram swung around the bend, he said, 'Come on, quick, jump on.'

She was already on the tram when she realised she hadn't brought any money.

'It's a cinch,' he said. 'When the conductor comes into our compartment, we'll pretend we're getting off, and then we'll get on again when he's gone.'

Hania felt uneasy. She hadn't envisaged catching trams or hitching free rides, but she didn't want Meggsie to think she was a scaredy-cat.

The tram clattered towards the beach and Meggsie craned his head out of the window as they passed a poster of a man in a red cape and black top hat pasted crookedly onto a wall.

'That's Morris the Magnificent,' he told Hania as he jiggled around in his seat. 'He's going to do the bullet trick. It's so dangerous that a magician once got shot doing it, and dropped dead on the stage in front of everybody. I'm saving up so I can see it. I can't wait!'

They jumped off the tram at North Bondi. At the end of the beach, Meggsie pointed to a flat rock at the base of the headland. 'I used to come here with my dad,' he said.

'Where is your dad?' Hania asked.

He shrugged. 'Dunno. Mum said he shot through like the Bondi tram and never came back. Where's your dad?'

'He's dead. He was killed during the war.'

Meggsie dropped his voice to a reverential whisper. 'Was he a soldier?'

She didn't know what to say. It was impossible to explain about round-ups, concentration camps and gas chambers, and she didn't want to try. It was simpler just to nod.

The sun was about to set and the sandstone cliff glowed with a honey-coloured light.

'It's up there,' Meggsie pointed. Suddenly he stopped walking and leaned against the rock, biting his lip. 'It's just my head,' he said. 'It hurts sometimes.'

Alarmed by his pale face, she suggested going back, but he shook his head. 'I'll be right in a minute.'

It was an easy climb to the spot where the ground flattened out and was covered in dense bushes. With their leathery foliage and sharp serrated leaves, the plants looked so tough that they seemed to dare you to touch them. Even their flowers had menacing shapes: the spiky brushes of the banksias and the blood-red grevilleas like spiders. The wildflowers looked softer: tiny pink flowerets of diosma with their dry bushland smell, and creamy flannel flowers. When she touched the petals, they felt like suede.

'They reckon the Abos left some cave drawings or carvings somewhere up here,' he said.

'Abos?'

'You know, blackfellows.'

She frowned. Apart from Bennelong, who was Captain Phillip's guide, the teachers never mentioned the Aborigines. She'd thought they all lived in the desert or in the bush, and was astonished to hear that they'd once lived in Bondi.

'Get down and don't make a sound,' Meggsie whispered. 'The house is just over there, past those bushes. We don't want him to see us.'

'I thought the place was empty,' she whispered back.

'He's there all right,' Meggsie hissed. 'Comes back at night. Some nights I used to see a light flickering in one of the windows when I came with my dad.'

Hania felt the skin prickling on the back of her neck.

They crept forward until they saw it, a simple timber cottage with a steeply sloping roof, behind two windswept Norfolk pines.

Hania hung back. 'I'm not going in,' she said, and flopped onto the sandy ground. 'What if he's there?'

Meggsie laughed. 'You wouldn't see him even if he was,' he said. 'Nosey's too smart to let anyone see him. Come on, I dare you!'

While they crouched behind the trees, he told her about the man who'd once lived there. 'He had one of those horse cabs, but one day the horse kicked him in the face and smashed his nose, and after that he looked so scary that nobody would get in his cab, so he couldn't earn any money and had to become a hangman.'

Hania shuddered and, pleased with the effect of his story, Meggsie told her more stories about the hangman. Like the weird way he went hunting for sharks, hooking the shark with some bait, wading in and grabbing its tail, and then dragging it out of the water by a rope he'd fixed to the horse's tail. His dad had told him that Nosey's horse was so used to going to the pub that it used to trot there by itself, with a pannikin fixed to the saddle. The publican would fill it with beer, and the horse would trot all the way back to Nosey.

'Why didn't Nosey get the beer himself?' Hania asked.

'He didn't like people staring at him. His kids stopped going to school because the other kids made fun of them 'cause their dad was a hangman and didn't have a nose.'

'That was mean,' Hania said. 'It wasn't their fault.'

'Kids at school laugh at me because my dad ran off and my mum's a barmaid,' Meggsie said, then blushed. 'I've never told anyone that before.'

Hania stole a glance at him. 'If I ever hear them making fun of you, I'll tell them off,' she said.

Meggsie scrambled to his feet and brushed the sandy soil off his legs. 'Come on, let's have a look at the house.'

Hania hesitated. The sun was about to sink below the horizon and the light was fading. She wanted to go home but she didn't want him to think she was a sissy. Before she could speak, he grabbed her hand. 'Race you up there.'

They peered through the broken window of the abandoned cottage. Most of the floorboards were rotting, and bits of corrugated iron lay against the mildewed walls. On the weathered sill of a small window stood a dust-encrusted beer bottle, and the enamel sink was piled high with blackened pots, rusting knives and grimy ladles.

Hania looked down and saw that a plant with lush green leaves had taken root in a hole in the floorboards and had pushed its way into the abandoned cottage. She was about to point it out to Meggsie when something crashed down, and she screamed. A rusty frying pan had toppled off the pile in the sink.

'I thought it was the ghost,' she said, still shaking.

'Maybe it was.'

He was teasing but the hair stood up on the back of her neck again. 'I want to go now,' she said.

Meggsie didn't reply. He was sitting on the doorstep, holding his head in his hands.

'It's my head again,' he mumbled. 'Feels like it's going to split open.'

She looked outside. It was already dark, and there was no one around. Meggsie's mother would be home from the pub by now, and her mother would know she wasn't with the other children in the paddock. Scared and nervous, she sat down beside him.

'Shall I go home and tell your mum you're sick, so she can come and get you?'

'Nah, Mum'll worry. I'll be okay.'

As they stumbled down the slope, Hania wasn't sure what she dreaded more: getting Meggsie home on the tram, or facing her mother and explaining where she'd been.

Chapter 14

As soon as he heard the tapping, Meggsie opened his eyes and felt the throbbing in his head again. Ever since the headaches had started, he hadn't been sleeping as soundly as usual. On these nights, when the house was quiet and dark, he often thought about his father, but that afternoon on the cliffs with Hanny, he couldn't bring himself to talk about him. It was all too complicated, the roller-coaster of fun and fear that his home life had been when Dad was there.

In the good times, he and Dad would go to the rock pool near Ben Buckler at night, and he'd hold the hurricane lamp while his dad set lobster traps. Sometimes they'd kick a ball around the paddock. But then there were dark days when Dad staggered home late, singing at the top of his voice and stinking of beer, and then the shouting would start, and he'd lie in bed and hear plates crashing and chairs being thrown across the room, shouting, then a terrible silence followed by his mother's curses and screams. Next morning she'd have a dark bruise on her cheek or a dark ring around her eye and pretend she'd had a fall, and he hated his father and couldn't look at him, especially when he saw him kissing and cuddling her.

Then one day Dad didn't come home and Meggsie couldn't figure out if he was relieved, sad, angry or disappointed. He was glad that the turmoil was over, and at last he could look after his mum and be the one she could rely on, but at the same time he missed his father and felt abandoned because his dad had never tried to see him after that.

The tapping grew louder and he slid out of bed, padded across to the window and pulled aside one corner of the curtain. It was dark outside, and a crescent moon floated in and out behind black clouds. The tapping came from the house next door, and when he looked out he saw a light shining from a small window at the back.

Perhaps their mysterious neighbour was a spy, tapping out Morse code messages to the Commies and passing them secret information. The more he thought about it, the more plausible it seemed. For one thing, there was the man's weird behaviour, the way he never spoke to anyone but seemed to melt into the air and disappear like a phantom. All that had to mean something.

Remembering the pact he'd made with Hanny and Beverley to keep an eye on Mr Emil, Meggsie had stopped Ted Browning in the street the day before and asked if he thought the man could be a spy. Ted had listened attentively, and then said with a serious face, 'I'd watch him if I were you. For all we know, he could be plotting to overthrow the government.'

This was all the encouragement Meggsie needed. Ted might even write an article about him — how a twelve-year-old boy from Bondi Junction had risked his life to capture a Commie spy. That would stop the bullies at school making fun of him because his dad had run away and his mum was a barmaid. He could already hear them saying, 'Gee, Meggsie, I never knew you were so brave. Can I be your friend?' And he'd say —

A sudden bang ended his reverie. Something heavy must have crashed to the ground next door. This was it. Time for action. He pulled on the Fair Isle jumper his gran had knitted for his tenth birthday. It was too tight now but he refused to pass it down to Ray because it was his favourite. He wished she'd knit him another one, but Gran hadn't been around for quite a while and, to hear Mum talk, it didn't sound like she'd be coming any time soon. If only he had a normal home life like the other kids who had a dad, grandparents and lots of cousins, so that his mum wouldn't have to be a barmaid and he wouldn't have to do paper rounds every day and be laughed at. His mum said it didn't matter what anyone said, if you were a decent person you could hold your head up and take no notice; but it was all right for her, she was grown up and didn't have to put up with bullies.

Meggsie crept through the darkened house, stopping and holding his breath each time the floorboards creaked. They creaked extra loud just outside his mother's bedroom where his little brother Pete slept in a fold-up bed.

He glanced in as he passed. Pete was on his back with his arms on either side of his head on the pillow in a gesture of surrender, his pink mouth wide open. His mother was lying on her side, with the blankets pulled up and her hair over her face. He imagined how proud she'd be when she read about him in the paper. He might even receive a bravery award from the police.

He opened the front door very slowly, pausing every few inches until it was just wide enough for him to slip through. The night air wreathed his breath around his face, and he shivered, wishing he'd pulled on his woollen socks. Now that he was outside his neighbour's place, he didn't know what to do. Perhaps he should wait and ask Ted. But now he'd got this far, he had to see it through. Once you started something, you had to see it through — that's what Biggles always said.

As Meggsie pushed open the gate, it dragged along the ground with a grating noise, and one of the dogs down the road let out an angry growl and started barking. It was Timmy, Pop Wilson's flea-bitten mongrel. Meggsie crouched beside a clump of spindly mauve hydrangeas until the barking stopped, then ran towards the front door. He tried turning the handle but the door was locked, and when he tried to raise the front window it didn't budge. Meggsie tried to rally his flagging spirits. You couldn't expect a spy to leave his front door and window wide open for anyone to walk in and see what he was up to.

A wooden gate secured by a metal bolt led to the side passage. He slid open the bolt and tiptoed down the passageway until he was standing outside the room where the light was coming from, but the window was too high up for him to see inside. An iron bucket stood at the end of the passage. Placing it upside down, he climbed onto it and looked over the edge of the weathered windowsill.

The Holland blind covering the window obscured the room, but there was a small hole in the blind a few inches above Meggsie's head. By standing on tiptoe and squinting, he could look through it. Mr Emil was bending over a work table, with his back to the window. In one hand he held a long thin metal tool which might have been a chisel or a pick, and in the other he held a small hammer with which he was tapping the chisel. There was no receiver or wireless in sight, and no matter how he craned and squirmed around for a better view, Meggsie couldn't see what his neighbour was doing.

He was ready to admit defeat and jump down when Mr Emil moved away. Meggsie's mouth dropped open. He was looking at a wooden box shaped like a rectangle. It tapered a little towards one end and then squared off. It was a coffin, and its lid was carved with flowers and fancy leaves. He pressed his face against the glass and saw another coffin lying on a pile of wood shavings on the floor. So that's what the hammering and tapping had been for. Meggsie shivered again, and this time it wasn't from the cold.

He stretched as high as he could until he was clinging to the windowsill with his fingertips and standing on the tips of his toes. Suddenly the bucket overturned with a clang and he fell to the ground. A moment later he heard the snap of a blind being rolled up and the window opening. He flattened himself against the wall, nursing his bleeding knee, and held his breath, praying that his neighbour hadn't seen him.

When it seemed safe, he pulled himself to his feet and began to hobble down the passageway. He'd almost reached the side gate when he felt himself being yanked backwards. Too terrified to scream, he tried to bolt, but the man's grip was too strong, and he felt like a fish wriggling helplessly from a hook.

'What you want?' Mr Emil said.

'Nothing,' he stammered.

'Why you are here? You come to steal something?'

Meggsie shook his head, appalled at being taken for a thief.

'So tell me. What do you look for?'

Meggsie was shaking, terrified by what he'd seen in the room, and his teeth were chattering so much that he couldn't speak.

Mr Emil was looking at him with piercing dark eyes and Meggsie was scared by the sudden transformation. It was as though he'd become another person, like those split personalities in the films, who were smiling one minute and killing people the next. He had a funny accent and there was something shifty about him. Maybe he was a Nazi.

Finally Meggsie found his voice. 'I won't tell anyone, honest,' he stammered.

The man was still staring at him, probably weighing up whether he could be trusted. 'You have good mother,' he said.

Sensing a threat, Meggsie repeated, 'I won't tell. Promise. Anyway,' he added, 'I didn't see nothing.'

'Good,' the man said. 'You see nothing and I see nothing. Go. Next time, ring bell. Not like thief.'

Meggsie ran home, threw himself into bed without taking off his pullover and covered himself with his blankets, but he couldn't stop shaking. He couldn't get the two coffins out of his mind. He'd heard on the news that two little kids were missing. They'd been playing on the swings in Waverley Park, but when their mum looked for them, they were gone. It all added up. Two coffins and two missing kids. So that's why he kept to himself and never talked to anyone. Who knew how many people he'd killed and buried in his coffins?

He tossed and turned, trying to figure out what to do. He longed to tell his mother but he'd promised Mr Emil he wouldn't tell. He'd made that promise on the spur of the moment, to save his skin, so did that count? But if he told, he'd have to admit he'd sneaked out of the house in the middle of the night and gone to spy on their neighbour, and his mum would tan his hide with the leather belt she kept on the hook in the hall. Worse than that, she'd look at him with that sad face and say she was disappointed in him. But if he kept his promise and said nothing, wasn't he guilty of being an accomplice, or an accessory, or whatever they called people who knew something and didn't tell the police?

On the way to school the next morning, he was relieved to see Hanny walking by herself. She wasn't silly like the other girls who were always whispering secrets and giggling behind their hands, and he was fascinated by her funny accent. He caught up with her, but whistled, kicked pebbles and swung his school case around as if he hadn't noticed her in case some of the bullies saw him walking with a girl.

As they were passing the Waverley Police Station, he blurted out what he'd seen through Mr Emil's window last night. The notices pasted on the wall, all headed *WANTED* in large capitals, included a poster about the missing children.

'Should I go in and tell them?' he asked, and added, 'But if I do, I'll get into trouble from my mum.'

She thought about it. 'We can't let him get away with it, but I don't think policemen would believe us. They only believe grown-ups.'

As soon as she said 'we', he shot her a grateful look.

They were at the school gate and he was about to go into the boys' playground when she said, 'I know. We'll write a note to one of the grown-ups and tell them about it. Then they can tell the police.'

He looked dubious. 'But then they'll know it was me.'

'No they won't,' she said. 'We won't sign it.'

'But what if they don't do anything about it?'

The school bell started clanging, and as they ran through the schoolyard, she called out, 'Don't worry, they will. I know exactly where to send it.'

Chapter 15

Sitting in her straight-backed wooden chair in the kitchen, Maude McNulty reread the note she'd found in her letterbox. The first thing that struck her about it was the paper. It was lined and had obviously been torn from a child's exercise book, so the writer probably had school-age children. As it was written in printed capitals and had some spelling mistakes, she figured that the writer wasn't well educated. Also, it wasn't signed. People had various reasons for choosing anonymity but she guessed it was because the writer had something to hide.

The melodramatic style of the letter, which began TO WHOM IT MAY CONCERN, and contained phrases such as *Be warned!* made her suspect that the person who'd written it spent too much time listening to popular serials on the wireless or reading trashy novels. But the message itself was intriguing, and Maude McNulty reached for the tea caddy and brewed herself another pot of Kinkara tea before settling down to read it for the third time.

A warning! The man in the house across the road
makes cofins at dead of night. Rember the missing kids?
Be warned! Whose next?

Bing Crosby was crooning one of her favourite songs, 'I'm Dreaming of a White Christmas', but she turned down the volume to concentrate on the note.

Everything pointed to the barmaid: the handwriting, the style, the paper, and the fact that the man accused of the crime lived right next door to her.

A triumphant half-smile played across Maude McNulty's face. From the moment she'd heard the hammering coming from the foreigner's place, she'd known he was up to no good. You only had to look at him, with his odd little hat, shifty glance and peculiar way of walking, to know that.

All her life Maude McNulty had felt that people looked down on her, and of course they had, and she knew why. All through her life she'd had the feeling that people were gossiping and tittering behind her back. Well, now they might stop.

She took off her apron and hung it on the hook at the back of the kitchen door, put on her lace-up shoes over her beige lisle stockings and buttoned the herringbone tweed coat she'd bought the year Jack Lang opened the Harbour Bridge. Hurriedly ramming a felt cloche hat on her head, she placed the letter in her worn leather handbag and, switching off the wireless while Dinah Shore was singing 'Buttons and Bows', went out.

At the end of the street she passed the new foreign woman standing in front of the boarding house. 'They're overrunning the place like a swarm of locusts,' she muttered to herself. She inclined her head slightly in greeting, just enough to show that she was polite but not sufficient to encourage conversation.

But politeness was in short supply at the police station. In fact, the officer behind the desk barely deigned to lift his head when she told him she had some important information.

'Got a note in the letterbox, did ya?' He yawned, showing the inside of his cavernous mouth.

He was very young, as all the policemen seemed to be these days. Young and incompetent.

'Young man,' she said in an icy tone. 'If you can't see the importance of this letter, I'll speak to your superior who will explain it to you.'

'Okay, Grandma, let's have a gander at it.'

Pursing her lips in disapproval, she handed it to him with a look that indicated she didn't expect him to understand its contents.

He took so long reading it that she was tempted to make a comment about his reading skills, but she thought better of it: it probably wasn't wise to get a police officer offside, however young and incompetent he might be.

He rubbed his hand over his chin. 'Who did you say sent this?'

She let out a hiss of exasperation. 'It's anonymous,' she said, enunciating the word very slowly. 'A-non-y-mous. That means —'

'I know what it means,' he said. 'Any idea why someone would send this to you instead of coming straight to us?'

This had occurred to her as well, while walking to the station. Perhaps Kath felt, quite rightly, that the police would be more likely to listen to a respectable old lady like her than to a barmaid.

'Perhaps they thought that being a respectable member of the community, I was the right person to —'

He cut her short again. 'Just wait here, will you? I'll be back in a minute.'

He disappeared behind a swinging door and reappeared a few minutes later with a blank form. 'Your full name and address, please,' he said.

She was taken aback. She preferred lighting the fire to standing near the flame. 'What do you need that for? I'm not the one with the coffins in my house.'

'You've lodged a complaint so we need your details. We're not putting you in jail. Not yet, anyway,' he added jocularly while she filled in the form.

He glanced down at the note. 'This man lives in your street. Have you seen or heard anything yourself that could help us with this?'

'Well he's foreign,' she began.

'So's most of Bondi these days,' he chuckled.

'I've heard funny noises coming from his place late at night, when decent people are sleeping. It's been going on for weeks now. From the moment I heard that hammering I knew he was up to something.' She hadn't meant to say any of this, and rummaged in her handbag for a handkerchief to stop talking.

'Did you ever ask him what he was doing?'

She stared at him. 'I told you, he's a New Australian gentleman. He never talks to anyone.'

The policeman gave her a shrewd look but said nothing. After asking a few more asinine questions, he thanked her for coming in and told her they'd look into it.

When Hania came home from school that afternoon, she threw down her school case and ran outside. She couldn't wait to talk to Meggsie. If only there was some way of knowing whether Miss McNulty had read their note and done anything about it.

Meggsie was nowhere to be seen, but Beverley was leaning over her gate, waving to her.

'Come and play jacks,' she called out. 'I've got a cold and Mum said I have to stay inside.'

In the kitchen, Aunty Muriel was cutting a loaf of crusty white bread and spreading the spongy slices so generously with golden syrup that the thick amber liquid oozed over the edges.

'Come on, love, have some,' she said as soon as Hania came in.

Aunty Muriel had a merry laugh and brown eyes that looked straight into Hania's in the kindest way. As Hania bit into the soft bread and licked the malty treacle from her fingers, she envied Beverley.

While they were playing, Hania stole guilty glances at her friend, wondering whether to tell her about the note she and Meggsie had concocted. In the end she decided to keep it their secret — the fewer people who knew about it, the better.

She kept glancing out of the window, and as soon as she caught sight of Meggsie's red hair, she made an excuse to finish their game and ran outside.

'Do you think she's seen it?' he whispered.

'I don't know,' she whispered back. 'How can we find out?'

While they were trying to work out what to do, Miss McNulty appeared on her verandah. Hania whispered something to Meggsie and a moment later they ran across the road.

'Can I run a message for you, Miss McNulty?' Meggsie asked.

'I could do with a shilling's worth of devon, some Kinkara tea, two eggs and a jar of Kraft spread,' she said, handing him a pound note. 'And you can keep a penny for yourself.' She looked at Hania. 'I suppose you'd better have one, too,' she added.

At the corner shop they took a long time deciding between the humbugs, jelly beans, musk sticks and liquorice all-sorts that Mr Johnson the grocer kept in large glass jars on the counter. When they'd finally made their selection, he counted out the sweets and placed them on a small square of brown paper which he twisted into a cornet. All the adults let the kids spend a penny on lollies or ice blocks, but they liked running messages for Pop Wilson the best because he always gave them threepence, which was enough for a packet of chips or an ice cream at the Saturday matinee.

Sometimes Pop Wilson would hand Meggsie a small wad of money wrapped in newspaper, and tell him to run to Birrell Street where the SP lady lived. She kept chooks in the yard and he always thought she looked a bit like a chook herself, with her fluffy orange hair, bright red mouth and fat little body. Meggsie always hoped Pop's horse would win because then he'd get a shilling.

Sucking their humbugs, Meggsie and Hania walked back to Miss McNulty's place with the shopping. Before ringing the doorbell, Hania raised the lid of the letterbox and looked inside.

'It's gone!' she whispered. 'She must have read it. I wonder what will happen now?'

Standing by the gate of the boarding house, waiting for Szymon to come home, Sala saw Eda's daughter and the red-headed boy hovering around the house of the cranky old woman. She wondered what they were up to. For Sala, Miss McNulty personified everything that was wrong with this suburban existence: its complacency, hypocrisy, monotony and xenophobia. People were courteous and pleasant, but you could never tell what they were thinking behind their polite greetings and false smiles.

Szymon came around the corner and she saw him stop by the house of the man they called Pop Wilson. A moment later she heard them laughing. Unlike her, Szymon took the neighbours' greetings at face value, marvelled at the good nature of Australians and, undeterred by his broken English, chatted about the weather, the housing shortage and the Communists. And everybody loved him.

'The foreman said I wasn't a bad bloke for a reffo,' he told Sala with a laugh when he came inside.

'Was that supposed to be a compliment?' she asked.

'Coming from him, it was.'

She watched his face light up when he saw the table. For once she'd covered it with a cloth, and a loaf of white bread sprinkled with poppy seeds lay on a cutting board. As soon as he sat down, she lit a match and held it against the base of two candles until the wax started to drip. Then she stood them on a plate.

'That'll do for a candlestick,' she said. 'The poppy loaf will do for the *challa*, and I've managed to make some chicken soup, but you'll have to say the blessings because I don't know them.'

Having absorbed her parents' secular way of thinking, she found it ironic that the believers had perished along with the apostates, and she wondered why the God they had worshipped hadn't saved them. But her argument didn't sway Szymon.

'I don't know what God thinks or wants,' he said. 'All I know is that it's my sacred duty to continue what my parents taught me. I promised myself in Buchenwald that if I survived I'd carry on the traditions I saw at home.'

He threw his arms around her and hugged her so tightly that she could hardly breathe. 'You don't know how much it means to me that you're doing this,' he whispered.

As he thanked God for the gift of the Sabbath, his eyes were moist with emotion. 'The last time I said these prayers was in 1939, when all eleven of us sat around the table at home and my father passed around the Kiddush cup and blessed us all.'

He turned to Sala and, taking her hand, looked straight into her eyes and recited the tribute a Jewish husband pays his wife on Friday nights, concluding with the words, 'All women have done worthily, but you've excelled them all.'

Disengaging her hand, Sala rose hastily and began ladling the soup.

Chapter 16

It was the usual morning chaos at Kath's place, with four boys to get off to school. She was running backwards and forwards, stirring the porridge, which was sticking to the bottom of the pan, darting into their bedroom to hurry them up and threatening them with the wooden spoon if they didn't get a move on. The smell of burnt porridge had her rushing back into the kitchen. After pouring some water into the pan and giving it another stir, she was spreading Velveeta on their sandwiches when she heard giggling and scuffling in the bathroom. Exasperated, she banged down the knife and marched down the corridor.

'Stop acting the goat and get ready or you'll get the wooden spoon on the back of your legs!' she shouted.

The door slammed, there was a clatter of shoes along the corridor, and she'd just got back to the kitchen in time to save the porridge when she heard Meggsie calling out, 'Mum!' And then a second time, more urgently, 'Mum!'

Something in his voice made her drop the knife and run into the room he shared with Alan and Ray. He lay sprawled out on the floor.

'What on earth are you doing, mucking around like that?' she asked. 'You're supposed to be getting ready for school.'

In an unsteady voice, he said, 'I fell over when I tried to get out of bed. My legs have gone funny, and when I tried to push myself up, my arms went weak. I can't get up. And my neck hurts.'

If it had been Alan or Ray, she would have thought they were putting on an act to get out of school, but Meggsie wasn't like that. And he'd never missed a paper round, rain or shine.

She saw the glassy look in his eyes and felt his forehead. It was hot.

'Got funny legs, have you?' she said lightly. 'Let's have a look.'

Her mind was racing with wild thoughts. Surely it couldn't be anything serious, not Meggsie, he was such a strong boy. Kids were always hurting themselves. He'd probably fallen over and been bruised. Or maybe he'd got into another fight at school.

Keep calm, she told herself. There was always a simple explanation. Perhaps he'd cramped up during the night or caught the flu.

She tried to pull him to his feet and get him back into bed but he was a dead weight. She called out to Alan and Ray. 'Quick, come and help.'

With the boys holding his legs and Kath lifting him under the arms, the three of them managed to haul him onto the bed.

'What's the matter with Meggsie, Mum?' Ray asked as he was putting the brown paper bag with his lunch into his school case.

'He's probably strained something. He'll be right as rain by tomorrow,' she said with a certainty she didn't feel.

As soon as she'd seen the boys off to school, she rushed to the shelf in the dresser where she kept her books. Wedged between *David Copperfield*, which she'd won for coming top in sixth class, and *Black Beauty*, which Gran had given her for her tenth birthday, was the Pears Cyclopaedia, its jacket frayed from decades of use. Her mother had always referred to it whenever one of them was ill, and she'd usually found a remedy in there. With trembling fingers Kath flicked through the pages that dealt with childhood ailments, but she couldn't find Meggsie's symptoms.

She ran to the red phone box on the corner to tell Mr Aldred she wouldn't be coming in to work today, and held her tongue while he complained about unreliable staff taking time off when they were most needed. Since the last time she had repulsed his advances, he hadn't missed an opportunity to have a go at her, and it took all her self-control to suppress the urge to say that her son hadn't got sick just to nark him.

She checked on Meggsie every few minutes, hoping for some sign of improvement, but by the afternoon he still couldn't move his legs and was complaining that his neck hurt even more.

He'd been complaining of headaches for a while, but she'd

just put it down to growing pains and dosed him up with Bex powders.

By the afternoon she was at her wits' end. His legs were still like blocks of wood, and the Bex hadn't stopped the pain. In desperation she raced back to the phone box. In her haste to call Dr McCallum, she kept dropping the pennies she was trying to insert into the slot.

She hadn't called him since Alan had had appendicitis nearly two years before. She'd been trying her own remedies for a couple of days, and had finally called him because Alan was writhing in pain and screaming. After the operation, Dr McCallum had fixed her with his penetrating look and said, 'You called me in the nick of time. Another hour and it would have ruptured.' He said he knew it was hard for her, bringing up four kids on her own, but she shouldn't wait so long next time because he wouldn't charge her.

Although she had been grateful for his kindness, his words had needled her. They made her feel like a charity case.

'It's Meggsie,' she blurted as soon as she heard the doctor's voice. 'I'm sorry to bother you, but he's burning up and he can't walk. Do you think you could drop in and see him?' Before hanging up, she added, 'And I can pay you.'

As soon as Meggsie saw Dr McCallum he knew he was really crook. As far as he could remember, the doctor had only ever come to their place twice: when Ray fell out of a tree and broke his arm, and when Alan had to have his appendix out.

Dr Mac, as everyone called him, drove an old Austin that was so dusty the kids in the street used to write their names with their fingers on the sides. One cheeky kid even wrote, *Wash me!* Dr Mac always wore a grey hat and a suit that looked as if he'd slept in it, and when he opened his scuffed leather bag, it was full of weird-looking instruments.

Sitting on the edge of Meggsie's bed, he said in his jovial way, 'Now what's all this about, young man? I hope you're not trying to get out of going to school!'

Meggsie swallowed and tried to smile because he didn't want Dr Mac to think he was a sissy. The doctor asked him to move his limbs. Although his arms felt weak, he could move them a little, but when he tried to move his legs, the pain made him cry out, and they flopped down as if they didn't belong to him. Dr Mac made that 'mmm' sound he made when he didn't want his patient to know what he was thinking. He listened to Meggsie's chest with that funny metal disk attached to a rubber tube, tapped his back, held his wrist for a minute and stared into space. Then he stuck a thermometer under Meggsie's tongue and told him to keep still. When he looked at the thermometer, he made that 'mmm' sound again and told Kath he'd like to talk to her.

When they went out of the bedroom, Meggsie strained to hear what they were saying but all he heard was a low murmur of voices. He hated those hushed voices, just loud enough for him to know they were talking about him, but too quiet to catch what they said. He heard the front door open and close, and a moment later he heard the Austin's motor starting up and the car driving away.

When his mum came back to the room, she said in a voice as bright as a new penny that there was no need to worry but Dr Mac was going to call an ambulance. Meggsie could tell she was just pretending to be cheerful because of the look in her eyes.

'What's the matter with me, Mum?' he asked. 'Why can't I move my legs?'

But all she said was, 'You'll be right, love, we'll take you to the kids' hospital and they'll fix you up in no time.'

Fifteen minutes later he heard the high-pitched wail of a siren and saw red lights flashing as the ambulance pulled up outside their place. He heard his mother opening the front door, and then two ambulance officers, important-looking men in navy trousers and high-collared navy shirts, came into his bedroom.

As soon as they heard the siren, most of the residents of Wattle Street hurried to their windows or out into the street to see who the ambulance had come for. The children were already home from school, and a curious crowd gathered on the pavement, whispering and pointing.

'I hope it's not Kath,' Verna said to Maude McNulty. 'What'll happen to her boys if she goes into hospital?'

'They'll run riot, that's what,' her neighbour said tartly. She clucked her tongue. 'It's no wonder she got ill with that job of hers.'

While Maude McNulty listed all the diseases Kath might have contracted at the pub, Verna was trying to figure out who'd be able to help out. Kath couldn't count on her sister, who had moved to the country with her large brood of kids, or her two brothers, both of whom had joined the navy. Kath's grandmother used to visit from time to time, but she hadn't been around since they'd had an argument about sending the boys to a Catholic school. Kath had told her they weren't on speaking terms, so it wasn't likely that the old woman would come around unasked, and Kath was too proud to ask for help. Verna decided she'd keep an eye on the boys and cook their tea.

As soon as Hania heard the siren, she ran to the front window to see what was going on, When she saw it pull up outside Meggsie's place, she rushed to the front door but her mother was already standing there, hands on hips.

'You're not going out,' she snapped. 'It's common to stand around in the street gawking at people's misfortunes. Anyway, I've told you to keep away from that boy. He's a bad influence.'

When Hania had come home late from Nosey's cottage the previous week, her mother had been hysterical.

'Where have you been?' she'd shouted. 'I was about to call the police. I can't trust you for a minute. And don't think I don't know what you got up to that Sunday you told me you were going to Tina's place. Mrs Browning mentioned this afternoon that you were at the Sunday school picnic. You lied to me! And today you told me you were going to play in the paddock, but you ran off somewhere with that larrikin. You're not going out of the house for two weeks, except to go to school. I'll teach you to tell lies, you deceitful girl.'

'I hate you!' Hania shouted back. 'I hate you!'

Her mother stared at her without speaking. After a long pause, she said softly to herself, 'For this I survived Auschwitz?'

'You spoil everything! I wish you were dead!' Hania shouted.

She fled to her room and, slamming the door behind her, flung herself on the bed, but a moment later her mother threw open the door, dragged her to her feet and slapped her face so hard that she staggered and fell back onto the bed.

'You wait and see, God will punish you for talking to your mother like that!' she shouted, and stormed out, banging the door so hard that the walls shook and *Alice in Wonderland* with the gold cross hidden inside the cover crashed to the floor.

As Hania rushed to pick it up, she heard a sound she had never heard before. Her mother was sobbing. Hania told herself she didn't care. She was sick of her mother's hysteria, sick of competing with phantoms who played a bigger part in her mother's life than she did. Talking to her mother was like trying to find a comfortable spot between the broken springs of their lumpy couch. Wherever you sat, part of you landed on something sharp.

Now, anxious to find out what was going on at Meggsie's place, Hania waited until she could hear her mother clattering pots and pans at the back of the house. Then, creeping back into the front room, she pressed her face against the window to see what was happening.

Sala came out onto the verandah of the boarding house to see what all the commotion was about. She saw the crowd standing around the ambulance and wondered who was ill. She hoped it wasn't the young woman with all the boys.

At the far end of the street, she saw Pop Wilson putting down his shears and resting his elbows on the gate. Verna had told her that Pop had once been a lifesaver and had rescued people at Bondi Beach, but looking at him now, with his protruding belly and red face, she found that hard to believe.

Verna was talking to the old woman next door, and as soon as she spotted Sala she waved for her to come over.

'How's your job going, Sally?' she asked.

Sala pulled a face. The work was easy, and Franka Feldman always had a friendly smile for her, but the nasty woman she worked with never missed an opportunity to make a crack about foreigners or to tell her she'd used the wrong cleaning fluid, or the wrong mop, or that the French polish had left streaks on the sideboard. That morning Beryl had railed at her for not moving everything on the director's desk before dusting it. 'But you said I not move things on director's desk,' Sala had protested. In reply Beryl had made a derisive comment about hopeless bloody wogs.

'You don't want to let her get you down, pet,' Verna said. 'She's probably got a husband who beats her up.'

'He wouldn't dare,' Sala said, and they both laughed.

While they were chatting, Maude McNulty was scrutinising Sala with narrowed eyes. She didn't take part in their conversation but as soon as they stopped talking, she turned to Verna.

'Did you see that lovely photograph of Princess Elizabeth's baby in the paper yesterday? Charles, they've called him. They make a lovely couple, don't they, the Princess and the Duke of Edinburgh. His uncle is Earl Mountbatten, you know.'

Verna sometimes wondered if Maude McNulty's obsession with the royal family stemmed from her having no family of her own. In all the years Verna had lived in Wattle Street, she'd never heard her neighbour mention any relative, not even her parents. No friends ever visited her either, but the old woman's personality didn't encourage any close relationships, and probably that was how she wanted it.

Kath's door opened and they all fell silent. Striding to the back of the ambulance, the officers asked the bystanders to move away and give them room, as they unhooked a stretcher and carried it into the house.

'She must be real bad,' Maude McNulty said. 'Last time an ambulance took someone away was when they came for Violet Wilson.'

The door opened again and everyone craned forward. Someone was being carried out on the stretcher and it wasn't Kath. It was Meggsie, and he looked so pale that even his freckles seemed to have faded. Kath was walking beside him, holding his hand; her face was strained and white.

Verna stepped forward and squeezed her arm. 'I'll see to the boys until you come back.'

Kath gave her a grateful nod, and Verna watched as Meggsie was loaded into the back of the ambulance. Poor lad, she thought, and poor Kath.

Inside the ambulance, Kath took Meggsie's hand and tried to reassure him, although her heart was pounding so hard she was sure he could hear it.

'You'll be right when you get to the hospital, love,' she said. Something was stuck in her throat and her voice was a hoarse whisper. 'The doctors there'll fix you up in no time.'

Her eyes strayed down to his legs. They were covered by a grey blanket, but his left foot was sticking out and it was curled inwards at a peculiar angle.

They sped along Oxford Street, past shabby shopfronts half hidden under corrugated-iron overhangs: Attwaters, Woolies, Taylor's Shoes and Lopes fruit shop. Cars pulled over to let them pass and shoppers stopped to watch the ambulance, no doubt wondering about the unfortunate souls inside, and relieved it wasn't them, as Kath usually was. But now she was inside, looking out, and it was her son whose life might be in the balance. She swallowed hard and blinked away the tears.

Meggsie was mumbling something and she leaned forward to catch what he was saying.

'Mum, I won't miss Morris the Magnificent, will I?'

He'd been fascinated by magic ever since he'd read his first Mandrake the Magician comic, and she knew he'd been saving his pennies for a ticket from the moment he'd seen the poster advertising the show.

'No fear. You'll be running around in no time, you'll see,' she said.

But the words sounded hollow, even to her.

Chapter 17

As soon as Emil heard the banging on the front door, his heart stopped beating for a moment, and then began thumping wildly against his ribs. Strange how after all this time the reaction never changed, even though he knew his life was no longer in danger. Ever since he'd caught the boy next door snooping around the week before, he'd felt uneasy. He didn't think there was any malice in the lad, but there was no knowing what he'd seen, or what he'd make of it.

Throughout his childhood Emil had hated the buttoned-up suits and polished shoes he had to wear, and the hushed apartment with its Biedermeier sideboards and Persian rugs, and the Rosenthal porcelain he wasn't allowed to touch. He addressed his emotionally distant parents in the third person and ate his meals with his warm-hearted nanny. 'You have to behave like a decent German boy, not like an uncivilised lout,' his father would scold whenever he let out a joyous yell or slid across the polished floors pretending to be a cowboy. 'If you don't study hard, you'll never amount to anything,' his father warned. No matter how Emil racked his brains in later years, he couldn't recall anything else his father had ever said to him.

But he hadn't studied hard. In fact he hadn't studied at all and, as his father had predicted, he hadn't amounted to anything. At least, not anything his father valued. He remembered the day his life changed. He was ten at the time, and when he closed his eyes even now he was back in that darkened theatre in Berlin, holding his breath as the magician in a satin suit swirled his cape and pulled a rabbit from his top hat. With the help of his pretty assistant in a short satin skirt that barely covered her bottom, he sawed a woman in half and later made a man levitate above the table.

It was Emil's first glimpse of another kind of existence, one which lay outside the realm of diligence and discipline. This was a world where normal rules didn't apply and anything was possible. He knew then that this, and not his father's tightly circumscribed existence, was what he wanted for himself. The world of illusion, magic and transformation. He hadn't known then that this world also relied on appearances, and required just as much discipline and deception, and that, in the end, whichever world you chose, you could never escape your destiny.

The illusion that had made his heart pound, the one few magicians could perform, was the one in which the magician cut off a man's limbs as well as his head, tossed the parts in the air, and then restored the body to its normal shape. Much later, when he got his first job with an illusionist, he discovered how this trick worked. He was one of the assistants dressed in black who moved silently and stealthily against a backdrop of black cloth, while the stage was brightly lit to distract the audience from what was going on. Unnoticed, they slipped the man's arms behind the cloth and hooked on dummy limbs. At a crucial moment they unhooked them and flung them in the air. The supposedly severed head was also a dummy, stuffed with rags. Emil had been thrilled by the power of creating such a deception and making the open-mouthed audience believe the unbelievable.

The knocking grew louder and more peremptory, and he hurried towards the door. Surely the boy hadn't seen anything. Even if he'd stood on the bucket, he couldn't have seen through the blind. Just the same, he was worried by the boy's insistence that he hadn't seen anything. He opened the door and saw two uniformed policemen standing there, and the blood drained from his face. They didn't have to wear black uniforms or jackboots to make his heart race.

'I'm Sergeant Frank O'Connor from Waverley Police Station, and this is Constable Tom Adams,' the older one said, indicating his colleague. Frank O'Connor had sandy hair and a mottled complexion that reminded Emil of minced veal.

'It's come to our attention that there's been a lot of hammering coming from your place at night,' the sergeant explained. 'Could you tell us what you're doing there, sir?'

'I fix things, that is all. Sorry for disturbing the neighbours,' Emil said. He spoke quickly to sound confident.

'Can you show us where you do all this fixing?'

Waving his arm in the direction of the back of the house, Emil said, 'Just an ordinary room.'

'We'd like to see it, if you don't mind.'

Emil's eyes darted around for an escape route as he tried to quell the panic. There was no way out.

He led the way. Their expressions didn't change and he realised that this was what they had expected to see.

'The boy told you, yes?'

'We're not at liberty to say who it was,' O'Connor said

Emil supposed it was the boy's mother. She smiled to his face and helped him mend his shoe, yet she'd gone behind his back and reported him. He wondered why she hadn't talked to him instead of going straight to the police. Perhaps that's what people did in this country.

The two policemen were walking around the coffins, looking at them gingerly from various angles as though expecting someone to jump out.

Finally the sergeant spoke in an affable tone. 'Is this what you've been hammering here at night?'

Emil nodded.

'And what's inside them?'

His mouth was so dry that his tongue was stuck to his palate and he had to clear this throat before he could answer. 'Nothing.'

'Do you mean to tell us they're empty?'

He nodded again.

The policeman seemed to be considering how to phrase his next question. 'Can you tell us who they're for?'

Emil shook his head. 'Not any person.'

The younger officer was pacing out the length of the coffin on the workbench and writing down the measurement in a notebook. He said something to his associate, who nodded and turned back to Emil.

'Do you expect us to believe that you spend night after night making coffins for nobody? They're not very big, are they? I reckon they'd be the right size for kids, don't you?'

He thrust his face closer to Emil's, and placed his big hands on his hips.

'Can you tell us where you were on the afternoon of 22 May?' he said in a threatening tone.

Emil froze. 'Please, I do not understand. Why you ask me this?'

'We'll do the asking, if you don't mind. If you don't want to answer here, you can come with us down to the station.'

Emil tried to calculate what day of the week the twenty-second had been, but his mind was paralysed and there was a dull humming in his head.

'Let's jog your memory,' the police officer said. 'Were you in Waverley Park by any chance?'

Again Emil tried to think but anxiety increased his confusion, and he couldn't remember where that park was. He had the urge to bolt past them and escape, but managed to calm himself. This was Australia in 1948, not Berlin in

1938. He tried to focus on their question. He often walked for hours without seeing where he was going. Perhaps he did walk across the park that day, but he couldn't be sure. If only he knew why were asking these questions.

'So you refuse to tell us where you were that day, or who these coffins are for?'

'I do not refuse, I said you already. The coffins are for no one. And I do not remember where I was that day. Maybe I walked, maybe not.'

'Well that's not very satisfactory,' the police officer said. 'I'm afraid I'm going to have to ask you to accompany us to the station.'

As Emil pulled on his coat and the hunting hat with the green feather, he understood something for the first time. It was so clear that it made his head swim. Starting a new life in another country wasn't as simple as crossing a border. It meant entering a new world of deception and illusion. Like a magician, a migrant had to reinvent himself or be destroyed.

When Verna Browning looked out of her window that afternoon and saw two uniformed policemen escorting the foreign gentleman across the road and pushing him into the back of the black Holden, she caught sight of his pale, frightened face and felt sorry for him. The man was strange, there was no doubt about that, but she didn't think he was a criminal, and as the car sped from Wattle Street she wondered why they'd taken him away.

She looked around to see if any of the neighbours had witnessed the arrest, and noticed Maude McNulty standing on her verandah. She held shears in her hands, seemingly focused on trimming her hedge, but Verna knew this was merely an excuse to watch what was going on. Perhaps the old gossip knew something.

Leaning over the low brick wall that separated their verandahs, she said, 'I wonder what he's supposed to have done. He seems so inoffensive.'

Miss McNulty gave a thin, knowing smile. 'Still waters run deep,' she said. 'I always knew there was something fishy about him.'

When Ted came home that evening, his mother told him the news. 'I think Miss McNulty knows more than she's letting on,' she added.

'That wouldn't surprise me,' he commented.

'Seriously, though, you should look into it. I can't imagine why they took him away. He looked so frightened. It could be an interesting story.'

Ted shrugged, and from his dismissive manner she realised that he wasn't interested in Wattle Street gossip. Turning the chops under the grill, she asked instead, 'How's the romance going?'

'Pretty rotten,' he said moodily. 'Her father's a real tyrant. Doesn't like her going on dates or having boyfriends.'

She nodded sympathetically. 'Some of these New Australians have funny ideas. But if she really likes you, she'll find a way of talking him round. Maybe if he met you he'd change his mind.'

'I doubt it,' he muttered. He was about to tell her what he thought of Lilija's father but she'd already switched on the wireless and settled down to listen to one of her favourite serials. The ghostly creaking of the asylum door indicated that *Inner Sanctum* was about to begin.

Chapter 18

When Pop Wilson came over to fix the leaky tap in their bathroom a few days later, Ted found the solution to a problem that had been on his mind ever since his meeting with George Addison.

When they had met at Cahill's restaurant, the former teacher from the Bonegilla migrant camp had turned out to be as pedantic as his letter had indicated. It wasn't until he'd finished his steak-and-kidney pie and folded the edges of his napkin until they were perfectly aligned that he'd been ready to reveal what he'd witnessed.

Ted was shocked to hear that the Jewish migrants at the camp, who were vastly outnumbered, were often victimised by other migrants who threatened, ambushed and beat them up. Their complaints, however, were ignored by the manager of the camp, whom Mr Addison suspected of a shady wartime past.

'He said he'd been a farmer in Lithuania,' he told Ted, 'but when I looked at his hands I knew he'd never done any farm work. The thing that bothered me was that he was responsible for issuing identity cards to other migrants who arrived here without any documents. Who knows what some of these people got up to during the war? I wouldn't be surprised if some of them had been in the SS.'

'But how did they get into Australia in the first place?' Ted asked. 'Surely the screening officers would have looked for the blood group tattooed under their left armpit?'

George Addison gave a thin smile. 'Yes, but most of them had the tattoo surgically removed in the DP camps. And if a medical officer happened to notice the scar, they said they'd had a boil lanced, been stabbed or hit by a bullet.'

While the waitress served their blackberry flummery dessert, George Addison opened his briefcase and handed Ted a letter one of the inmates had written.

Honoured Sir

I am Jewish man from camps in Europe for six years and now again I am in camp with Nazis. One Jew in barrack with nineteen fascists. The Baltics and Ukrainians mens tell about Jews they killed. They show nife across throat and say look how we kill Jews. They sorry not kill more. They laugh and say you next. Did I survive war to live with Nazis in Australia?
Help please.
With respect,
Itzak Klein

George Addison had shown the letter to the Australian major in charge of the camp, but when he had confronted the attackers, they had denied everything.

'The major thought he was Eisenhower,' George Addison said. 'He ran the camp like a military establishment, and barked at the migrants like a sergeant major addressing soldiers on the parade ground. He didn't want anyone criticising the way he ran the place, and he dismissed the whole affair as nonsense. And that's probably why I lost my job,' he added. 'I was poking my nose into matters they wanted to keep quiet.'

He sat forward and lowered his voice. 'I've heard something interesting recently, but it has to be off the record. I don't want my informant to lose his job.'

He waited until Ted put down his pen before continuing in a conspiratorial whisper, 'A friend of mine who works for the Commonwealth Investigation Service told me that the Yugoslav government has applied for the extradition of two war criminals who are staying at Bonegilla, but our government has been ignoring their request.'

Ted had felt his adrenalin pumping. He'd known he would have to find some way of getting into Bonegilla to investigate the allegations; they'd never let him in if they thought he was a journalist stirring up trouble. Now, as he watched Pop Wilson taking screwdrivers and spanners from his old tool bag, and inserting new washers, he figured out how to do it.

The next day he rang Pop's front-door bell. As he waited on the verandah, alcohol fumes rose from a pile of empty wine bottles. The door opened and there was Pop in a singlet and baggy shorts.

He beamed when he saw Ted. 'Come in, son, come on in,' he

said. 'Been breaking lots of hearts, have you?' he asked in his jocular way.

Ted grinned. 'Been beating them off with a stick.' He could never figure out why people thought he was some kind of Casanova, or why all throughout his teenage years attractive girls had flirted with him even though he'd been too shy to approach them himself. When he looked in the mirror he saw an ordinary face with a square jaw and no distinguishing features.

Pop was already twisting the cork from a half-empty bottle of sherry on the sideboard. 'Will you join me?' he asked as Ted sat down.

Without waiting for an answer he started pouring the sherry into two tumblers with hands that shook so much he splashed some of it onto the sideboard.

While he went into the kitchen for a cloth, Ted looked around the room. The curtains, which hung unevenly, were still drawn, and the musty smell suggested that the windows hadn't been opened in a long time. Old newspapers were scattered all over the worn settee, and the current issue of the *Sportsman* was spread out on the table. Pop had obviously been studying the form guide.

It was Saturday afternoon and Ted could hear Ken Howard calling the races on 2UE.

'Wonder where he's calling them from today,' Pop said, wiping the sideboard with a rag which smudged the sticky liquid. 'They barred him from calling the races from the track, so every week he has to find a different vantage point nearby. Last week at the Hill, he hid above an oil storage tank to see the races,' Pop chuckled. 'And the week before, at Canterbury, he climbed up a tower above a chookhouse! One of the racing blokes at Randwick threatened to turn a shotgun on him for broadcasting from the roof of a block of flats, but that never put him off. They reckon once he even used a hot-air balloon!'

Pop turned up the volume. 'Hang on a sec,' he said. 'I've got a bet on this one.'

A moment later Ken Howard's distinctive voice filled the room. *'They're lunging for the wire, and it's London to a brick that Fancy Pants will make it a hat-trick. Here they come, turning into the home stretch, they're settling down for the run to the judges, and,'* his voice rose to a new pitch of excitement, *'it's Scarlet Pimpernel coming round the straight, Scarlet Pimpernel's the one to watch, he's gaining on Fancy Pants, it's neck and neck, he's edging ahead now. Boilover!'* he shouted as the outsider won.

Pop Wilson tore up his SP slips in disgust and switched off the wireless.

'You'll have to excuse the mess,' he said as he handed Ted a glass printed with finger marks. 'I don't have many visitors these days.'

Ted took a sip of the sickly wine and glanced at the two framed photographs on the mantelpiece.

In the formal studio photograph of a bridal couple, the bride had a kiss-curl over her forehead and a lace veil that trailed over her slinky satin gown. Standing beside her, the groom, stiff in a dark suit, held her arm as he stared into the camera. There were no other family photos. Ted thought about Pop's daughter Nola and remembered his mother's advice, but curiosity got the better of him.

'I was thinking about Nola the other day,' he said. 'What's she doing these days?'

Pop looked out of the window for a moment, drained his glass and, without giving any indication that he'd heard the question, pointed to the other framed photograph. It showed ten lifesavers in woollen swimsuits and head-hugging caps tied under their chins.

'You wouldn't know it, but that's me in the middle,' he said, pointing to an earnest-faced young man. 'Of course, I was better-looking in them days.'

Ted studied the photograph. 'When was that taken?'

'Just after Black Sunday,' Pop said. 'We made lifesaving history that day.'

He didn't need any prompting to tell the story, and as he talked Ted sensed that he was reliving the whole incident.

'It was a stinking hot Sunday in summer, and there were so many sunbathers on the beach that you couldn't see the sand for people. There were lots on the sandbank in the surf as well. Suddenly the water went flat and it was deathly quiet. Then these massive waves rushed in, one after the other. They crashed into the sandbank and it collapsed, and hundreds of surfers were swept out to sea.'

Pop was shaking his head. 'I reckon God was watching over Bondi that day because we'd arranged to have a race in the surf that afternoon, so there were at least sixty of us on the beach. Otherwise, Lord only knows what would have happened.'

'What did happen?' Ted asked.

'We manned all the surf-reels, grabbed all the rubber floats, surfboards, whatever we could lay our hands on, and plunged into the surf.

'The trouble was, the surfers panicked and started pulling at the surf-lines and got in our way. They made it even harder for us to get people out, and all this time huge waves were breaking over us. By the time we managed to get everyone out of the water, there were about seventy people lying on the sand like beached whales, and some of them were unconscious. By then people were running around the beach in a panic, looking for relatives and friends, while us lifesavers, ambulancemen and doctors were going all out trying to revive the victims. It was a miracle that out of all them people only a handful died.'

Pop was shaking his head in wonderment as he took some tobacco from a pouch, spread it on cigarette paper, rolled it up and lit it. 'In all me years as a lifesaver, I never seen anything like it.'

He closed his eyes and inhaled, and as the smell of tobacco filled the room, he said, 'Funny, the things you remember. Whenever I think about that day, I still see dozens of straw hats floating on the waves and disappearing over the horizon.'

Ted looked at his neighbour with new interest. 'You must miss your lifesaving days.'

'Yeah, well, you miss a lot of things when you get older.' He sighed. 'A lot of things and a lot of people. But I'll tell you one thing. The sea plays silly buggers with you — you never know what's going on under those smooth-lookin' waves. Like people, I suppose.'

Ted suddenly remembered why he'd come. 'Will you be needing your tool bag over the next few days?' he asked.

Pop chuckled. 'Don't tell me you're changing jobs?'

'I just need to borrow it for a couple of days. And do you think you could give me an idea how to use the tools?'

Pop disappeared into another room, and returned a moment later with his tool bag. He took out the wrench, screwdrivers and pliers, and ran through some of the things that could go wrong with plumbing, explaining which tools a plumber would use to check water pressure, unclog drains and change washers. Ted tried to remember everything. He couldn't afford to make a mistake.

On Monday morning Ted spent half an hour trying to convince Gus Thornton to let him follow up the story about Bonegilla.

'Don't tell me you're planning to waste two days chasing some cock-and-bull story in Albury?' Gus shouted, his jowls wobbling like a Christmas turkey.

Ted stood his ground. 'I don't think it will be a waste of time. I reckon I'll be able to file a good story about conditions in the camps. Especially now they're in the news. '

His luck was in. The *Sydney Morning Herald* had just run a short news item about the death of two babies at another migrant camp, and one of the weeping mothers had blamed the government for not providing adequate medical facilities for the migrants.

'Of course the medical facilities are inadequate,' Gus scoffed, pushing his cigarette into his cigarette-holder with such force that it broke in half. With a curse he tossed the two pieces into the ashtray. 'There aren't enough medical facilities anywhere, so why would it be any different in the camps?'

But he acknowledged that with the right kind of reporting, dead babies at a migrant camp could be a big story. Nothing got readers worked up as much as medical negligence, especially when children were involved. It might even lead to a series on infant deaths all over the country for which doctors and hospitals could be blamed.

Ted didn't bother to explain that investigating medical mistakes wasn't his reason for going to Bonegilla. He reckoned that if his story turned out to be as big as he hoped, Gus would forget all about sick children.

But as he walked out of his boss's office he wondered what his father would have thought if he'd known that his work involved so much manipulation and deceit. It was the only way to find out what was going on, but Ted had a nagging feeling that his father wouldn't have approved.

Chapter 19

Three days later Ted was sitting in the Parthenon Café in Albury's main street, about to tuck into a big plate of steak, eggs and chips. When he asked the dark-eyed young waitress for the tomato sauce, she shook her head and said something in Greek to the man behind the counter, who came over to ask what he wanted.

'She no speak English,' he said.

Until recently Ted hadn't taken much interest in newcomers, but now as he looked at the timid waitress he wondered if she'd just stepped off a migrant ship and landed in a strange city where she couldn't understand what anyone said.

He opened the *Albury Banner* and saw that it was full of ads for sheep and stock sales. Farmers' and graziers' co-ops were selling Herefords, Shorthorns, Romney and Merino sheep. There were even notices that promised to teach wool-classing by mail. Australia was certainly riding on the sheep's back, but even here, in the heart of rural Australia, with all those cows grazing in the meadows, butter was still rationed. It made Ted angry that in this land of plenty, more than three years after the war had ended, they still had rationing, but he knew it was because Australia's butter was being exported to

Britain. 'They're milking us dry,' Gus often said, and for once Ted agreed with him.

He looked at his watch, put down the paper, grabbed the tool bag and hurried from the café. He reached the bus stop just as the bus for Bonegilla was about to pull out. 'Come on, mate, get a move on, we can't wait all day,' the driver growled good-naturedly as he jumped on.

The only other passengers were two elderly women who had been shopping in Albury. As the bus jolted past the outskirts of the town, one of them began complaining. 'It's not right having a migrant camp in the town, putting all of us in danger,' she said. 'I reckon some of those foreigners would stick a knife in you as soon as look at you.'

Her companion was nodding. 'And they don't even speak English.'

Looking through the streaked bus window, Ted saw the landscape as the girl in the café, or Lilija, or any of the new migrants might have done. He noticed that the grass on the pastures was sparse, and the leaves on the trees were grey rather than green. In spring, the fine-leafed acacias would dazzle with a froth of yellow flowers, but now the winter foliage was bare and brittle, and the ground was parched and brown.

To people coming from the lush meadows and dense forests of Europe, it must appear as though the pitiless sun had sucked all the juice from the land. Ted loved the vast horizons and harsh colours of this country, but it was the possessive feeling of a parent who loves a child without understanding it.

'Bonegilla!' the bus driver called out.

As soon as Ted got off the bus, he took off his jacket and put on a pair of overalls and a tradesman's cloth cap. The gum trees by the side of the road smelled dry and sweet, but as he walked up to the camp he saw a sandy wasteland where army huts with corrugated-iron roofs were surrounded by cyclone fencing. It looked like a prison, and he could imagine the despair that former internees of concentration camps and DP camps must feel on arriving here, and what impressions they would form of their new country in this desolate place.

There was a sentry on duty at the gate and Ted sauntered up in his workman's gear as though this was just another routine job. When the guard asked to see his permit, he nonchalantly raised the tool bag to show why he'd come, and mumbled something about the drain blocking up again in the washroom. The man on duty had his eye on a pretty brunette swinging her hips as she strolled towards the gate, and he waved Ted through without checking his credentials.

Ted wandered around the camp and peered inside the dormitory-style huts, counting the number of beds. Twenty-five per hut. Accommodation was segregated, and in one of the huts four men were leaning over a card table, puffing away at cigarettes. He watched them for a while through the open door, and when one of them looked up and caught his eye, he called out, 'Does anyone here speak English?'

They glanced at him, moved closer together and spoke volubly in their own language. An unshaven fellow in a baggy woollen sweater threw down his cards and shambled towards Ted. He was a big man with dark stubble, and as he leaned against the door he folded his beefy arms and gave Ted a suspicious look.

'Vat you vant?' he asked.

'I'm looking for the communal bathroom,' Ted said, then added with an air of bonhomie, 'How are they treating you in here, mate?'

The man studied him for a moment, then, without a word, spat into the dirt and turned his back on him.

Outside the women's huts some of the mothers were chatting as their tow-haired children played in the dirt. Some of them looked up when they saw him, and smiled back, but no one seemed to speak English. If he didn't find some way of communicating with these people very soon, he'd end up with no story and a furious editor on his back. He needed to find someone like the migrant who'd written to Mr Addison.

Finally someone pointed to the washroom, down the main path past the mess building. It was late afternoon and he saw a few men going in with towels around their necks.

Whistling 'Rum and Coca-Cola' to sound nonchalant, he went inside.

'Been told the plumbing's crook,' he said to no one in particular. 'I reckon I'll get it going in no time.'

He took a plunger from his bag, ran some water into one of the large metal sinks and pushed down on it several times, shaking his head and muttering about the poor water pressure.

He took apart a few taps, replaced them and then knelt down beside the drain and poked around as Pop Wilson had shown him, hoping that none of the men in there were plumbers.

Men came and went, all speaking different languages. Some showered in the open cubicles while others pulled their shirts down to their waists and leaned over the sinks as they washed their hands and faces and splashed water over their heads. Every few minutes Ted looked up, and then put his head down again. He had already been there close to an hour without finding any evidence that might substantiate the story Mr Addison had told him, and he knew he couldn't hang around much longer.

He was putting the tools back in the bag when a man at one of the sinks stripped to the waist and started soaping himself. He raised his left arm and there it was. A red scar raised in the middle, with lumpy edges. Ted looked away quickly so that the man wouldn't realise he'd seen it. He kept his head down to conceal his excitement. Finally he'd seen something that substantiated Mr Addison's allegation about removed SS tattoos.

As he snapped the tool bag shut he sensed that someone was watching him. He looked up; at the far end of the washroom a young man with a shock of fair hair was looking at him with a sardonic smile. There was something familiar about him, but Ted decided he must have imagined it.

The young bloke kept his gaze on Ted's face. 'Yesterday you journalist, and today you fix pipes?'

Ted spun around, hoping no one had overheard the comment. He looked at the fellow more closely and knew he was in luck. It was Peter Czerny from the SS *Napoli*, who had told him about the fascists on board.

Glancing around to make sure they weren't being watched, Peter took Ted's arm and propelled him along a path behind the toilet block. They sat on a bench in a secluded corner of the camp, facing beds of spindly stocks and wilting marigolds that some of the migrants had planted in the sandy soil. The sun was going down and long shadows fell across the ground.

'The man you saw in washroom,' Peter said. 'American doctor in DP camp in Germany did skin graft.'

Ted felt a quiver of excitement. 'Can I quote you?'

Peter shrugged. 'Why not? Tomorrow I go from here. To job.'

Ted whipped out his notebook and fountain pen and started jotting down what Peter had said.

'I will be happy to go from here,' continued Peter. 'They beat Polish man yesterday because he try to defend Jewish man they beat up. Not only Waffen SS are here. Hungarian man in kitchen, he say he was Arrow Cross. He talk how he and friends round up Jews in Budapest and shoot them, then they throw bodies in Danube River. He is proud of that.'

'Arrow Cross? Who are they?'

Ted listened while Peter listed extremist groups that had willingly collaborated with the Nazis in murdering hundreds of thousands of defenceless men, women and children with machine guns, bayonets and axes, in camps, forests and prison camps all over Europe. He mentioned groups Ted had never heard of: Croatian Ustashe, Hungarian Arrow Cross, Slovenian Domobran, Latvian Arajs Kommando, Carpathian Hlinka Guard, and the Brotherhood of Ukrainian Nationalists.

By the time Peter had finished, Ted's jaw was clenched so tight that it ached. He could see now why it had been easy to pull the wool over the eyes of so many Australian screening officers. It wasn't just that they couldn't speak the languages of the people whose applications they were processing. Like him, most of them didn't even know about these fascist militias and thought that the only war criminals were Germans.

'The Ustashe did things that shocked even the Germans,' Peter was saying. As he described some of their atrocities, using gestures when he couldn't find the words, Ted's stomach rose into his throat, and he held up his hand for Peter to stop.

'Two Ustashe men in my hut,' Peter said. 'They keep photograph of Ante Pavelić, Ustashe leader. He is hero for them. They say one day they get weapons and train. Then they go back to Yugoslavia and kill Communists.'

Ted stopped writing. 'Get weapons and train where?'

'In Australia. They want to have Ustashe militia again. They want to kill more peoples.'

Ted let out a breath he didn't realise he'd been holding. How much of this incredible story was true? His instinct told him that Peter knew what he was talking about, but without any proof it was just another unsubstantiated account that could easily be refuted.

Seeing Ted's expression, Peter shrugged. 'My friend, I see you do not believe.' He looked at his watch. 'Now is dinner. Come. You will see.'

As they walked along the dirt path towards the huts, ducking several times behind some bushes to avoid being seen, they heard the clatter of cutlery, the clink of glasses on wooden tables and a hubbub of voices coming from the mess hall. 'Now they eat,' Peter said. 'We have time.'

Peter's hut stood at the far end of a row of identical army-style barracks with corrugated roofs. They peered through the window to make sure there was no one inside, and opened the door. Inside, Peter pointed to a small brown suitcase with the corners bashed in, which lay on the grey blanket on his narrow bunk. 'Tomorrow morning I go to job in Griffith.'

He walked along the row of bunks, motioning for Ted to follow him, and stopped at the last bed on the right. Glancing around, Peter opened a drawer in the small wooden bedside table and took out a small figurine. It was a crudely made likeness of Hitler with the swastika armband, the hair plastered over the forehead and the clipped black moustache.

'Look,' Peter whispered. He pressed a button at the base and the right arm began to swing up and down in the Nazi salute.

Ted was shocked, angry and excited all at once. If only he had a photographer with him.

'Look, here is more,' Peter said. He replaced the figurine, walked over to the next bedside table and pulled out the drawer so that Ted could see an armband with a swastika. He opened another drawer, took out a Bible and turned it upside down until a photograph fell out.

'Ante Pavelić, Butcher of Croatia,' Peter said, and added, 'Some of them keep German bayonets in suitcases.' He glanced at his watch. 'We go now.'

He was closing the drawer when the door opened and a bald man with broad shoulders came into the hut. From his expression Ted could tell that he knew what they'd been looking at. The man let loose a barrage of what sounded like abuse. Shaking his head, Peter pointed at Ted's tool bag and at a loose piece of galvanised iron hanging from the roof, as though to explain their presence. As they left the hut, the man gave Peter a look that made the hairs at the back of Ted's neck stand up.

They were walking towards the camp gate when Peter turned to Ted. 'Tell me, my friend, what will happen when you write about this?' he asked.

'I hope it will cause an outcry, embarrass the immigration department and make them realise they have to smarten up. They've got to stop these fascists from coming here.'

At the gate Ted shook Peter's hand and wished him luck in his new life in Griffith.

'And I wish you good luck also,' Peter replied, and Ted thought he detected irony in his voice.

Back in Albury Ted returned to the Parthenon Café. As he watched the shy young waitress carefully placing his fish and chips in front of him, he remembered reading that thousands of young Greeks were being kidnapped by guerrillas and sent to youth camps in Communist countries. In spite of all the jubilation about Allied victory, the war still wasn't over for some nations.

He would have liked to ask the girl whether she had migrated here to escape being abducted and forced to become a fighter in a foreign country for a cause she didn't believe in, but he smiled at her instead.

In his small room at the Albury Hotel, he lay on the hard bed with his arms clasped behind his neck. It was a typical room in an old country pub: poorly lit, with heavy old-fashioned furniture stained with a dark varnish, ill-fitting curtains which didn't keep out the light, and a monastic bathroom down the hall with toilet cubicles and cracked sinks on wobbly stands.

He opened the novel he'd brought with him, but the weak electric bulb in the bedside lamp gave very little light and he put the book aside. His mind kept wandering back to what he'd seen and heard at Bonegilla. As he turned off the lamp, it struck him that the lives of perpetrators and victims were closely intertwined in their new country.

* * *

Two days later Ted's article, FASCISTS FIND SANCTUARY ON OUR SHORES, appeared in the *Daily Standard*, and for once Gus Thornton didn't blast him for being wishy-washy. The article described what he'd seen in the hut, quoted what George Addison had observed and what Peter Czerny had told him. He criticised the ignorance and naivety of the screening officers, and the smug attitude of the immigration department, whose officers denied the defects of a system that enabled perpetrators of atrocities to enter Australia. He'd intended to include an account of the Ustashe atrocity Peter had described, but Gus decided it was too shocking to print.

Ted was disappointed by the response to his article. There were a few sympathetic letters calling for an overhaul of the screening system to exclude the very people Australia had gone to war against, but it seemed as though his exposé had played into the hands of the xenophobes. Most of the letter writers praised him for revealing that the current immigration policy was a failure, and urged the government to restrict immigration to British citizens, while some writers dismissed his claims and accused him of being a Communist sympathiser.

Several days later, the secretary of the immigration department wrote to the *Daily Standard* to refute Ted's article and said that Ted had probably got confused between the tattoos of concentration camp inmates and those of SS men. In a scathing riposte, Ted replied that, unlike the letter writer, he could tell the difference between a forearm and an armpit.

Chapter 20

It had been exciting, hearing the wail of the siren and knowing that the ambulance had come for him, Meggsie thought. Seeing everyone out in the street watching him being carried out on a stretcher, he'd felt like the hero of one of his adventure stories, especially when he'd seen Hanny's worried face pressed against the window. But as soon as the ambulance had sped from Wattle Street and rushed along streets he'd never seen before, he'd thought about his useless legs and had trouble getting enough air into his lungs.

He'd tried to sit up but the ambulance officer had told him to lie still.

'The paper round!' he'd cried out, his eyes wide with alarm. 'Mum, I didn't do the paper round this morning! Mr Smithson will go crook. He'll give the round to someone else and then I won't get any money.'

Taking his hand, his mum had said, 'Don't worry about it, love. I'll tell him you're sick and he'll keep the job for you. You'll see, you'll be running around in no time.'

The ambulance had pulled up in the driveway of a brick building with big pillars and before Meggsie knew what was happening he was being wheeled away without having a chance to say goodbye to his mother. At the end of a long corridor, in a brightly lit room, they placed him on cold white sheets on a hard table under a lamp that shone into his eyes. Everything in there was cold and white, even the caps and coats the doctor and nurses wore, and the masks that hid their faces.

'Are you a brave boy?' the doctor asked.

Meggsie nodded but his stomach was churning round like the time he'd had a roller-coaster ride at the Easter Show.

'What's your favourite book?'

'Biggles,' Meggsie said in a whisper that didn't sound like his own voice.

'Well, let's see how brave Biggles can be,' the doctor said as the nurses rolled him over on one side. 'This might sting a bit, but we need you to keep very still so we can do a little test to see what's wrong with you. Do you think you can do that?'

Meggsie nodded but his heart was pounding. He wished his mother was there. He felt like crying but he wanted to be brave. Two nurses were holding him down and suddenly he almost leapt into the air with a pain that took his breath away as the doctor stuck a needle into his spine. He thought it would come out on the other side and stab him to death, and he heard himself screaming in a way he'd never screamed before. He was mortified. He'd let Biggles down.

The next day the doctor came to see him.

'Dr McCallum was right,' he said. 'It's poliomyelitis. We're going to put your legs in splints.'

Meggsie didn't know what poliomyelitis was, or why the nurses were putting something hard at the back of his legs and padding it with a soft mesh-like fabric, and then placing something under his feet. He heard them saying something about stopping foot drop, and he thought it meant his foot was going to fall off.

In the isolation ward he was dimly aware of other beds and other children, but he felt hot and cold and shivery and didn't feel like talking and, he supposed, neither did they. In his feverish state he saw white-clad figures with masks covering their faces hovering around his bed like ghosts. They spoke to him but the masks muffled their voices and he was too exhausted to reply. He thought they said his mother wouldn't be allowed to come and see him for some time, but his head was too fuzzy to take it all in. All he could do was mumble through his cracked lips.

He didn't know how long he'd been there by the time his head and neck stopped aching and he heard the ladies in the white masks saying that his fever had dropped.

'How're you going? All right?' one of the masked nurses would ask with a sympathetic smile whenever she brought his dinner tray with shepherd's pie, sago and stewed apples. 'Not much fun in here, is it? But only another week and you'll be in the orthopaedic ward, and then your mum will be able to visit you. But your brothers won't — children aren't allowed into the polio wards.'

He didn't know what the orthopaedic ward was, but from

her tone it sounded like an improvement on the isolation ward where he couldn't see his mum or anyone he knew, and there was nothing to distract him from his misery, not even the sound of a wireless. Lying in the bed with his useless legs, he wanted to scream at the nurses to take off the splints and the bandages so he could get out of there. Through the window he could see tiny motes of dust suspended on shafts of light high above his bed. When a breeze swayed the branches of the gum trees outside, they brushed against the panes in ever-changing patterns of light and shade, and occasionally he heard a bird chirping and saw the shadow of its wings as it flew past, and wished he was a bird and could fly away.

Whenever a nurse came in, his eyes followed her hungrily, hoping that she'd stay and talk to him, but the nurses were always rushed off their feet and only had time to exchange a few words as they straightened his bed or took his temperature.

Most of them were kind but some were as crisp as their starched uniforms and veils; they told him they had their time cut out trying to get their work done and didn't have time for idle chitchat.

The prettiest young nurse, whose name was Cecily, often stopped by his bed and tried to cheer him up.

'Buck up,' she'd said one day. 'Next Sunday you'll see your mum. She won't be able to come into the ward, but you'll be able to see her through that window. She came last Sunday, but you were too sick to know she was there.'

He had counted the hours until Sunday, and now it was here he was counting the minutes. Finally two o'clock arrived, and when he looked towards the door, there she was, her pale face looking at him through the window, but all they could do was look at each other and make miming gestures. She kept wiping her eyes and trying to smile as she waved to him. When the bell rang and visiting time was over, she blew him one last kiss, and as he listened to her slow footsteps growing fainter he felt more alone than before.

In the long, lonely hours after she left, Meggsie went over the events of the past few weeks and came to the conclusion that God had punished him. He thought about all the bad things he'd done, like fighting in the schoolyard, breaking Pete's wooden train and not telling Alan that Gran had left a bag of lollies for him when he was sick, and eating them all himself. When he got out of hospital, he'd buy Alan a big bag of liquorice all-sorts, fix Pete's train and never fight again. Suddenly he remembered Mrs Browning telling his mum that two policemen had taken Mr Emil away, and he felt sick. That was why God had punished him. For spying on his neighbour and dobbing him in.

When Nurse Cecily brought his porridge next morning, she was holding a book. 'I've brought you something,' she said, placing *The Count of Monte Cristo* on the bed. 'When I was sick, my mum gave it to me. I loved it. I'll bring you a reading stand so you can put the book on it. Try and turn the pages yourself, but I'll come in and turn them for you whenever I can.'

He wondered whether she'd had polio as well, and had her legs in splints, but she'd gone before he had time to ask.

At first it took so long to read each page that he became discouraged. The print was small, there weren't any pictures, and he couldn't understand many of the long, unfamiliar words. The detailed descriptions bored him, and he couldn't follow who was who, or what was going on. But with nothing else to do, he read each page several times, and before long he became so fascinated by the story of Edmond Dantès that he couldn't wait to find out what happened next, especially when the hero began to dig a tunnel to escape from the Chateau d'If.

Each night before falling asleep, Meggsie would relive each scene in his head. He seethed with indignation at the injustice of Edmond Dantès's sentence and wondered if he would ever escape and get his own back on the horrible man who'd had him imprisoned. He became so absorbed in the story that he began thinking of himself as Dantès. After all, he was imprisoned in this hospital, far from everything and everyone he loved. If Dantès could escape from his island fortress, then perhaps one day he might be free too.

Finally the day he'd been longing for arrived. The three-week infectious period had passed, and he cheered when Nurse Cecily told him that he was going to be moved into the orthopaedic ward that morning.

'I bet you're glad to be rid of me!' she laughed.

His face fell. He hadn't realised that moving out of the isolation ward meant changing nurses.

Seeing his dismay, she said, 'It's funny, isn't it — whenever we get something we've been wishing for, it never turns out exactly the way we expected.'

He was struggling with that idea when she added, 'I suppose you'll know the book off by heart by the time you go home.'

'I won't be in here that long,' he said.

As soon as they transferred him to the orthopaedic ward and he saw the row of beds on the long verandah with other children in them, he forgot his disappointment about Nurse Cecily. In the bed next to his lay a boy about his own age, and on the other side was a little kid who reminded him of Pete. At the far end was an inquisitive little girl with a mop of curly hair. Betty, who was five, immediately wanted to know all about him and his brothers: what were their names, how old were they, which one did he fight with the most, and which one did he like the best?

Facing him stood a large metal contraption. At first glance it looked like one of the coffins he'd seen the night he spied on Mr Emil. Then he decided it was more like the boxes he'd seen in magic shows, the ones where the magician pretended to cut his assistant's head off. He was surprised to see a girl's head poking out of the box.

But he didn't have time to find out what it was because a woman in a white uniform came towards him and told him she was the physiotherapist and she'd come to remove his splints and put his legs in plaster ones instead. The moist plaster felt pleasantly warm as she slathered it all over his legs. When it was dry, she picked up some cutters and cut away the top part so that his legs rested in the plaster cases.

'That's so you'll be able to get your legs in and out of the plaster,' the physiotherapist said in a reassuring voice. 'Just imagine that your legs are wearing half a sock to keep them warm.'

After the physiotherapist had gone, he looked at the metal contraption again, trying to work out what it was for. When he looked up he saw his mum standing there. At first his mind was as numb as his legs, and he couldn't think of anything to say because there was so much he wanted to say that it got all jumbled up inside his head. She just stood there looking at him with tears pouring down her face. He hadn't been able to touch her since the day the ambulance brought him to the hospital, and he reached out and clutched her hand. He hadn't seen her cry since the day his dad walked out, and although he felt like crying too, he felt embarrassed in case someone was watching.

Suddenly his mum was hugging him and they were both talking at once. He wanted to hear about his brothers and his friends. Did Alan get into the cricket team at school, did Hanny ask about him, was Mr Smithson keeping his job for him? She wanted to know whether his legs hurt, what were the nurses like, and what he ate for dinner. Then she started taking things out of her shopping bag: his balsawood plane, some Batman, Superman and Mandrake the Magician comics, a lamington and two iced finger buns. He wanted to tell her all about Nurse Cecily, and the wonderful world of the Count of Monte Cristo, and about the grumpy old nurse, but suddenly the bell shrilled. Visiting time was over.

'I'll come again on Sunday, love,' his mum said, and with one last hug she disappeared through the door.

This time his sense of loss was so intense that he bit his lip hard to stop himself from crying. His joy at seeing her turned to sadness. After not seeing her for so long, having to part after such a short time was like being offered a gift and then having it snatched away before he could open it.

He felt sad for another reason he couldn't quite understand or put into words. Something had changed between him and his mother. Too much had happened to him that she didn't know about and he couldn't express. He wondered whether that was what Nurse Cecily had meant, that the things we long for never turn out the way we imagine.

'Hey! You!' The girl in the metal box was calling him in a hoarse whisper.

'Hey!' she said again. 'What's your name? Mine's Dawn.'

'You can talk!' he said.

'Of course I can talk,' she retorted. 'I'm paralysed, not dumb. Was that your mum? She looks really nice. She brought you things and said she'll be back next Sunday. You're lucky. My mum can't come every week. She just had a baby.'

Dawn had been in the iron lung for seven months. When

she explained that it breathed for her, Meggsie peppered her with questions.

'See that thing on the side? That's a sort of pump. It's connected to the iron lung by a tube that moves my chest so I can get some air in,' she said. 'Otherwise I'd be dead.'

Meggsie was impressed. This was better than anything he'd ever seen in the comic books, better even than the serials they screened at the matinees on Saturday arvo, where spacemen travelled in those weird aircraft. He wished he could have a closer look at the pump and see how it worked.

'Gee, that's like a magic trunk,' he said. 'When I get out of here, I'm going to see a real magician, Morris the Magnificent.'

Then he stopped talking as a frightening thought took his breath away. What if he didn't get out in time?

Chapter 21

As Sala walked to the tram stop she was enchanted by the light pouring down from a sky tinted with gauzy wisps of pink. It was spring, or what passed for spring in this strange country which had no real seasons. The trees didn't change colour in autumn, and there were no crocuses or primroses at the end of winter. The only difference she'd noticed was in the quality of the light, which shone with a golden radiance. There was one other difference — something in the air made her sneeze so much that her head ached.

'Hay fever' was what Mrs Browning had called it when she'd heard her sneezing. That made no sense as there was no hay anywhere around. Sala wondered if she'd ever become familiar with these illogical English expressions. Szymon, who never let his lack of vocabulary stand in his way, just laughed at her frustration. He forged ahead, misusing words and phrases in a way that made her cringe, but somehow he made himself understood and everyone thought he was a 'bonza bloke' for 'having a go', whatever that meant.

Slipping onto a slatted wooden seat that had been buffed to a high gloss by passengers over the years, she thought about their latest argument which, as usual, had been about her work. Suddenly a paperboy jumped onto the running board and poked his cheeky face into her compartment. 'Py-pah, read all about it!' he chanted, and leapt down again just as the tram was moving off.

A moment later the tram guard came into the compartment, his battered cap slightly askew. 'Lovely morning, eh?' he said as he tore a ticket off the large leather ticket holder scuffed from decades of use. 'Soon be beach weather, I reckon. You like the beach?'

'I like very much,' she said, handing him her fourpence.

This time she got off the tram in Taylor Square near the court house, whose Grecian columns she found so incongruous in this slummy area of boarding houses, sly grog shops and poky corner stores. On the corner she stopped for a moment to look at the array of abandoned possessions in the pawnbroker's window: watches, bracelets, a tarnished trumpet, an old Leica camera and a pearl necklace that looked as if it had never been taken out of its crimson velvet case. There was probably an interesting story behind each one, and she wondered what it was.

Turning into Darlinghurst Road she walked past old terraces with splintered doorways, cracked tiles and sagging verandahs. Behind the leaning fences and broken palings, uncut grass straggled in neglected front yards. A young woman in a tight red skirt was puffing on a cigarette as she leaned suggestively against the open door of a terrace, eyeing the passers-by. Inside, the wireless was on full blast, and Sala slowed down to listen to Peggy Lee's husky voice singing 'Mañana'. The record finished, and with a bored look the young woman tossed her cigarette butt onto the cracked tiles, ground it out with the toe of her black ankle-strap shoe and disappeared inside.

A few doors further down, a toothless man sitting in a frayed wicker chair on his verandah waved at Sala as she passed. Beside him hung a birdcage whose occupant, a large grey-and-pink parrot, made her jump as it screeched 'Hello cocky!' in a hoarse drunken voice.

There were few people in the street so early in the day, and the corner shops hadn't yet opened, but high in the acacia trees, small birds twittered and whistled. Sala filled her lungs with the cool freshness of the September morning, and she could feel the muscles in her neck loosening up. She and Szymon had had an argument that morning, but by the time she pushed open the door of the Jewish Welfare Society she no longer felt angry and she resolved to be less critical.

She opened the door to the cleaning closet, reached for her crossover apron on the hook, and almost fell over Beryl who was propped up against the wall, her head slumped on her chest.

'Strewth, I feel that crook,' she mumbled, holding her head.

'You should go home,' Sala said. 'I will tell Mrs Feldman you are sick.'

Beryl looked up, her bloodshot eyes wide with alarm. 'Don't say nothink. It's not the first time, see. If you tell her, I'll lose me job. I'll be okay in a minute.'

A moment later she vomited. Curds of undigested food lay in her apron, and threads of yellowish liquid hung down her chin.

'Sorry, love. Just bring me a glass of water and I'll be right as rain.'

Sala brought Beryl a glass of water, sponged her face and carefully removed her apron, surprised at her own lack of rancour. Ever since she'd started working there, she had seethed over Beryl's nasty comments and had brooded about revenge, but suddenly the old dragon looked no more menacing than a deflated balloon.

'You should go home,' Sala repeated, looking at Beryl's face, which was as sallow as candlewax. 'I won't say anything to Mrs Feldman, and I'll do your rooms so she won't know you weren't here.'

Staggering to her feet, Beryl nodded gratefully. 'Ta, love. Hooroo.' She steadied herself against the wall and waddled out of the building.

Sala ran around whisking the feather duster over the furniture, emptying the ashtrays and sweeping and polishing the floors. She was putting on her coat when Franka Feldman put her head around the door and asked her to come into the office. None of the typists had arrived yet and they were alone.

After a brief chat, Mrs Feldman said, 'Tell me, was your maiden name Preiss by any chance?'

Sala nodded, surprised by the question.

Mrs Feldman opened a copy of the previous week's *Jewish News* and turned to the Personal Notices section at the back of the paper. 'Someone is looking for you,' she said.

Sala's hands trembled as she took the paper. So many Jewish survivors had migrated to Australia after the war that it wasn't unusual for family members to place advertisements in the local Jewish press in the hope of finding relatives. Perhaps an aunt or cousin had survived after all and was searching for her.

But the notice hadn't been placed by a relative. There was to be a court hearing in Poland and they were looking for witnesses. Too agitated to read the notice word by word, she scanned it, and her heart pounded. One name leapt from the page.

Behind her large shiny glasses, Franka Feldman watched with her calm, sympathetic gaze.

When Sala finally looked up, her face was taut and pale. 'How did you know it was about me?' she said.

'Well, you told me you came from Łódż, so when I saw that someone was looking for Sala Preiss from Łódż, I thought it might be you,' Franka said. 'I can see you're upset. If you ever feel like talking about it, come and see me any time.'

Thoughts coiled and uncoiled themselves in Sala's mind as she sat in the tram on her way home. In the seat in front of her two women were talking in loud staccato voices in what she recognised as Hungarian. In the quiet compartment their voices sounded shrill, and she heard an Australian saying,

'Shuddup, you bloody reffos. Go back where you came from if you can't speak English.'

Sala spent the rest of the day wandering around aimlessly, her mind in turmoil, and when Szymon came in she realised that she'd forgotten to buy meat for dinner. They'd parted on bad terms that morning and she braced herself for more recriminations about her job and her forgetfulness, but to her surprise he didn't seem to mind that she'd forgotten the meat.

'Don't worry, Salcia, tonight we'll be vegetarians. Too much meat isn't healthy anyway.'

He was in an expansive and forgiving mood, and it didn't take her long to find out why.

'Fela wants us to come for dinner next week. It's Rosh Hashana,' he said eagerly.

Sala hadn't seen Szymon's cousin since they'd moved out after the episode of the spilled borsch. She was reluctant to go there but, remembering the notice in the newspaper, she decided to be conciliatory.

She found some cauliflower, a few potatoes and an onion in the cupboard and took them into the kitchen. She prepared the cauliflower the Polish way, sprinkled with buttered breadcrumbs, and she fried the grated potatoes and onions the Jewish way, into the flat pancakes called *latkes* which were Szymon's favourite. This time she had the communal kitchen to herself, but for once she didn't dwell on the state of the greasy Kooka stove, the rancid smell or the fly-spotted ceiling. She had something else to think about.

She dreaded the prospect of broaching the subject in case Szymon started dragging up the old suspicions and accusations; she couldn't face going over all that again. But apart from worrying about Szymon's reaction, she felt confused. How should she respond to the notice? There were so many rights and wrongs, so many excuses and rationalisations, that it was impossible to disentangle one from the other. Perhaps she should wait. She needed to assess the situation with a calm mind before deciding what to do.

Relieved that she'd found a way of delaying the confrontation, she carried the vegetables to their room and forced herself to smile.

A week later they rang the bell on Fela's door. Sala pulled nervously at the jacket of the outfit Szymon had bought her in Marseilles, wondering if she was overdressed. As soon as the door opened, Fela threw her arms around their necks and wished them '*Shana Tova*' in her effusive manner, while behind her Lutek was fussing around, straightening the fringes of the Persian rugs.

Sala looked at the dining table with the silver candelabra and the round *challa* studded with raisins and wanted to cry. This was an empty ritual attempting to re-create a vanished world in a country where there was no room for imported nostalgia. Instead of clinging to old rituals, they should concentrate on adapting to their new environment.

Szymon, as usual, saw it differently. 'Look, Salcia, isn't this fantastic! Who would have thought during all those terrible years that one day we'd be celebrating Rosh Hashana again in a free country?'

She glanced at him, handsome in spite of his broken nose, his thick dark hair brushed back from his wide forehead and cresting into a wave, and his face glowing like a child who has just received a longed-for gift. It irritated her that, despite everything that had happened, he persisted in clinging to this optimistic view of the world. But at the same time she envied his childlike capacity for unquestioning faith.

They had just sat down when the doorbell rang and, with little shrieks of welcome, Fela ushered in another couple. The newcomers were Alex and Genia Engelman. Like their hosts, the Engelmans had also arrived in Sydney before the war. Alex had been a public prosecutor in Warsaw, but instead of repeating his law studies in a foreign language and learning a new legal system, he'd started a business manufacturing men's shirts, and from what Fela had told them, he was doing very well.

Lutek wiped each delicate crystal glass and held it up to the light to make sure there were no smudges, then poured the Cherry Heering while Fela went into the kitchen to put the finishing touches to the festive meal. Szymon was drawn into the men's conversation about Australia's dependence on Britain, the crippling cost of imported textiles, the need for locally produced merchandise, and the escalating cost of flats and houses.

'This is a very peculiar country,' Alex was saying as he placed his empty glass on the walnut coffee table. 'They think it's bad manners to talk about sex, religion and politics. Doesn't leave much!'

'That's why all they talk about is the weather,' Lutek said as he whisked away the glass and placed it onto a tray. 'It's the only topic left.'

Szymon was shaking his head. 'Well, I've had enough discussions about religion and politics to last the rest of my life. But as for sex ...'

The men burst out laughing, and on the other side of the room Genia leaned towards Sala and giggled. 'I bet they're telling dirty jokes.'

Looking at Genia's fashionably short hair, which was cropped around her animated face, and her crisp taffeta dress with its big portrait collar and full skirt, Sala was glad she'd worn her New Look suit, but when she caught a glimpse of her own hair in the gilt-framed mirror above the mantelpiece, she wished she'd arranged it in a more sophisticated style. It had already worked loose from its roll and was hanging in a riot of curls around her face

Genia's hands were weaving arabesques in the air for emphasis as she compared Sydney with prewar Warsaw. She extolled the latter's cafés, nightclubs, boutiques and beauty salons, and sighed with nostalgia as she reminisced about Warsaw's operettas, concerts and plays.

'Sydney is a cultural wasteland,' she said. 'People here are quite backward and hardly anyone worth listening to ever gives concerts or recitals. What they do have is a wonderful climate, but it hasn't occurred to them to have outdoor cafés and restaurants. All they do is fry at the beach.'

From the other side of the room Alex broke in good-naturedly. 'Genia, what are you talking about? It's not so bad. In June we saw Laurence Olivier and Vivien Leigh at the Tivoli, and last week we went to hear Elisabeth Schwarzkopf at the Town Hall. As a matter of fact, I've just bought tickets for *Tosca* at the Elizabethan Theatre.'

He smiled across the room at Sala. 'Genia always exaggerates. That's part of her charm.'

Genia rolled her eyes and gave Sala a conspiratorial look. 'And Alex always takes everything literally. Have you noticed how men do that?'

Alex looked at Sala's hair and turned to his wife. 'See, darling, not everyone has shorn their hair.'

He looked at Sala again, and she was aware that he held her gaze far longer than was socially acceptable. She blushed and looked down, but when she glanced up again he was still watching her.

She liked the direct gaze of his dark blue eyes and the shape of his full lips, which were accentuated by his neatly trimmed moustache. She blushed again and was relieved when Fela called them to the table.

When they were about to begin the traditional new year meal, Szymon said, 'Mind if I say the *brochas*?'

Sala felt herself shrinking with embarrassment, but the men quickly took folded handkerchiefs from their pockets and covered their heads while he intoned the Hebrew blessings for the bread and wine.

After they'd dipped slices of apple in honey to symbolise a sweet year, Fela served chicken soup with matzo balls.

Genia closed her eyes in ecstasy. 'I've been looking for matzo meal everywhere. Where on earth did you find it?'

This led to an animated exchange of information about the grocers who sold continental goods, the butchers who knew how to cut veal fillet into schnitzel, and the continued lack of unsalted butter.

While Lutek carved the roast chicken with the precision of a surgeon, Genia turned to Sala. 'Fela said you spent the war in Poland.' Her eyes were soft with sympathy. 'You must have had a terrible time.'

Invisible ropes yanked Sala's stomach so tight that her breath came in rapid gasps. She felt everyone's eyes on her. Somehow she had to forestall the inevitable question.

'Yes,' she said, and turned to Lutek. 'Could you pass me the salt, please?'

Fela and Lutek exchanged glances, and for a few awkward moments no one spoke.

Alex was looking at her with an expression that implied an unspoken collusion. 'It's Rosh Hashana,' he said. 'Why talk about the past? Let's talk about the future.'

Sala agreed, grateful that he'd understood her reluctance to discuss the war.

Lutek opened a bottle of sparkling burgundy and poured the foaming liquid into their glasses. 'Let's drink a toast to the new year and to our new country,' he said.

As they raised their glasses, Sala saw that Genia was leaning against Alex, her hair brushing against his cheek, and she was aware of a feeling that disturbed her.

'I've got good news,' Genia said. 'We're going to have a real New Australian!'

Before the news sank in, Fela was at her friend's side, hugging her and uttering little screams of delight.

'That's wonderful,' Szymon said, and gave Sala a meaningful glance, but she was studying her wine glass.

She couldn't wait for the evening to end. As the night wore on, she realised that she felt more comfortable with her Australian neighbours, women like Verna Browning who never asked about the past. With them she could be whoever she wanted to be, but here she had to be on her guard because they were obsessed with a past she was determined to leave behind.

As they waited for the tram, Szymon reached into his coat pocket, and handed her something small and flat. 'Go on, open it,' he whispered.

It was a bankbook, and under the deposit column, in neat handwriting, the bank teller had written *Twenty-five pounds*.

'I've saved that already,' he said. 'Mr Furstenberg said he'll give me a raise soon, and when I've saved a hundred pounds we'll get a loan from the bank and start looking for a place of our own.'

He squeezed her arm. 'You didn't look happy tonight, Salcia, but don't envy them. You'll see, one day you'll have everything.'

She sighed. As usual, he had got it wrong.

Chapter 22

To add to Kath's problems while Meggsie was in hospital, Alan, Ray and Pete were sent home from school in case they were infected as well. None of the children in the street were allowed to play with them and, as if she didn't have enough to worry about, the Pitts, a stuck-up couple who lived at the Barton Street end of Wattle Street, pointedly crossed the road and placed handkerchiefs over their mouths whenever they saw her. The third time they did it, Kath sang out, 'Meggsie's got polio, for Christ's sake, not the bloody plague!'

With a self-righteous air, the Pitts repeated what she'd said, and soon embellished versions of her retort went around the neighbourhood. By the time the story reached Verna Browning, their encounter had turned into a screaming match, with Kath about to throw a punch at the defenceless Mrs Pitt.

'You'd think people would have more sense, to say nothing of Christian charity, gossiping like that,' Verna Browning said indignantly as she put junket and tinned peaches into Ted's dessert bowl.

Ted nodded absentmindedly. He was brooding about an upsetting encounter with Lilija three days before. When his article about Bonegilla had been published, Gus had given him a small raise, and he'd decided to splurge it on a romantic candlelit dinner in a swanky restaurant like Prince's or Romano's. She would gaze at him adoringly while waiters in dinner suits and haughty expressions filled their glasses and flamed crepes suzette at their table. But this time he resolved he wouldn't wait until he met her in secret on the tram. He would go to her house to ask her out.

His heart had pounded when he'd rung her doorbell and he'd rehearsed what he would say to convince Mr Olmanis that he loved his daughter and would bring her back at whatever time he stipulated. Lilija's mother answered the door; her nervous expression and stiff movements reminded him of a marionette whose strings were being pulled offstage. The skin on her face was taut, and she fiddled with the collar of her dress. Her eyes darted sideways and she muttered something he couldn't understand, fluttered her hands, and said, 'Wait a moment please,' and left him standing on the doorstep.

Peering into the hallway, he saw that it was decorated with intricately hand-embroidered pictures depicting women in folk dress, snow-capped gingerbread houses and verses he supposed were in Latvian. From inside the house he heard a man and woman arguing in loud, angry voices.

A few moments later Lilija appeared and he felt that shock of delighted incredulity he experienced each time he saw her.

Her face was paler than usual, and her arms were tightly folded as though she was trying to hold herself together.

She didn't invite him inside. Not meeting his gaze, she said in a tremulous voice, 'I'm sorry, you cannot come here. I can't see you any more.'

'But I came to ask you out,' he began, but she shook her head and quickly closed the door.

Since then he'd gone over every conversation they'd ever had, but he was still baffled by her odd behaviour. Why had she closed the door on him and said she couldn't see him any more? She'd defied her father before to meet him, she'd let him hold her hand and kiss her, so why had she suddenly brushed him off like that? And what did her father have against him anyway?

Too restless to stay inside, Ted went out onto the verandah and lit a Capstan. It was one of those delicious spring evenings when the air was warm with the promise of summer, and the light breeze carried the scent of wood smoke. The sun was starting to set and the horizon was the colour of ripe strawberries. As he inhaled, he felt the nicotine relaxing him. Next door, the Polish girl was sitting on the doorstep, her face in her hands, and he wondered what was wrong. Probably another fight with her mother. Across the road Kath was shouting at the boys to sit down for dinner before she took the wooden spoon to them.

A clinking sound made him look around, and there was Pop Wilson placing another empty bottle onto the pile on his verandah. Without the jovial mask he put on for others, his bloated face sagged and seemed to collapse into itself.

Ted suddenly remembered that after returning the tool bag he'd promised to drop in for a chat, but he still hadn't got round to it. Feeling guilty, he hurriedly tamped out his cigarette and went inside before Pop saw him.

He threw himself dejectedly into an armchair and pulled at the loose threads of the crocheted throwover.

His mother cast him a sympathetic look over her knitting. 'She might change her mind one of these days. You never know.'

'Not with that tyrant of a father, she won't. What he says goes.'

'Then you're well out of it,' Verna said. 'You know, it's hard enough to understand someone from the same background as yourself, let alone a foreigner.'

Settling down to listen to the latest episode of *When a Girl Marries*, she clicked away with her knitting needles without dropping a stitch as she watched Ted pacing around the room. 'You're like a caged tiger tonight,' she said, looking up from her knitting. 'Why don't you go out and see some of your mates?'

Ted shrugged. Ever since he'd started work at the *Daily Standard* he'd drifted away from his old friends. Most of them had become schoolteachers, bank tellers or clerks in the public service, and their stories about naughty children, office politics and banking problems bored him. They'd all become staid and smug, and all they talked about these days was finding somewhere to live or saving enough for a deposit for a house. Although they kept trying to pair him off with someone, he always made excuses. There was only one girl he was interested in.

Syrupy theme music came over the wireless, indicating the end of the episode, and Verna turned the dial to *Pick-A-Box*.

'I've been thinking,' she said as Bob Dyer's strident American voice introduced the program. 'Why don't you write something about poliomyelitis?'

'It's not news, Mum.'

'Well I think it is,' she said. 'It said in the paper the other day that there were even more cases this year. The poor kids have to lie in hospital day in and day out, and their parents are only allowed to visit them once a week. When Kath tried to find out how Meggsie was going, some old battleaxe told her that anxious mothers slowed up their children's recovery! What a nerve!'

Ted chuckled. He could imagine Gus Thornton's reaction if he suggested writing about kids with polio. Unless they were dying in droves as a result of medical incompetence, it wasn't a story. But his mother was right. He did need to get out for some fresh air. He'd go down to the beach and stretch his legs on the promenade, and then get a malted milkshake on Campbell Parade.

Ten minutes later he was on the green-and-yellow tram that swung around Five Ways and rattled along Bondi Road, past blocks of redbrick flats, boarding houses and car-repair workshops. As it rattled past the picture theatre, he saw that the poster for Morris the Magnificent had been replaced by an advertisement for a new movie with Virginia Mayo. He swivelled around for another look at the film star whose ravishing face reminded him of Lilija.

The tram driver pressed the foot gong to let passengers know they'd reached the North Bondi terminus. With the clanging still in his ears, Ted strolled along Campbell Parade, watching the waves roll in, their foamy crests lit up by the lamps along the promenade. Although it was a pleasant evening, there was hardly anyone about, and when he looked around he saw that the shops were closed. It struck him that this was very different from the lively promenades in European cities, and realised that he was seeing Bondi through Lilija's eyes.

The aroma of frying onions made his mouth water, and before he knew it he was walking in the direction of the smell. Squeezed into the recess between a stucco-faced hotel with an Art Deco roof and a dingy block of flats with a dance studio on the first floor was a hamburger stall. Standing behind it, an olive-skinned man with a handkerchief knotted in four corners over his curly brown hair was placing lumps of minced beef onto a hot griddle and flattening them with a spatula. While the meat patty was frying, he threw a sliced onion and two rashers of bacon onto another part of the griddle, and broke open an egg. A few moments later he inserted the lot between two slices of thick toasted bread, added sliced beetroot, tomato and lettuce, and handed it to a stout man in a beige windcheater who bit into it as he strode away.

Ted leaned against the wall while he waited for his hamburger. Most people were already home from work and, apart from an occasional Austin or Vauxhall, there were few cars on the road. As soon as his order was ready, Ted crossed the road, walked past a row of Norfolk pines and sat down on a bench facing the sea. He was glad that no one could see him as he tried to get his mouth around the hamburger, with the egg yolk oozing down his chin, onions spilling onto his paper bag and tomato sauce dripping onto his fingers. It wasn't until he'd swallowed the last morsel that he noticed he wasn't alone. Sitting at the other end of the bench, still and silent as a statue in a museum, was the peculiar man from Wattle Street, and he remembered the mysterious coffins Meggsie had told him about.

'I need a bath after eating this,' Ted chuckled, licking the sauce off his fingers and scrunching the greasy bag into a ball.

The man didn't reply, and Ted watched the white-tipped rollers on the dark water whose treacherous depths concealed sharks and created unpredictable rips. He turned towards his neighbour to warn him about the dangers of the surf but the man had slipped into the night.

Emil knew that the young man lived with his mother across the road, but since his ordeal at the police station the week before, he'd become more reclusive and withdrawn than ever.

You couldn't trust anyone, he decided. The boy next door had broken his word and his mother had reported him. Although Emil no longer believed in God, he did believe in divine retribution. He also believed in the devil because he'd met some of his disciples here on earth. Once he'd believed in the power of magic, but his skill had become tainted, the magic had turned out to be a farce, and the only one who had been deceived was himself.

Inside the dimly lit interviewing room at the back of the police station, the policemen who had questioned him had tried to make him admit he'd been at Waverley Park that Sunday, or at least to confuse him so they could accuse him of lying. He didn't know why they had kept on about it, or why they had refused to give him any information, but he assumed that something must have happened in the park that day and they wanted to pin it on him.

He had tried to say that they had no right to detain and intimidate him, but he'd had trouble putting the words together, and while he'd been stammering about his rights, Frank O'Connor had pushed his wooden chair backwards so it was balancing on its back legs, and given him a mocking smile. Emil was no stranger to men like O'Connor, whose uniforms gave them power over others, and whose lips smiled while their fists lashed out. The younger man, Constable Adams, looked more intelligent and seemed less of a bully, but Emil supposed that he'd go along with whatever his superior said.

O'Connor leaned forward and turned to Adams. 'Listen to this. Our friend here wants to teach us about his rights,' he sneered, rubbing the knuckles of his right hand with his left palm. 'Of course our laws aren't as good as the ones where he comes from. Where do you come from, mate?' he asked Emil with false bonhomie.

'Berlin,' Emil said.

'Berlin! Well that explains everything! No bloody wonder you want to teach us about laws. You lot know all about that.' He jumped to his feet, clicked his heels and gave a mock Nazi salute. 'Heil Hitler!'

Emil felt sick. He tried to explain that he wasn't a Nazi, that the Nazis had deported him to a concentration camp, but before he could get the words out, O'Connor grabbed him by the shoulders, pulled him to his feet and landed a punch to his stomach that made him gasp and double up with pain.

'Hey, you blokes,' O'Connor shouted, opening the door. 'You want to come in here and listen to a bloody Nazi telling us about the law?'

Two young policemen trooped in and mockingly called him 'Herr Bloody Hitler'. Emil blinked nervously, and his hands were clammy with sweat but he didn't make a sound. He wouldn't give them the satisfaction of crying out. He'd been through worse.

After a few punches they lost interest and drifted back to their desks, shaking their heads and muttering about the government letting in bloody Krauts when decent Aussie diggers had nowhere to live.

Thrusting his face right up to Emil's, O'Connor hissed, 'You'd better come clean about them coffins. Who are they for?'

'For no one.'

'Are you taking the mickey out of me?' The sergeant banged his fist on the table so loudly that Emil jumped. 'Are you trying to tell me that you make coffins in secret for nobody?'

'I work for carpenter. Is against law to make coffin?' Emil asked.

The sergeant stared at him, his eyes bulging with fury. 'It's against the law to make a fucking racket and disturb people at night.'

'So I will not do it at night.'

Rubbing his knuckles, O'Connor glared at Emil and told him to clear off. 'And watch out, 'cause I'll be watching you!'

Emil had trembled all the way home, but he had felt a sense of triumph. He hadn't told them the truth about the coffins and he never would.

Chapter 23

The big red crosses woven into the white cotton covers of the beds were so bright that when Meggsie closed his eyes they were still imprinted on his eyeballs. He always closed them as soon as he saw the ward sister coming. Everything about Sister Davis was starched, from her white veil and stiff uniform to her rigid back. She always sounded put upon, as though they were all in hospital just to nark her, and he noticed that the younger nurses were scared of her and scurried about with nervous faces whenever she was around in case they hadn't made the beds with perfect corners or had forgotten to give someone their medication. He thought of her as Sister Danglars, after the man who'd betrayed the Count of Monte Cristo and caused his misfortunes. Her eagle eye never failed to spot a sheet that hadn't been perfectly tucked in, and she bossed the nurses around and told them off at the top of her voice, even when there were visitors in the ward.

Once a week the consultant came in. Dr Tennyson Wilkie was a tall, lean man with eyes that reminded Meggsie of lozenges with all the colour sucked out of them. His distant gaze rarely rested on his patients as he walked at the head of a respectful entourage of junior doctors, registrars and senior nurses who always had a joke or a friendly word for the children but deferred to the consultant with murmurs of agreement bordering on reverence. Meggsie had never heard any of them offer a different opinion or ask a question in case he thought they were challenging his judgement.

During one of his rounds, when Dr Wilkie stopped beside Meggsie's bed and cast his eyes on the notes proffered by the ward sister, Meggsie suddenly spoke up.

'Please, when will I be well enough to go home? I've been here for ages and I miss my mum and my brothers.'

The residents and registrars looked at him as though they understood how he felt, but the ward sister had a murderous look on her face. 'Don't be cheeky,' she said.

Ignoring her, Dr Wilkie scrutinised Meggsie with concern in his tired eyes. 'What's the matter, lad? Sister tells me you're managing to sit up a bit longer every day. Is something worrying you?'

He sounded kind, and Meggsie longed to tell him how unhappy and worried he was, and how he detested the painful physiotherapy sessions which left him exhausted and upset, but with all their attention on him, he felt shy and hung his head in silence.

When his mother came to see him the following Sunday, he was brimming with news. They'd started taking him down to the indoor pool for something they called hydrotherapy, which was the highlight of his day.

'It's so good, Mum, I wish I could stay there all day!' he said.

Submerged in the warm water, he felt weightless and didn't feel any pain. For that brief period of time he almost forgot he had polio and imagined he could move his legs.

Sometimes he dreamed that he was running and jumping and acting the goat with his brothers, but then he woke up and saw the red cross on the bedcover and knew he was still in the hospital, still living the nightmare. He'd squeeze his eyes shut and try to will himself back into that wonderful dream, but it never worked. That's when the panic grabbed hold of him. What if he never walked again and became a cripple and had to be in a wheelchair all his life? Everyone felt sorry for cripples but no one wanted to play with them. And how would his mum manage without his help? It was all his own fault. If only he hadn't spied on Mr Emil and sent that note to Miss McNulty, none of this would have happened. Maybe he was no better than Danglars, who had written a letter about Edmond Dantès and been punished in the end.

Tears rolled down his face but he blinked them away. If the nurses saw you crying, the nice ones tried to cheer you up but some of the others told you to stop feeling sorry for yourself or you'd never get better. He'd even heard Sister Danglars say that to little Betty, and she was only five.

When he'd first met Betty, she'd been a lively little chatterbox with sparkling eyes. She'd never stopped talking, and had entertained everyone with her questions and comments. She'd been the nurses' pet as well, and he'd noticed that they lingered beside her bed and sometimes brought her a soft toy or a picture book while she quizzed them. Why had they become nurses, what did they have to do, did they mind emptying pooey bed pans, and did they like Sister Davis? Her questions had made them laugh. He had often heard her talking to her knitted blue bunny, telling him to lie still and take his medicine so he'd get better.

Every morning she would ask the nurses if her mum was coming, but they usually shook their heads. From what they said, Meggsie gathered that Betty came from the country somewhere, and it took her mother most of the day to get to the hospital for the Sunday visit. Then she had to stay in town overnight to catch the train home on Monday morning. With a sick husband and five other kids to look after, she couldn't afford the money or the time.

On the rare occasions she did come, Betty's excited little voice could be heard all over the ward telling her mother all about the other kids and the nurses and the yukky food, but when the bell shrilled to announce that visiting time was over Betty clung to her mother with her hot little hands and shouted, 'Don't go! I don't want you to go! Take me with you! Don't leave me here!'

She screamed so loudly that her voice could be heard in the corridors and Sister Davis would stride in, pull Betty's tearful mother away and tell Betty to stop playing up.

Long after her mother had left, Meggsie would hear Betty's gulping sobs, until one Sunday she gagged and started vomiting. One of the nurses came running, cleaned her up and tried to comfort her but Betty was inconsolable because she'd vomited all over her blue bunny and they had to take it away to wash it. 'I want my mum. I want my blue bunny,' she kept shouting.

'Don't cry,' Meggsie whispered. 'They'll bring it back all nice and clean.' But she was too distraught to listen.

When the nurse brought the bunny back two days later, Betty wept again because it had shrunk in the wash and its pink tongue was missing. Gradually her chattering stopped and she just lay there, hardly saying a word. The nurses brought her little treats and read her fairytales; some of the other children in the ward told her riddles, and Meggsie told her stories from his Biggles books, but as the days wore on, Betty became more and more withdrawn, clutching her bunny and staring at the ceiling. Her sadness affected the entire ward, including the nurses, but Sister Davis insisted that the child was only seeking attention and shouldn't be rewarded with special treatment.

When Kath came into the ward the following Sunday, Meggsie asked her to go and talk to Betty even before he glanced at the comic books she'd brought him.

'Her mum hardly ever comes, and her bunny's wrecked,' he explained. 'She used to talk all the time but now she's gone all quiet.'

But when Kath sat down beside Betty's bed and started talking to her, the child muttered, 'I don't want you. I want my mum,' and turned her head to the wall.

'Would you like me to bring you something next time I come?' Kath asked.

Betty shook her head. 'I only want my mum.'

Kath came back to Meggsie and squeezed his hand. 'You're a good boy,' she said. 'I know you want to help her.'

Meggsie glanced over at Betty. 'I just wish her mum would come. That's the only thing that will make her better.'

'Poor little mite,' Verna Browning said when Kath told her about Betty. She fossicked in her purse, counted out nine shillings and handed them to Kath. 'It's not much, but it'll pay for her mother's train fare and accommodation at the YWCA in town.'

Kath looked at her friend with admiration. Verna had given her an idea.

At the pub the next day the men were crowding around the counter, guzzling their beer as the hands of the clock moved inexorably towards six. Kath knew they were a bunch of drunken no-hopers, but their hearts were in the right place. At five-thirty, with only half an hour to go before closing time, they pushed forward, four-deep, jostling and calling out, and the wooden doors swung to and fro as more customers rushed inside to drink as much as possible while there was still time. The winos were slumped against the bar in a beatific stupor, while the whiskey drinkers had become more pugnacious and were picking fights with anyone who bumped into them or spilled their drinks. The air was thick with cigarette smoke, the language grew more foul, and drunken arguments raged about the favourite for the two o'clock at Rosehill on Saturday arvo. Bets were laid, and when swearing and cursing failed to convince or silence opponents, fists settled the argument.

Kath heard someone retching in the far corner of the pub, and recoiled in disgust as the stench of vomit filled the air. Her arms ached from drawing one schooner after another, her legs ached from standing at the bar for hours, and her head ached from all the shouting and swearing. Thank god in twenty minutes they could close up and she could go home.

'Hey, Rita, step on it, love, four schooners over here.' It was Mick Kelly, the big bloke with a purplish bulbous nose who had given her the nickname.

'Mick, how'd you like to do a good deed and go to heaven instead of the place you're booked in for,' she called out above the racket. Blokes were leaning on the bar, clamouring for another beer, and while she was serving them, she told them about Betty.

Bob Longley, whose front teeth had been knocked out in a brawl the previous Saturday, hitched his baggy trousers over his beer belly, whipped off the battered felt hat he wore at the back of his head and held it upside down, showing its sweat-stained lining.

'Come on, if youse can afford a schooner, youse can spare a bob or two to bring a smile to a sick little girl's face,' he slurred in his thick nicotine- and alcohol-ravaged voice as he pushed his way through the crowded pub.

Without missing a beat, Mick stepped forward and put in a quid and, not wanting to be shamed by his generosity, others followed suit. Most of the blokes dropped a few bob into the hat, and some even put in a quid, and by the time Bob placed it on the counter, it was full to the brim.

'Here y'are, love,' he slurred. 'Let's get that woman on the train.'

As soon as the hands of the clock pointed to six, Cyril Aldred stood by the door and sang out, 'Time, gentlemen, please.' There was the usual grumbling when his customers heard that their drinking was over for the night and they had to go home to face their angry wives. Gulping down the last of their beer, they banged the glasses on the counter and staggered out into the street, swaying and belching.

Cyril locked the door and turned around to see Kath putting money into a large paper bag. 'What's this all about?' he demanded. 'Someone been paying for your favours?'

Ignoring his malicious comment and the way he eyed her as though she was the kewpie doll on top of the chocolate wheel, she explained why the blokes had donated the money.

He was still eyeing her. 'When my customers part with their money, they get something back for it,' he said.

'They got something back,' she retorted, edging away from

him. 'A good feeling. For once they've spent their money on something worthwhile.'

'This is a pub, not bloody St Vincent de Paul's, and I won't have you organising charity drives here.'

Furious at his petty-mindedness, she pulled on her old coat and picked up the money, but it slipped from her hands and the coins scattered all over the floor. 'Bloody hell!' she exclaimed. She bent down to pick them up, and he was on his knees beside her, grabbing her shoulders and breathing heavily into her face. Pushing him away, she scrambled to her feet. His face reddened and his neck swelled so much that she thought the top button of his shirt would fly off.

'I'd like to remind you, Miss High and Mighty, that you owe me something for all the time you've taken off over the past month since your boy got sick.'

Unable to control her temper, she shouted, 'I'm sick to death of you leering and groping, and if it wasn't that I needed this job to feed four kids, I'd've walked out ages ago, but that's it. I've had it. And I hope your wife finds out about you and kicks you out.'

She hadn't intended it as a threat, but from the look on his face she realised he'd taken it that way. Too bad. Telling her employer what she thought of him was a luxury she had never allowed herself, but the stress of the past few weeks had suddenly overwhelmed her. She was shocked but also relieved by her outburst. Finally she'd said what she thought, and to hell with the consequences.

Chapter 24

Over the past few weeks Kath had become increasingly concerned about the changes in Meggsie. There was a dull look in his eyes and he talked in a flat voice. She had other worries as well. Christmas was approaching and she regretted her reckless outburst at the pub. Now that she'd lost her job, she wondered how she'd make ends meet, let alone provide Christmas dinner and buy gifts for the boys. She felt she'd fallen into a deep well without a rope or a ladder to climb out. She'd never felt so alone or so desperate. Jobs were scarce, and with Christmas only weeks away, her chance of finding one was slim. And to make things even worse, Meggsie wouldn't be home for Christmas.

That's what the medical registrar had told her when she'd made an appointment to see him. She hadn't understood the medical terms he'd used, and she'd been too intimidated to ask what they meant, but she'd understood that the physiotherapy and hydrotherapy hadn't worked as well as they'd hoped.

The registrar had looked at her over his glasses and spoken in such a soft voice that she'd had to strain to hear him.

'When do you think Meggsie will be well enough to go home?' she had asked.

'I wish I could give you a definite answer. Only time will tell how long recovery will take.' Then, in his barely audible whisper, he'd added, 'If at all.'

That had stung her like an electric shock.

'But he will recover, won't he?' she'd asked, fighting the panic.

He'd paused too long before replying. 'These things are in the lap of the gods, but your boy is in the best possible hands,' he'd said. But instead of being reassured, she'd left his office feeling more downhearted than ever.

Apart from her own problems, Kath wondered how to get the money she'd raised to Betty's mother. Sister Davis had said she had her hands full running a ward without taking on the duties of a bank, and when Kath had asked the superintendent's secretary about it, she'd been told that although they appreciated her concern, passing on money to the children's parents wasn't one of the hospital's functions and there was no precedent for that kind of transaction.

Kath sighed. Problems wherever she looked. Gran was right; she had made a mess of her life.

Meggsie had read *The Count of Monte Cristo* several times by now, and each time he'd discovered something new in its pages. The first time, he'd been caught up in the sheer excitement of the story; the second time, he'd been inspired by Dantès's determination to escape; and the third time, it had been his quest for justice and revenge that had enthralled him.

But as the weeks passed, Meggsie began to doubt whether he himself would ever escape from the prison he was in. Some of the children in the ward had already gone home, and others had improved sufficiently to be sent to a convalescent hospital, but he was still here, anchored to his bed, like a wrecked ship at the bottom of the sea. Sometimes he felt so desperate that he wanted to shout the place down, hurl himself onto the floor and crawl out of the ward on his hands and knees.

Betty was still here too. She rarely even cried these days, so he was surprised when he heard her calling frantically for the nurse one morning, and he raised his head to see what was wrong.

Sister Davis was striding across the ward. 'What's all this rumpus about?' she said gruffly. 'As if I haven't got enough to do. Well, what is it?'

Meggsie didn't hear Betty's reply, but he heard Sister Davis shouting, 'You naughty girl! A big girl like you wetting the bed! You should be ashamed of yourself.'

He watched as she pulled the wet sheet out from under Betty and rubbed it all over the little girl's face. While Betty screamed, Sister Davis called for a nurse to change the bed, and stomped out of the ward.

Meggsie was so shocked that it took him some time to get his voice out. 'Don't cry,' he whispered. 'She's just a bully. One day she'll pay for this.'

For the next few days the thought of revenge buoyed his spirits. His mum had always said that bullies were really cowards, and when someone confronted them they always backed down, so if someone picked a fight with him he should give as good as he got and then they'd leave him alone. But this was different. Betty couldn't fight back and neither could he. He had to be like Edmond Dantès and search for some way of making Sister Danglars pay for what she'd done. He thought of telling one of the friendly young resident doctors about it, but he knew that she'd deny it, and then she'd be meaner than ever.

The following Sunday, while his mum was taking the latest Superman and Captain Marvel comics from her bag, Meggsie said, 'Mum, if you wanted someone to get into big trouble, what would you do?'

'That depends.' She looked searchingly into his eyes. 'What's this about?'

'If someone important, like Sister Davis, did something bad and you wanted to tell on them, who would you tell?'

'Why don't you tell me what happened and then I'll see.

'Are you quite sure?' she asked when he'd described the incident. 'You actually saw her do that?'

He nodded. 'It was horrible. How could she do that to Betty? What can I do, Mum? Should I tell someone?'

His mum shook her head. 'She might take it out on you if she found out you'd reported her. Sometimes there's nothing you can do in situations like that, but bullies always get found out in the end.'

He stared at her. 'So you'd let her get away with it? You always told me to stand up for myself and now you're telling me to be spineless and let the bully win. And what about Betty? Who's going to stand up for her?'

Meggsie's words had stung, and Kath was thinking about them while she was doing the dishes that evening when, to her surprise, Ted Browning dropped in to see her. Although she'd watched him grow up from a boy into a young man, she hadn't seen much of him since he'd become a journalist, and she wondered what had brought him here.

'I'm going to write an article about children with polio and I was wondering if I could interview you,' he said.

While she was getting out the teacups and putting the kettle on the stove, he explained that people would be touched by the plight of a sick little girl fretting for a mother who couldn't afford to visit her. 'Besides,' he added, 'ever since Meggsie got sick, Mum's been on at me to write about polio.'

'Well,' Kath said while they were drinking their tea, 'I can tell you something else that'll really make your readers sit up and take notice.'

From his excited reaction to the story about Sister Davis, and the way he wrote down everything she told him, Kath could tell he'd include the incident in his article. It was late when he left, but she continued to potter around the kitchen, too stirred up to sleep. She couldn't wait to see Meggsie's face when she told him that the bully wouldn't win after all.

* * *

Dr Wilkie was doing his ward rounds and Sister Davis was fussing around him as usual. The entourage came to a halt by Meggsie's bed and Sister Davis handed Dr Wilkie a folder with an ingratiating smile that set Meggsie's teeth on edge.

He waited expectantly as the doctor flicked through the notes. Perhaps he'd say he could go home soon.

The doctor pulled back the cotton cover and proceeded to poke and prod Meggsie's legs, using words that Meggsie couldn't understand.

Then he snapped the folder shut and, without a glance in Meggsie's direction, said to the other doctors, 'This boy will never walk again.'

With that, he thanked Sister Davis, handed back the folder and walked out of the ward.

There was a dull humming in Meggsie's ears as the doctor's words kept going through his head.

'That's a lie!' he muttered to himself. 'I *will* walk again!'

Chapter 25

After Sunday School, Beverley Noble sashayed into the street in her new dress and twirled around so that the full skirt flared out like an open umbrella. All the other girls sighed in envy.

'Oo-wah, I can see your pants,' her little sister Daisy said in her singsong chant, but the older girls hushed her as they gazed in wonder at the ice-blue organdie dress with its sash, Peter Pan collar and short puffed sleeves. While their eyes were devouring the dress, their fingers stroked the crisp fabric.

It was the most beautiful dress Hania had ever seen, even nicer than the communion dress her foster mother had made for her in Poland, from white silk trimmed with lace.

She was still thinking about that dress when Beverley ran up to her. 'My mum said you can come and have tea with us tonight. Say you'll come!'

Eventually Hania persuaded her mother to let her go. The Nobles were already at the table when she ran inside and as soon as she sat down, they clasped their hands together and closed their eyes while Uncle Bill said grace. 'For what we are about to receive, may the Lord make us truly thankful,' he said.

While he carved what was left over from Sunday's roast lunch into thin slices, he said, 'When I was little we kids used to say, "Two, four, six, eight, bog in, don't wait".'

They all laughed, but Hania's laughter was tinged with envy. They always had so much fun at Beverley's place.

'Beverley said you liked the dress I made her for the school dance,' Aunty Muriel said as she placed a slice of cold lamb and a few slices of cucumber and tomato on Hania's plate. 'I can make you one like that if your mum gets the fabric.'

'You'd better make it in a different colour or they'll look like the Bobbsey twins,' Uncle Bill joked.

'The Beverley twins, you mean,' Aunty Muriel said, and they all pealed with laughter again.

The school year was drawing to a close, and Beverley couldn't wait for the Christmas holidays to begin. Her little sister was impatient for the family's annual pilgrimage to the city to sit on Santa's knee at Anthony Hordern's department store and tell him what they wanted for Christmas.

'Make sure you leave some water outside your room for Santa's reindeer on Christmas Eve, 'cause they'll be thirsty after that long sleigh ride from the North Pole with all those presents,' Uncle Bill said to Daisy, with a wink at Beverley and Hania.

'What do you mean, she'll make you a dress like Beverley's?' Eda Kotowicz demanded when Hania came home. 'Did you ask how much she wants for making it?'

Hania shrugged. 'Aunty Muriel just said for you to get the material, that's all.'

'How many times have I told you, she's not your aunty. And how do you know she won't charge me? Why should she make a dress for nothing?'

'You just don't understand,' Hania said. 'She wants to do it for me because I'm Beverley's friend.'

Eda scrutinised her daughter. 'If you need a new dress, why don't you come to me instead of to the neighbours? You think I can't make you a dress as good as Beverley's mother?'

Hania let out a long, exaggerated sigh. Trying to talk to her mother about anything was like crossing a field of stinging nettles. You might manage to avoid one, but you'd be sure to be stung by others.

'It's not fair!' she shouted. 'Why do you always have to spoil everything? I just wanted a dress like Beverley's for the dance.'

And she flounced out of the room before her mother had time to ask where to buy the material.

Hania hated the idea of Christmas in Australia. In Poland, with her foster parents, it had been different. Shivers still ran down her spine whenever she thought of the hushed atmosphere in the church on Christmas Eve, with the flickering candles, the smoky smell of incense and the soulful voices chanting and praying. After Mass, she'd looked forward to the traditional spicy beetroot borsch with potato *pirogi*. Her foster father would lug home a huge fir tree and the house would be filled with a sharp piney smell. Then they'd hang shiny baubles and coloured stars on the ends of the branches and arrange gifts around the tree. She'd been Catholic then like everyone else, but now that she was Jewish she didn't belong anywhere. She was excluded from the preparations, decorations and celebrations, the beautifully wrapped gifts and the visits the other children looked forward to from aunts, uncles, cousins, godparents and grandparents. Even Tina, who was usually as much of an outsider as she was, celebrated Christmas with her Greek family.

Her mother had tried to console her by saying that Jews observed Chanukah instead, a beautiful festival that also fell in December, but as far as Hania was concerned Chanukah didn't count. Who had ever heard of it?

'Jewish children, that's who,' her mother had retorted. 'There must be some Jewish girls in your class. Why don't you make friends with them? Or you could join a Jewish youth group like Habonim. There must be one around here, with all the Jewish migrants. There's a synagogue on the corner of Grosvenor and Grafton Street. Why don't you talk to your scripture teacher at school?'

Hania had shrugged. She hadn't told her mother that she never went to the Jewish scripture classes. Instead, she always sneaked into the Church of England classes with Beverley.

'I don't want Jewish friends and I don't want to go to Habonim, whatever that is,' she'd grumbled.

But what she wanted most of all, she didn't dare to tell her mother.

Across the road Kath sat up at the kitchen table trying to figure out how she could stretch her meagre savings to put Christmas dinner on the table and buy something for the boys as well.

A few times lately, whenever she'd passed the red telephone box on the corner, she'd been on the verge of swallowing her pride and ringing Gran, but at the last moment the thought of going begging, and then having to listen to her grandmother's acid comments, had changed her mind. Help from Gran came at too high a price.

Kath didn't care about Christmas for herself but she did want to try to make it special for the boys, especially little Pete. But what kind of Christmas would it be, with Meggsie still in hospital, unable to walk, and no one knowing when he'd recover?

'I'd better start praying for a miracle because that's the only thing that'll help me,' she muttered to herself.

She glanced out of the window, and noticed the timid foreign woman standing at her front gate, lost in thought.

Marija Olmanis was thinking about Christmas too. Christmas in Latvia. Walking to church on Christmas Eve on snow that creaked under her fur-lined boots, placing Advent wreaths in the front of her home, watching the mummers who visited homes to bless the occupants and drive out evil spirits. And preparing the traditional food: brown peas with bacon, beef pies filled with cabbage, yeast cake with chopped almonds and cardamom, and ginger biscuits that made the whole house smell wonderful and which they ate with a drink made from honey, cranberries, rye bread and whipped cream. In Latvia, St Nicolas didn't arrive with gifts on just one night, he stopped by every evening for twelve wonderful nights.

She sighed as she looked out into the street. The frangipani trees were in full bloom, and she picked up three brown-edged flowers that had fallen onto the verandah and breathed in their cloying perfume. Apart from a scrawny ginger cat that shot across the road and disappeared, and a black mongrel that lay panting in front of one of the semis, there was no other sign of life, although Marija knew that most of her neighbours were home.

She would never understand life in Sydney. In Riga there was no distinction between the residential and commercial parts of town, and people lived in apartment blocks all over the city, so flats, stores, cafés, workshops and offices were close together. There was always plenty of activity, with people strolling around, shopping or meeting their friends in cafés, but here no one lived in the business part of town, and no one went out at night in the residential area. People kept to themselves and didn't seem to have much social life. They said that an Englishman's home was his castle, but it must be a lonely castle.

Marija wiped the sweat from her forehead and neck. Christmas in sweltering heat, without snow or ice, skating or tobogganing, wasn't Christmas. Even the sky here was different. Whenever she looked up at night, she couldn't find any familiar stars. But she consoled herself with the thought that Australia was only a temporary haven. As soon as the Communists were overthrown, they'd be able to go back home.

From inside the house, Paulis was calling her in the peremptory tone to which she'd become accustomed. Marija sighed again. Her mother had begged her not to marry him. Even on the day of her wedding, as she was adjusting the Chantilly lace veil on her head, she had shocked Marija by saying it wasn't too late to change her mind. 'It's better to admit a mistake than to live with it all your life,' she'd said. Marija had turned away without replying. Her mother had been a domineering woman, and being silent and stubborn had been Marija's only weapons.

As the years went on, and Paulis became more dogmatic and overbearing, there were many times when she'd thought of leaving him, but she hadn't wanted to give her mother the satisfaction of knowing she'd been right.

Marija had started watering the geraniums on the windowsill when she heard the postman's shrill whistle and looked down the street. He was chatting to the plump woman with short white hair, whose son liked Lilija. She couldn't understand what Paulis had against this fellow or why he told Lilija that if she kept seeing him, he'd throw her out of the house. Poor Lilija was very keen on the boy, and Marija couldn't see anything wrong with him, but you couldn't reason with Paulis once he'd made up his mind about something. She finished watering the geraniums, and went inside the house.

Chapter 26

At the Department of Immigration, Sir Lachlan McKenzie surveyed Ted with an expression of such distaste that Ted wondered whether he'd stepped in dog shit on his way to the office.

After weeks of phone calls and letters, the department head had finally agreed to an interview. Although Gus still had reservations about the Nazis-in-Australia story, he had agreed to let Ted travel to Canberra. Ted was in his good books because his article about the little girl in the Children's Hospital had aroused an unprecedented reaction, with offers of money and accommodation for the mother pouring in from readers all over the State.

Ted knew that Gus welcomed the opportunity to needle Sir Lachlan. When Arthur Calwell had announced his new policy of allowing non-British migrants into Australia, Gus had written a blistering editorial accusing the Minister for Immigration of starting the rot which would undermine the British character of the country. In a scathing reply, Sir Lachlan had written that the only rot he could detect so far was the editorial written in the *Daily Standard,* whose editor he accused of unbridled jingoism.

Gus never forgot and never forgave. In Ted's story about war criminals, he saw a vindication of his stand against non-British migrants. And he relished the prospect of scoring points off his adversary in Canberra.

'Hammer him about those Yugoslavs and don't let him off the hook,' Gus had barked, spraying mixed metaphors around his office. 'If we really are harbouring criminals and ignoring the Tito government's request for extradition, I want to know why. But McKenzie's a slippery customer, so don't let him sidetrack you.'

It was Ted's first visit to the nation's capital. Unlike Sydney's undisciplined sprawl, Canberra seemed the essence of controlled planning with its straight tree-lined avenues, leafy parks and architect-designed buildings. But for all its chaos and disorder, Ted found Sydney's vitality exhilarating, while Canberra reminded him of a neat stage set, with every tree and flowerbed placed according to a predetermined design. Sterile and artificial, it was an ideal setting for politicians, diplomats and bureaucrats, he thought as he entered the imposing building that housed the Department of Immigration.

He'd just been ushered into Sir Lachlan's office when there was a deferential tap on the door and a young woman in a demure white blouse and pleated grey skirt came in with a manila folder. While Sir Lachlan excused himself and looked over the documents, Ted studied the man who had started his working life as a messenger boy in the defence department and worked his way up to become one of the most powerful bureaucrats in the country. With his sparse sandy hair, lashless eyes and round face, Sir Lachlan looked more like an inoffensive country parson than a top-level public servant.

Sir Lachlan took out his fountain pen, signed the document, blotted it and handed it back to his secretary. Then he passed a hand across his eyes and leaned against his high-backed chair.

'You're the author of that' — he paused as though searching for the right word — 'colourful article about Bonegilla. I'm not surprised. The *Daily Standard* has always favoured fiction over fact. As you probably know, I don't have a high regard for your newspaper, but the minister felt we should take this opportunity to set the record straight for your readers.'

Ted whipped out a notebook from his pocket and assumed what he hoped was a humble tone. 'That's why I'm here, sir.'

Knowing that Sir Lachlan had the unenviable task of trying to sell the government's radical shift in immigration policy to an antagonistic public, Ted didn't interrupt his statements about the far-sightedness of the minister, or the care with which the right migrants were selected, but when he started extolling the high standard of their migrant hostel in Albury, Ted couldn't keep quiet any longer.

'Are you aware that some migrants have been bashed by other inmates at Bonegilla, and that some of them have brought Nazi memorabilia to Australia?'

Sir Lachlan made a dismissive motion with his freckled hand. 'None of the bashing allegations have been proven. And as for memorabilia, surely souvenirs are harmless.'

Sir Lachlan looked pointedly at his watch and Ted realised he'd better move on with the interview.

'I've heard that the Yugoslav government has requested the extradition of some of their nationals whom they accuse of war crimes,' he said. 'Could you tell me why their request has been ignored?'

A sharp look crossed the bureaucrat's face, and he glanced at the door as though hoping his secretary would come back and give him an excuse to end the meeting.

'We never ignore the requests of democratically elected leaders,' he said smoothly. 'However, it takes time to investigate these matters, and what may be taken for negligence is actually diligence.'

'I didn't realise it was up to Australia to investigate allegations made by other governments about their nationals,' Ted said innocently. 'I would have thought that would be a matter for the government concerned.'

Sir Lachlan passed a hand over his eyes again.

'These are complex issues. With so many agitators among us stirring up trouble and dissension, we can't be too careful.'

He gestured towards a bulging dossier on his desk, as though to illustrate what he was saying. Ted craned forward and saw that the folder was labelled *The Anti-Fascist Society*.

'Agitators, sir?' he asked. 'Could you tell me who you have in mind?'

'I'm sure you know I'm talking about Communists who are trying to destabilise our system of government and overthrow it.'

As Ted jotted down Sir Lachlan's answer in his notebook, something occurred to him and he looked up. 'If a country that didn't have a Communist government had made such a request, would we consider it more favourably?'

Sir Lachlan studied Ted for a moment, then said, 'You're wasting your time with this line of inquiry.' Pressing a button on the black telephone on his desk, he said, 'Miss Shaw, could you please see Mr Browning out?'

Turning back to Ted, he added, 'If I were you, I'd stop pursuing this topic. It won't do you any good.'

The early-afternoon sun shone through the plane trees, whose branches formed a canopy over the avenue and made lacy patterns on the footpath. With an hour to spare before catching the Sydney train, Ted sat on a park bench and thought about Sir Lachlan's parting remark. Was it well-meant advice or a veiled threat? He checked his shorthand notes and decided to look up the Anti-Fascist Society.

As he gazed through the dirt-streaked window of the train, the small country towns flashed past in a blur. What he kept seeing was Lilija's face, tense and white, perhaps even frightened, the time he'd gone to her place. His efforts to see her since that day had proved fruitless, and the letter he'd slipped into her letterbox had gone unanswered — he suspected her father had intercepted it and torn it up. If only he knew why her father was so adamant that she have nothing to do with him.

Although he'd tried to take his mother's advice and find someone else, the girls his friends introduced him to were plain or vain, and either tongue-tied or gushing. None of them had the astonishing face that made his body tingle. The more he tried to put Lilija out of his mind, the more he thought about her.

With a hiss of pistons, the train pulled into Sydney's Central Station. Coated with soot, which he could even taste in his mouth, Ted made his way along the dusty platform towards the exit. Under the Art Deco glass dome of the vast station building, a fat girl with a lace-edged petticoat showing under her full skirt paced back and forth in front of the railway clock. As Ted walked past, he wondered whether her date would turn up, and whether they'd make the train in time.

It was a sultry night and not a breath of air blew in through the open window above Ted's pillow. Ted tossed from side to side, unable to sleep. Every night his mind roiled with fantasies of what he'd like to do to Lilija, and what he'd like her to do to him. The strange mixture of violence and tenderness of his erotic imagination both disturbed and excited him, and he always made his bed quickly in the mornings so his mother wouldn't see the damp patch on the sheet.

Finally he dropped off to sleep. In his dream Lilija told him she would meet him under the big clock at Central Railway Station and go away with him. In a frenzy of anticipation he rushed to the station, delirious with joy. So she did love him after all. He waited, craning his head this way and that, but the clock ticked on, and the hours went by, and still there was no sign of her. He wondered whether the tram cables had loosened and come off again, or if her father had locked her in. When he finally realised that she wouldn't be coming, his disappointment was so bitter that he could taste it, and he woke up drenched with sweat.

Exhausted, he dragged himself to the office the next morning, hoping to find some angle for his interview with Sir Lachlan. He'd just hung his hat up on the hook in his cubicle when he saw some of the reporters in the newsroom crowding around Joe Black's desk. As usual, they were arguing about Chifley.

Joe, whose belligerent manner indicated an unlucky streak at the gambling tables the night before, was shouting above the others. 'What was it Chifley said the other day? "We MPs are only servants and no more"?' he bellowed. 'Well I don't know about you lot, but I haven't heard of any lift drivers or street sweepers voting themselves a raise of eight pounds a week after a few years' work!'

A couple of voices murmured assent, but Hal Monk, one of the old hacks, whose gravelly voice matched his deadpan expression, retorted, 'Arrgh, you rookies don't know what you're talking about. Chifley's a man of the people.'

Ted moved closer to listen to them arguing. He wasn't interested in politics, but he was fascinated by the Cinderella story of the engine driver who'd become prime minister. These days, however, Mr Chifley's love affair with the people had run its course, and there were rumours that the prime minister, who represented decency and working-class values, had a secret mistress.

Even though for diehard Laborites like Hal Monk, Chifley was the hero of the workers, some criticised him for being soft on Communists, some of whom held important posts in the defence department. Gus had recently written a scathing editorial accusing Chifley of helping to harbour enemy agents.

By now Joe and Hal were so het up that Ted thought they'd come to blows. They were arguing about a secret document that had recently been leaked from the House of Representatives. According to this document, the Americans had refused to share atomic research information with Australia because they didn't trust the government's security measures where Communists were concerned.

Joe was jabbing his finger in Hal's face. 'When your hero was confronted with the news about that embarrassing leak, did he deal with the actual issue, which was America's lack of confidence in this country because of his attitude to Communists? Not on your life. The devious mongrel turned the tables on the opposition, calling them dishonest for leaking the document, and now he's got the Commonwealth Investigation

Service to spy on them! If that's not police state tactics, I don't know what is!'

From hero to Gestapo in the space of one year, Ted thought, reflecting on the vagaries of politics. What was it his father used to say about the fickleness of fame? One minute you're a rooster, the next you're a feather duster.

Back in his cubicle, he flicked through his files and dialled the police station to follow up the story of an eighteen-year-old youth who'd killed his father with a knife. As it happened, Detective Sergeant Jim Mitchell was in charge of the case. Ted still couldn't get Scarlett O'Halloran out of his mind, and sometimes late at night the image of her bloodstained blouse and unlit cigarette floated into his mind. But when he asked Mitchell if the police had made any progress in the case, the detective snapped that they didn't have any leads and hung up on him.

Chapter 27

Verna Browning surveyed herself in the bedroom mirror and pulled a face. With her white hair, billowing breasts and pear-shaped body she might have been looking at her own mother. The extra butter that had recently been made available on their ration cards hadn't done her figure much good, and she told herself she'd better cut down. Christmas was coming, and she'd been looking longingly at the pretty muslin and dimity dresses in the windows of Mark Foys and Farmers, but with their fashionable nipped-in waists and mid-calf flared skirts, they were designed for slim young women like Kath, not matrons of ample proportions like her.

These days the newspapers were full of ads for things she'd never dreamed of, and would probably never own on her widow's pension. She'd often eyed the portable mantel radio at Anthony Hordern's, and she would have willingly exchanged her small ice chest for one of those new Silent Knight refrigerators. Then there was that clothes wringer she'd seen, with wide rubber rollers and a reversible water drainer, but it cost five pounds and sixpence, and even if she put it on lay-by, she couldn't justify the expense. She felt guilty about wanting such luxuries, but they kept bringing out all these new-fangled goods to tempt people to buy things they didn't really need. Still, Verna rarely dwelled on things she couldn't afford, so she told herself to snap out of it and put on her navy blue felt hat with the wide grosgrain ribbon and headed to Attwaters to find a McCall's pattern for a dress. Something loose-fitting that might conceal the bulges.

On her way to the counter with the pattern books, she paused beside the haberdashery shelves and looked at the rolls of elastic. During the war you couldn't get elastic for love or money, not even for your panties. She used to hold them up with buttons, but once the buttons had snapped off when she was in Mark Foys and she'd had to rush red-faced to the ladies' room, trying to hold them up.

She was browsing among the pattern books when she saw Muriel Noble at the big brass cash register, buying some pale pink organdie which the saleswoman was measuring out by stretching out her arm twice, to gauge two yards.

'I'm making a dress for Hanny,' Muriel explained. 'You wouldn't believe the fuss her mum made before she finally agreed I could make it. Can't understand that woman.'

'Some people find it hard to accept presents,' Verna said. 'Maybe she doesn't want to be beholden.'

Muriel shrugged. 'She's always making Hanny's life difficult. If it's not one thing it's another. I feel sorry for the poor girl.' Leaning on the wooden counter while the saleswoman wrapped the organdie, she warmed to her theme. 'If you ask me, people that come here from other places should fit in with us and not stick to their old ways.'

Picking up her parcel, she wandered over to the section with trimmings and fastenings, to look for a zipper and buttons to match the organdie.

Verna took a long time deciding on the material for her dress. The shot silk was too expensive, the jacquard was too fancy, and the linen would crush like a concertina. Finally she settled on a fresh-looking lemon seersucker and put it on lay-by.

Pleased with her purchase, she was walking towards the exit when she noticed Mr Emil, the foreign gentleman from across the road, examining bolts of satin with a look of total concentration. You couldn't miss him with that funny little hat he always wore, and those tan-and-white shoes. He was the only man in the haberdashery department, and several women turned to look at him, but he seemed oblivious of their attention.

It was odd for a man to be looking at fabrics, but he was certainly odd. Maude McNulty was always on about him, saying that he was up to something, with all that banging and hammering. A few weeks ago she'd told Verna that Kath had put a note in her letterbox, something about coffins. Verna thought the old biddy was losing her marbles.

'Kath never wrote it,' Verna said. 'She's not the type to send anonymous notes.'

Verna was surprised that a shrewd old bird like Maude McNulty hadn't figured out that even if Kath had wanted to send someone a note, she certainly wouldn't have sent it to her.

'If Kath saw something odd going on, she'd report it herself, not leave notes in someone's letterbox,' she added. 'She wouldn't do anything underhand or sneaky.'

A few days later Verna had seen two policemen knocking on Emil's door and watched him getting into the back of their Holden. It had dawned on her then that the old busybody must have dobbed him in.

Verna watched as Emil compared several bolts of pastel-coloured satin, holding them up to the light one at a time to check the colours, and unrolling one of them to gauge how much he needed. When he'd made his selection, he lugged two bolts over to the counter, one shell pink and the other a baby blue.

She would have liked to go over and ask him what he was going to make, and perhaps offer some help, but there was something about his purposeful movements and focused gaze that stopped her. It didn't look as if he'd welcome any well-meant advice.

Half an hour later, back in Wattle Street, she looked around for Kath, to tell her what she'd seen at Attwaters, and to ask if she knew anything about Maude McNulty's note. Kath wasn't home, but a flutter of the curtain next door told her that her neighbour was watching as usual. The only person she could see in the street was the tall foreign woman she called Sally, who was standing alone at the gate with a faraway look in her eyes, probably waiting for that nice husband of hers to come home.

Chapter 28

Sala was walking towards the tram stop after work, thinking about her conversation with Beryl that morning. She had put away the brooms and dusters in the closet and hung up her pinafore when Beryl planted herself in front of her. With her arms akimbo and her small eyes darting sideways, she'd said, 'Ta for helping me out the other day. I've got a bit of a problem, see. Went on a bender the night before. Know what I mean?'

Sala had no idea what a bender was, but from Beryl's changed tone she realised that she now regarded her as an ally.

Lost in thought as she walked, she didn't notice that someone had fallen in step with her until she heard a man's voice.

'It's Sala, isn't it?'

She looked up and saw Alex Engelman looking at her with his searching gaze, and the blood rushed to her cheeks.

'What are you doing here so early in the morning?' he asked.

He didn't take his eyes off her while she told him about her job.

'You're really something!' he exclaimed. 'Most women would have made up a story rather than admit they were working as a cleaner.'

He took her elbow in a firm grip. 'I don't know about you, but I could use a cup of coffee. Have you been to Repin's? They've got the best coffee in Sydney. Let's go.'

And before she could reply, he was already helping her into the tram.

As soon as they got off the tram in Market Street, she could smell the pungent aroma of roasting coffee beans, and although the department stores and offices weren't open yet, the coffee lounge was already full.

Inside the café, Sala could see her reflection in a wall mirror with a sunburst design. She tried to smooth her hair, some of which had escaped from her roll and curled around her face. She hoped there was no one here she knew, and then told herself to stop feeling guilty. After all, there was nothing wrong with having coffee with a friend. It wasn't as though she'd planned a *rendezvous*. She felt excited whenever she caught Alex looking at her with that admiring expression, and wondered what Szymon would say if he came in and saw her sitting there with him.

'The Repins are white Russians,' Alex was saying as she looked around the crowded coffee lounge with its snappy green-and-white decor. 'They were the first to roast beans on the premises, and to charge for coffee. Everyone said they'd never get Australians to come to a place like this and pay for coffee, but look how wrong they were. Australians may not like us foreigners, but we're dragging them out of their dull English existence. Before they know it, they'll be a nation of gourmets.'

She nodded, but she wasn't really listening because while he was gazing into her eyes in that disconcerting way of his, he'd picked up her hand and was massaging each finger in turn, with a touch that was light but tantalising. Then he started kneading her palm in such a sensual and intimate way that the blood rushed to her face and her body tingled. It was like making love in the middle of the crowded café.

He was watching her closely as she felt herself slipping into a languorous trance. With an effort, she withdrew her hand, but she could still feel the warm pressure of his fingers and their seductive touch. It was a relief when the waitress brought the menu.

'The other night at Fela and Lutek's, when Genia asked you about the war,' Alex said, 'you didn't want to talk about it, did you?'

She shook her head. 'I didn't feel like being quizzed about my life at the dinner table.'

She looked down at the menu to avoid his gaze and wondered if he guessed what she didn't want to reveal.

'There's a determined look comes over your face when you don't want to say something,' he said. 'You must have looked like that when you were a little girl. Did you stamp your foot as well?'

They both laughed, and the laughter defused her uneasiness.

'You're a very interesting woman. I'd like to know all about you,' he said.

She laughed again. 'How long have you got?'

'All day. And all night,' he said, and she suppressed a smile at his insinuating tone.

She told him about her home in Łódż, her parents who had both been doctors, her plans to study medicine, which had ended with the war, and her recent decision to enroll in a part-time course to become a medical technician.

The waitress brought their mocha coffee, and Sala breathed in the rich, dark aroma that brought back memories of afternoons in outdoor cafés with her parents in the main square in Łódż.

'If you want to be a doctor, why are you settling for being a lab technician?' he asked.

She shrugged. 'Studying medicine takes too long. I'd be thirty by the time I finished.'

He leaned forward until she could feel his warm breath. 'And how old will you be in six years if you don't study medicine?'

'That's all very well, but I have to earn some money.'

'If medicine is what you really want to do, don't settle for second best,' Alex said. 'Life's too short. If you really want something, work out how to get it.'

'Do you practise what you preach?' she asked.

He lowered his gaze from her face and rested it on her breasts. 'I always get what I want.'

Her face was still burning when she left the café.

* * *

Sala went over their conversation as she waited for the Bondi Junction tram. She had pushed the idea of becoming a doctor to the back of her mind, and had resigned herself to doing a part-time course, but Alex's words had challenged her. Perhaps she should consider studying medicine after all. Franka Feldman had said that was what her husband was doing. Instead of going home, she caught the tram back to Darlinghurst.

But when she sat on the hard wooden chair in front of the social worker's desk, she didn't know how to begin.

'Starting life in a new country is terribly hard, isn't it?' Franka Feldman said. 'The worst thing is being torn in all directions and not knowing the right thing to do. When we got here, my husband and I quarrelled all the time. There were times I wanted to leave him, and times I thought he was having a nervous breakdown. That was the worst time in our married life.'

Sala listened with interest. 'How long did that go on for?'

'Until he sorted out what he really wanted to do.'

'I just don't know if I can do it,' Sala said after a long pause. 'Medicine, I mean.'

'Do you mean because of the language? Or financially? What does your husband think about it?'

Sala looked away and bit the inside of her lip. She didn't want to admit that she hadn't talked to him about it.

Changing the subject, Franka asked, 'What happened about that notice I showed you in the *Jewish News*? Did you ever find out why they were looking for you?'

Sala suppressed a sigh. That was another issue she had pushed away. It was too hard to tackle.

'Lately I can't seem to make my mind up about anything,' she said slowly. She tried to blink away the unexpected tears that filled her eyes.

Franka nodded. 'It's hard to know what to do sometimes. Especially when you've been through so much. Everything here is so different and confusing, and there's no one to turn to.'

Her empathy made Sala's tears flow faster and suddenly her shoulders were heaving and she was sobbing aloud.

Franka let her cry without trying to console her. By the time Sala left the office half an hour later, she felt less confused. It was time to talk to Szymon about the notice in the *Jewish News*.

The late-afternoon sun gilded the front of the cottages on the eastern side of Wattle Street with a glow that transformed their usually drab façades, like plain girls enhanced by skilful make-up. The brilliance of the light made Sala shield her eyes with her hand as she stood at the gate waiting for Szymon to come home. It was only the first month of summer, and as she wiped beads of sweat from her neck she wondered how much hotter it would get.

The rhythmic thud of skipping made her turn around. In the middle of the road two girls in navy pleated uniforms were turning a skipping rope while a smaller girl jumped in and out, her plaits bouncing on her shoulders with each skip. 'Blue bells, cockle shells, eevie ivy over,' they chanted. Sala didn't understand the words but found herself repeating the rhythm in her head.

Further along, Eda Kotowicz's daughter, Hania, was drawing a hopscotch grid on the pavement with a piece of white chalk. Two boys were weaving among the girls, occasionally pulling their plaits and evoking a chorus of complaints as they whooped and shouted, playing cowboys and Indians. Another little boy stood on the edge of the pavement, a shirt tied around his neck like Superman's cape, shouting, 'Up, up and away!' Sala smiled to herself. Children were the same the world over.

She watched the reclusive man who lived across the road as he turned into their street carrying a small parcel under his arm. He kept his head down as he passed the children and didn't seem to notice them or, perhaps, Sala thought, he didn't want them to notice him. Without appearing to move, he slipped inside his gate and disappeared. From the way he dressed, and his little hunting hat and brown shoes with white caps, she could tell he was a migrant. She wondered where he came from, but she'd never heard him speak.

The sun was going down, and mothers called their children in for tea. Within a few minutes the street was empty except for a lone tabby cat sprawled on a patch of sun-warmed pavement. Sala paced back and forth, too restless to read the newspaper or to look up new words in the dictionary as she did most afternoons. Several times she tried to plan what to say, but it sounded too rehearsed, too stilted. She'd have to come out with it in a normal, matter-of-fact way.

At last she heard Szymon's light springy footsteps as he turned the corner into Wattle Street, the *Daily Standard* neatly folded under his arm. Her heart beat a drum roll against her ribs. At home, whenever she wanted to ask her father for anything, her mother always told her to wait until he'd hung up his hat, put on his slippers and eaten his dinner. 'Men are more likely to say yes if they've had time to relax after a day's work,' she would say. It all seemed a hundred years ago, as though it happened in another world, and in a sense it had.

Sala watched while Szymon ate the schnitzel and potato *latkes*, but she couldn't swallow anything. They chatted about their day, and she told him about Beryl's surprising confession, but she didn't say anything about running into Alex.

'That was a terrific dinner, Salcia,' he said, putting his arms around her, and for once she didn't wriggle out of his embrace.

She watched him speculatively while he sipped his tea. Finally she decided that the time was right. She took a deep breath. 'Szymon, there's something I've been meaning to tell you.'

Before she had time to say any more, his face lit up and he swept her up in his arms. 'Don't tell me! Let me guess! You're expecting!'

His exuberance made her close her eyes and groan. Now he'd be disappointed, and the receptive mood she'd tried to foster by cooking his favourite dinner and being affectionate would be wasted.

'It's not that.'

The eager gleam went from his eyes. 'So what is it?'

'A few weeks ago there was a notice in the *Jewish News*. They're looking for me. There's going to be a court case in Łódź, and they want me to give evidence.'

She paused to give him time to absorb what she'd said, then added, 'It's about Ernst Hauptmann.'

His eyes were flints. 'Good. Now you can tell them what a Nazi bastard he was.'

There was a buzzing in her ears. 'But Szymon, he saved my life.'

'And what about the people he betrayed or killed?'

She was trembling now. 'That's nonsense,' she said, 'He was a *Volksdeutsch*, not Gestapo or SS.'

'But he hobnobbed with them. You told me so yourself.'

He leaned towards her, shaking a finger in her face for emphasis. 'I saw how the ethnic Germans welcomed the Nazis in 1939, with cheers and flowers. And you know how happy they were to turn the Jews over to the Gestapo.'

'All I know is that if it wasn't for him I wouldn't be here.'

'He saved you because he wanted to fuck you!' Szymon shouted as he stood over her, his face contorted with fury. 'Go on, tell them all about your hero, how good he was to you in that cellar of his.'

She thought she was going to be sick. With an effort, she said, 'I couldn't live with myself if I helped to convict the man who saved my life.'

Szymon gripped her arms. 'If he was so innocent, how come they're putting him on trial? How come he's been charged with war crimes? Tell me that.'

She pulled free and looked at the imprint of his hands on her arms. 'You're being melodramatic. I just want to do the right thing.'

'The right thing is to tell them how he kept you locked up in that cellar for eighteen months. That's the right thing. Unless you enjoyed yourself in there with him.'

She sprang up and pummelled his chest with her fists.

'How dare you say that to me?' She was screaming at him while she lashed out with her hands. 'You didn't know him. You weren't there. He risked his life hiding me all that time. You don't know what you're talking about.'

He caught her wrists. 'You're right,' he said sarcastically. 'What would I know about what went on? I was having a picnic in Buchenwald at the time, watching everyone around me turning yellow and starving to death. And you know why some of us were in there? Because heroes like your Ernst Hauptmann turned us over to the Gestapo, that's why.' He gave her an ironic look and tapped his temple. 'And you're actually defending him! You're not right in the head, you know that?'

Her body felt so taut that she thought it might snap. 'I should have known there was no point trying to talk to you.' She was sobbing now. 'You're vulgar, you don't understand anything, and you drag everyone down to your own level.'

Before she could say another word he'd snatched his hat from the hook, flung open the door and slammed it so hard behind him that the walls shook.

For a long time Sala sat on the edge of the bed, shaking with rage. Then she sprang up, swiped their cups off the table and watched the tea spray all over the room, leaving brown stains on the greasy wallpaper as the china flew across the room and shattered.

She sobbed as she pulled out the drawers where Szymon kept his shirts and underwear in neat piles and flung them all over the floor. Now everything was smashed and wrecked, like her life. Exhausted and out of breath, she sank onto the bed. She closed her eyes and she was in the cellar again. She could smell the musty air, feel the coolness of the tightly packed soil under her feet, hear the floorboards creaking overhead as the heavy footsteps came closer and closer.

Sometimes she heard them yelling at each other, Ernst and his wife Urszula, after he'd gone back upstairs and closed the trapdoor. Urszula would scream that she knew what he was up to in there, and she threatened to go to the Gestapo and tell them he was hiding a Jewish girl so they'd take her away and their life would go back to the way it used to be.

Sala would hold her breath and tremble. Then Ernst would yell that she was imagining things, nothing was going on in the cellar, what would he be doing with such a young girl, and a Jewish one at that, and anyway she was stupid because if she said anything about a Jewish girl hidden in their cellar, they'd shoot her as well. Eventually the arguing died down and Sala breathed out again.

They kept sacks of potatoes down there, and barrels of apples and pickled cabbage. Firewood was stacked up for winter behind bottles of *wisniowka,* the bitter-sweet spirit that Ernst made from the cherries in their orchard. He'd given her a drink that first time, when she'd cowered in the corner, pressing herself against the cool wall because she had never seen that look on his face before and she was frightened.

His face was red and distorted with lust as he unbuckled his leather belt and threw it down on the ground. It made a dull sound as it struck one of the wooden barrels. When he grabbed her by the shoulders she struggled to free herself and screamed, but he placed his large hand over her mouth and whispered for her to be quiet or someone would hear and know she was there. He pinned her against the wall and fumbled under her skirt.

She squeezed her thighs together and punched him, but he was too strong for her. He picked her up and carried her to the mattress, while she kicked and flailed her arms and tried to free herself. 'Lie still,' he kept murmuring, and she could smell the alcohol on his hot breath. 'Lie still. It won't hurt.'

Afterwards, she turned away from him, her face flaming with hatred, disgust and shame. Avoiding her eyes, he uncorked one of the bottles and handed it to her. She shook her head and refused to look at him. 'I trusted you.' She spat the words out. 'You said you wanted to help me. You're disgusting. I wish you'd left me where I was.'

He didn't look at her and, without saying a word, he buttoned his trousers and went upstairs. Alone in the cellar, she folded her arms around herself to stop the trembling and took a slug of the *wisniowka* straight from the bottle, and then another and another, until her eyes closed and she fell asleep.

The sound of his heavy tread on the wooden ladder the next day made her start. Before he stepped off the last rung she was already standing in the far corner of the cellar, behind the barrels of pickled cabbage, holding a length of wood behind her back, ready to strike. But he didn't come near her. He sat down heavily on the last rung without saying a word and held his head in his large hands.

He was a farmer from the outskirts of Łódż who had delivered butter, cream and cottage cheese to her parents' home in his horse and cart before the war. The cook and the maid had made fun of him behind his back because he spoke ungrammatical Polish with the guttural accent of the ethnic Germans, but she'd heard them whispering and giggling that they wouldn't mind having his shoes under their bed, even if they were big farm boots.

She'd been twelve or thirteen at the time and hadn't understood what they were talking about, but she'd found their bawdy laughter and suggestive glances titillating.

When he made his delivery the following week, she looked at him more attentively and saw that he was good-looking in a different way from the city men who visited her parents. There was a physical strength in his large head, sinewy arms and broad shoulders, and he smelled of hay, earth and sweat in a way that was unfamiliar but not unpleasant.

'Do you think Mr Hauptmann is handsome?' she asked her mother, who was amused by her question. 'I suppose he is, in a rustic way,' she replied. For her mother, refinement in all things was the goal that civilised people should aspire to, but the lack of it made the farmer more interesting in Sala's eyes. From the way the cook and the maid made eyes at him and bantered with him, she knew they were flirting.

She remembered the time when, ignoring them, he turned towards her and chatted with her for a long time about her school and her friends, to the obvious irritation of the two women. The cook put her big red hands on her hips and said provocatively, 'I can see we're not good enough for you, you like little girls.' She made out it was a joke but Sala could sense the resentment in her voice.

The Germans invaded the following year, and they lost very little time in implementing their stated aim, to rid Poland of its Jews. Sala and her parents were horrified to find themselves interned in the overcrowded ghetto with tens of thousands of Jews from Łódż, other Polish cities and Czechoslovakia as well. Even now, eight years later, Sala tried not to remember how degraded, hungry and frightened she had felt in the ghetto where people dropped dead in the street, and ragged, starving children sat on the footpaths, too weak to beg.

Sala had lost hope when Ernst Hauptmann miraculously appeared. He told them that the ghetto would soon be liquidated, but promised to find some way of getting Sala out. She protested that she wouldn't leave her parents, but they insisted. She had to survive. Several days later he turned up with his horse and cart, and after delivering cabbages and potatoes he rushed into their room, covered her with rough blankets which prickled and stank of horse sweat, and smuggled her out of the ghetto. Throughout the long and bumpy journey to his farm she wept because in the panic to get away she hadn't kissed her parents goodbye.

How he'd managed to get into the ghetto twice without being stopped by the guard at the gate, she never knew, but she suspected that he'd probably bribed the SS officers in charge. He took her to his village and, to allay the neighbours' suspicions, told everyone that she was his wife's niece who had come to give them a hand around the farm.

Sala's heart stopped beating whenever Gestapo officers or SS men came to visit the Hauptmanns, as they often did. They would sit around the rough-hewn oak table in the kitchen for hours, drinking *wisniowka* and bellowing rousing German songs. As soon as they left, Sala could hear Urszula Hauptmann urging her husband to get rid of her, but Ernst always argued that the SS officers would never suspect he was hiding a Jewish girl under their noses.

Sala couldn't understand why he was risking his life and that of his wife to save her but, not being an introspective or articulate man, he never talked about it. His wife plaited Sala's hair and pinned it on top of her head like a coronet, the way country girls did, and no one questioned her presence until the day she was serving lunch to some SS officers. Her hands always shook on those occasions, but she knew she had to overcome her fear and look relaxed. She had just placed a platter of pork cutlets and pickled cabbage on the table when one of the Germans asked if she was the cook. Laughing, she'd replied that she wished she were as good a cook as Frau Hauptmann and hoped one day she would be. As she spoke, she was aware that he was looking at her in a strange way.

It wasn't until Ernst Hauptmann broke in and told her in slow, emphatic Polish to stop chattering and bring the potatoes that she realised her mistake. By replying in German, she'd given herself away as a Jew.

After lunch, the SS officer took his host aside and said, 'I don't want to see that girl here next time I come.'

Since then, Sala had been hidden in the cellar, and Urszula's recriminations had become even more strident.

Now, as Ernst Hauptmann sat on the bottom rung of the ladder the day after he'd assaulted her, Sala watched him warily from the other side of the cellar. Behind her back, her hands tightened around the wood. She was ready for him. But he continued to sit there in silence, and gradually she relaxed her grip.

Several weeks passed before he spoke to her again. He was almost incoherent with embarrassment. 'You're right,' he mumbled. 'I'm a pig. Too much to drink.' He waved his arm in the air as though to forestall an argument. 'That's no excuse, God knows.'

He lapsed into another long silence, still avoiding her eyes.

Suddenly he burst out, 'I'll be honest with you. When I saw the Jews being thrown out of their homes and losing everything, I can't say I was sorry. But the day I saw you in the ghetto, there was nothing left of you, just skin and bone, and that empty look in your eyes. I knew I had to save you. I've always been a sinner, but for once in my life I wanted to be a good Christian. And now you can't even look at me.'

While he was talking, Sala kept her face averted. She didn't want to see him or hear his feeble excuses.

Without another word he pulled himself to his feet, set down the bread, buttermilk and boiled potatoes he'd brought her, and trudged back up the wooden ladder. A moment later she heard the front door slam, and she knew he'd gone out to plough the potato field.

Alone in the cellar again, Sala paced around, seething. She mustn't drop her guard. Today he was contrite but tomorrow he'd probably be drunk again. Never again would she trust him. In the weeks that followed, whenever he came down with her food she turned her back on him, and he went back upstairs without a word.

Sometimes Ernst's wife brought her food. Urszula was a large woman with her hair pulled severely back from her flat face. She never looked straight at Sala and never spoke to her, and only the tight set of her mouth, and the way she banged the plate on the box that served as a table, expressed her resentment. Sala knew that only Ernst stood between herself and death.

Crazed with anxiety about her parents, and hungry for human contact, Sala paced around the small cellar and fought the urge to escape from her prison and breathe fresh air again. Anything would be better than being cooped up in this musty cellar, at the mercy of this ruffian and his churlish wife. Surely she'd survive somehow. Perhaps she'd work on another farm, or go back to the city. But when she recalled the conversations she'd overheard between Ernst and his SS guests who were congratulating themselves on making Łódź *Judenfrei*, she knew it wouldn't be long before someone recognised her and betrayed her to the Germans. The cellar was her only hope of survival.

She was so deep in thought when Ernst came down with her food the following day that for once she didn't have her back to him, and he was the one who looked away. After that, whenever he came down he'd spend a little longer in the cellar, not speaking, but watching and waiting for some reaction. And like a wild animal gradually becoming accustomed to human proximity, she began to feel less threatened.

In time he started talking about the farm and the outside world, still keeping his distance. Although she listened with grudging interest, she didn't reply. But the day came when she couldn't control her anxiety any longer and asked about her parents. He couldn't conceal his relief that she'd finally broken her silence. Several days later he told her he hadn't been able to find out what had happened to her parents, but according to his SS acquaintances, all the Jews in the ghetto had been sent to a concentration camp in Auschwitz.

When he went back upstairs, she felt more alone than ever, and over the next few days she listened for his footsteps and, to her surprise, found herself waiting for him to come down again. About a week later she heard the Germans carousing upstairs. And this time when Ernst came down to the cellar for another bottle of *wisniowka* she didn't move away but looked straight into his eyes. Suddenly she was in his arms and he was covering her face with kisses. He stroked her head and held her so tightly that she could hardly breathe, while he murmured endearments she had never heard before.

'I love you, Sala,' he whispered fiercely. 'I love you and I want you. More than anything. More than my life.'

She looked up and saw that his eyes were moist with emotion. He bent down to kiss her lips, gently at first, and then crushing them under his, and to her own surprise, she was pressing her lips against his and wrapping her arms around his neck and losing herself in the embrace.

He disengaged himself and stood back, looking into her eyes. 'I'll never do anything you don't want me to.'

The blood rushed to her face and she nodded. This time she believed him.

From that day she lived in a delirium of anticipation, waiting for his footsteps on the stairs and his touch on her skin. She felt alive only when he was with her. He spent more and more time with her in the cellar, and when he went back upstairs she heard the bitter arguments and his wife's threats to denounce her to the Gestapo.

'Let them come and get both of you,' she screamed. 'It would serve you right.' Sala didn't know what he said or did to calm her down, but she didn't carry out her threat.

As time went on, the visits of the SS officers became less frequent, the singing stopped, and one day Ernst came to tell her that the war was over. They held each other for a long time without speaking. The news was too overwhelming to comprehend. She had waited so long for this, but now she was in turmoil. She would have to leave the dark, confined space that had become her sanctuary and venture into a strange, empty world she hardly knew. She would have to start living a normal life again, but she no longer knew what was normal.

'I want to stay with you,' she sobbed, clinging to him. 'I don't want to leave you.'

'I'm a farmer, Sala,' he said slowly, and there was so much pain in his eyes that she had to look away. 'That's all I know. But you're a smart city girl, you're not cut out to bury yourself in a village and be a farmer's wife. You owe it to your parents to make something of your life.'

Urszula was washing dishes at the sink and didn't turn around to say goodbye, but as Sala climbed into the horse cart she saw her standing at the window, a triumphant smile on her broad face. On the long journey back to Łódż, as the cart rumbled over the dirt road, Sala sat beside Ernst with her head on his shoulder, too numb to speak.

She returned to her family home where the smell of her mother's perfume and her father's pipe tobacco still lingered in the silent, empty rooms. A Jewish welfare centre had opened in the square, and she went there every morning to scan the lists of survivors, in case some relative had returned alive. She hung around the centre for most of the day, hoping to run into someone who might tell her what had happened to her parents. One day she saw their old housekeeper crossing the square and started running towards her, but the woman hurriedly turned into a side street and disappeared, and Sala wondered whether she was the one who had betrayed them to the Gestapo.

Depressed after two years of fruitless searching, she met Szymon at the Jewish welfare office. They'd both lost their families, were alone and desperate to find someone to cling to, to fill the void in their lives. But even though three years had passed since the war ended, Sala could still feel the urgent touch of Ernst's hands on her body. With him she'd discovered a wildness in herself, an uninhibited capacity for sexual pleasure that surpassed anything she'd ever felt with her husband.

Alone in the room on Wattle Street, Sala sat on the edge of the bed, confused and depressed. Perhaps Szymon was right. There had to be some reason why Ernst was being charged with war crimes. After all, she didn't know what he'd done when he wasn't with her. It was true he'd hobnobbed with SS men, but he might have done it to allay their suspicions that he was hiding a Jewish girl. And the charges against him could have been trumped up by a jealous neighbour or a fanatical patriot who hated ethnic Germans, or even by his jealous wife.

The more she thought about it, the more possibilities she concocted, until her head ached and she became more confused. She wondered what was wrong with her. Surely a normal woman would know what to do.

Exhausted by the turmoil, she finally fell asleep. She dreamed she was in Sydney, living in a house with Szymon. 'See, you wanted to rent a flat, but I've bought you the whole house,' he boasted. But she didn't like anything about the house and knew she never would. She was trapped in an ugly house she hadn't chosen. As she paced around from room to room, she noticed a trapdoor she hadn't seen before. She raised it and couldn't believe her eyes. She was looking at a cellar stacked with sacks of potatoes, wooden barrels containing apples and pickled cabbage, and bottles of *wisniowka*. Her spirits soared as though she'd just uncovered buried treasure. There was a cellar here after all! It was there all the time and she hadn't even noticed!

When she woke up, the exhilaration evaporated in the sultry air. She was still in the boarding house in Wattle Street and there was no wonderful discovery awaiting her. In the dark, she could make out Szymon's shape in bed beside her. She turned over very carefully so as not to wake him, and lay awake until the alarm went off at dawn.

Chapter 29

In the corridor outside Meggsie's ward, the orthopaedic specialist took Kath aside. His lips were moving, but there was a ringing in her ears and the words made no sense.

Seeing her bewildered expression, he repeated it more slowly. 'I'm sorry to have to tell you this, but I'm afraid your son will never walk again,' he said. 'I believe you're divorced, and have other children. My advice to you is to put him in a home for crippled children. He'll be well looked after, and you'll be able to devote yourself to the rest of your family.'

She slumped against the wall, staring at the scuffed beige lino floor whose lozenge design made her feel giddy. 'A home for crippled children?' she whispered hoarsely. 'For how long?'

'Until he's old enough to be transferred to an institution for adults.'

The doctor's face suddenly became blurred and Kath fumbled in her bag for a handkerchief.

'Isn't there anything else you can do?' she pleaded.

'Unfortunately some cases just don't respond to treatment,' he said. 'I know this is difficult, but the sooner you accept the situation, the easier it will be for him. Children adapt much better than you imagine.'

She stumbled from the hospital and started walking towards Parramatta Road, her chest so tight she could hardly catch her breath. Too agitated to wait for the tram, she walked on. At Central Railway Station she sank onto a wooden bench under the clock, and sat there for a long time, unable to gather her thoughts.

It couldn't be true. Perhaps the doctor had made a mistake. Sometimes patients recovered despite the doctors' predictions. You only had to look at little Betty. After Ted Browning's article, a fund had been set up to help the family. Betty's mother now came to Sydney every week, and the little girl had started chattering again. Kath gave a bitter laugh. Her intervention had helped Betty, but she didn't seem able to do anything to help her own son.

Put Meggsie into a home for crippled children, to live among strangers and be at the mercy of nurses like the ward sister? The thought of it made her feel sick. There must be something she could do. If only she could bring him home, but that was a pipedream. She had to find a job, and he wouldn't be able to stay home by himself. Besides, he'd need nursing.

Heavy-hearted, she forced herself to get up. The boys would soon be home from school.

An hour later, she turned into Wattle Street. Verna Browning, standing at her front gate, took one look at Kath and said, 'Been to the hospital, have you? How was Meggsie today?'

Instead of answering, Kath burst out crying.

Verna took Kath's arm. 'Come and have a cuppa,' she said.

Although they'd been neighbours for fifteen years, this was the first time Kath had ever been inside Verna's house. There was a solidarity among the women of Wattle Street, but they confined their chats to the front gate or the back fence and didn't invite one another inside. Home was a private place, and no one wanted to breach the unspoken rule that safeguarded their privacy.

Verna put the kettle on the stove and kept up a stream of light-hearted chatter as she took her Royal Doulton cups with the country roses design from the dresser. 'You wouldn't believe it, they were a wedding present from Alf's mum and dad but I've never used them. I always kept them for best, but I'm beginning to wonder who I'm saving them for. So I reckon now's as good a time to get them out as any.'

Kath nodded absentmindedly. She realised that Verna was trying to distract her, but she was too upset to respond.

Verna bustled about setting out shortbread biscuits on a plate, and poured their tea. As the steam rose from their cups and swirled towards the ceiling, Kath told her what the doctor had said.

'That's terrible,' Verna said, shaking her head. 'No wonder you're upset. Isn't there anything else they can do?'

Kath's eyes filled with tears again. 'Apparently not. I can't bear to put him in a place like that, but I don't know what else to do.'

'Don't give up hope, love,' Verna said. 'Sometimes help comes when we least expect it.'

'It'll certainly be unexpected,' Kath sighed.

'I've been wanting to ask you something,' Verna said as they drank their tea. 'Did you know that Miss McNulty got an anonymous note in her letterbox a few months ago?'

Kath shook her head. 'What did it say?'

'It was about Mr Emil, the foreign gentleman. She thinks you were the one who sent it.'

Kath's eyes widened. 'Me?' she exclaimed indignantly. 'Why on earth would I be writing anonymous notes about that man, and to her of all people! I know she looks down on me, but this is going too far, accusing me of things like that. As if I didn't have enough to think about!'

'That's what I told her,' Verna said. 'I knew it wasn't you.'

Kath was fuming. 'She's got a nerve, spreading rumours about me. Why did she think it was me anyway?'

Verna shrugged. 'Old people get funny ideas sometimes. Don't take it so hard.'

But Kath wouldn't be mollified. 'She can't go around accusing me of sending anonymous notes.' Then a thought struck her. 'Did that note have anything to do with the cops taking Mr Emil to the police station?'

Verna nodded.

'So the old busybody must have given the note to the police. I bet she told them I'd written it too. So any day now they'll be coming for me as well, to charge me with creating mischief or something like that. I'm going to go and give her a piece of my mind.'

Verna sighed. 'I shouldn't have said anything. I didn't mean to upset you.'

Without waiting to finish her tea, Kath thanked Verna and rushed out. A moment later she pushed open Maude McNulty's gate, stormed up to the front door and pressed the doorbell. The white lace curtain over the front window fluttered and the old woman opened the door.

Kath thought she looked like one of the dried-up grey moths she sometimes found under the sofa.

'Yes, what is it?' Maude McNulty said in her querulous voice.

'I have a bone to pick with you,' Kath said.

'What about?'

'The anonymous note you took to the police.'

The old woman's sunken eyes darted from side to side to make sure no one was listening.

'You'd best come in then,' she grumbled. 'But don't be long about it.'

Ignoring the fact that she wasn't asked to sit down, Kath threw herself into one of the armchairs, ruffling the lace antimacassar on the back. Maude McNulty sat straight-backed on the edge of a wooden chair as though to indicate that she expected their conversation to be brief.

Kath came straight to the point. 'What do you think you're doing, telling people I sent you an anonymous note?'

'Who told you that?'

'Never mind. The point is, I want to know why.'

Maude McNulty looked down and Kath saw that her eyelids were as crinkled as tissue paper. She started to explain about the torn page from the exercise book and the childish handwriting when Kath interrupted.

'Well I don't go round sending anonymous notes about my neighbours, and even if I did, I certainly wouldn't be sending them to you.'

Maude McNulty was fidgeting in her chair.

'But if you thought I wrote it, why didn't you just come and ask me? And what about Mr Emil? You know you got him arrested, don't you?'

Kath was shocked at her own belligerence, but she couldn't control herself. All her pent-up anger was pouring out. 'Don't you think I've got enough trouble? I've lost my job, my son is ill in hospital, and the doctor said he'll never walk again.'

She hadn't meant to say any of this, or to show any weakness in front of the heartless old witch, but it had just slipped out, and now Miss McNulty was staring at her like a rabbit caught in the glare of headlights on a country road.

Bidding her neighbour a hasty goodbye, Kath strode out, but her relief at venting her anger was short-lived. It had done nothing to resolve the real cause of her distress.

After Kath had left, Maude McNulty continued sitting there. No one had spoken to her like that in all her adult life, but she had made sure no one would ever have the opportunity to hurt her again the way they'd hurt her when she was young.

It hadn't taken long for the other children to find out her father was the hangman, and they'd tormented her in the playground, chanting nasty things that made her cry. They never let her join in their games, and whenever they played that horrible game called Hangman, they'd point at her and giggle.

In the end, she had what the doctor described as a nervous breakdown. Thinking back, it struck her that, in a way, she'd been as paralysed then as Kath's son was now. She never went back to school after that, and her mother taught her at home.

In spite of her limited education, she was bright enough to be admitted to a secretarial college and get a job in the public service. She was a quiet girl, not pretty, but neat and well turned out, in her high-necked blouses with the leg-of-mutton sleeves that were fashionable at the time, and her thick brown hair coiled on top of her head. Unlike the other girls, she didn't giggle and whisper about the boys in the office, but kept her head down and took dictation without a single spelling mistake or misplaced comma.

She was twenty-two when she caught the eye of the second in charge of her department. She couldn't believe her luck when this dashing man, with his luxuriant moustache and celluloid collar above his dark suit jacket, singled her out. When they walked out together through Centennial Park on Sunday afternoons, her arm through his, she felt she was walking on air. She had never imagined she could be so happy. They spoke of getting married, and he was about to come and ask for her hand when someone took him aside and told him about her father's occupation. After that, he made lame excuses about being too busy to see her and got himself transferred to another department.

She suffered another breakdown, more serious than the first, and it took many years before she felt strong enough to go out by herself or hold down a job, and when she did, she kept to herself and didn't mix with any of her workmates. She wasn't going to be rejected again.

When her parents died and left her the cottage at the top of the cliff at Ben Buckler, she preferred to let it go to rack and ruin than to admit she had any connection with it. She didn't mind that some people thought Nosey's cottage was haunted. As far as she was concerned, it was.

She hadn't thought about the past in a long time, and she sat in the dark with her memories. She glanced at the calendar and realised it was her birthday. She had just turned ninety-two, and no one knew or cared.

Chapter 30

Kath sat on the edge of the hard wooden chair in Dr Tennyson Wilkie's waiting room clasping and unclasping her hands. She looked at the sketches on the wall depicting characters from children's stories and decided they must have been pasted onto the cardboard backing a long time ago because most of them were coming away at the corners. In between Alice in Wonderland and Peter Rabbit, Christopher Robin was kneeling at the foot of his bed, hands clasped in prayer. An apt image, Kath thought, in a place where people often prayed for their children's recovery.

She wondered how doctors coped when they had to give parents bad news about their children. It was sad to think how quickly people hardened their hearts to the tragedies of others. Even where their own family was concerned. Her sister, who lived in the country, was run off her feet looking after the property and her large family and had no time for Kath. Her brothers had joined the navy, probably to escape from the responsibilities of everyday life. Apart from exchanging Christmas cards, they had little contact. And then there was Gran, hard and unforgiving.

Kath looked up when she heard a meek voice saying,

'Thank you, doctor.' The door opened and a thin woman with downcast eyes came out, blowing her nose into a handkerchief patterned with rosebuds.

As soon as Kath felt Dr Wilkie's clinical gaze on her face, her composure faltered, and a swarm of butterflies fluttered wildly inside her stomach.

'I came to thank you for everything you've done for Meggsie now that he's leaving the hospital.' She spoke quickly to get it over with.

He tamped his cigarette in the glass ashtray and nodded. 'You've made the right decision. As I told you, the home for crippled children is the best place for him.'

She tried to keep her voice steady. 'But I'm not putting him in there. I'm taking him home.'

He stared at her, at first in astonishment, and then with disapproval. 'I see,' he said in a tone that showed he was affronted by her defiance. 'I can only repeat what I told you before: for the boy's sake, for yours and that of your family, he should be in a home for crippled children where he can be looked after properly.'

Her heart was beating fast, but she stood her ground. 'I'm sorry, but I'm his mother and I feel in my heart that I'm doing the right thing.'

Dr Wilkie shrugged, and his voice was cold and dry. 'What you're doing is not only foolhardy, it's against the boy's best interests, and you'll regret it. But you've decided to ignore my advice, so I have nothing more to say to you. Good day.'

As Kath walked from the surgery, her knees were wobbling so much that she had to lean against a wall to steady herself. She didn't know how she'd found the courage to confront this eminent specialist and tell him she was about to ignore his advice. Nor did she understand how she'd come to this unexpected decision after having convinced herself that it was impossible. Perhaps she was being foolhardy in allowing her heart to rule her head, and perhaps she'd come to regret her impulsive decision, but her instinct as a mother had triumphed over all other considerations.

Meggsie cheered when his mum told him she was taking him home. 'Yippee! This is the best day of my life,' he exulted.

He told Nurse Cecily that he felt like Edmond Dantès when he'd finally tunnelled his way out of his prison in the Chateau d'If.

'Keep the book. Whenever things get you down, just think about Edmond Dantès and remember that nothing is impossible,' she said, and gave him a hug. 'And don't forget, one of these days I expect to see you walk in through that door.'

Nurse Cecily was the only one he would miss. He certainly wasn't sorry to see the last of Sister Danglars. He couldn't believe his eyes when his mum had shown him Ted's article, and he'd read it over and over again. Now everyone knew what a rotten bully she was. When, a few days after the article appeared, she had been moved to another ward, Meggsie was jubilant.

He often went over the sequence of events in his mind, proud that he'd played such a big part in getting rid of her. This was how Edmond Dantès must have felt when he finally got his revenge. And it had all happened because he'd asked his mother to see Betty, and she'd talked to Mrs Browning, who had told Ted, who had written the article which had made so many people send in money for Betty's mother. And Betty had been transferred to a hospital for children who were getting better. But he was the one who'd started the ball rolling. Then he thought about the note he'd written, which had got Mr Emil into so much trouble, and he didn't feel proud of himself any more. It took only one person to make trouble for others, but a lot of people were needed to put things right.

The next day, as the ambulance sped him away from the hospital, Meggsie thought he'd burst with impatience. He couldn't wait to be home again, in his own bed, seeing his brothers and Hanny. But in spite of his elation, he felt a nagging sense of guilt. He didn't deserve this lucky break. He hadn't told his mother about the night he'd sneaked out to spy on Mr Emil, or about the note he and Hanny had written and slipped into Miss McNulty's letterbox. His mother didn't know, but God did, and that's why He'd struck him down with infantile paralysis.

Chapter 31

The rare sound of a car engine in Wattle Street made Emil look out of his window in time to see the ambulance pull up next door. He watched as the ambulance officers jumped out, opened the back door and carried the red-headed boy out on a stretcher. The mother walked beside them, carrying her worn leather bag in one hand and a small brown Globite case in the other.

Emil had never forgotten Kath's kindness the day of the bonfire, when the sole of his shoe had come unstuck, but that had made her treachery all the more difficult to understand. Her son must have told her what he'd seen that night, but why had she gone behind his back to report him, when she could have just asked him what he was doing? She was the only person he'd met in Sydney he felt he could trust, but he'd obviously been wrong about her.

It had taken him several weeks to get over the shock of being interrogated and humiliated at the police station, but he'd learned his lesson. From now on, he wouldn't trust anyone. These people smiled to your face but you never knew what they were thinking. At least the old battleaxe across the road made her dislike of foreigners quite clear, but the others were hypocrites. Just the day before when he was in Attwaters, he'd seen the white-haired woman from across the road watching him. He could tell she wanted to come over and start talking, probably so she'd have something to gossip about.

He unwrapped the material he'd bought in Attwaters that day, and spent a long time looking at the two lengths of satin, lost in thought. With a sigh he opened one of the coffins and tried draping the blue satin inside it in various ways. When he was satisfied that he'd figured out how to line the coffin, he cut a small piece of the fabric. Then he took a brown paper bag from under the table and pulled out a thick wad of cottonwool, letting his hands luxuriate in its fluffy softness before he spread it on the base of the coffin. When the cottonwool was evenly spread, he tucked the blue satin around it like an eiderdown cover. Next, he filled the small offcut with cotton wool, shaped it into a pillow and placed it on top of the eiderdown, patting it down to make sure there were no lumps.

When the first coffin resembled a cosy little bed, he repeated the same procedure with the pale pink satin. When both coffins were finished, he lit two candles and sat in front of them for a long time, his head in his hands, harsh sobs escaping from his throat.

If he still believed in anything, he would have said it was the prayer they used to recite for the dead, in the days when God still existed. In those days he'd regarded God as a kind of benevolent elderly relative who lived far away but watched out for you. He hadn't needed God back then. As the Great Novello, the legendary magician of Berlin, he'd created his own world and made his own rules. People spoke about him in hushed tones, wondering whether they had really seen the miraculous feats he performed in front of their eyes. All over Europe people queued to see him, but his biggest following was in his own country. And that was his salvation as well as his downfall.

Not satisfied with tricks other magicians performed, he perfected acts that left his audiences open-mouthed. He thrilled them with the substitution trunk, the bullet-catch trick, and the buzz-saw illusion. Death sat constantly on his shoulder but he didn't see its face. Not yet.

'You think people come to see how clever you are,' an old magician once told him with a mocking smile. 'But you're wrong. They come to see you fail. Sometimes to see you die.'

At the time Emil had been shocked at the old man's cynicism, but these days he no longer had any trouble believing in the dark side of human nature.

Like him, the old magician was Jewish, and that's when Emil realised that magic and Judaism were somehow connected, and that he was part of an ancient tradition. Back in the days of the Old Testament, the Jews had survived by performing magic tricks.

How else could you explain Moses walking across the Red Sea, or Aaron's rod turning into a serpent and swallowing up the serpents of the Egyptians? Like all magicians, Moses had made use of natural phenomena to produce what to the gullible appeared to be magic effects. In the New Testament another Jew had seduced his simple followers with a series of magic tricks like walking on water, turning water into wine and producing the miracle of the loaves and fishes.

You could win everyone over with magic. Lurking in the depths of human nature, concealed by a gossamer-fine layer of sophistication, education and rationalism, lay a primitive belief in the supernatural, and a childlike willingness to believe in the occult, and that was what Emil exploited, exulting in the power it gave him.

But Emil had overestimated his power. When Hitler began waging his war against the Jews, Emil had thought himself immune. His father had fought for Germany during the First World War and had been awarded the Iron Cross. Kristallnacht had shocked Emil, but he regarded it as an aberration, a hate crime committed by a group of brown-shirted thugs who were out of control. He thought that Dachau was a prison for society's undesirable elements, that the Nuremberg laws would never work, and that the Nazis were a flash in the pan and would soon be ousted. In any case, being Jewish was an accident of birth, and he and his wife Gisela were patriotic citizens, even more German than Hitler himself, who was Austrian.

Late one night, two Gestapo in belted trenchcoats and grey fedoras pulled low over their foreheads banged on his door and, ignoring his protestations and explanations, pushed him, together with Gisela, five-year-old Heinz and seven-year-old Renate, into their black Opel.

It took Emil a long time to comprehend that although he didn't go to synagogue or observe the dietary laws, to Hitler he was as Jewish as the rabbi, and his fame wouldn't help him. In those first disorienting days in the camp, his protestations that he was a famous magician met with derision. 'If you're a magician, why don't you disappear?' the SS guards mocked him. While flogging him, they laughed and goaded him to turn their whip into a rabbit. Gisela and the children had been taken to the women's part of the camp. Desperate to help them, he often saved half his piece of clay-like bread and slipped it across the fence to them.

He'd been in the camp for six months when one of the SS guards recognised him and the word soon spread that he really was the Great Novello. Now the Nazi devils came to his wooden bunk every night, shook him awake and dragged him to their quarters, ordering him to entertain them while they drank. Without even the basic magic apparatus, he'd put together a show using coins, cigarettes, a grimy pack of playing cards and a piece of string. Like children, they were fascinated by his tricks and demanded to see them again and again. He despised these sadists and murderers, and wished he had the moral strength to refuse to perform for them, but his new status as the camp magician meant special privileges, which included a little more food and a little less brutality.

Best of all, it meant he was protecting Gisela and the children, because the commandant assured him that as long as he continued to entertain them, his family would be safe.

Deception is a magician's stock-in-trade, but as Emil was to discover, his masters surpassed him at this art. He believed them when they told him that Gisela and the children had been moved to a camp where they would have more food and better conditions. But they'd double-crossed him. By the sleight of hand that the Nazis had perfected, the bodies of Gisela, Heinz and Renate had been transformed into the sweetish black smoke that poured from the chimneys looming over the camp.

Emil was one of the walking skeletons the liberators found among the stinking pile of cadavers in the camp, staring into space, almost too weak to blink or to swallow his own saliva. He no longer cared whether he lived or died. He hated the Nazis but he hated himself even more. One thought burned in his brain. Never again. As long as he lived, he would never perform magic again.

As he watched the ambulance officers carrying the sick boy into the house, he stroked the satin lining of the coffins his children had never had. He'd kept his vow. But he had performed one final trick: he'd made himself virtually invisible. Magic had now become irrelevant. His whole life had been a sickening illusion, and Australia had become his own substitution trunk.

Chapter 32

School had broken up for the Christmas holidays, and from his chair by the window Meggsie could hear the girls giggling as their skipping ropes thudded on the footpath. Jimmy Noble's dad had made him a wooden billycart, and Meggsie could hear it rattling as the wheels scraped along the ground. Jimmy was giving some of his mates a turn, pushing them down the street, while the kids waiting impatiently on the pavement urged them to hurry up. Every now and again he heard a girl whining, 'Stop pushing! I'm telling on you!' or 'That's not fair, it's my turn!'

Meggsie couldn't see much through the window but he listened out for Hanny's voice and hoped that she'd come over. Although her mother had forbidden her to visit him for fear of catching polio, Hanny would sneak across the road, stand on tiptoe on a couple of bricks and talk to him through the window. Sometimes when her mother was at work, Hanny came inside and talked to him from the doorway of his bedroom. Unlike almost everyone else who came to see him, she talked to him just as she always had, and for those brief moments he felt normal again. In between her visits she sent him little notes and sketched funny little cartoon faces at the bottom which made him laugh.

Beverley sometimes dropped in with a book. Last week she'd lent him *Treasure Island,* but he couldn't concentrate on it. He'd been home for two weeks now, but he couldn't get interested in anything. In the hospital all the other children were sick too, but here he was the odd one out. His arms and hands were still weak, and all he could do was lie in bed or sit in his chair, listening to the other kids running around and having fun, and he felt more like a prisoner than ever. Whenever he heard them talking about going to the beach, he realised with a shock that he might never paddle in the waves again, or feel the warm sand between his toes. At their mothers' prompting, some of his mates dropped in now and again with a dog-eared comic book, or his brothers would come in and sit on the edge of his bed and give him a game of checkers or fiddlesticks, but they didn't know what to say to him now that he couldn't play footie or cricket. Outside, the sun was shining, and after a few minutes they'd start fidgeting and find an excuse to run off again.

Uncle Bill, who was always collecting old tools, discarded appliances and bits of scrap metal, loved tinkering and fixing things, and soon after Meggsie had come home he had presented him with a contraption he'd made. It was something between a pushchair, a wheelbarrow and a pram, with a flat base and small wheels, so that Meggsie could get out into the street if someone pushed him. He hadn't been able to wait to go outside with the others, but as soon as his mother had wheeled him out, the other kids had rushed up to ask if they could push him, and he'd felt like a sideshow freak at the Easter Show. When he'd seen some boys pointing at him, whispering and giggling that Meggsie was a cripple, he had asked to be wheeled back inside. After that, he had refused to go outside again.

He looked around when his mum came in to make the bed. As she helped him into his armchair, she said, 'Come on, love, go outside for a bit. You're looking that peaky, you need some sun on you.'

But Meggsie shrugged and shook his head. 'I'm not going out there for them to make fun of me,' he muttered, and his mum reluctantly gave in.

Back in the kitchen, Kath opened the *Daily Standard*. Reading about the terrible things that befell others sometimes helped to take her mind off her own problems. There were the usual sensational stories about murders, bashings, thefts and tragedies, but today they only added to her despair. She was about to put the paper down when a small article caught her eye. It was headed KENNY POLIO CLINICS A SUCCESS IN THE UK.

The article was about a bush nurse from Queensland called Sister Kenny who had apparently found a way of helping kids with polio, using methods that differed from those used by the doctors. Kath sat forward and read on. Although Sister Kenny had encountered considerable opposition in Australia, from the medical profession as well as from the massage association, her unorthodox treatment had been accepted in America and in the United Kingdom, where clinics using her methods had been established.

Kath reread the article carefully to make sure she had understood it. Why had no one ever told her there was another way of treating polio? No matter how strange it was, it might be worth trying. According to the article there was a clinic at the Royal North Shore Hospital in Sydney that used the Kenny method. Kath underlined the name and cut out the article. For the first time since bringing Meggsie home, she felt a little hope.

Chapter 33

On the evening of the school dance, Hania put on her pink organdie dress, did up her new black ankle-strap shoes, let her thick dark hair out, parted it in the middle and slipped blue clips on either side. Her mother hadn't made any comment about the dress Aunty Muriel had made. When Hania had carried it home, she'd looked expectantly at her mother, who had given it a brief, critical glance and turned away without a word. But now, when she saw Hania wearing it, she caught her breath. 'You look beautiful,' she said as she tied the sash around Hania's waist. She blew her nose several times even though Hania knew she didn't have a cold. But her mother's reactions were always strange and inexplicable so she didn't give it another thought. Impatient to go to the dance, she gave her mother a perfunctory peck on the cheek and ran across the road to Beverley's place.

The two girls were chattering excitedly and walking so quickly that Beverley's mother could hardly keep up with them. The hall, which was usually bare except for the photograph of King George VI on the wall, had been decorated with balloons and streamers, and when Hania went inside she glowed with pleasure at the envious glances of the other girls. She felt like Cinderella at the ball.

Miss Charlton, Hania's teacher, went over to the gramophone, placed a record on the turntable, cranked the handle, and the music started. Standing around the edge of the hall, the girls looked eagerly at the boys, trying to catch the eye of the good-looking ones. With their hair slicked down and parted on one side, and their white short-sleeved shirts neatly tucked into their long trousers, the boys didn't resemble the untidy tearaways who chased each other around the playground on school days. But now, subdued by the formality of the occasion and the expectation of having to ask girls to dance, they hung back, fidgeting and looking at the floor, until one of the male teachers pushed them forward. When they'd chosen their partners, they stumbled around, often treading on the girls' toes as they lolloped in the wrong direction in the progressive barn dance or forgot the Canadian two-step, which their PE teacher had been drumming into them over the past few weeks.

Shortly after the record started playing 'Come Back to Erin', Barry Skelton planted himself in front of Hania and mumbled something that she took to be an invitation to dance. Barry was the most popular boy in sixth class. The girls swooned over him because he was tall, had a lock of fair hair that almost covered his left eye, and a devil-may-care smile. What made him even more attractive was the fact that he never took any notice of them. As Hania walked onto the dance floor with his arm clamped around her waist, she saw her schoolfriends watching enviously.

But they'd hardly done two turns of the Pride of Erin when her neck began to itch. Within a few minutes her eyes were red and streaming, her nose was running, and there were big red welts on her neck which she couldn't stop scratching. To make things worse, everyone was staring at her, pointing and whispering. She tried to keep dancing, but the itching was so bad that she had to stop, and she stood there, not knowing what to do until Aunty Muriel rushed forward and said she was taking her home.

Midnight had struck for Cinderella, and as Hania walked from the hall, feeling as though everyone was staring at her, she wished the ground would swallow her up.

As soon as her mother saw her, she ran to the telephone box to call a Polish doctor she'd met on the ship to Australia. He arrived within an hour, and after examining Hania he said that it was an allergic reaction, but whether it was to a plant, an insect bite or something she'd eaten, he couldn't tell. Her mother, however, had no doubts. 'It's that dress,' she said, barely able to suppress a note of triumph. 'You're allergic to that material.'

By the following morning the swelling had gone down, the welts had disappeared and there was no sign of the allergy that had ruined her night. And to add her to misery, Christmas was only a few days away.

After giving Meggsie a bed bath and massaging his back and legs, Kath went into the kitchen to make the Christmas pudding. Whenever she thought about Christmas, she let out a long sigh. She'd managed to scrape together a few shillings to buy the boys some comic books, socks and a cricket ball, but she'd only be able to put rabbit on the table this year — a turkey was out of the question. Lost in her thoughts, she was stirring her worries into the dough along with the sultanas, and throwing in a few silver threepences, when the doorbell rang.

She wiped her floury hands on her apron and hurried to the door, but before she got there she could hear hoarse voices singing 'Jingle Bells'. Collecting money for some charity, she supposed. She opened the door and was about to say she was sorry she couldn't spare anything, when she stepped back in surprise. On her doorstep stood Mick Kelly and Bob Longley from the pub, and they were struggling with a large cardboard box.

'This fell off a truck the other day and we thought maybe you could use it,' Mick said. Thrusting the box into her hands, he mumbled, 'Merry Christmas, love,' and before she could thank them, they'd gone.

Inside the box was the biggest turkey she'd ever seen, a leg of ham, a bag of potatoes and a box of biscuits.

Kath rushed to Meggsie's room. 'It's a miracle, that's what it is,' she kept saying as she sat down on the edge of his bed. 'We'll have a proper Christmas now. All we need is another miracle to make you well.'

Chapter 34

For weeks Hania had heard the other children talking about Christmas. Beverley and her family were going to Thirroul to visit her Aunty Tessie, but when Aunty Muriel invited Hania to go with them, her mother tried to talk her out of it.

'Christmas is a family day for Christians,' she said. 'You'll be out of place.'

But Hania was adamant. It was bad enough missing out on the Christmas tree, the presents and the festivities she loved; she wasn't going to miss out on the outing as well. Away from her mother, with Beverley and her family, she'd be able to forget she was an outsider, and feel she was part of something for once.

On the train she sat next to Beverley, her nose pressed against the grimy window as she stared out at the backs of red-tiled cottages with their outdoor wooden dunnies and the skinny dogs running around and barking in backyards. Every few minutes the train ground to a halt at another station, until finally they reached Thirroul.

Aunty Tessie, Uncle Dick and their three children lived in a fibro cottage facing the beach. They kept chooks out the back, and as soon as they arrived, all the children rushed out to see if there were any eggs. Inside, the men were arguing about football, and Uncle Bill told Hania that his brother used to play for the Butchers, the local rugby league team. There was a strong piney smell in the lounge room where the Christmas tree stood, hung with brightly coloured paper chains, tinsel, shiny baubles, and an angel with a silver star on top. As they stood admiring the tree, Uncle Dick said that now the cedar forests around Thirroul had been logged, real Christmas trees were hard to come by, but he'd managed to get one for the kids.

Exciting boxes and parcels wrapped in bright Christmas paper were piled up under the tree. Except for the fact the tree stood in a bucket and was propped up with bricks, it reminded Hania of Christmas at her foster parents' home in Poland. Despite her mother's warning that she'd be intruding, they all made her feel as if she were part of the family, and Beverley's aunty told her to call her Aunty Tessie like the other kids did.

After the roast turkey, ham and baked potatoes, Aunty Tessie brought out a steaming Christmas pudding and warned them to eat slowly to make sure they didn't swallow the threepences she'd put inside. Beverley's little sister Daisy was the first to squeal that she'd bitten into one. Aunty Tessie had been very generous with the coins, because by the time the pudding was finished, all the children had found at least one.

When they'd finished lunch, Hania hung back while Beverley and her little sister and cousins were given their presents but, to her surprise, she hadn't been forgotten. Aunty Tessie handed her a small parcel wrapped in Christmas paper, and said, 'Merry Christmas, love.' It was a book called *Seven*

Little Australians. Hania was thrilled to be given the book, but the best thing was being included.

As they travelled home on the train, Hania found it difficult to join in Beverley's light-hearted chatter. The elation she'd felt at Thirroul was replaced by a feeling of sadness. Being included in the Nobles' Christmas celebration didn't mean she belonged. As the train rattled towards Sydney in the soft darkness of the summer night, it struck her that being included had accentuated the fact that she was different.

There was only one way to stop being different, and for the rest of the journey she thought about the idea that had been germinating in her mind for some time.

Hania had often passed St Xavier's church while walking home from Bondi Junction, and she had sometimes paused, wondering whether she dared go inside and carry out her plan, but a few days after Christmas she summoned up the courage to enter. Tentatively she swung open the heavy wooden door of the old parish church and looked inside, surprised at the austere interior. It didn't have the rich ornamentation, vivid paintings and dramatic atmosphere of the churches in Poland, but as soon as she came to the stone baptismal font and the half-burnt votive candles, a feeling of peace descended on her. It was like being held by strong, loving arms.

In front of the altar the priest was talking to the old sacristan, and she crept in and sat down on a wooden pew. She breathed in the smell of incense and candle wax and gazed at the white lace-edged cloth over the altar, with the bowl of roses on top and the crucifix above it.

Their conversation over, the sacristan hobbled across the transept and his limping footsteps resounded in the empty church. He disappeared through a side door, and the priest, a tall figure in a black cassock, entered the confessional. Wondering what to do, Hania crept towards it and stood outside, peering through the latticed screen.

'Have you come to confess, my child?' the priest asked.

Taken aback, she didn't know what to say or how to address him in English. 'No,' she stammered.

'I haven't seen you in here before,' he said. 'Are you from this parish?'

Hania stood there, not knowing what to say.

'You seem troubled,' he said.

She took a deep breath. This was much harder than she'd expected. 'I'm Jewish,' she said.

The door opened with a soft click and the priest came out. He stopped and looked at her so intently that she felt he could read her mind.

'I'm Father Keegan,' he said. 'Would you like to come to the presbytery? We can sit down and talk without being disturbed, and you can tell me what's on your mind.'

A cement path lined with straggly petunias and wilting dahlias led from the church to the presbytery, a small brick building behind a weathered paling fence. Inside, a round-shouldered woman with a scarf tied over her grey hair sprang up from the couch where she'd been reading the parish newspaper and hurriedly grabbed her feather duster.

'Could I trouble you to make us a cup of tea, Mrs O'Reilly?' the priest asked. 'With some biscuits, please.'

As Hania sat down on the edge of a stuffed armchair, she noticed that the flowered material on the couch was threadbare in places, the sideboard had the corners chipped off and the armchairs didn't match, as though the furniture had come from a second-hand shop.

While they waited for the tea, Father Keegan kept chatting. 'I've only been here at St Xavier's for six months, and I'm still making terrible mistakes and getting myself into all kinds of trouble,' he chuckled. 'Only last Sunday I didn't recognise Mrs Fennelly and called her Miss Doyle, which wasn't very smart, seeing she had the five children with her!'

He gave Hania a conspiratorial look. 'New beginnings are hard, aren't they?'

As he told her about his problems, Hania began to relax. She sensed that beneath the light-hearted chatter, he was letting her know that he understood how she felt.

Mrs O'Reilly's heavy tread made the room vibrate, and a vase nearly fell off the sideboard as she came in with a tray and placed it on the small glass table. She filled their cups from the pot, which was covered by a tea cosy crocheted from multicoloured wool, and set down a flowered plate of Iced Vo-Vos, then left.

As Hania sipped her tea, she studied Father Keegan. Unlike

the old grey-haired priest she remembered from Poland, he was young and handsome, with brown hair parted on the side and regular features that reminded her of her favourite film star, Errol Flynn. But it was his boyish manner that surprised her the most.

Biting into a biscuit, he said, 'I can't decide whether I like these or Anzacs the best. Which ones do you like?' and soon they were chatting about their favourite biscuits.

After they'd finished their tea, Father Keegan pushed away his cup and reached for a cigarette. He lit it, then sat forward and asked where she came from, and whether she was having a hard time at school on account of being foreign and speaking with an accent.

'Is it hard to make friends here?' he asked.

She shook her head. Apart from turning around to stare at her each time her unpronounceable surname was read out at rollcall, and giggling at the funny way she pronounced some words, the other children were nice to her. Once a girl from another class had called her a 'bloody reffo' but Hania's friends had told her off and she'd never said it again.

He looked straight into her eyes. 'So will you be telling me what's on your mind now?'

Hania twisted her handkerchief around her thumb several times before she spoke. 'I want to become Christian,' she blurted out.

She thought he'd be shocked, but he simply nodded, as though it was the most natural thing in the world for a twelve-year-old Jewish girl who spoke with a Polish accent to come and see a priest about changing her religion.

'Have you talked about this with your parents?' he asked.

She shook her head vehemently. 'There's only my mother, and she wouldn't understand.'

She didn't tell him that if she had dared to mention such a thing, her mother would have become hysterical. She would have ranted about dead relatives, persecution, heritage, and probably Auschwitz as well.

He seemed to be waiting for her to go on, so she added, 'I can't talk to her about anything.'

'Mothers are sometimes like that, to be sure,' he said sympathetically. 'I always found it hard to talk to mine. I never thought she really listened, or tried to understand me.'

He took a puff of his cigarette, closing his eyes as he inhaled. 'I'm interested to know why you want to convert. Will you tell me?'

Before she knew it she was telling him about the day her mother had appeared in her life like the witch in a fairytale and abducted her from the Catholic foster parents she loved. By the time she'd finished, she was crying.

'I was so happy there,' she sobbed. 'For once I was like everyone else. Why did she have to take me away?'

He reached out to take another cigarette from the pack on the table but seemed to change his mind. 'Terrible habit,' he murmured, and turned his attention back to her. 'I can see why you were so upset when your mother turned up, but you weren't really like everyone else, were you? You only thought you were.' He paused while she blew her nose. 'I suppose your mother didn't want to lose you after all she'd been through. You were all she had left.'

'If she really loved me she would have left me there,' Hania said sullenly.

They sat in silence for a while.

'So is that why you want to become a Christian?' he asked. 'So you can be different from your mother, or so you can pay her back?'

She stared at him for a moment before shaking her head, and a note of irritation crept into her voice. 'I'm sick of being Jewish, that's all. I hate being different. Wherever we are, I'm always different from everyone else. I'm always worried in case people say something bad about Jews, and I can't do what the other kids do or have the same holidays as they do.'

As she spoke, she suspected that she sounded childish, not like a mature person embarking on a major life change.

'Ah, yes,' he was nodding again. 'I understand what you mean. It's certainly hard to be different. Take me for instance.'

She looked up at him.

'I'm different from most people. All my brothers and sisters are married and have children. That's what my mother wanted for me as well, but here I am, sworn to remain single, married to the Church instead of a woman!'

'But you chose that yourself,' she argued. 'I didn't choose to be Jewish and I didn't choose my mother.'

'Well now, that's a very interesting point you've raised,' he said. 'Do we choose our lives or do our lives choose us?'

She frowned, and he changed the subject. 'Tell me about your friends.'

When she'd told him about Meggsie, he said, 'I wonder how Meggsie feels about being different.'

She was frowning again. 'What do you mean?'

'Well, he hasn't got a father and he can't walk. I'd say that makes him different, wouldn't you?'

The conversation seemed to be spinning out of control and she looked at him helplessly. She hadn't come here to discuss Meggsie, and she felt that irritation again. Father Keegan seemed to be challenging her.

'What I'm saying is that Meggsie is even more different than you are,' he said. 'And if you look around, you'll see that everyone is different in some way. Come to think of it, I don't suppose life is very easy for your mother, either, being a foreigner in a new country and bringing you up on her own.'

Hania didn't know what to say.

'I know this isn't what you came to hear,' he was saying, 'but we're not put on earth to be the same as everyone else, in religion, ability, looks or anything else. Our Lord was different too. He was a Jew.'

'But he became a Christian!' she cut in.

Father Keegan shook his head. 'No, He didn't become a Christian. He remained true to His Jewish faith. His followers called themselves Christians.' He rested his gaze on her. 'We're all different, but I believe we're here on earth to make the most of our differences.'

At the front door he put his arm around her shoulders and said, 'It was very brave of you to come and see me. But what you're considering is a very big step, and you should think it over very carefully. If you still want to go ahead, come and talk to me again. But I'd like you to think about it this way: a bird might decide to live in a stable, but that doesn't make it a horse.'

With a wry smile he added, 'And I should be warning you that in Australia many people don't like us Catholics any better than they like you Jews.' Then in a more serious tone he said, 'But if you still want to convert, come and see me again. Even if you decide you don't, whenever you have anything on your mind, don't hesitate to come, and I'll make sure Mrs O'Reilly gets in some chocolate biscuits.'

Hania walked home slowly, dragging her feet. The elation she'd felt when she arrived at her decision had evaporated, and she felt as though Father Keegan had thrown a bucket of iced water over her. For all his pretence at being sympathetic and understanding, she felt that he had talked down to her and had given her a lecture. She was disappointed and embarrassed, and his suggestion that she was doing this to get back at her mother lingered uncomfortably in her mind.

Chapter 35

For the first few weeks after Meggsie had returned home, everyone had rallied round to help. Neighbours brought bowls of junket, pots of Irish stew or trays of Anzac biscuits, and even Mrs Adamson, who lived in one of the posh houses in Barton Street, surprised Kath by sending over a passionfruit sponge which the boys devoured at one sitting. Then there was that nervous foreign woman from across the road who thrust a bowl into Kath's hands and scurried away. Kath had no idea what this strange dish was, and supposed it was some continental speciality, but she was touched by the kindness of someone she knew only by sight.

But as time went on, most of the visitors drifted away, and apart from Muriel Noble and Verna Browning, no one came to see them. Kath's heart ached whenever she looked at Meggsie but she did her best to conceal her distress. If only there was some cure. She thought about the article she'd read about the bush nurse who had found a different way of treating polio. It was probably a long shot, but she decided to make some inquiries about the clinic that used her methods.

Skimming through the telephone directory in the phone box, she found the number of the Royal North Shore Hospital. The receptionist said in a businesslike voice that she didn't know anything about a Sister Kenny or her clinic, but when Kath explained about Meggsie, she sounded more sympathetic. She asked Kath to hold on and a few moments later she returned to the phone with the clinic's direct number.

Kath's fingers trembled as she dialled. The nurse who answered the phone explained that this was an outpatients' clinic, but she did know of a nurse who had been trained there and who, as far as she knew, visited people's homes. She didn't know her phone number or address, but if memory served her right, her name was Joan Gately.

Gately wasn't a common surname, and scanning the columns in the phone book, Kath found a *J Gately* listed in Kingsford. Nurse Gately had a brisk, matter-of-fact manner and came straight to the point. Yes, she did home visits; Bondi Junction was not out of her area, and she charged seven and sixpence per visit, plus bus fare. In an unsteady voice, Kath thanked her and walked slowly back home. How could she have been stupid enough to think that she'd be able to afford private treatment?

As it was, she didn't know how she'd manage when her meagre savings ran out. Now that the Christmas break was over, she planned to do the rounds of local pubs and shops to see if she could get a part-time job. If she couldn't find anything, she supposed she'd have to swallow her pride and ask Gran for help.

Worn out and dispirited, Kath stood waiting for the gas copper to boil. Monday was washing day, and she was throwing shavings of Sunlight soap over the sheets and towels in the laundry tub when the doorbell rang. Monday was also rent day, so it was sure to be the rent-collector. Giving the bubbling water a quick stir with the broomstick to dissolve the soap, she took her moneybox down from the dresser.

It was one of the few souvenirs left over from her childhood, a music box that her father had given her when she was ten years old. The music had stopped playing long ago, and the ballerina in the pink tutu no longer turned on her pedestal. The tutu was encrusted with years of dust and grime, and the fretted metal edge of the box had become tarnished, but Kath couldn't bring herself to part with it. It was one of the few treasures she had clung to on that terrible day they were thrown out of their home and stood shivering on the pavement beside their bundles and their bedding. If Gran hadn't come to the rescue, her parents would have become vagrants and she would have ended up in a children's home, and Gran never let them forget it.

Kath counted out twenty-five shillings and opened the door, expecting to see the rent-collector with his tan leather bag slung around his shoulder. But it was Mr Emil from next door, looking down at his shoes and holding his funny little hat in his hands.

'How is the boy?' he asked Kath, turning the hat in his hands as he spoke.

Kath shrugged. 'Much the same, I'm afraid.'

Emil didn't move or speak, and to break the awkward

silence, she looked down. 'I see your shoe is still in one piece. So you still have your sole!'

'My soul?' he repeated.

He stood there and, not knowing what to do with him, Kath asked him to come in. She hoped that he wouldn't be long because she still had the washing to do.

Emil followed Kath into the cramped kitchen and wondered how she managed to cook and feed her boys in here. Plates and bowls were stacked up in the sink and on a dresser whose cream paint was peeling off. A strip of sticky orange flypaper hung from the light globe. As he watched, a fly landed on it and buzzed as it tried to extricate itself.

Waving her arm in the direction of the dirty dishes piled up in the small enamel sink, Kath said, 'Excuse the mess. I haven't had time to clear up after breakfast.' There was a strong smell of laundry soap and bleach, and she jumped up. 'Back in a minute,' she said.

Through the open door that led to the back of the house, he watched her pulling clothes from the copper and feeding them through the wringer. Ever since he'd seen the ambulance bringing Meggsie back home, he'd been thinking about the boy and his mother. Although he felt let down by her underhand behaviour in reporting him to the police, he still wondered how she was managing, and how the boy was getting on. But there was another reason why they were constantly in his thoughts, one he had tried for a long time to block from his mind: the boy was about twelve, the same age Heinz would have been.

He waited until Kath came back into the kitchen, and while she was wiping her soapy hands on a tea towel he stammered, 'Can I see the boy?'

When Meggsie saw who it was, his stomach lurched and he felt sick. He knew why Mr Emil was here. Now it would all come out, how he'd sneaked out of the house that night to spy on him, and then written the anonymous note that had got him arrested. Mr Emil would tell him off, and his mum would be upset and angry. He closed his eyes. If Mr Emil thought he was asleep, maybe he'd go away.

But when he peeped, he saw that Mr Emil was looking at him with a strange expression, as if he were seeing something that wasn't there. Meggsie steeled himself for the scolding and waited, so Mr Emil's question took him by surprise.

'Is it maybe disappointing to be home again?'

No one had asked him that before, and he had to think how to reply.

'It's real boring. I hate being in here when all the kids are running around outside, but I hate being out there as well because I can't play with them.' He swallowed. 'They call me a cripple.'

He stopped, not wanting to sound like a whinger, but Mr Emil didn't contradict or say anything to cheer him up. He was nodding as if he understood.

'Do you sometimes dream that you can walk?' he asked.

Meggsie's eyes lit up. This was something else no one had ever asked, something he'd longed to talk about, but the people who came to see him didn't know what to say to him, and he didn't think they'd want to hear things like that. They were either embarrassed or else they felt sorry for him and avoided the one subject that was always on his mind.

'Sometimes,' he said. 'They're my best dreams. But then I wake up and it's all bad again.'

'And then you wish you could go back to sleep and keep having that wonderful dream,' Mr Emil said.

Meggsie nodded, wondering how come Mr Emil knew so much about his dreams which, like magical time machines, sucked you back into the past only to drop you back into the present with a horrible thump.

When Kath put her head around the door a few minutes later to rescue Meggsie from their strange visitor, she found them deep in conversation, although she couldn't imagine what this peculiar foreigner could possibly say that would interest her son.

Walking with Emil to the door, she said, 'Thanks for dropping in. I can see that Meggsie really enjoyed your visit. Please come again.'

He hesitated for a moment, then he said, 'Thank you. I will come. But tell me please. Why you did write a letter about me to the police?'

She stared at him. 'Me? Write a letter to the police?'

This was the second time she'd been accused of writing a note about him, and she wondered if the old busybody across the road had told him she'd written it.

'What on earth makes you think I'd do that?' she asked him.

'I think so your son told you what he saw.'

Kath frowned. 'Saw what? Can you tell me what this is about?'

By the time he'd described Meggsie's nocturnal escapade, it all made sense. The childish scrawl, the paper torn out of an exercise book, and the melodramatic message that sounded like something from a Boy's Own mystery.

'I never wrote that note,' she said, and from the look on his face she realised that he'd figured out who the writer was.

'We will not talk about it any more,' he said.

After he had gone, Kath sat on the edge of Meggsie's bed. 'I know about the note you sent Miss McNulty, and I'm surprised at you,' she began, and he hung his head.

'Look at me when I'm talking to you,' she said. 'First of all, you shouldn't have sneaked out of the house at night and spied on Mr Emil. But the worst thing was writing that note. Did you stop to think what you were doing? You've made a lot of trouble for the poor man. I want you to remember one thing: if you write a letter, always sign your name. Only crooks and cowards send anonymous notes.'

She saw tears in his eyes and softened her tone. 'You're

lucky that Mr Emil isn't angry with you, but it's time you learned that everything we do has consequences, so you've got to think before you do anything that might hurt someone.'

Alone in his room again, Meggsie sighed as he looked at his stiff legs. He knew more about consequences than his mother realised. It was all very well to say Mr Emil wasn't angry, but what was much worse was that God was angry, and that's why He'd punished him for what he'd done. He wondered what Mr Emil would think about that.

Chapter 36

On Sunday afternoons Hania's mother usually invited her friends home for coffee and cake. In the mornings Hania would watch her bustling around the tiny kitchen as she stirred the bubbling yeast mixture in a bowl, placed it in a warm spot and covered it with a tea towel until the dough began to rise. Within an hour, their semi smelled of freshly baked yeast cake filled with poppy seeds or vanilla-scented cream cheese.

The guests were always Polish migrants like themselves. There were two widows and a married couple her mother had befriended on the voyage to Australia, her neighbour Sala, two women who worked with her at the clothing factory, and a woman who lived nearby and mended nylon stockings so that her husband could repeat his dental studies. The husbands rarely came to these Sunday afternoon gatherings. Some were poring over lecture notes in a language they barely understood, while others were taking advantage of their free time to play bridge.

Two of the women usually brought their daughters, who were about Hania's age, and Hania supposed that this was her mother's way of encouraging her to have Jewish friends.

That was enough to put her back up even before they tried to talk her into joining their Jewish youth group. Despite their similar background, Hania felt that she had nothing in common with these girls who, according to her mother, always did as they were told and were perfect in every way. Her mother's praise made Hania dislike them even more. Their strong accents and foreign way of dressing made her cringe, and she hated being in the street with them in case Beverley and the other girls saw them. She wished she could spend Sunday afternoons with Beverley or Tina, but her mother told her to stay home and be hospitable, which she did grudgingly.

She wasn't very keen on her mother's friends, either, especially Pani Niusia, an opinionated little woman with a pursed-up mouth who had a high-pitched voice and an argumentative way of talking. She often tried to talk Hania into going to Habonim with her daughter and pointed out that it was important to maintain a Jewish identity now that they were living in Australia. Her comments irritated Hania, who couldn't resist retorting that she had lots of nice Australian friends and wasn't interested in joining Jewish youth groups.

The only person whose company she enjoyed on those long Sunday afternoons was Sala, who alone seemed interested in Hania's opinions and asked her what she thought about the issues they were discussing.

'Hania has a point,' Sala said when the topic of Jewish youth groups came up yet again one Sunday after Christmas.

'We've always complained about being pushed into ghettoes in Europe, so why are we creating them for ourselves? We're in Australia, so we should mix with Australians.'

Her words caused an uproar. 'Are you suggesting we should stop being Jews?' Pani Niusia demanded, pursing her mouth even more than usual.

'No, all I'm saying is that we should mix more, and become part of the community instead of isolating ourselves. There's enough anti-Semitism without creating more.'

'Do you really think that if we mix with Australians they'll forget we're Jews and treat us as equals?' The speaker was Pani Tosia, who was older than the others. She was a tall woman with regal bearing, and when she spoke in her slow, quiet voice, the others listened.

Her mother's friends were nodding. 'Before the war, my family was assimilated,' Pani Marysia was saying, and her pale blue eyes looked more watery than usual. 'We considered ourselves Poles first and Jews second, and my closest girlfriends were Polish. But as soon as the war started, most of them avoided me like the plague. That's when I realised I'd been kidding myself. In their eyes I was always a Jew. I'd never been one of them.'

Pani Niusia sat forward, ready for an argument and, turning to Sala, she said, 'How can you say we should spend more time with Australians? They have no idea what we went through, and they don't want to know.'

'That's why I like being with them,' Sala said.

Hania sighed. They all lived in the past. No matter what they were talking about, whether it was the recent Vivien Leigh film, Elisabeth Schwarzkopf's recital at the Town Hall, or the latest scandal about Errol Flynn, in no time at all they were back in Poland, discussing their wartime experiences.

On the few occasions when her mother's friends visited without their daughters, Hania would go over to Tina's, but after a few games of jacks or countries, she usually went home because Tina had to help in her parents' milk bar. She resented having to do this as much as Hania hated her mother's social afternoons, and they often commiserated with each other about their old-fashioned parents and restrictive lives. Hania and Tina only had to exchange long-suffering glances to know what the other was thinking. Although she loved Beverley's easygoing company, Tina understood her in a way that Beverley never could.

In the summertime, picnics often replaced the afternoon teas, and her mother's group sat by the duck pond in Centennial Park, talking about old times as they cracked the shells of their hard-boiled eggs and ate rye bread sandwiches spread with *liptauer*, a mixture of cottage cheese, paprika and caraway seeds which Hania didn't like. While the other girls sat beside their mothers, listening to the conversation or chatting to one another, Hania often sat a small distance away, her back against the rough trunk of a stringy-bark as she read *Seven Little Australians* for the third time and tried not to hear what they were saying.

From time to time she was distracted by sulphur-crested cockatoos screeching as they flew among the branches, their wings translucent in the sunlight, or by the ducks quacking in the reed-fringed pond. Sometimes she glanced up as boys playing cricket with their fathers yelled 'Out!' or let out a deafening cheer. Occasionally she heard a peal of laughter from her mother's group. In between their nostalgic and tragic reminiscences, they made fun of their efforts to speak English.

Pani Tosia was telling them about her Australian neighbours, and in spite of herself Hania listened to her pleasant voice. 'They told us they'd just dropped in for a few minutes, but they were still there at midnight, and I thought they'd never go home. Finally they got up to go, but when they were at the front door, they said, "See you later." I was panic-stricken. I thought they were coming back!'

They all laughed and Hania turned her attention back to her book. After a while she was aware that the background noises had stopped, and in the silence she heard her mother's voice.

'I'll never forgive myself as long as I live.'

Hania stiffened and became very still. What was her mother talking about? She had a sense that her mother wouldn't want her to hear what she was saying, and without looking up, she strained to hear, but her mother had lowered her voice and she couldn't catch a single word. When her mother stopped talking, no one spoke, and Hania heard someone blowing their nose.

As usual, Pani Niusia was the first to speak. 'That's terrible, but it wasn't your fault. You couldn't possibly know what would happen.'

There was a pause, and then Hania heard her mother's low voice. 'But it *was* my fault.'

'There are things we all would have done differently if only we'd known what would happen,' Sala said. 'I'm sure that most of us feel guilty about something we did or didn't do during the war. Or just for surviving when the rest of our family didn't.'

When Hania looked up, she saw that Sala had her arm around her mother's trembling shoulders.

The sun was going down, and the stringy-barks glowed in the late-afternoon light. Hania thought there was an air of mystery and magic in the park. They had been reading *A Midsummer Night's Dream* in class, and she could imagine Puck and his elves and fairies peering through the gilded branches of the trees. The women packed up the leftover food in their string bags and headed towards Oxford Street along a path lined with fan palms and stiff-stemmed canna lilies.

'I wish you wouldn't argue so much with Pani Niusia,' Eda said while they were waiting for their tram. 'You always have to have the last word. The other girls don't argue.'

Hania pulled a face. 'Of course not. They're all angels.'

Eda was preparing dinner that evening when, to her obvious surprise, Hania offered to help. In an unusually companionable mood, they began singing 'Buttons and Bows' and 'How Much is that Doggie in the Window' while wrapping minced beef and rice in cabbage leaves and placing them in a large saucepan to simmer with tomatoes.

While they waited for the cabbage rolls to cook, Eda picked up her sewing, and Hania watched her, biding her time as she tried to figure out how to broach the subject that was on her mind.

Her stomach was churning as she said, 'In the park this afternoon you said you could never forgive yourself. What was that about?'

Eda stopped sewing and gave Hania the look that normally silenced her.

'Nothing important,' she said, biting off the thread. 'Can you get me that green spool of cotton from the table?'

'It sounded important,' Hania persisted, handing her the spool.

'Well you shouldn't have been eavesdropping,' Eda snapped.

'How was I to know you were telling secrets?' Hania retorted. 'And how come you can tell those women but not me?' Then she added, 'But of course why would you bother telling me? I don't count.'

She waited for the usual comment about being insolent, but her mother was silent. The lamp cast a shadow over her bowed head. It looked as though she was looking down at the skirt on her lap, but Hania knew she was gazing at the invisible, inaccessible landscape of her past, and, as usual, its gate was locked.

Eda raised her head and looked at Hania searchingly. This time there was no anger in that glance, only great sadness, almost resignation. Putting aside her sewing, she took off her thimble and leaned back in her chair.

'All right, I'll tell you, but you have to promise not to interrupt until I've finished.'

She took a shuddering breath. 'I've never told you this before, but you had a brother.'

Hania opened her mouth to speak but closed it again.

'He was nine when the war broke out. You were two and a half. As soon as the Germans marched into Kraków, they started rounding up the Jews. One day your father went out and never came back. I was frantic and didn't know what to do. I didn't know where to go or who to ask, and all the time I knew I couldn't risk arousing suspicion or they'd take me away too. My parents — your grandparents — were living in Lwów, in the eastern part of Poland. It was occupied by the Russians at the time, not the Germans, so they kept writing to tell me to go there because we'd be safer, but I couldn't think straight. And by the time I decided to join them, there was a border between the German and Russian sectors. Crossing it was illegal, so I had to find someone to smuggle us across.'

Her voice faltered and she pressed a hand over her heart as though to make sure it was still beating.

Hania was staring at her mother and seeing a stranger. Her face, whose contours were usually so well defined, with her high cheekbones and finely moulded features, had sagged, and her eyes had a faraway look.

'I found out there was a fellow who smuggled Jews across the border if you paid him or gave him a diamond. I didn't have much money, so I gave him a gold necklace. We arranged to meet him at the crossroads just outside town, at dawn.'

She swallowed and pressed her handkerchief to her mouth, shaking her head to indicate that she couldn't go on. Hania waited on tenterhooks, but her mother was staring into space.

Eda would never forget the terrible beauty of that morning, with the night frost still glittering on the hard ground, the birch trees powdered with snow, and the steam from her breath warming and moistening the woollen scarf she had wrapped over her mouth.

The three of them were creeping towards the shrine at the crossroads. She was carrying Hania, still warm and drowsy from sleep, with nine-year-old Rysio striding manfully beside them, carrying the big canvas rucksack and protesting that it wasn't heavy.

She could see it all as though it was happening in front of her now, and her heart was knocking against her ribs just as it had that morning when they stood on the dark deserted road as their shadows grew longer and the cold wind blew through the bare branches of the poplars. What if a German patrol drove by? What if a farmer spotted them and reported them to the Gestapo? What if the guide didn't show up? People had warned her that some guides took the money or jewellery and then abandoned the Jews, or denounced them to the Gestapo. She shivered, more from apprehension than from the cold, and looked desperately up and down the road. The minutes seemed like hours until she heard hooves and the clattering of cart wheels along the empty road, and recognised the man in the battered hat holding the reins. She almost collapsed with relief.

He jumped down from his seat, rubbing his big rough hands together to warm them, but he didn't look at her. He was looking sideways and stamping his feet against the cold as he stammered that he was sorry but there was a problem near the border, and he couldn't smuggle all three of them across. He could only take two. Eda stared at him, numb with panic. 'But you promised, you must, you can't do this to us, what am I going to do?' she kept saying. Just thinking about it, she could feel the panic suffocating her all over again.

But her pleas were in vain. He couldn't take three of them and that was that. He suggested that if Rysio stayed in town, he'd come back for him in two days' time. 'We haven't got time to stand here and argue,' he said. 'A German patrol car will be coming past in a few minutes and we'll all end up in a police cell.'

Eda looked around helplessly. She had to think quickly but what should she do? If they all stayed behind hoping to find another guide, they might all be caught. Jews were being rounded up and interned in a camp in Płaszów every day. Their only hope of survival was to head eastwards, away from the Germans. But how could she leave Rysio behind? Could she trust the guide to keep his promise and come back for him?

While she was trying to decide what to do, the guide climbed up onto his seat and picked up the reins. 'Make up your mind quick, missus, because I'm not hanging around here.'

'You go, Mama,' Rysio said. 'I'll be fine.'

Her teeth chattering with panic, she told him to go straight to her aunt's place near the square, and not to move from there until he got a message from her or from the guide.

'Don't worry,' he said, wriggling out of her tight embrace. 'I'm not a baby. I know what to do.'

Her hands trembled as she held them above his head and murmured a blessing in Yiddish for the Almighty to keep him safe.

Still sobbing, she turned to take one last look at him as she climbed into the cart. He was still waving as they turned off at the crossroads. She clutched Hania as they jolted over rutted village roads and already she was reproaching herself for leaving her son. What have I done? I must be insane, she kept telling herself. How could I have agreed to such a crazy plan?

About an hour later the cart stopped at the back of a darkened farmhouse and the guide led them into a barn.

In the dim light she could see a group of silent people with worried faces huddled together on the straw.

She turned angrily to the guide. 'If you can take them, how come you couldn't take my son?'

But he just shrugged and spat into the straw. 'If you don't like it, missus, you can go back.'

She supposed that the others had given him more jewellery. Taking him aside, she undid her gold brooch, the last piece of jewellery she owned, and made him promise on his mother's life that he'd go back for Rysio.

'Sure thing, missus,' he said. 'What do you take me for?'

Eda found a clean spot on the straw for herself and Hania, and took out a piece of bread and some milk for the child. The tension in the barn was palpable. Two middle-aged couples sat in silence but a third couple argued incessantly in querulous voices until Eda felt like shouting at them to be quiet. A young man took out a penknife and started peeling an apple: seeing Hania eyeing the fruit, he sliced off a piece and gave it to her.

Soon the guide returned. 'Time to go,' he whispered.

Warning them not to make a sound, he led them through the back of the village into a birch forest. It was dark, and the white patches on the trunks glowed with an unearthly light. As they stumbled through the woods, they tripped on tree roots or got hooked on the bare branches. Hania whimpered that she was tired, but Eda couldn't carry her all the way because she had the rucksack on her back. She had to stop frequently to catch her breath and give the child a rest while the others trudged on lugging their valises, bags and bundles.

Twigs snapped under their feet as they followed the icy path for almost an hour until they reached the river.

The water had frozen and, to Eda's horror, the guide told them that they had to walk across. By now Hania was exhausted, so Eda unslung the rucksack and put the child on her back. She was about to pick up the rucksack when the young man with the apple took it from her. 'My case is quite small,' he said, 'I can put your rucksack on my back.' She almost cried with gratitude.

A chilly mist rose from the river, and after a few minutes her feet ached with cold. She was terrified of slipping on the ice, or taking a wrong step and falling through a crack into the freezing water. Looking at the tense faces of those around her, she knew that if she fell and injured herself, she'd be left there, and she and Hania would die. She didn't know if it was fear or determination that gave her strength, but somehow she reached the other side, and collapsed onto the frosty ground, sobbing.

As Eda described that unforgettable day, she almost forgot where she was. Suddenly she looked at her daughter. 'You were such a good child. You didn't cry once, or complain. Little as you were, you seemed to understand that we were in danger and you had to be very quiet.

'Our guide left us on the other side of the river, but before he went I made him swear again that he'd pick up Rysio the following day and bring him to Lwów. A peasant was waiting for us with a cart, and he took us to Lwów. From the moment we got to my parents' place, I paced up and down the flat like a wild animal in a cage. I couldn't relax. I kept calling my aunt's house but no one answered, and when I tried to get in touch with the guide, the people who had recommended him said I had the wrong number and hung up. From their tone, I guessed he must have been caught. I was hysterical. I rushed from room to room like a madwoman. I wanted to tear my hair out. My parents tried to calm me down. They told me not to panic, that there was probably a simple explanation. Our relatives must have moved, or gone to hide in someone's place, but I knew that the worst thing that could possibly happen had happened, and that it was all my fault.'

She buried her head in her hands and sobbed. 'It felt as if my heart was being ripped apart inside my chest. I howled like an animal and banged my head against the wall and I wished I could die because I'd left my son to die alone.

'And when I thought things couldn't get any worse, the Germans invaded the eastern part of Poland, and another bloodbath started. And this time the Nazis were hunting down Jewish children.

'There were hardly any Jews left in Lwów by then. My parents had been taken away, and I knew it was just a matter of time before someone pointed me out to the Nazis. Whatever happened to me, I had to find someone to look after you, so you'd survive. And that's how I came to choose Mr and Mrs Majewski.'

The Majewskis, a Catholic couple who lived in the apartment next door to her parents, had no children, and Eda had noticed that whenever Mrs Majewska saw Hania her usually stern face softened and she stopped to talk to her, and sometimes gave her a small toy or a sweet. In desperation, Eda knocked on their door and begged them to take the child. At first they hesitated. They loved little Hania, but everyone knew they didn't have any children, so it would be obvious they were looking after a Jewish child. But the thought of Hania being thrown into a truck and killed kept Mrs Majewska awake at night, and she came up with a solution. They would move to her parents' village. Life in the country would be safer there for them as well as for Hania. As they hadn't been there for several years, they could pass Hania off as their own child. 'Thank God she doesn't look Jewish,' Mr Majewski said. Although Eda tried to put a positive interpretation on his words, they chilled her. But there was no choice. The child's survival was all that mattered.

Eda looked at Hania and hoped that her daughter would finally understand, and stop resenting her. 'I was so grateful to them for taking you that I didn't dwell on the possibility that they might put anti-Semitic ideas in your head, or that they mightn't want to give you back. Knowing that you were safe was the only thing that kept me going all the years I was in the camp. That, and the hope that one day I'd find Rysio and your father. I used to dream of the day I'd see you again and hold you in my arms. It never occurred to me that when I finally came back you wouldn't want me.'

Hania looked close to tears. 'I miss them so much,' she whispered. 'They loved me. They saved my life.'

'*You* are my life,' Eda replied.

A hundred questions were racing through Hania's mind. There was so much she wanted to know about the brother she hadn't known. Within a single hour she had found him and lost him. What did he look like? What did he like doing? Was he good at school? Did he like playing with her? Did he love her? Did she love him? It was unbearable to think that she'd had a brother whom her mother had never even mentioned. She'd kept him a secret and, as usual, she'd locked Hania out of her life.

Several times Eda started to say something but Hania was too distraught to listen. 'I bet you wish I was the one you left behind, and he was the one who survived,' she burst out, and rushed from the room sobbing.

She had to be alone. Too much pain, too much guilt, too many secrets. She curled up on her bed and clasped the little gold cross in her hand. She tried to recall the big brother she had probably adored, but she couldn't remember anything about him, and a wave of confused emotions swept over her. Anger towards the Nazis, pity for her mother, grief for her brother, regret for her foster parents, and sadness for herself.

The war had always seemed to be her mother's tragedy, but now for the first time Hania realised that she had lost far more than just her foster parents. She saw herself as that scared child in the barn with strangers, crossing the frozen river and then witnessing her mother's hysteria and grief, and sensing that something terrible had happened and that her mother wasn't strong enough to protect her.

It was too much to absorb, too much to cope with. Her brother had died but she had survived. Why? Was that pure chance, or part of a divine plan? But what kind of God lets children be killed, and favours one child over another? And what about Jesus and what he said about little children? Were those just empty words?

She didn't know how long she lay on the bed, clutching the cross so tightly that it became imprinted on her hand, and feeling overwhelmed by questions that had no answers, and emotions that threatened to pull her into a whirlpool in which she would drown. With a cry she gripped her throbbing head with both hands, and didn't notice that the cross had slid to the floor.

After a time, the darkness lifted and, through a narrow crack in her confused mind, a chink of light appeared. She slipped off the bed, tiptoed down the dark hall to the lounge room. Her mother was slumped in her chair under the lamp, her head in her hands. She started when Hania's shadow fell across her face and she caught her breath, as though she'd seen a ghost.

'That day we escaped across the border and you left Rysio behind,' Hania said slowly. 'You really chose me, didn't you, Mamusia?'

Tears filled Eda's eyes. 'Of course I chose you,' she whispered, and drew her closer.

Hania flung her arms around her mother's neck, and they clung to each other without speaking.

Chapter 37

Verna Browning hurried across the road with a batch of scones she'd just baked, and found Kath sitting alone in the kitchen.

'I've found a nurse who might be able to help Meggsie but I can't afford to pay her,' she sighed.

Verna put her hand on Kath's shoulder. 'Isn't there anyone who could help you out?'

Kath shrugged. 'My sister lives out west, and my brothers are in the navy. I've never been able to rely on any of them for anything. If I don't find a job soon, I'll have to ask Gran to lend me some money to tide me over. She thinks I'm a no-hoper as it is, so I'll never hear the end of it.'

Verna walked home slowly, on a carpet of bruised frangipani flowers which released their perfume as she stepped on them. Life was so unfair. Her husband dead in battle, Kath deserted, and Meggsie stricken down. The minister in her church always said that everything happened for a reason, but you had to wonder what reason there could possibly be for all that unhappiness.

As she opened her wooden gate she heard the dry scritching

sound of a whisk broom on the tile verandah next door, and knew that Maude McNulty was out there, watching everything as she swept.

'So what's the latest with the barmaid?' she asked in her reedy voice.

Although Verna made a point of not discussing Kath with her cranky neighbour, she was so upset by Kath's predicament that she blurted out, 'The poor thing's having such a bad time. That boy of hers is just wasting away, and there's a nurse who could help him if only Kath had the money.'

She shook her white head and sighed. 'Lord only knows what will become of him.'

'I always said she should put him in one of those places for cripples,' Maude McNulty said, leaning on her broom.

'Well that's very helpful,' Verna snapped, and without another look in her neighbour's direction, she went inside, slamming the door behind her.

'Nasty old witch,' she muttered to herself, and wished she'd held her tongue.

The plight of the boy next door was on Emil's mind too. Every evening when he came home from the furniture factory he would sit in front of the coffins and light the candles, his head bowed and eyes closed, as if in prayer. But as soon as he rose and started pottering around the kitchen to make himself some dinner, it was the red-headed boy next door who occupied his thoughts.

A week after his first visit, he rang their doorbell again. This time Kath beamed when she saw him, and without waiting for him to speak, she led him straight into Meggsie's room.

'Mr Emil, do you think God always punishes us when we do something wrong?' Meggsie asked.

'Sometimes He punishes people even when they don't do anything wrong,' he said bitterly.

Meggsie looked puzzled. 'How do you know?'

'Believe me, I know.'

They sat in silence while Emil looked around the room. A half-empty glass of water stood on a pile of tattered comic books on a small plywood table, and beside the comics stood a balsawood model of a Spitfire. On top of the crocheted patchwork quilt on the bed lay an open book, face down, and when Emil bent his head to read the title, he caught his breath. It was Heinz's favourite story, the one Emil used to read to him in their Berlin apartment every night before he went to sleep. The memory was so sharp that he clutched his chest as though he'd been stabbed.

'Are you okay, Mr Emil?' Meggsie asked.

Emil nodded. When he could speak again, he said, 'This book is wonderful.'

'It's my favourite book,' Meggsie said.

When Kath put her head around the door half an hour later, they were discussing tunnels and whether it was possible to dig your way through stone to escape.

She cleared the small table, placed a tray with two cups of tea and some scones on it, and went out again.

As they sipped their tea, Emil looked at Meggsie.

'Why do you ask if God punishes people?' he asked.

Meggsie shrugged. 'Just wondering. There are so many people on earth, how does God know what everyone's been doing? And how does He arrange the punishment?'

Emil knew why Meggsie felt guilty, and he sometimes wondered if the boy would ever admit what he'd done.

'I'm sure God understands that even good boys sometimes do naughty things,' he said.

'But you said that He punishes good people too.'

The conversation had moved into treacherous depths, beyond metaphysics and philosophy into the personal experience of evil, and Emil didn't know how to extricate himself from it. The boy had a good mind and deserved sensible answers, but Emil didn't want to disillusion him. In any case, he wasn't a philosopher or a clergyman, and he didn't feel qualified to engage in such a discussion. Or perhaps he was too well qualified.

'God did punish me,' Meggsie was saying. He spoke so slowly and quietly that he might have been thinking aloud. 'That's why I got sick and won't ever be able to walk again.'

Emil leaned towards him. 'Why do you say that? That's not true. You will get better and then you'll walk again.'

But Meggsie was shaking his head. 'No I won't. It's impossible.'

Emil jabbed his index finger at Meggsie. 'Nothing is impossible. Remember Edmond Dantès.'

Meggsie looked taken aback by Emil's forceful tone but he shrugged and looked away.

'That was just a story,' he said dully.

That night, as he tried to get to sleep, Meggsie couldn't get the image of Mr Emil's momentary transformation out of his mind. He'd never heard him speak so forcefully before. It was almost as though he'd turned into another person. Mr Emil was the most terrific person he knew and he hoped he'd never find out why Meggsie was being punished. He knew he should own up and say he was sorry for what he'd done, but if he did, Mr Emil might never come to see him again. He couldn't risk that.

Late at night, after the boys had gone to bed and she had finished all the chores, Kath sat in the kitchen, racking her brains for a way out. There weren't many options. She'd done the rounds of the local stores and restaurants, but those that had vacancies wanted someone full-time, and she had to be home part of the day to look after Meggsie. If only she could find the money to pay that Kenny nurse. Her only chance was to ask her former boss at the pub for help. He'd probably lend her the money, but she knew what he'd expect in return. She would do almost anything to help Meggsie, but not that.

* * *

Kath's problems had played on Verna's mind all day, and over dinner that evening she turned to Ted.

'You reporters spend most of your time writing about crooks and swindlers, but what about all the ordinary decent people who have to battle all the time?'

'Vice sells papers, virtue doesn't,' he said as he cut his steak. 'That's a fact of life.'

'Well I think it's a bloody shame.'

Ted raised his eyebrows. His mother really had a bee in her bonnet about the kid across the road. But he had his own obsession too. He caught himself searching for Lilija on the tram, in the city streets or at the beach, always scanning the crowd for a glimpse of her dazzling face. At home he often hung around the front gate, smoking a cigarette or pushing the leaves and fallen flowers backwards and forwards on the tiled verandah just in case she happened to walk past.

On a warm summer evening with a clear starlit sky and a bright crescent moon, Ted stood in the doorway blowing smoke rings into the air, fighting an aching feeling of emptiness.

Although he'd dismissed his mother's comment, it bothered him. There was no denying that his profession focused on the worst traits of human nature. Something his father used to say flashed into his mind. 'You can't do anything about the length of your life, but you can do a lot about the width and depth of it.' He dismissed the uncomfortable thought. After all, he had plenty of time to create some depth in his life.

Grinding his cigarette butt on the verandah with his shoe, he kicked it into the dirt and took another look at the empty street. Somewhere a cat on heat was yowling, and the strident sound made his scalp prickle. And then he saw her. Closing her front gate carefully behind her, she crept along the street, keeping to the shadowy part of the footpath. He flattened himself against his front door, wondering where she was going alone at night; then, to his amazement, she stopped outside his gate, glanced around and placed her hand on the latch.

As he came out of the shadows, her hand flew to her mouth to suppress a cry of surprise. Her face was as white and taut as the time he'd come to her home and, despite the warm air, she was trembling.

'I waited for them to sleep so I could come.'

She spoke in a whisper and kept looking around.

He drew her onto the verandah, breathing in the floral fragrance of her skin. It had been so long since he'd heard the Baltic lilt of her voice and seen the little pointed tips of her ears showing through hair that gleamed in the moonlight.

'How come you wanted to see me?' His voice was muffled, and for some reason he had to keep clearing his throat.

She looked down at her hands. 'I think about you. All the time.'

Ted was grappling with so many conflicting emotions that

he couldn't think clearly. Resentment, anger and confusion were mixed up with the rapture of seeing her again and hearing the words he'd dreamed of for so long. She shivered again, and he put his arm around her slim shoulders and drew her down onto the doorstep beside him. They sat in silence, her head resting on his shoulder.

He drew away and looked into her eyes until she met his gaze. 'Why did it take you so long?' he asked.

She bit her lip. 'You do not understand. You are Australian. I am Latvian. What my father says, I must do.'

'But you didn't tonight,' he said.

She glanced around again. 'I couldn't wait more. But I cannot upset him. He had bad time in war. Sometimes he shouts in sleep. He has, how you say it, night horses?'

Ted's resentment rose up again. 'What on earth does your father have against me? Is it because I'm an Aussie?'

She nodded. 'And you are journalist. He says journalists are, how you say, animals that eat dead bodies.'

'Hyenas,' he said bitterly. 'So he's got it in for me because I'm a reporter.'

'He don't — doesn't like things you write.'

He was about to ask which of his articles had upset her father so much, when he looked at her, leaning against him with her hair spread out on his chest. Why waste time trying to analyse her father and his wartime nightmares? Bending down, he kissed her lips and pressed her so tightly against him that he could feel every contour of her soft body.

'I love you, Lilija,' he said in between kisses. 'I can't live without you. You're all I think about. We're going to be together, no matter what your father thinks of journalists or Australians. This is Australia, he can't lock you up and tell you how to live. You're not a child.'

The cat was still yowling, and she turned in the direction of the sound before replying.

'You do not understand,' she said. 'He loves me. He wants to protect me.'

Ted opened his mouth to argue but stopped himself. She was right. He didn't understand this mentality and never would, but it didn't matter. One day he'd have to confront this tyrant and tell him that he couldn't live his daughter's life, but now he just wanted to relish this fantastic moment.

She was stroking his cheek. 'We will meet in town. Like first time, yes?'

She was looking up at him and he bent down and crushed her mouth with kisses while his hungry hands slid down the front of her blouse, tentatively at first, until they found her breasts and he almost stopped breathing as he felt their softness and warmth.

She made a small movement as though to stop him but closed her eyes and threw her head back as she surrendered to the urgency of his touch.

The cat was shrieking in the relentless throes of mating, providing an unsettling soundtrack to their lovemaking.

'I'm so happy, I could die right now,' he murmured. His own words took him by surprise, and the rawness of his emotion brought tears to his eyes. No matter what happened, he would never let her go again.

Chapter 38

Kath was sweeping the hall when she noticed the corner of a white envelope poking under her front door. She rested the broom against the wall and picked it up. Apart from the occasional get well card for Meggsie, and a few words of encouragement written by one of the schoolteachers or someone in a nearby street, she rarely received any letters. The envelope didn't have her name or address on it. Perhaps it was a notice of some kind, advertising a sale or the opening of a new store.

When she tore open the flap and looked inside, her eyes widened. The envelope contained the thickest wad of pound notes she'd ever seen outside the cash register in the pub. She checked the envelope again but there was no letter. Sinking into a kitchen chair, she glanced around to make sure she wasn't being watched, and enjoyed feeling the weight of all that money before starting to count it. Fifty pounds! A fortune. She riffled through the notes to make sure she hadn't overlooked a letter, glanced around, and stuffed the notes hurriedly back into the envelope, elated and uneasy at the same time.

Someone had slipped that money under her door, but who and why? She'd seen enough crime movies with James Cagney, Edward G Robinson and Humphrey Bogart to suspect some ulterior motive. Maybe someone had stolen it and ditched it in a hurry. Perhaps she was being framed.

It flashed through her mind that she could hide the money and pretend she hadn't seen it, but the crook would probably knock on her door one day and bash the truth out of her. But by then she would have spent it all, and then they'd either kill her or set the cops on her for stealing it.

She slipped her hand into the envelope again and felt the thickness of the wad with longing. All that money. If only she could keep it. She took her old jewellery box from the top of the dresser and jammed the notes inside. For once the box was so full that she had trouble closing the lid. Pushing the box under her pillow, she covered it with her candlewick bedspread and ran across the road to tell Verna Browning.

Grabbing Kath's arm in excitement, Verna said, 'What a windfall! Well, you asked for a miracle and you got one.'

Kath looked dubious. 'But who is it from? I don't know anyone with that much money. And why didn't they include a note, or at least write their name?'

'Maybe they're shy and don't want any thanks. In the papers they're always writing about people making anonymous donations to flood victims, cancer sufferers and suchlike.'

'Well I'm not a flood victim, and anyway, I can't think of anyone who'd do that.'

'Don't let it worry you,' Verna said. 'It's not as if you found it in the street and didn't hand it in. Whoever left it meant you to have it.'

'Maybe I should go to the police and ask if anyone has reported it missing, in case it was stolen,' Kath said slowly.

Verna was shaking her head. 'I wouldn't do that, love. Someone put it there because they know you need it, so use it.'

The first thing Kath did when she returned home was to make sure the money was still where she'd left it. Then she went in to check on Meggsie. Night fell quickly on these midsummer evenings, and the children had stopped their games and gone home for tea, so there were no sounds in the darkening street. In his room, Meggsie was staring into space, sad and listless. Seeing him like that made her feel like crying, but she swallowed hard to stop the tears.

She turned up the volume on the radio in the kitchen and switched the dial to his favourite serial, *Yes, What?* But for once the exasperated schoolteacher and his cheeky pupils didn't bring a smile to his pale face.

Putting her head around the kitchen door she shouted, 'Alan! Ray! Come in here at once and play with your brother!'

'Aw, not now, Mum, we're building a tower with the blocks Uncle Bill gave us for Christmas,' Alan called back.

She rushed into their room, grabbed them by the arms and pulled them to their feet. 'Did you hear what I said? Or do I have to take the wooden spoon to you so you do as you're told?'

She could hear them muttering as they stomped around their room. Selfish little brutes, only thinking of themselves. Only little Pete showed any spontaneous feeling for Meggsie.

Without being told, he often perched on his bed and chattered about school and the footie or played snap with him until Meggsie's arms grew too tired to hold the cards.

'It's okay, Mum, I'll read my book,' Meggsie called out.

She felt guilty now for rousing on the boys. They were only kids and it wasn't their fault they had a sick brother and a mum who'd just about reached the end of her tether. While she stirred breadcrumbs into the mince, and shaped the mixture into rissoles for dinner, she thought about what Verna had said. Perhaps she should keep the money and use it to get Meggsie treated, so one day maybe he'd walk again …

Lost in her daydream, she hadn't noticed that the meat had caught on the bottom of the frying pan and the smell of burning filled the kitchen. 'Bloody hell,' she muttered as she wiped the spattering fat off the stovetop. Now the rissoles were ruined. Cursing under her breath, she moved the blackened patties around with her spatula and added some water to the pan to stop them drying out when the doorbell rang. She ran to the door, half expecting to see a policeman standing there with a search warrant, or a mean-eyed character in a long trenchcoat and black fedora. Thank goodness it was only Mr Emil, who gave her his stiff little bow and headed straight for Meggsie's room.

As Kath scraped the burnt bits off the rissoles it suddenly struck her that it might have been Mr Emil who'd slipped the money under her door. He was exactly the kind of person Verna had mentioned, shy and self-effacing. He'd be one of those anonymous donors who'd hate being thanked. Then there was his recent friendship with Meggsie. And it couldn't be mere coincidence that he had turned up half an hour after she found the money. It all added up. And since no one knew anything about him, he could easily have lots of money stashed away. He could even be forging it. She stopped stirring the rissoles. What if the money was counterfeit and she was caught passing it? The cops would never believe that she'd found it under her front door. If only she knew what to do.

As soon as Meggsie saw Mr Emil, he put down the book he was reading but he didn't smile.

'That show I wanted to see, you know, Morris the Magnificent, well it's finished, and now I'll never get to see him,' he said.

It was strange that he found it much easier to confide in Mr Emil than in anyone else. He didn't want to add to his mother's distress by telling her how miserable he was, and as for the neighbours, he knew it wasn't nice to complain or make a fuss. In any case, they wouldn't know what to say if he told them how he really felt.

As for the other kids, he already felt he was living on a different planet from them. By the way they wriggled, sighed and kept asking the same questions without waiting for his answers, he knew he made them uncomfortable. They couldn't relate to his life and he couldn't relate to theirs any more. The only one he would have liked to talk to was Hanny because he knew she'd listen and understand, but she still wasn't allowed to come and see him, and dropped in only when her mother was out.

'Morris the Magnificent?' Emil repeated.

'He was supposed to do the bullet trick in his show,' Meggsie said. 'You know, the one where the magician's helper points a pistol at him and really shoots him. Did you know that's the most dangerous trick in the world?'

Emil nodded. 'How do you know about it?'

'There was a book about magicians in the library at school and I borrowed it before I got sick. One magician got killed doing it. Chinese, I think he was.'

'Chung Ling Soo,' Emil said.

'How did you know that?' Meggsie asked, amazed. There was no end to Mr Emil's surprises. Not only had he read *The Count of Monte Cristo* and loved it as much as Meggsie did, but he knew about the bullet trick as well.

'Like you, I read about it,' Emil said. 'But he wasn't really Chinese at all. Chung Ling Soo was his stage name. He was American, but he didn't speak very clearly so he pretended to be Chinese and did his show in silence.'

Meggsie was looking at him with awe. 'Gosh, Mr Emil, you know everything. Do you know anything about Houdini?'

Emil smiled at the boy. Houdini had been his inspiration from childhood. He'd read everything he could find about the phenomenal escapist, and became convinced that Houdini's

343

performances weren't merely shows, they were real-life dramas in which he was always alone, fighting for his life, as he struggled to free himself from situations where the odds were always stacked against him. To Emil there was something mysterious in the way Houdini's acts crossed the boundary from magic to mysticism. In his feats of unpicking locks and escaping while tied up in chains even when he was underwater, Houdini seemed almost to want to escape from himself, to test the limits of his strength and challenge his own mortality. That was something Emil could understand.

'Houdini did not like people who said they could contact the dead,' he said to Meggsie. 'Have you heard of Arthur Conan Doyle who wrote the Sherlock Holmes stories?'

Meggsie nodded, and he went on. 'He and Houdini became friends, but there was one thing they never agreed on. Conan Doyle believed the psychics who said they could contact his dead son, but Houdini thought they were charlatans who were tricking him.'

Meggsie was staring at him round-eyed. 'And what do you think, Mr Emil? Who was right?'

Emil shrugged. 'I do not know, but I understand Conan Doyle. When you have lost someone you love, you want to believe the clairvoyants.'

He sighed and changed the subject, and for the remainder of his visit they talked about Houdini's miraculous escapes from locks and chains.

* * *

Kath had been listening out for Emil, and as soon as she heard his soft footsteps in the hall she came out from the kitchen, wiping her hands on her apron. She had been rehearsing how to thank him for his gift in a way that wouldn't embarrass him.

'I wanted to tell you how much we appreciate your kindness,' she began, but before she could say any more, he gave a curt nod, rammed on his little hat and hurried from the house.

Chapter 39

Ever since their fight about Ernst Hauptmann, Sala and Szymon had hardly spoken to each other. Usually their arguments ended quickly, but this time she couldn't forgive him for what he'd said. As for Szymon, he'd become unusually quiet and brooding, like a volcano about to erupt. Although she kept to her side of the bed and shrank from any accidental touch, she resented that he didn't reach for her any more, and no longer called her Salcia.

They were having dinner in silence a week after the argument when, exasperated by his morose expression, she banged her knife and fork down on the table. 'How long are you going to keep this up? What's the point of dwelling on the past?'

He looked up from his plate, met her eyes for a moment and looked away again.

'It's not the past I'm upset about,' he said. 'It's the present. I knew you didn't love me when we got married, but I hoped things would change. Well they haven't, and I've been thinking maybe we should separate.'

Sala stared at him. Although she'd often thought the same thing, and sometimes said so to provoke him during an argument, she was shocked to hear him say it. More than the words, it was the deadly calm with which he spoke that stung the most. Instead of shouting or spitting out hurtful words, he spoke quietly and with great sadness. He'd obviously been mulling over it for some time.

In the emotional seesaw of their relationship, she had always held more power. She was the one who threatened to leave because she knew that he couldn't bear the thought of losing her, and that her threat would put an end to the argument and lead to renewed affection. Now the ground had unexpectedly shifted under her feet, and she was struggling to find her balance.

'Do whatever you like,' she said coldly, and started clearing away the dishes.

The following morning they dressed, gulped their coffee standing up and left for work without exchanging a word. It was New Year's Eve and they had been invited to Fela and Lutek's place that evening. If it hadn't been for the fact that Alex would be there, Sala would have made an excuse not to go, but the urge to see him again was too strong to resist.

On her way home from the Jewish Welfare Society that morning, she bought a white pique blouse with a plunging neckline which revealed her cleavage. She experimented with her hair and decided to leave it loose for a change, parted on the side.

When Szymon came home from work, neither of them spoke as they dressed. Sala was pleased with her reflection in the fly-spotted mirror, but for once Szymon didn't comment on her appearance.

'Look at you!' Alex exclaimed and came towards her with his arms outstretched as soon as they walked into Fela and Lutek's flat.

Turning to Fela, he said, 'You didn't tell me Lauren Bacall was coming tonight!'

He was squeezing Sala's waist, pressing her against him, and as she wriggled out of his playful embrace, her face was flushed and she laughed for the first time that week.

She was relieved that Fela and Lutek had invited three other couples, so that she could avoid Szymon without making the strain in their relationship obvious. Looking around the room, Sala saw Franka Feldman deep in conversation with a short man with bushy hair. She hadn't expected to see her there, but it wasn't surprising that members of the Polish Jewish community knew each other.

Franka introduced her to her husband Zenek, whose watchful, heavy-lidded eyes had a bemused expression that made Sala feel uncomfortable. She was trying to think of something to say when she remembered that he was studying medicine again.

'How are you finding your course, Dr Feldman?' she asked.

With a short laugh, he ran his small hands through the clumps of crinkly hair on either side of his pink scalp.

'How do I find it? Not so good. Look, I was a psychiatrist in Warsaw for over twenty years, so being treated like an ignorant student by lecturers half my age is pretty hard to take, but I'm regarding it as one of life's never-ending lessons. For most of the students I'm something of an oddity, an old man who can hardly speak English, can't play poker, doesn't drink and doesn't understand cricket. Luckily there are a few returned soldiers doing the course who are a bit more mature.'

He rested his somnolent brown eyes on her. 'And what about you? How are you finding life?'

Knowing that he was a psychiatrist made her choose her words with great care, and she gave a brief, noncommittal reply. He nodded and waited but, wary of revealing the turmoil she was in, she said lightly, 'Language problems, money problems, just the usual things.'

She found his gaze disconcerting and scanned the room for Alex, but he was murmuring something to a pretty brunette, so she turned her attention back to Dr Feldman. From his half-smile she could tell he'd followed her glance.

'The first year in a foreign country is very tough on migrant couples, don't you think?' he said.

'I always thought only the first twenty years were tough,' she quipped.

He was studying her with obvious interest and, regretting her flippant remark, she added, 'I always thought that starting a new life together would bring people closer.'

He shook his head. 'Grief, loss and trauma tear most couples apart.'

She wondered why he'd brought up the subject of marital problems, but she remembered Franka saying that their first year in Australia had been traumatic, so perhaps Dr Feldman was probing to see if other couples experienced similar difficulties.

Her mother used to say that psychiatrists chose their speciality in the hope of solving their own problems, and she wondered if that was the case with him. Or perhaps he'd seen her looking at Alex and suspected something. Psychiatrists were good at getting people to expose their innermost thoughts and feelings, and she felt increasingly uncomfortable, as though her mind had suddenly become transparent and he could see her naked thoughts. But although she wanted to keep her feelings secret, at the same time she felt tempted to reveal her turmoil, in case he understood what she was going through and could tell her whether she was normal or not.

Choosing her words carefully, she said, 'When you said that grief and trauma tear couples apart, did you mean grief and trauma they'd gone through together, or individually?'

He raked his fingers through the clumps of crinkly grey hair again. 'Either. The point is, if people haven't confronted their past and dealt with it, it can destroy their life and their relationship.'

The speed with which he'd summed up her dilemma was unnerving, and Sala was relieved when Lutek played an imaginary fanfare with a rolled-up serviette and asked everyone to sit down for dinner. When Fela came in carrying a large platter, all conversation stopped. As Lutek carved the crisp skin of the roast ducks stuffed with apples, a mouth-watering aroma filled the room and evoked a flood of nostalgia.

'I haven't seen ducks like that since Friday nights at my mother's house,' Franka sighed.

The others began reminiscing about festive meals they remembered from home, and the women exchanged recipes for roast goose, chicken soup, chopped liver, and honey cake.

'When I was in the camp,' Franka mused, 'all we talked about was food. We exchanged recipes as though talking about food would fill our stomachs. I couldn't stop thinking about all the wonderful food I used to leave on my plate at home. I thought God had punished me for wasting so much food.'

'Ah, the free-floating guilt that hovers above us all, ready to weigh us down,' Zenek Feldman said, and the corners of his mouth turned up mischievously as he spread his small pink hands. 'Where does it come from?'

He intended it as a rhetorical question, but it provoked a heated discussion about the relative roles of religion, society and upbringing in the creation of guilt.

Alex turned away from the brunette, who was laughing at something he said. 'And what about Jewish mothers?' he exclaimed. 'Aren't they the ones who filled us all with guilt?'

He was smiling, and from his light-hearted tone Sala wondered whether guilt ever intruded on his pleasures.

In the midst of the discussion, someone called out, 'Hey, listen, everyone, it's midnight!'

While the other couples embraced, Sala hung back, aware of Szymon's eyes on her, but neither of them moved. Franka was the first to step towards Sala and wish her a happy new year. 'You'll be starting your course soon, won't you?' she asked, and clinked glasses. 'Here's to your success.'

Sala looked around for Alex and felt a jealous twinge as he put his arm around his pregnant wife and whispered something in her ear.

She turned away but a moment later she felt an arm squeezing her waist. 'Happy New Year!' Alex whispered. 'I hope all your wishes come true. And I hope at least one of them is the same as mine.'

She leaned towards him, aware that his hungry eyes were on her cleavage. Blushing, she stepped back. She didn't want to be undressed twice in the same evening.

That night she fell asleep thinking about Alex, but she dreamed about the cellar again. She'd had the dream so often that even while she slept she knew it was a dream. Again she was wandering through her empty house when she saw the trapdoor; she knew straightaway that it led to the cellar. Her fingers trembling with anticipation, she opened it, but when she looked inside, it was Alex in there, waiting for her, and she woke up with a start and a strangled cry.

She threw off the damp sheet and staggered to her feet, still dazed by the dream. Her eyes, puffy after a restless night, strayed to the calendar. She tore it off the wall and tossed it into the wastepaper basket. It was the first day of the new year. She had come to a country that was a blank slate on which she could rewrite her life, but so far the slate was full of errors. By day she dreamed about a man who was married, and by night she was haunted by a man accused of war crimes.

She heard children shouting and realised it was a public holiday, and she was alone. Szymon had left early, probably to avoid being with her. She pulled the cord of the brown Holland blind with a jerk and the cord came away in her hand. It was a brilliant summer's day, the kind of day she and Szymon had dreamed of when they'd thought of Australia, and as she breathed in the scent of frangipanis from the tree next door, she sank onto the bed again and wondered what Dr Feldman would make of her dream.

Chapter 40

The small brass plaque screwed onto the façade of the office building was so tarnished that Ted could hardly make out the words. Few passers-by would have noticed that this building housed the headquarters of the Anti-Fascist Society, but perhaps that was the idea. The building was behind the Hotel Australia, in a narrow street where arty coffee shops and quaint tearooms attracted painters, students and intellectuals, while boutiques with Paris hats and American costume jewellery catered for women willing to pay for imported accessories.

To the left of the building a tiny shop sold gramophone records and sheet music, while to the right a boutique called Couture displayed a chic black dress in the window, hinting at the exclusive nature of its merchandise.

The music shop was playing 'Because' and Ted paused to listen to the mellow voice of Perry Como crooning the song which was on the hit parade. Once, he would have cringed at the sentimental lyrics, but now he marvelled at how well they expressed his own feelings. Mesmerised by the romantic mood of the song, he was looking through the shop window at photos of Peggy Lee, Doris Day and Bing Crosby when he saw reflected in the glass a man standing in front of the Edna

May tearoom across the road, reading a newspaper which covered his face.

The last chords of the love song faded away and Ted watched the sales assistant take the seventy-eight off the turntable and replace it in its brown paper sleeve. When he turned around, the man had gone, swallowed up in the lunchtime crowd of office girls in their summer dresses, sales assistants in their black skirts, and bookkeepers in grey suits, all rushing to pay off their lay-bys, meet their boyfriends or to eat their sandwiches on the lawns of Hyde Park in the brilliant January sunshine.

Ted had rushed from the newsroom to keep his appointment with the President of the Anti-Fascist Society. For the past ten days Gus had kept him busy chasing up stories for his series on juvenile crime, and this was his first opportunity to find out about the group whose name he'd seen on the file in Sir Lachlan's Canberra office.

The society's office was on the third floor. Ted took one look at the antiquated lift with its brass buttons and concertina-style wrought-iron door and decided to use the stairs. Ever since his reunion with Lilija he'd felt like an elastic band stretched to snapping point, too restless to keep still. He glanced at his watch for the tenth time. They'd arranged to meet outside Cahill's in Castlereagh Street at six o'clock, and time was moving very slowly.

He stopped on the first landing to catch his breath and look around. Most of the offices on the first floor were tenanted by jewellers, whose showroom doors were secured by iron bars. There was A Finkelstein and Sons, Diamonds; Thomas Crawford, Estate Jewellery; and Joseph Berry, Antique Jewellery. Perhaps one day he'd bring Lilija here to choose an engagement ring. That thought gave him such a boost of energy that he sprinted up the next two flights without stopping for breath.

There were only two tenants on the third floor. Facing the lift was a glass door whose assertive black letters proclaimed *Frank Daley, Private Investigator Extraordinaire. Divorce Cases a Speciality.*

A small round hole in the centre of the door indicated that someone had taken exception to his investigating style. Ted wasn't surprised. Frank Daley was frequently mentioned in salacious divorce cases, and a stock photograph of his pugnacious face often accompanied the newspaper reports.

Only a few days before, the *Daily Standard* had reported on a divorce case in which Frank had provided the crucial piece of evidence. He had testified that he'd caught the couple in question *in flagrante delicto*. 'In the act,' he'd explained with a smirk, in case the presiding judge wasn't familiar with Latin. Pressing his face against the car window, Frank had asked the woman, 'Girlie, have you got your panties on?' whereupon her companion had punched him in the nose.

When Ted's mother had read this article, she'd thrown the newspaper into the wastepaper basket in disgust. 'Do we really need all those details in our daily papers?' she'd said with a reproachful look at Ted, as though he was responsible for his paper's contents.

Perhaps the fellow he'd noticed outside the building had a grievance against Frank Daley and was waiting to give the private eye another punch in the nose. Ted chuckled at his own suspicious nature. That was the trouble with being a reporter: you were always snooping around, ferreting out information and looking for sinister motives. The bloke might simply be waiting for his wife.

Past Frank Daley's rooms, Ted came to the office of the Anti-Fascist Society. The wooden architrave had once been painted cream, but much of the paint had peeled and was hanging off in strips, showing mottled patches of timber underneath. A Venetian blind the colour of stale tea hung crookedly over the glass. The name of the organisation was printed in small letters on the right-hand side of the door, and again Ted had the feeling that this group didn't want to attract attention.

He pressed the buzzer and waited. Through the grimy slats of the blind he could make out people moving around, and he could hear voices, but no one came. He pressed the buzzer again, and the door was opened by a flustered young woman with frizzy hair, which stood out from her head like a halo, and a blouse that needed tucking into her dowdy skirt.

'I've got an appointment with Mr Klein,' Ted told her.

Gesturing towards an unravelling cane chair in the corner, she said, 'I'll let him know you're here,' and walked away.

He looked around the office. Six or seven people, mostly men, were sitting around a long table behind piles of newspapers and magazines. Every so often someone picked up a pair of scissors and cut out an item which they passed to the only other girl in the room, who slathered it with glue and pasted it into a bulging scrapbook.

'Not another Communist threat to democracy!' she groaned in mock dismay when the fellow on her left leaned over to pass her a clipping.

'Listen to this,' someone called out in a foreign accent. 'Is letter from man in camp in Bathurst. He say Nazis in his hut want kill him.'

Chairs scraped on the wooden floor and within a few moments the others were leaning over his shoulder as he read out the letter.

'Bloody mongrels,' someone drawled in a broad Australian accent. 'They keep harping on about Commies, but they don't give a bugger about the fucking fascists they've let into the country.'

The girl who had opened the door gave the speaker a disapproving look. Someone gestured towards Ted and, glancing uneasily in his direction, they lowered their voices. As he strained to hear what they were saying, he had the feeling he'd infiltrated a clandestine society.

They were still whispering when a tall man in shirtsleeves strode towards him, hand outstretched, and apologised for keeping him waiting.

The moment Harold Klein appeared, the energy in the office changed. His grey-speckled hair curled tightly around his head as though about to spring out; his blue eyes burned with intensity; and when he spoke, his London-accented words tumbled out so fast that he was continually interrupting himself.

Placing his hand on Ted's shoulder, he ushered him into the recess in the far corner of the room which served as his office. It consisted of a small pine desk, a black bakelite telephone, a few books stacked on a shelf, and one chair.

'Wait, wait, I'll be back in a minute,' he called, and returned a moment later dragging a chair for Ted.

'Coffee's coming,' he said. 'Instant, is that okay? We're not very flush here, you understand. We're all volunteers. The donations only cover the rent. Thank goodness we have enough for that, otherwise … Oh, and by the way, we did appreciate the article you wrote about Bonegilla.'

'But it didn't change anything,' Ted said.

'It told the bleeding truth, didn't it?' Harold said. 'That was a change.'

Leaning towards Ted, he asked, 'Tell me, how did you hear about us? Wait, wait,' he waved his hand as Ted began to explain. 'I just wanted to say, as you can probably tell, we don't go out of our way to attract publicity.'

The young woman with the frizzy hair brought their coffee in thick mugs.

'So how did you find out about us?' Harold asked again.

When Ted explained that he'd seen their name on the desk of the Secretary of the Department of Immigration, Harold's laughter boomed across the entire office. 'Don't tell me, let me guess — it was a very thick file, right? We're a thorn in Sir Lachlan's side, you understand. By the way, it's poetic justice, isn't it? I mean, you finding out about us from the very person who wishes we didn't exist!'

'What do you actually do?' Ted asked.

Harold explained that they compiled survivors' stories, collected information about the Nazis and collaborators who had emigrated to Australia, and wrote letters to the newspapers and members of parliament about their findings.

'The trouble is, they either ignore our letters or thank us for our concern and assure us about their careful screening methods.'

'But if the immigration department is keeping a file on you, they must be taking your letters seriously,' Ted said.

Instead of replying, Harold sprang up from his chair, strode to the window and glanced down. 'Did you see a middle-aged man reading a newspaper outside our building?' he asked.

Ted nodded.

'He comes here every day and watches everyone who comes in and out of our office, and reports on them to his boss. So I'm sorry to tell you this, but now they'll have a dossier on you as well.'

'And who is his boss?' Ted asked.

'The Commonwealth Investigation Service.'

'Why on earth would they be spying on you?'

'Because they reckon we're a bunch of Communists.'

'And are you?'

Harold paused. 'I can't speak for all of our members, of course, but some of them are. As for me, I'm against "isms" of every kind. Don't get me wrong, I like ideas, but when an idea becomes an ideology, it always leads to violence. Give someone a uniform, a stick and permission to bash people, and you'd be surprised how many will do it. And I'm not just talking about Germans either, or people in backward countries. Look, I lived in London, right? I saw Oswald Mosley and his Nazi supporters with their swastikas on their sleeves marching in the streets. They threw him in jail, thank goodness, but if Hitler had invaded England, believe me, he would have found lots of willing collaborators.'

Ted looked up from his notebook. 'So why doesn't our government want to do anything about these fascists you keep telling them about?'

'Every government needs an enemy. Us and them. And today in the west the enemy is Communism, so because some of our members belong to the Communist Party, it's us. But that's only one side of the story. The other part is that the government has found a good use for the fascists, and we're getting in the way.'

Ted was looking perplexed. 'How on earth would the government use fascists?'

Harold leaned across the table. 'Think about it. In Europe, all those Nazis hated the Communists, just like our government does, right? So they're using them to spy on the Communists, and report to the CIS on their activities. Forget the war, the death camps, and all the rest of it. Today's all that matters, and today they need the fascists to help them spy on Communists. The enemy of my enemy, that kind of thing. Get it?'

He looked at Ted's face and laughed. 'You look shocked, my friend. You obviously have a lot to learn about politics.'

Again Ted had the sense that he was being sucked into a cynical, shadowy world of espionage, counter-espionage and political intrigue. It sounded like the creation of a writer with a vivid imagination, but he had to admit that the basic premise — fear of Communism — was very sound.

Ted gestured towards the people in the office. 'If what you've said is true, you're all wasting your time in here. What's the point? It must be pretty dispiriting.'

Harold shrugged. 'It would be much more dispiriting to do nothing. Anyway, I believe that sooner or later the time will come when the government will want to do something about these war criminals and then they'll be glad to have our files. I just hope it won't be too late.'

He jumped up. 'But wait, you wanted to know what we do in here. Come, I'll show you.'

Ted had intended to have a quick look through the files and leave, but once he sat down and started reading, he couldn't tear himself away. As he read, he had to loosen his tie, undo the top button of his shirt and ask for a glass of water. It wasn't just the sun blazing through the window that dried his throat. It was the feeling that he was being suffocated by the weight of what he was reading.

Since he'd met Redvers Morrison and visited Bonegilla, he'd learned more about the collaborationist militias in various European countries, and about the activities that had turned the cool pine forests of Europe into blood-soaked killing fields. But reading these eyewitness accounts, he could feel the terror and the panic inside his own skin. He could hear children screaming and women pleading for their children's lives as they were being stripped naked; he could hear the sputtering of machine-gun fire, and then the black silence, louder and more frightening than any rifle shot.

Sickened by these descriptions, Ted looked up at the shafts of light slanting through the window. His head swam, and he felt he was immured in a chamber whose windows and doors had been bricked in. There was no escape.

Among the accounts of the mass killings, he came across descriptions of the killers, apparently unremarkable-looking men who joked among themselves, took swigs of vodka and swore as they wiped off their victims' blood which occasionally spattered on their faces.

He thought about the men who'd machine-gunned tens of thousands of men, women and children without compunction, cold and mechanical as the barrels of their weapons. And yet before becoming mass executioners they had probably been normal men leading normal lives, buying their wives flowers and playing with their kids. Despite the heat in the room, which had made him perspire so much that his shirt clung to his back, Ted shivered.

A separate file contained photographs and sketches showing the uniforms of ultranationalist militias in Ukraine, Croatia, Latvia and Lithuania. Ted stared at the photos, hoping to discern something in these faces that might mark the men apart, or hint at the evil they had committed, but they looked disappointingly normal. You could pass them in the street or stand beside them in a shop and exchange the usual pleasantries, not suspecting what they'd done. And perhaps if circumstances had been different, they wouldn't have done any of those things and would have gone to their graves without ever discovering what they were capable of. Perhaps we should be grateful to them, Ted thought, for revealing how much darkness lurked beneath the superficial civility of everyday life.

He closed the file and stared into space.

'Makes you wonder about humanity, doesn't it?' Harold's voice booming in his ear made Ted jump.

Overwhelmed by the accounts of the massacres, Ted had almost forgotten to ask about the issue that had been uppermost in his mind when he'd made the appointment — the request by the Yugoslav government to extradite some of their war criminals from Australia.

'Well, like practically everything else in life, it's political, and politics is a dirty business,' Harold said. 'Yugoslavia's government, which happens to be Communist, has requested the extradition of members of a fascist group that fought against them. But because our government has found a use for these bastards, and disapproves of the Yugoslav government, they've found it convenient to regard their request as an internal political matter and not a war crimes issue.'

'And what do you think?' Ted asked.

'It's no secret that the Yugoslav Communists are dying to get revenge on these fascists. But we know for a fact that some of the members of the Ustashe who migrated here are plotting to train in secret so they can regroup, rearm, attack Yugoslavia and reinstate their fascist regime. But when we try and warn Australian authorities about it, they laugh at us. They reckon we're just parroting the Yugoslav government's propaganda.'

Harold spoke in such a rush that Ted's head was spinning, and he was still trying to absorb what he'd been told as he walked slowly down the stairs. The lane outside resounded with carefree laughter as students with art folders under their arms headed for the Lincoln Inn Coffee Shop and disappeared through the narrow entrance leading to the basement. The sun had already slipped behind the office buildings, which cast long shadows on the street as offices began to empty at the end of the day.

Ted looked around for the fellow who'd been watching him behind his newspaper, but he was nowhere to be seen, perhaps gone to report on his visit to the Anti-Fascist Society. Ted patted his jacket pocket for the notebook and felt the blood racing in his veins. Now he had enough material for a hard-hitting article about the government's attitude towards war criminals.

Back in the newsroom, Ted spent the rest of the afternoon writing a story about the rising divorce rate, another of Gus's pet themes, probably because his wife had left him, Ted supposed. It was a relief to switch from war atrocities to a social issue. The article was based on his interview with Dr Ewart White, a prominent medico who wrote an advice column in the *Women's Weekly*. Dr White always blamed women for the problems they were experiencing with their boyfriends or husbands and advised them to be more feminine, less demanding and more conciliatory. As Gus concurred with Dr White's views, he'd told Ted to interview him.

According to Dr White, the biggest problem in most marriages these days, apart from the demanding nature of women, was sexual incompatibility, a topic most women as well as men were too embarrassed to mention. There was widespread ignorance about sex, and classes were urgently needed to give couples some basic anatomical and physiological information so that they could learn how to give each other pleasure instead of disappointment and frustration.

Gus liked the sexual angle of the story, and envisaged a headline screaming SEX CLASSES NEEDED FOR MARRIED couples. Ted typed the last word just before five-thirty, called for the copyboy and rushed out of the office to meet Lilija.

She came running into his arms and he scooped her up and covered her face with kisses. He'd spent much of the day looking into the darkness, and an evening with Lilija was just what he needed to restore his faith in humanity.

Chapter 41

In the silvery light of morning the tramlines gleamed and quivered. It seemed to Sala that these were the veins of the city, connecting its main arteries. Unlike her life, where everything was pulling apart. And the only stable thing in her life, her marriage, had become the most uncertain.

She sensed that her relationship with Szymon held the key to her future. She still hadn't decided whether to enroll in the part-time course that would qualify her to be a medical technician, or to take the plunge and study medicine. It was already mid-January, and she'd soon have to enroll, but she couldn't make that decision because, without Szymon's financial support, she had no hope of studying medicine. The threads of her life were bound together, and she was entwined in the centre, incapable of untangling the knots.

Beryl, who now regarded Sala as her mate, often grumbled about her husband as she changed into her pinafore and picked up a broom and feather duster. 'Me old man's a real bugger,' she often said. 'Rolls home drunk of a night after closing time, goes to the races on Sat'days, never takes me nowhere, and won't do nothink round the house, not even mow the bloody lawn.'

From what Beryl said, Sala got the impression that Australian men weren't considerate husbands. They went to the pub after work and drank until the doors closed at the uncivilised hour of six o'clock. On Saturdays they went to the races with their mates, on Sundays they went to the footie, and the rest of the time they hardly talked to their wives unless they wanted sex which, from what she'd heard, they performed without much thought for their wives' pleasure. But when Sala asked Beryl whether she'd ever thought of leaving, the older woman put her hands on her hips and stared at her in amazement. 'Leave 'im? What for? He's no worse than what the rest of 'em are. And I'm no spring chicken. Where am I goin' to go, and what'll I do on me own after all these years?'

If there was one person who got Beryl more worked up than her husband, it was the Leader of the Opposition, Robert Menzies, to whom she referred by his nickname, Pig Iron Bob. 'Got his nickname 'cos he wouldn't sell iron to the Japs. Only good thing he ever done,' she used to mutter as she sloshed a mop across the lino floor. 'The enemy of the working man, that's what he is. Give 'im half a chance and he'll ban the unions before you can say Heil Hitler.'

In the world according to Beryl, Chifley was the hero of the working class, but she was shrewd enough to mistrust his promises as well. 'A greedy lot of double-crossing parasites, the lot of them,' she'd scoff.

Sala enjoyed Beryl's tirades and learned a lot about Australian politics from them. This morning Beryl had been sounding off about the newspapers, which blamed the miners' union for the recent power cuts, describing their leaders as power-hungry despots who refused to negotiate.

With her soapy arms akimbo, Beryl had held forth about the exploitation of the workers by the greedy capitalists. 'If it wasn't for the ruddy unions, little kids'd still be goin' down the chimneys and crawling in the mines,' she'd said.

Sala was waiting at the tram stop, thinking about Beryl's views on politics, when she looked up and saw Alex walking towards her, swinging his leather briefcase. Ever since their chance encounter a few weeks before, she'd often imagined running into him again, and castigated herself for daydreaming like a silly schoolgirl. But the unhappier she was with Szymon, the more she longed for Alex. He was the kind of man she should have married, the exact opposite of Szymon. Suave, cultured and dangerously attractive.

He was standing so close to her that she could smell the brilliantine on his smooth dark hair. When he bent down to greet her in the traditional Polish manner, first pressing his lips to her hand and then to both cheeks, she was embarrassed and excited at the same time.

'You don't have to go straight home, do you?' he murmured, his warm lips brushing against her ear.

He was squeezing her arm as he spoke. 'It's a sin to waste such a beautiful morning. Have you been to the Botanic Gardens? Let me take you there.'

The prospect of spending an hour or two with him made the blood rush to her cheeks. She didn't hesitate.

They strolled along the winding paths of the Botanic Gardens, past herb gardens and lily ponds, until they found a secluded bench under a giant strangler fig whose matted roots hung down like uncombed tresses.

Alex put his arm around her shoulders and, gazing into her eyes, murmured, 'You're a very sexy woman. I'd like to take you to bed and make love to you.'

The unexpected directness of his words and the lust in his face shocked and thrilled her. Confused, she looked down, twisting the wedding band around her finger as she wondered what to say. His intimate tone and admiring glances were seductive, but an insistent voice in her head warned her to think what she was doing. It was wrong for a married woman to sit in a park with a married man, listening to flattery which could only end one way.

He was stroking her shoulder, lightly at first and then more insistently, and his expert hands slid down her back, promising more intimate and rapturous caresses.

'What about you?' he said, looking into her eyes. 'Do you want me as much as I want you?'

Before she could reply, his warm lips were pressing against hers, forcing hers to part, and as his tongue explored her mouth, she kissed him back with a passion she hadn't felt for a long time.

'I know a quiet little hotel in Kings Cross,' he said in a thick voice. 'Let's go there.'

Torn between desire, conscience and common sense, she hesitated. This was the point from which there was no return.

From the moment she'd met him, she'd dreamed of him being her lover, and now that her fantasy was about to come true she was elated, and tried to silence the negative voice in her head.

Her father, a keen chess player who believed that the game held the answer to many of life's problems, used to say that before making any decision you should always think three moves ahead. Suppose she started an affair with Alex, what would the consequences be, and how would it end? He was kissing the nape of her neck, and her whole body tingled with anticipation. Why shouldn't she succumb to this pleasure? She was still young and she'd gone through so much. Surely she deserved to have some joy in her life.

While Alex was checking in at the reception counter of the Federal Hotel, Sala pretended to study the painting on the wall in the neon-lit foyer. She heard him asking for a room with a view on the fifth floor, and as she turned around, she wondered if she'd imagined the smirk on the receptionist's face as she handed him the key.

The old lift heaved to a stop with a lurch, and they walked to the end of the dimly lit corridor which smelled of cigarettes. Alex turned the heavy brass key in the lock and, as they entered the room, her eye fell on a large dark stain in the centre of the faded Axminster carpet.

The double bed, which took up most of the room, was covered with a shiny bedspread, and the fraying brocade drapes over the window had some tassels missing. Sala breathed in the musty odour of unaired rooms.

She walked to the window and looked through the dust-streaked pane. William Street stretched into the heart of the city, and beyond the office buildings the iron bridge they called the Coathanger spanned the harbour. Sala was wondering whether her heart would ever belong to this city, when she felt Alex's hot hands on her shoulders.

He spun her around to face him and, edging her towards the bed, he undid the buttons of her dress. It slipped to the floor, and as she stood in her white slip, he held her closer and murmured, 'You're so beautiful.'

For some reason her eyes kept straying to the stained carpet, and in an effort to overcome her lack of responsiveness, he kissed her again, harder this time. 'I've never wanted any woman as much as I want you,' he whispered.

She was about to speak but he placed his hand over her mouth. 'Don't say anything. I know you want me too. We're both adults, so let's not waste this opportunity.'

His eyes were gleaming, and under his moustache his lips were full and red. She was excited by the lust in his face but there was something predatory in his expression, which thrilled and repelled her at the same time. It reminded her of an illustration she'd seen in a children's book of the wolf trying to lure Little Red Riding Hood into the hut.

She heard herself say, 'But what about your wife?'

The imperturbable smile was still on his face, and if he found her question disconcerting, he didn't show it. Without speaking, he began to rake her arm from the wrist to the elbow in a slow, sensuous way that sent little spasms of pleasure through her body.

'I have a wonderful wife and I'm sure you have a wonderful husband,' he said after a pause. 'So what? You can love more than one person. Love isn't a limited commodity like butter, it doesn't get used up.' He tilted her chin so that she had to look straight into his eyes. 'I knew the moment I saw you that we were going to be lovers. If we throw this chance away, we might regret it for the rest of our lives.'

His words were seductive, but they tripped off his tongue too easily. They sounded glib and insincere, and she sensed he'd said these things before, perhaps in this very room, to other gullible women. Like a pianist giving a well-rehearsed performance of a familiar piece of music, he'd struck the wrong note and ruined the crescendo he'd so carefully planned.

She felt deflated. Deluding herself about romance and passion, she had mistaken this cheap imitation for the real thing. What a fool she'd been. But what had she expected? Illicit trysts in a sleazy hotel room, deceiving her husband, and his wife, sneaking around and hoping not to be discovered. And then, looking several moves ahead, she saw herself being ditched for another paramour. Was that the new life she'd come here to rebuild?

'Maybe you're right and I will regret it.' She had picked up her dress and was buttoning it hurriedly as she spoke. 'I'm sorry if I led you on, but I just can't do this.'

'I think you'll be sorry if you don't,' he said, and his smile looked forced. 'We regret missed opportunities far more than our mistakes.'

She shrugged. 'Perhaps on my deathbed I'll wish I'd said yes. But now I'm going home.' She picked up her handbag and walked quickly from the room without looking back.

Instead of feeling a sense of triumph, she felt depressed, and when the tram conductor gave her his usual cheery greeting, she felt like crying.

There's something wrong with me, she thought. I can't live a normal life or have normal relationships. Why didn't I die with the rest of my family? They were all better people than I am. What's the point of living if I'm always miserable?

By the time she alighted from the tram, tears were flowing down her cheeks. When she turned the corner into Wattle Street, she saw Verna Browning sweeping the fallen frangipanis from her verandah.

'Lovely day, isn't it?' Verna called out, but Sala just nodded and kept walking.

Resting her chin on the broom, Verna looked at her neighbour's slow gait and downcast gaze. Something was obviously wrong, and Verna wondered if she should try to find out if Sally needed help. The last thing she wanted was to intrude, but Sally did look very upset. Maybe she needed someone to talk to.

It was hard to know what to do for the best sometimes, she thought, and continued sweeping.

A moment later Maude McNulty popped her head over the fence. 'I read in the paper that the royal tour might be going ahead after all,' she said. 'Thank goodness the King's got over his chest infection.'

In a confidential whisper, she added, 'He hasn't been the same since his brother married that awful Mrs Simpson.' Although thirteen years had passed since Edward VIII had abdicated and married Wallis Simpson, Maude McNulty couldn't forgive him for giving up the English throne for a scheming American divorcee.

Verna nodded, wondering why her neighbour hadn't found something worthwhile to do in the course of her long life except spy on her neighbours and collect useless information about the royal family. It was hard to imagine Maude McNulty as a young woman, but perhaps like Miss Havisham in the Dickens novel, she'd been jilted. Maybe that was why she'd never married or had children and had turned into such a misery.

Kath was rubbing Meggsie's arms and legs when she looked out of the window and saw Verna talking to her next-door neighbour.

'What's the old bag been haranguing you about?' she asked when Verna came over a little later. But she was too excited to wait for Verna's reply. Pushing her thick auburn hair back from her flushed face, she said, 'You know that nurse I found out about? The one that uses the Kenny method? I rang her up this morning and she's coming next week! There's enough money in that envelope to pay her to keep coming every week till the end of the year!'

'That's terrific, Kath,' Verna said while Kath put the kettle on. 'I bet that's bucked Meggsie up.'

Kath's smile faded. 'When I first got him home, he was always talking about walking again, but he doesn't talk about it any more. I think he's given up hope.'

She placed the tea on the table but left hers untouched. 'Sometimes I wonder if I did the right thing bringing him home,' she said. 'Maybe it's just made things worse.'

Verna shook her head. 'Don't think that for a second. Of course you did the right thing. Anyway, this nurse will probably get him on his feet again.'

Kath didn't answer; she didn't want to tell Verna that she was close to losing hope herself. 'What about your gran?' Verna asked. 'Are you going to let her know about Meggsie?'

Kath's mouth stretched into a thin line. 'She doesn't care enough to find out if we're alive or dead, so why should I?'

They sat in silence, then Kath shot Verna a sharp look. 'Why, do you think I should?'

'Just wondering. He *is* her grandson, after all. You're waiting for her to get in touch, and she's probably waiting for you to make the first move. Maybe you're both cut from the same cloth. What was it that Indian fellow used to say, you know, the one in the loincloth that got killed last year? An eye for an eye leaves everybody blind?'

Kath looked at Verna in astonishment. It wasn't like her to interfere.

As if she'd read her mind, Verna said slowly, 'I didn't talk to my father for the last three years of his life and I've always been sorry. He went off with someone else and left Mum when I was fifteen. She was bitter and never forgave him. He tried to stay in touch with me and wrote to me, but whenever I mentioned wanting to see him, Mum hit the roof. I didn't want to upset her so I didn't write back. I didn't know what to say. Anyway I thought he'd always be there, so there'd be lots of time to see him, but he died a few years later, and I never did.'

Kath studied her hands for a long time without replying. 'I know you're right,' she said at last, 'but I just can't take that first step. And even if I did, it wouldn't work because I'd be too resentful. Maybe one day I'll get in touch with her, and maybe I won't and I'll be sorry, but I just can't do it now.'

'Sorry, love,' Verna said. 'Didn't mean to preach. I was just thinking aloud. I hadn't thought about my dad for a long time, that's all.'

As Verna walked back to her place, she wondered whether she would have braved her mother's anger and contacted her father if someone had told her that time was finite, and missed opportunities caused more heartache than misguided actions.

Chapter 42

The sultry days of February had begun, and at night the air was heavy, still and moist. Clammy after a night spent tossing from side to side on rumpled sheets, Ted sprang out of bed as soon as the first rays of the sun lit up his room. It was Sunday, the sky was a Namatjira blue, and he was going to spend this golden day at the beach with Lilija.

Too excited to wait until it was time to meet her, he sprinted to the tram stop and found, to his delight, that Lilija was already there. Her red sundress accentuated the creamy European pallor of her skin and the silvery blondeness of her hair, and he couldn't stop looking at her.

'You know what I wish?' he murmured into her ear. 'I want you to be the first thing I see in the morning and the last thing I see at night.'

She blushed and nudged him because the middle-aged couple standing nearby were watching them.

'They're just jealous,' Ted whispered, squeezing her hand as they climbed onto the tram. 'They wish they were as happy as we are.'

For the past six months, the Bondi tram had stopped running on Sundays due to power cuts, but now that the service had been resumed, thousands of sunbathers had come to Bondi Beach. Ted and Lilija stood at the top of the wide flight of stairs leading down to the sand, and looked down on the mosaic of beach towels, umbrellas and suntanned bodies sprawled on sand as pale as lightly baked shortbread. Ted breathed in the sharp and salty air, sniffed the nutty sweetness of coconut oil, and smiled as he felt the tension leave his body.

He spotted a space between the flags, took Lilija's hand, and they ran down the steps, past the foreign teenagers sitting there. They were an animated lot, and Ted admired their exuberance and camaraderie, but he wondered how any of them ever managed to finish a sentence with everyone calling out, gesticulating and interrupting. Most of the blokes were short but well built, while the girls had hourglass figures accentuated by their tight shorts and halter tops.

'They call this the Jerusalem Steps, because of the Jewish kids who sit here on Sundays,' he told Lilija, who turned to have another look.

They spread out their towels, and he lay on his side watching Lilija as she stepped out of her sundress. He swallowed hard as he looked at the swell of her breasts and her small nipples pressing against her black swimsuit. She flopped onto her towel and turned her back to him, twisting her hair away from her neck as he rubbed coconut oil on the soft skin on her long, smooth back. Occasionally his hands slid to the front and brushed against her breasts and he almost stopped breathing. When he'd finished oiling her back, she lay on her stomach, but he stayed on his side with his head propped on his hand, watching the dip of her back and the curve of her buttocks, glad that she couldn't read his mind.

He sat up and looked at the sunbathers around him. The beach was the city's social and economic leveller. Outside their homes and offices, without their everyday clothes and trappings of power, the men smoking cigarettes and exchanging pleasantries could be postmen or politicians, doctors, company directors or dustmen. Here, under the blazing sun, in their swimsuits, they were all equal. And those New Australians on the steps, who had brought with them their strange languages and sad memories, they too were part of the fabric of the new Australia that was being woven right here in front of him. Ted thought about his own street, where the newcomers had moved in among the Aussies. Lilija and her parents, Hanny and her mother, and the mysterious Mr Emil. Life was changing and he was witnessing something important, something that might even be worth writing about.

He heard a roar and saw groups of athletic, suntanned men climbing up on each other's shoulders, forming pyramids. Every few minutes they shouted as the pyramid collapsed and they tumbled down, laughing and spraying sand in all directions.

Two suntanned lifesavers, with caps tied under their chins, ran past him, and he recalled that seven years before, a Japanese shell had hit the clubhouse. As he watched them changing the position of the flags, he remembered Pop Wilson's story about Black Sunday. Next weekend he'd definitely go and see him.

Too hot to sunbake any longer, he tapped Lilija's reddening shoulder. 'Let's go in and cool down,' he said and, taking her hand, pulled her towards the sea.

She ran into the water but recoiled whenever the cold waves broke and sprayed her sun-warmed body.

'Come on, you're in Australia now, you've got to learn to bodysurf,' he said. 'Don't be scared, I'll show you what to do. See that wave? Dive under it now, before it breaks. Now!'

But she hesitated too long, and a moment later a roller whacked into her back, knocked her off her feet and dragged her under, buffeting her as she tumbled in the water like a strand of seaweed. She came to the surface, coughing and gasping, grazed by the sand and spitting sea water. Glaring at Ted, who was wading towards her, she punched his chest. 'I nearly drowned,' she gasped. 'I want to come out.'

But Ted held onto her hand. 'Don't be a quitter,' he said. 'You can't give up after one go. If you fall off a horse, you get straight back on again.'

She frowned. He could see that she didn't understand about the horse, but she stayed in the water clutching onto him. On her second attempt she got the timing right and surfaced on the other side of the wave with a triumphant smile.

They were running towards their towels when they saw the beach inspector, in his white singlet and Panama hat, bearing down on a young woman in a brief two-piece swimming costume which consisted of a tiny red-and-white polka dot brassiere and a skimpy triangle that barely covered her shapely bottom. She was surrounded by a group of young men whistling, howling and making catcalls. And small boys chanting 'Hubba hubba, digga digga! Strike me lucky, what a figure!'

Before the girl had time to dip her scarlet-varnished toes into the water, the inspector barred her way.

'Cover yourself up, young lady, or you'll have to get off the beach.'

She started to protest in a foreign accent, but the inspector broke in and told her to leave the beach.

Lilija turned to Ted. 'What does he want? Why does he tell her to go?'

'Inspectors have the right to order girls off the beach if they're wearing indecent bikinis,' he explained.

Lilija looked amazed. 'Australians are very old-fashioned.' While they were drying off, she poked him playfully in the ribs. 'But you thought girl in indecent bikini looked beautiful, no?' she said.

He flicked her bottom with his towel. 'Not as beautiful as you. Come on, let's have lunch.'

As they walked past Ravesi's Tearooms, he recalled that his mother had taken him there for a treat on his tenth birthday. He had never seen such a classy place, with starched white cloths, potted palms and waitresses in white caps and aprons, and he still remembered the cupcake with the vanilla icing that dissolved in his mouth. He would take Lilija there for afternoon tea one Sunday. He squeezed her hand in anticipation of all the wonderful Sundays ahead of them.

They bought mint freezes from Bates's milk bar, hamburgers and chips from the hole in the wall next door, and strolled towards Ben Buckler with their arms around each other.

Outside the boatsheds, an old fisherman was scaling fish and throwing them onto chipped ice in his wicker basket. As they peered at his catch, he pushed his battered hat back from his weather-beaten face and looked up. 'Two of my mates went out in a dinghy a couple of months back and landed a fourteen-footer. Razor-tooth he was. Just over there,' and he pointed to the spot where surfboard riders were catching waves a few yards away.

Lilija looked at Ted in alarm. 'I will not go in the water again.'

He laughed and, taking her hand, helped her climb up the steep vine-carpeted slope above Ben Buckler. The slope flattened out at the top into a tangle of bushland and they made their way past diosma bushes covered in tiny pink flowerets, their branches twisted by wind which blew up from the sea. Lilija pointed at the erect candle-like flowers of the banksia trees and gingerly touched their straw-coloured spikes, delighted by their unexpected softness and cushiony centre.

They found a small shady space between a stand of casuarinas and sat on a soft blanket of fallen needles to eat their hamburgers.

'I used to come here a lot when I was a kid,' he said, his voice soft with nostalgia.

In the distance, a large tanker, like a painted ship, sat on the horizon. Closer in, two frail-looking yachts were sailing towards the Heads, and the lifesavers' boat was speeding towards a swimmer caught in a rip some distance from the beach. Lilija shaded her eyes with her hand and squinted at the waves, trying to spot razor-tooth sharks lurking in the depths below them. Seagulls screeched overhead, swooping down with their sharp predatory beaks on the potato chips Ted threw to them, and flying away with the food before their rivals could snatch it away.

Suddenly he was telling Lilija about his childhood. With her head resting in his lap, and her fair hair fanned out on the dark green needles, he told her that he used to come here as a kid to play cops and robbers with his mates. He pointed to Nosey's cottage and told her that sometimes they'd dared each other to go into the haunted house and stay there alone at night. Later, as a teenager, he'd come here whenever he wanted to be alone. Like the time he'd found out that his father would never come home again.

Then he told her about the war years, about Japanese submarines in the harbour shelling Sydney and hitting a street not far from where they were sitting now. He told her about the blackouts, the drills, the buckets of sand in the classrooms, and having to crawl through wire entanglements to get to the beach.

Lilija stroked his cheek while he talked, but after a while he tailed off. How trivial those experiences must seem to her, compared to what she and her family had gone through, with so many of their relatives being deported to Siberia, and then going through the war in Latvia where her father had had such terrible experiences that he still had nightmares. And after all that, they'd had to flee from the Red Army, live in a displaced persons' camp in Germany, then start a new life in a foreign country.

As he lay beside her, he felt dizzy with romantic intoxication. It seemed as if his whole body was vibrating. He reached over and eased the straps of her swimsuit down over her shoulders and whispered, 'Let me look at you. I just want to look at you.'

A moment later he was kissing her breasts and sliding his hand down her belly until it rested between her thighs and he could feel the thrilling heat of her body.

'Not here,' she whispered, and pushed his hand away.

He looked into her face and kissed her. He could wait.

Hands linked behind his neck, he lay back and gazed at the vastness of the sky. He felt a surge of power, of faith in himself, and sensed the depth and width of existence that his father had hinted at. He gazed at Lilija and felt gloriously connected with the entire universe.

The late-afternoon sun was slanting through the branches and when Ted sat up he saw that the uppermost boughs of the eucalypts and acacias were glazed with a syrupy amber light. Without speaking, they held each other and gazed at the sun falling towards the sea and disappearing behind the horizon.

When the last tinge of colour had faded from the sky,

Lilija looked nervously at her wristwatch. As she turned her beachbag upside down to shake out the sand, her wallet dropped to the ground and a small photograph fell out.

'What's that?' Ted asked.

Gently she brushed off the specks of soil and handed it to him. It was an old, sepia-hued photograph of a wintry scene in Europe with snow on the ground. A pretty girl of about twelve, muffled in a woollen scarf and heavy hooded coat, was standing beside a uniformed man, her mittened hands clasping his as she smiled into his face.

'When was this taken?' he asked.

'In Riga in 1942, I think so,' she said. 'My father was on leave from army.'

'Which army was that?'

'Latvian army of course!'

Ted studied the peaked cap, khaki uniform and wide leather belt. There was an armband on the sleeve and as he looked at the emblem he felt as though he'd just been dropped from a great height.

'Something is wrong?' Lilija asked.

He shook his head. Despising himself for the deception, he said in a tight, thin voice, 'We've got a photographic section at work. If you like, I can get your photo enlarged for you.'

Then he pulled her to her feet. 'Come on, it's getting late. We'd better go.'

Suddenly it was evening, and as they walked back along Campbell Parade Ted saw that the beach had emptied. Its colours had faded like Lilija's old photograph, and its sounds had become dull and muted. Ted was aware that she was saying something but he found it hard to concentrate on the words.

Four years before, while he was still a cadet, he'd accompanied a reporter to an area of the Blue Mountains where bushfires had been raging. Ted had never forgotten the haunted expression on one man's face as he stared at the devastation that had once been his home. 'It's all gone,' he'd kept whispering over and over. 'It was there this morning and now there's nothing left.'

He'd felt sorry for the man in his numb, confused state, but now he understood. That was how you felt when everything you cared about suddenly disintegrated before your eyes and was reduced to a pile of ashes.

Chapter 43

Bent over the rolltop desk in the front room, with his Latvian–English dictionary open in front of him, Paulis Olmanis was composing his report. He usually gave it verbally to the Commonwealth Investigation Service agent whenever they met on Campbell Parade, but this time he felt a written report would better serve his interests.

The agent had intimated that the Commonwealth Investigation Service was about to be replaced by a new body, the Australian Security and Intelligence Organisation. Paulis knew from bitter experience that once these security departments changed names, they usually made drastic staff changes to justify their existence. Whether his contact was moved upwards, downwards or sideways, Paulis suspected that he himself would fall into the crack created by the shift, unless he moved fast to prove his importance to Australia's new security organisation.

Closing the door so that Marija wouldn't interrupt him with her tiresome questions and offers of coffee, he picked up his fountain pen and began to write.

Frequently consulting his well-thumbed dictionary, he worded his report with great care to indicate his respect for the current organisation and to compliment it on its vigilance in safeguarding the country from the evils of Communism, while at the same time expressing the conviction that the work of making the country safe from Communism would now proceed even faster and more efficiently.

He took the opportunity to remind them that he'd already justified their faith in him by reporting on the pro-Communist attitude of several Sydney residents, including a young reporter he'd been watching, and he hoped that he'd be permitted to continue assisting them in their important work. In fact, he now had firm evidence that this particular individual had made contact with a Communist action group calling itself the Anti-Fascist Society, and he was ready to provide them with more details. Wishing the new department every success, he signed his name with a flourish and blotted the report.

Paulis leaned back in his chair, reread what he'd written and smiled at his own subtlety. They'd soon see they weren't dealing with an amateur, and they were sure to take the bait he'd so skilfully dangled in front of them by hinting that he had more information.

On his way to the Bondi Junction post office to buy a postage stamp, he raised his hat to the white-haired woman whose son had written those malicious lies about Baltic migrants. Giving her a stiff bow, he said, 'How do you do,' as they did in the English films, and quickly crossed the road.

Paulis had spent the past two weeks observing the comings

and goings of the Anti-Fascist Society, most of whom he suspected of being Communists and Jews, and he hadn't been able to believe his luck when this reporter had turned up. Naturally he'd wasted no time in telling his daughter that it was a good thing he'd stopped her from seeing this fellow who was obviously a Communist. She'd just stared at him and walked out of the room without saying a word, but he knew that in time she'd realise he was right.

It was a steamy day and the air shimmered with heat. Under his grey felt hat his head began to perspire, and he had to stop several times to wipe the perspiration beading on his forehead. This oppressive humidity was the only thing he disliked about living in Sydney. Unlike Marija he didn't miss the snow or the church choirs. There were far more important things to be thankful for, things she had no idea about.

Australia had turned out to be a brilliant choice in every way. Australians were polite, trusting and ingenuous, and seemingly devoid of guile, which made life much easier than he'd expected. He still couldn't get over the naive Australian selection officers in Berlin who had believed everything he'd told them. He'd been on edge when he'd arrived for his interview, and he'd come well prepared with a fabricated story and forged documents, explaining that he was afraid to return to his native land because his anti-Communist activities would put his life in danger. This was true, but luckily the selection officer hadn't tried to find out why he was wanted by the authorities. Looking back on it, the interview had been a joke.

It was almost too easy, like training hard for a sporting event only to discover that your opponents were kindergarten children. He could see that what appealed to the Australian authorities about him was his hatred of Communists, and he harped on that, emphasising that he was willing to do anything to expose their subversive activities.

It was true. His abhorrence was closely linked with his patriotism. He'd been seven years old in 1918 when Latvia had been freed from the yoke of the Russian Empire. He could still recall the rejoicing in the streets of Riga as everyone waved flags and cheered at their nation's new freedom. His usually taciturn father had had tears in his eyes as he'd hoisted him up on his shoulders and told him never to forget this historic moment, and he never had.

While studying law at Riga University during the 1930s, Paulis met Viktors Arajs, a fellow student whose deep-set dark eyes and charismatic personality made a profound impression on him, especially when he spoke so eloquently about Latvian heritage and nationalism, and the need to protect it from foreign elements.

Latvia's independent days came to a brutal end in 1940 when the Bolsheviks invaded and shot or deported tens of thousands of Latvian dissidents, intellectuals and government officials to Siberia. Paulis remembered hearing the dreaded banging on the door at midnight. Two armed NKVD agents in long trenchcoats and hats pulled over their faces dragged his father and grandfather from their apartment because they were government officials and were considered enemies of the state. They never returned.

When, after two years of Soviet oppression, the Germans attacked the Soviet Union and entered Latvia, Paulis, along with many of his countrymen, greeted the Nazis as liberators. Delirious with joy and relief, thousands of Latvians lined the streets and welcomed them with flowers.

Not long afterwards, Paulis read a notice in the *Teviya* newspaper which called on patriotic Latvians to join a group that would help cleanse the country of Jews and Communists. He signed up at once. He couldn't wait to wreak revenge on the Communists, and he was delighted to discover that the leader of the new militia was his former university colleague Viktors Arajs, after whom the militia was named.

Paulis knew that many of the members of the Kommando were in it either for the money, the vodka, the plunder or the unbridled violence, but he had joined with loftier motives. The Germans had lost no time letting Latvians know that all Jews were Bolsheviks, and that they were their country's real enemies. They said Jews had been responsible for the repression and massacres during the Communist regime, and had to be eliminated.

At first, the Arajs Kommando played an auxiliary role. It seemed to Paulis that initially they displayed a lack of discipline: going on rampages, beating Jews and ransacking their homes, and setting fire to the main synagogue with a few hundred Jews inside. He didn't approve of them storming the Riga ghetto and shooting all those children and old people, then leaving their bodies in the streets. He preferred disciplined behaviour befitting a quasi-military group.

Paulis, who soon became the commander of one of the Arajs Kommando units, prided himself on the orderly way he organised the elimination procedure. First they lined up the Jews, then they loaded them into open lorries, claiming to be relocating them to a better place to prevent panic and hysteria. They drove them into the woods outside Riga where they pushed them towards pits that had already been dug. Then they formed a cordon to make sure none of them escaped while the German soldiers started firing. It was all done in a methodical, efficient way, although the Germans kept complaining that the killing wasn't going fast enough.

At first the Arajs Kommando's role was rounding up, escorting and guarding Jews, and to kick them into the trenches if they resisted, but eventually they, too, got their chance to shoot the naked men, women and children they pushed into the pits. Paulis's zeal in killing Jews and Communists sometimes exceeded even that of the Nazis, and he was proud that his enthusiasm was noticed and rewarded by his SS masters.

When the job of the Arajs Kommando was done, and Latvia was what the Germans called *Judenfrei*, Paulis was put in charge of a unit that was sent to Byelorussia where they carried out punitive operations against partisans. This entailed killing the inhabitants of entire villages as reprisal against suspected Communist sabotage.

What had spurred Paulis on during his unit's activities on foreign soil was the conviction that, in getting rid of Communists and their sympathisers, he was helping his nation regain its independence because the Germans had promised that as soon as the Jew-Bolshevik menace was eradicated, and Germany had won the war, they would make Latvia independent once more. The bitter irony of that promise enraged Paulis to this day. Unfortunately, Germany had lost the war, and Latvia was in the iron grip of the Bolsheviks once more.

Of those long days spent in the dappled forests, he remembered very little. It all seemed unreal now, as though it had happened to somebody else. And in a sense it had. He was no longer the soldier who had done those things. What he did remember was his shock when he realised how easy and meaningless it was to kill people, how hard it was to stop firing once you started, and how exhilarated you felt afterwards.

He didn't dwell on the inhuman shrieking of the women trying to protect their children, or their pleas to spare their lives. He was carrying out his nationalistic duty and was never swayed by their tears or entreaties. Some of them offered him jewellery but he wasn't tempted. He'd already amassed plenty of gold and jewellery from the houses of the Jews they'd rounded up, and it was thanks to some of this booty that he'd been able to buy forged documents and, later, to set himself up in Sydney.

It all seemed so far away now, as though it had happened to someone else, in another lifetime and in a different world. He didn't waste time shining a torchlight into those dark, unfathomable recesses of his soul. The past was past and couldn't be changed. But what he avoided thinking about in his waking hours often came back to haunt him at night, and he'd sit bolt upright in bed in the darkness, his heart pounding as he heard a woman begging him to spare her baby, or saw the pit heaving and oozing blood after it had been filled in.

Sometimes he dreamed that God, a bearded, white-haired patriarch, pointed an accusing finger at him and consigned him to eternal hellfire. Paulis was panic-stricken. He was a good person, a caring son and a devoted husband and father. He'd only done his patriotic duty as any soldier would have done.

People didn't seem to understand that war sanctioned violence, and once it began, it couldn't be controlled. If it hadn't been for the war, he would have finished law and fought for the rights of the poor and the downtrodden. He would never have become involved in such violence or discovered the godlike sense of power that war had given him.

Marija, who knew nothing about his wartime activities, had no idea why he so often woke up shaking and screaming. She thought he'd been an ordinary soldier and that his nightmares were the result of the terrible things he'd witnessed in the army.

He'd even lied to her about the *Kriegsverdienstkreuz* decoration he'd been awarded by the Germans. She and Lilija thought he was a war hero because he'd told them that he'd earned a War Cross of Merit for bravery in battle. Although he knew he should have left the German medal behind because it was incriminating, he hadn't been able to part with it. He'd brought it to Australia and kept it at the back of a drawer in his desk where he was certain Marija and Lilija would never find it.

As Paulis pushed open the door of the post office, he reflected that his only fear was that someone from Riga might recognise him, but as the Communists were still in power in Latvia, and most of the Jews had been deported to camps or killed on the spot, that wasn't likely.

Chapter 44

When Ted came into the newsroom the day after his beach date with Lilija, his mind was on the photograph in his coat pocket. Perhaps he'd been mistaken about the uniform. As soon as he could get away, he would drop into the Anti-Fascist Society and check it out.

He was brooding about it when a booming voice cut into his reverie. Norm Bell, the court reporter, was regaling the journalists with one of his court stories.

'You should've seen her, peeling vegetables in the front row of the gallery in her fur coat while the case was being heard,' he was saying.

'How come the judge didn't throw her out?' someone asked.

'He tried to shut her up a few times but she said there was no law preventing anyone from peeling vegetables in court!' Norm was laughing so much that his flabby stomach wobbled. '"I'm just an innocent housewife and I've got to get the veggies ready for dinner!" she says in this genteel voice she puts on, and all the time she's flashing her diamond rings and bracelets around, practically blinding everyone. Of course the whole courtroom cracks up, and the judge is banging his gavel, trying to restore order. And then the accused, a sinister cove you wouldn't want to run into on a dark night, takes the stand. Whenever he opens his mouth, she yells out, "You tell 'em, love. Don't let 'em bully you!" It was better than a three-ring circus.'

Norm, who had worked on the *Daily Standard* longer than anyone could remember, understood the legal system and was well acquainted with those who regularly featured on both sides of it.

He was a big bloke with a fleshy face, a nose the shape of a parsnip and a florid complexion that matched his colourful writing style. He pulled no punches, and after reading the front and back pages of the paper, most people turned to his column for inside information about crims, cops and lawyers.

It was around two o'clock and Norm's face was more flushed than usual, no doubt the result of yet another boozy lunch. Sometimes in the afternoons he sat hunched over his telephone, as though engaged in an intense and secret conversation, but they all knew this pose was designed to conceal a much-needed nap to sleep off the alcohol.

Curious to hear more about the case, Ted edged closer.

Being the youngest reporter on the paper, he didn't like to reveal his ignorance by asking too many questions, so it took him some time to figure out that Norm was talking about Trixie Slattery, who was usually described in the tabloids as 'the Queen of the Underworld'.

The case Norm was referring to involved the bashing murder of a notorious hitman, and for once Trixie was in court as a spectator and not as the accused. With his talent for colourful details, Norm described the scene outside the court as the portly woman lumbered out of a white Studebaker driven by her boyfriend and climbed up the steps of the Central Criminal Court in Darlinghurst, pursued by an eager mob of reporters and photographers. Pausing dramatically at the top, she had adjusted her silver fox cape with a flourish and, while the large-format cameras flashed like lightning during an electrical storm, she held forth with a straight face about the evils of violence and the wages of sin.

Norm turned to Ted. 'You're too young to know about Trixie,' he said, putting his legs up on his desk American-style as he puffed on his cigarette. 'In her heyday, she and her gang were the scourge of Sydney. Razorhurst, we called that part of town, because of all the slashing that went on. Old Trixie has been mixed up in everything — sly grog, prostitution, drugs, the lot. Her boyfriend used to get the girls hooked on cocaine to make sure they kept working.'

Ted jotted something in his notepad and looked up. 'Is she still in business?'

'Is she ever! She's got a string of brothels around Darlinghurst. Naturally she looks after the cops so they don't raid her premises unless they warn her beforehand.'

Jabbing Ted playfully in the chest, he said, 'Planning to pay her a visit, are you? Make sure you take a rubber!'

Ted flushed and wandered back to his desk. He was thinking about the callgirl known as Scarlett whose body still lay unclaimed in the morgue. He didn't know why the girl's murder haunted him. Maybe it was pity, or a sense of injustice, because no one else seemed to care. Or maybe because somewhere out there a mother needed to know her daughter's fate so that she could end the agonising uncertainty and finally mourn for her. But he suspected that it had as much to do with curiosity as compassion.

As soon as Ted filed his story that afternoon, he rushed from the newsroom and jumped on a tram to the city. At the Anti-Fascist Society, his impatient fingers leafed through the folder labelled *Latvia, Lithuania and Estonia*. When he came to a photograph of a member of the Arajs Kommando, he took out Lilija's photo and compared them. Despite the heat in the stuffy office, he felt cold. The uniforms and the armbands with the skull and crossbones were identical.

The folder contained two translated interviews with Latvian villagers who had been questioned after the war about what they'd witnessed in the woods. They said they'd heard lorries arriving, and heard crying and yelling. They'd seen hundreds of people being pushed along a path by men with rifles, then they'd heard screams that made their blood run cold, followed by machine-gun fire, and had seen bodies falling like stones into the open pits.

Ted's hands were clammy and his heart was thumping too fast. He poured himself a glass of water and gulped it down, trying to calm himself. Perhaps not all members of the

Arajs Kommando were cold, vicious killers. Perhaps among them were ordinary men like Lilija's father, who had joined up mistaking it for a regular fighting unit, not suspecting that their duties would involve murdering innocent people, but were unable to back out when they discovered the true nature of their duties. As he read on, however, he realised that this possibility was very remote.

As he waded through the file and tried to absorb the stupefying scale of the massacres, and the cold-blooded planning that had made them possible, he came across an article from a 1946 Riga newspaper. In the margin, someone had translated the headline: WAR CRIMINALS FLEE TO THE WEST. Although he couldn't understand the text, he noticed the words *Arajs Kommando* repeated several times.

The last item in the folder was a letter, and from the date at the top of the page he saw that it had been written by a Mrs Anna Vestermanis about five weeks before. Mrs Vestermanis wrote that while walking down a lane near the Hotel Australia, she'd caught sight of a man she recognised instantly. He was in charge of an execution squad in the woods outside Riga in 1942.

I was shocked to see this man in Sydney, she wrote. *He is a criminal and he should be in gaol. Please do something about him.*

For a long time Ted sat in front of the open file, staring numbly into space. While noting down Mrs Vestermanis's address, he was wondering how to tell Lilija that the father she loved and admired had been a member of a death squad that had killed women and children. Even if she believed him, she would despise him for destroying her lifelong trust. Ted knew that he was about to confront the biggest challenge of his life, and that nothing would ever be the same again, for him or for her.

Chapter 45

A few days later, with the help of Norm Bell, who'd pulled in a few favours from his underworld contacts, Ted got in touch with Trixie Slattery. Gambling on her huge ego, he'd written to her saying he was planning a feature about the wild women of Sydney. She was his first choice, but if she couldn't talk to him, he'd have to interview Babs O'Neill instead. Babs was Trixie's sworn enemy, and she'd fallen for his ruse.

As he walked past the row of old terraces in the quiet Darlinghurst street, the only sign of life was a middle-aged businessman in a grey suit and hat glancing around furtively as he emerged from one of the old terraces with a red light in its window.

The bodyguard who loomed in the doorway when Ted pressed the buzzer wore dark glasses, a long black leather coat and a menacing expression. From his cauliflower ears, broken nose and massive hands it was obvious that life had given him plenty of opportunities to indulge a taste for violence. Ted sensed that this was a man who would beat you to a pulp in cold blood and then resume eating his lunch.

He was glaring at Ted as though considering whether to bash him now or later when, from inside the house, a woman yelled in a voice altered by decades of smoking, drinking and carousing, 'Let the bugger in and shut the fucking door!'

No sooner had he entered the lounge room than he was beset by three Dobermans that jumped up at him, snapping and growling.

Ted was backing away when the woman yelled, 'Hey! Down! Stop the bloody racket, and get out before I take the whip to youse!'

The dogs slunk from the room.

The big-boned woman who fixed Ted with an intimidating stare of her cold hard eyes sent a shiver down his back, and he knew he was in the presence of someone who wielded unforgiving power. The Queen of Sydney's Underworld wore a close-fitting toque over her elaborately coiffed hair, and a fox-fur jacket over her kaftan-style dress. Bracelets glittered on both wrists, and each plump finger flashed with diamonds or precious stones as big as knuckledusters.

Like her attire, the decor of her lounge room was obviously intended to impress visitors with her wealth and sophistication. The room was cluttered with brocade couches, glass-fronted cabinets, cedar davenports, grandfather clocks and old paintings in heavy gilded frames.

Taking a crystal decanter from the carved chiffonier, Trixie Slattery offered him a Scotch. 'Go on, have one,' she boomed. 'It's double malt, the best.' She gave him a shrewd look. 'You look like you need one. Did they tell you I eat young reporters for breakfast?'

Although whiskey made him sick, he took a swig and tried to look as though he drank it every morning.

'I heard you were a sensation in court the other day with your vegetables,' he said, trying not to gasp as the peat-flavoured spirit hit his throat.

She gave a loud wheezy laugh. 'Made them sit up and take notice, didn't I? Fucking hypocrites, they think they're gods with their wigs and gowns, looking down on the rest of us.'

She looked at her diamond wristwatch. 'Get to the point. I haven't got all bloody day. What do you want?'

A few innocent questions about her life got her started on a monologue about all her good deeds. By the time she'd finished listing the gifts she'd made to children's charities, the funds she'd donated for homeless men, and the accommodation she'd provided for deserted wives, she sounded like Sydney's biggest philanthropist. He wrote it all down dutifully, nodding and making admiring noises while he wrote.

But when he asked her about Scarlett O'Halloran, her bonhomie disappeared and she glared at him with her calculating little eyes. 'What's she to you? What are you really after? If you've tried to con me, I'll fucking show you what happens if you mess with Trixie.'

Ted swallowed the rest of his Scotch and thought about asking for a refill. He knew it wasn't an idle threat.

'I'd just like to find out the girl's real name.'

'And what makes you think I know? I'm not a fucking encyclopaedia on all the slags in Sydney.'

At least she'd stopped yelling and threatening. Taking a deep breath, he plunged in, hoping not to provoke another violent outburst. 'Well, she was in the same line of business as you, and knowing how influential you are, I thought you might have come across her.'

'I'm not as black as what I'm painted, you know,' Trixie said as she poured her third Scotch. 'I've always treated my girls good and fair.'

Fuelled by the whiskey, she went off on another tangent, this time to boast about her benevolence towards the girls in her brothels.

'I've heard how well you treat your girls,' he lied.

She sat up, obviously pleased. 'You've heard that, have you?' Then her face darkened and her tone became menacing again. 'Who've you been talking to? What are you really up to? I'll get someone to rearrange that innocent-looking face of yours if you're lying to me.'

Being in Trixie's intimidating presence had proved more nerve-racking than he'd imagined, and Ted was fighting a strong desire to end the interview and get out.

He wished he hadn't drunk the Scotch because his head was swimming just when he needed to think fast. He had to reassure her that he was on the level, but his head felt fuzzy. It was like trying to solve a maths equation during an exam when your mind was in a panic because the clock was ticking and time was running out. Only in this case the wrong answer could prove fatal.

He calmed her down by saying there were a few more questions he needed to ask for his article. With the interesting life she'd led, had she learned anything over the years that she'd like to share with the readers?

She nodded, obviously mollified. 'Tell the sheilas they'd better make their own way in the world. You can't rely on men. And never give nobody a second chance. They'll do you if they can, so you've got to get in first.' She glared at him. 'That's why no one doublecrosses Trixie and lives long to enjoy it.'

She surveyed him for a moment. 'I reckon you're going to write a bloody good story about me, so if I find anything out about the dead bitch, I'll let you know.'

He was at the door when she called out, 'And you can tell the bugger who writes about the courts that I'll thank him not to harp on my fucking age.'

Chapter 46

Sala was dragging a mop across the beige linoleum floor in the corridor of the Jewish Welfare Society, sighing as she went. Thin and preoccupied, she slouched past Franka Feldman's office, keeping her eyes averted as though avoiding her.

Shortly after eight o'clock, Franka pushed back her chair, adjusted her thick glasses and walked over to Sala, who was bending over a bucket, her hands covered in suds as she rinsed the mop.

'I'm just going to have some coffee,' Franka said. 'Why don't you come in and have some with me?'

Sala was too dejected to chat but, not wanting to be rude, she hung up her pinafore, took the scarf off her head and followed Franka into the office.

It was quiet inside. There was no clatter of typewriters, scraping of chairs or murmur of voices.

'We've got the room to ourselves,' Franka said, pulling up a chair for Sala. 'The typists haven't come in yet and the director's secretary is in his office, taking dictation.'

She unscrewed her thermos, and steam rose towards the high ceiling as she poured out the coffee.

Sala cupped the thick mug in both hands and blew into it. She couldn't think of anything to say, but she was determined not to break down and cry like last time. She took small sips of the scalding liquid and responded to Franka's chatter with monosyllables.

'It's getting harder and harder to get dinner ready these days, with all the blackouts and power cuts,' Franka was saying. 'I've bought a pressure cooker, but I don't know how mothers with young children manage to bath them and do the cooking with all the restrictions. And they say that the trouble with the unions will get worse. How are you managing?'

Sala made a vague comment. She'd read something in the papers about demarcation disputes between various unions, and threats of more strikes on the coalfields, but most of her information came from Beryl, who sided with the workers and blamed the capitalist system for all the problems.

'But this government is Labor, isn't it?' Sala had ventured.

'Look, love,' Beryl had said, putting down her bucket and placing her hands on her hips. 'It's the system what stinks. Bloody politics. Ben Chifley was fair dinkum when he got elected. He tried to nationalise the banks but they wouldn't let him. I just hope that when push comes to shove, he'll have the guts to back the workers.'

With an effort Sala brought her attention back to Franka's question. 'The power cuts don't really affect me, because I don't do much cooking,' she said. She didn't add that Szymon often came in late, after eating dinner God knew where and with whom. And as for her, she'd lost her appetite.

Franka studied Sala for a time without speaking. 'I can see you're having a hard time,' she said after a pause. 'You haven't been yourself for weeks. Is there anything I can do to help?'

Not trusting herself to speak, Sala shook her head.

'Are you quite sure?' Franka persisted. 'Even if I can't do anything, you might feel better if you talk about it. Sorry to keep on, but I know you don't have any family here. It might sound silly but, because I hired you, I feel responsible for you, as if you were family. And I'm old enough to be your mother.'

Sala looked down at her hands without replying.

Franka blinked behind her glasses and said in a faraway voice, 'I had a daughter once.'

Sala looked up.

'Her name was Rutka. She was our only child. In 1942, when she was eighteen, the round-ups in the Warsaw Ghetto were getting more frequent, and they'd already deported tens of thousands of people to Treblinka. Zenek, Rutka and I made a pact. We wouldn't let them take us alive. Then, on a beautiful autumn day, the Nazis and their helpers surrounded our building. We heard them shooting and yelling, and we knew they were coming for us.'

Her eyes were fixed on something in the distance and her voice was so low that Sala had to lean forward to hear what she was saying.

'We were calm. We'd said our goodbyes. The only choice left to us was how and when we'd die, and we weren't going to let them take that away from us. Zenek had got hold of three cyanide pills, one for each of us, and we'd decided that as soon as they burst through the door, we were going to swallow them.'

Sala waited, her hands balled into tight fists.

'We could hear their boots thumping up the wooden stairs. They were banging on our door, yelling for us to open up. Any second now. I held my breath and stared at the door. But nothing happened. The door stayed closed and a minute later I heard them running down the stairs. I sank to the floor and closed my eyes. "Thank God," I kept whispering. "It's a miracle. They didn't come for us after all." I turned around and saw Rutka sitting on the floor, propped against the wall. "Come on," I said, "it's all right, they've gone." But she didn't move. I was looking at her and I still didn't know. Then I looked at Zenek's face and I knew. Rutka hadn't waited. She'd swallowed her pill. I heard someone screaming, screams that made the blood freeze in my veins, and I didn't realise it was me.'

Franka's eyes, magnified by the thick lenses of her glasses, quivered and swelled. Her voice trailed off.

Sala tried to swallow but her tongue was stuck to her palate and her breath was jammed in her chest.

She remembered Zenek's remark at the New Year's Eve party. Now she understood his comment about the destructive power of grief.

'It must be hard for you to talk about it,' she said finally.

'It is,' Franka replied, 'but not talking about it is even harder. I think about Rutka all the time. For the first two years I was in so much pain I thought I'd die. But you know, the sun keeps shining, the birds keep singing, and somehow life has a way of seducing you into staying alive even after you've lost the will to live.'

'So does it help you to talk about it?' Sala asked.

'While I'm talking about her, it feels as if I'm bringing her back to life.'

'What was Rutka like?' Sala asked.

Franka smiled. 'A real livewire. Always laughing, teasing, joking, dancing around, never still. She wanted to be an actress.'

'How did you get over it?'

'I'll never get over it,' Franka said. 'But when you look a ghost in the face and call it by its name, it loses some of its power to haunt you. When Zenek and I were asked to escort a group of Jewish orphans who were sailing to Australia, we were adamant we wouldn't do it. We were paralysed with grief, blaming ourselves and each other, and the last thing we wanted was to be with children who'd survived. But sometimes the thing you dread the most turns out to be your salvation. Being with young people again was like coming into the warmth of a spring day after a frozen winter.'

Sala's eyes glittered with tears. 'I admire you. You're so brave and resilient.'

Franka made a deprecatory gesture. 'You know what resilience is? It's getting up in the morning, making breakfast, going to work, coming home and cooking dinner. Managing to lead what people call a normal life.'

'And you're helping others,' Sala broke in. 'In spite of everything.'

'Not in *spite* of everything,' Franka said softly. '*Because* of everything.'

On the way home Sala thought about Dr and Mrs Feldman and she contrasted their strength with her own emotional paralysis. Silence and solitude had done nothing to banish her phantoms. Perhaps it was time to confront them. She thought about Dr Feldman, who seemed to see into the heart of things. Perhaps he'd understand.

Later that week, Sala sat in a tram that rattled along New South Head Road, and gazed at the succession of little bays, each one prettier than the last. Rushcutters Bay, Double Bay and Rose Bay. The water lapped gently against strips of sandy shore, launches bobbed in the marinas, and white yachts with their spinnakers billowing sailed across the harbour, tacking in between the wooden ferries.

Suffused in the golden light of the summer afternoon, with seagulls screeching overhead and low wooded hills rising above the water, Rose Bay had the laidback atmosphere of a holiday resort, and for the first time since arriving in Sydney, Sala felt stirred by the easygoing beauty of this city.

Alighting in Dover Road, she walked for several blocks until she came to a side street lined with brick bungalows. An elderly man standing by his front gate raised his hat in greeting as she passed. A few doors further on, a woman with a wide-brimmed sunhat tied under her chin was bent over a garden bed. She paused, trowel in hand, as Sala walked by, and smiled. 'Good day for gardening, isn't it?' she said, and resumed planting.

Sala slackened her pace. Now that she was almost there, she felt nervous, and wondered what she would say to Dr Feldman. 'Come by all means,' he'd told her when she'd rung that morning. 'The university year hasn't started yet so I'm home most of the time.' If he'd been surprised by her request to see him, he hadn't shown it. In fact, he sounded almost as though he'd been expecting her call.

The cottage the Feldmans were renting was the colour of the Toruń gingerbread her mother used to buy every year in December. When Zenek opened the door, he seemed older and more stooped than the last time they'd met, and the clumps of wiry hair on either side of his pink skull were greyer than she remembered. Or perhaps now that she knew his story, she was looking at him more attentively.

He ushered her into the small enclosed verandah which looked out onto the patch of grass in front. The medical books spread out on his desk were open at lurid photographs of diseased kidneys, and beside them lay a Polish–English dictionary.

'I have to look up all the strange words I write down in lectures,' he chuckled. 'You'd be surprised how few of them I manage to find in here. English is a peculiar language, calculated to confuse and bewilder us bloody reffos. Have you noticed that hardly any of the words are spelled the way they sound?'

She knew he was trying to put her at ease, but she was too tense to discuss the vagaries of the English language. He sat back in his chair and a large tabby cat crawled onto his lap. Encircling it in the crook of his arm, he stroked it and said, 'This is Felix.'

A moment later the cat jumped from his lap and sprang up onto the windowsill, its whiskers brushing against the glass. 'Let's have tea, shall we?' Zenek said. 'The coffee in Sydney is so terrible, I've learned to drink tea.'

She was about to tell him about Repin's Coffee Lounge but stopped herself. She didn't want to think about Alex.

Zenek padded down the hall in his tartan slippers, and a moment later she heard the clatter of cups and the hollow sound of water filling a kettle. While waiting for him to return, she crossed and uncrossed her legs, fidgeted with her bag, and got up and looked at the bookcase, but her eyes slid from one shelf to another without registering any titles.

Zenek came back with a tray which he placed on the edge of the desk, pushing away the books to make room.

'How brave are you?' he asked in a jocular tone. 'I baked some biscuits this morning but I think they're like bricks.'

As she bit into one of them, it broke off with a loud snap

and they both laughed. They finished their tea, and in the silence that followed she tried not to fidget, knowing his heavy-lidded gaze was on her.

He set aside his cup and looked straight into her eyes, making it hard for her to avert her gaze. 'How do you think I can help you?'

She sighed. 'I don't know if you can. I'm so confused, I don't even know where to start.'

'Let's see. Of all the things you've got on your mind, what's worrying you the most?'

'I keep wondering if I'm normal. I should be happy. I've survived the war, my husband loves me, and I've come to a good country where I can make a fresh start, but I can't sleep and I'm miserable.'

'Tell me about yourself. What was your life like before the war?'

She took a deep breath and her face glowed as though lit by an interior lamp as she described the life she'd led with her adoring parents. 'Then the war broke out,' she said, and stopped. Now she had to be on her guard.

'What happened then?' he asked.

She shrugged. 'Everyone I loved was killed. Mama, Tata, aunts, uncles, cousins. I was the only one left.'

'How did that happen?'

She bit the inside of her lip and looked out of the window. A woman was pushing a baby in a stroller while a toddler skipped beside her, singing. She turned back to Zenek.

'A wonderful man saved me. He risked his life to hide me in his house.'

Zenek was nodding. 'What was he like, this wonderful man?'

Again she seemed lit up as she told him how kind Ernst had been, and how he'd protected her, even from his wife.

Zenek was studying her with that gaze which seemed to focus on nothing yet saw everything. 'So here I am,' she concluded.

'Confused and miserable,' he said.

After a long pause, he went on, 'You mentioned that you had trouble sleeping. Maybe you need barbiturates or sleeping pills, but I can't help you with that. You'd have to go to a registered doctor for a prescription. Would you like to try that and see if it helps?'

Taking pills was a tempting option, but she sensed he was testing her to see how determined she was to solve her problems.

'I don't think pills are the answer,' she said. 'I have strange dreams.'

He raised his bushy eyebrows. 'The same dream, or different dreams?'

'The same one. About a trapdoor.'

'And where does the trapdoor lead?'

'To a cellar.'

They looked at each other like adversaries at the start of a boxing match, dancing around each other as they assessed each other's strength and weaknesses.

'Dreams often reveal what our mind would prefer to conceal,' he said. 'Would you like to tell me about that cellar?'

Her heart beat so fast that she could feel it thumping against her ribs. She wanted to run from the room and never come back, but she forced herself to tell him about Ernst Hauptmann's house, the arguments he had with his wife, and the trapdoor which led to the cellar. She told him how good Ernst had been to her but said nothing about the intimate side of their relationship.

While she talked, he made encouraging sounds without taking his eyes off her. When she'd finished, he rested his chin on his steepled fingers.

'When you wake up from that dream, are you upset because you're back in that cellar or because you're not?'

His question startled her with its unexpected insight, and she looked down without replying.

'Tell me how you feel when you open that trapdoor and see the cellar.'

She thought for a moment. 'I feel happy. Relieved.'

'Do you think you are happy because you've discovered that the house where you and your husband are living has such a cellar?'

She nodded and then shook her head. 'Yes. No. I don't know. My dream doesn't have anything to do with Szymon.'

'But you're happy when you discover that the house you've never liked actually contains the refuge you've been longing for.'

She shrugged. His interpretation placed too much emphasis on her relationship with Szymon.

'Do you have any idea why you're having those dreams at the moment?' he asked.

She told him of the notice about Ernst Hauptmann, and the chaos it had caused in her life.

He looked at her intently. 'If he was so good to you, why are you having so much trouble deciding whether to write a letter to help him?'

She stared out of the window.

'I know this is very hard for you,' he said after a long silence. 'Tell me, what made you decide to come and talk to me?'

'I had a feeling you'd understand.'

He nodded. 'And how do you feel now? Has our conversation helped to clear up some of the confusion?'

'I don't know. In a way I feel even more confused,' she said. 'I need to go home and think.'

Zenek stood at the window watching as Sala opened the gate, and his throat closed up. Rutka would have been the same age if she'd lived. He sighed and turned back to his textbooks. Transference was something that was supposed to happen to the patient, not the psychiatrist.

Chapter 47

Sister Joan Gately planted her large feet in the hallway, placed her bulky travel bag on the floor, unpinned her large black hat and took off her loose black coat with an air that showed she meant business. Refusing Kath's offer of tea, she asked to see the patient.

'No time to waste,' she said in a voice that indicated a lifetime of order and discipline.

Meggsie was sitting in the armchair beside his bed staring into space when Sister Gately came in. She sat on the edge of the bed and pulled back the sheet covering his legs. No matter how often Kath saw his thin, wasted legs, the sight always made her draw in her breath.

Sister Gately picked up each limb like a housewife feeling a leg of lamb, muttering to herself and shaking her head as she did so. 'We've got a lot of work ahead of us,' she said in a grim voice.

Upset by her brusque manner, Kath didn't know what to say, but the nurse didn't wait for a response.

'Sister Kenny has proved time and time again that a lot of the damage in polio cases is caused by the treatment and not the disease,' she said. 'She kept telling the doctors that immobilising the limbs of polio sufferers does a lot of damage, but they didn't listen to her, did they?'

Seeing Kath's confused expression, she pulled out a sheaf of papers from her travel bag, spread them on the bed and pointed to intricate diagrams of muscles and nerve pathways to illustrate her point.

Kath didn't understand the diagrams or the rigmarole about receptors, proprioceptors and subcutaneous tissues, but she was reassured by the fact that Sister Gately was so knowledgeable.

'Pity I didn't get to see him sooner, but better late than never,' Sister Gately said. 'We have to help those muscles recover. We'll stimulate them and loosen them up so they'll start working again. I'll give him hot, moist compresses and show you how to do the exercises and give him warm salt baths. But if you don't follow my instructions to the letter, I'm wasting my time and you're wasting your money.'

As she raised Meggsie's legs, one at a time, he groaned and shot Kath a beseeching look to rescue him. She bit her lip and looked away while the nurse continued to check the extent of the muscle wastage.

When she'd finished she gave Meggsie a stern look. 'I want you to remember two little rhymes,' she said, wagging her finger at him like a schoolteacher. '"No gain without pain", and "If you don't use it, you'll lose it." I want you to keep saying them over and over in your mind while you're doing your exercises,' she said. 'Will you do that? Good boy.'

After applying the hot compresses she called foments, she demonstrated the exercises, stressing that they had to be done frequently and with ever-increasing pressure. Then she looked at her watch.

'Time to go,' she said, ramming on her hat and pulling on her coat. 'Make sure you do the exercises three times a day.'

She was at the front door when Kath stopped her. 'Do you think he'll walk again?' she asked in a low voice.

'All I can tell you is what Sister Kenny once said. "Human hands are only the instruments of the great unseen hand which shapes our destiny."' She quoted the words as though reciting a holy text. 'But he'll have a good chance of regaining some movement if you follow my instructions.'

'Why aren't there more Kenny clinics in Sydney?' Kath asked.

Sister Gately put her bag on the floor, leaned against the wall and folded her arms. Now that they were talking about her favourite subject, she wasn't in a hurry to get away.

'Professional jealousy, that's why. The doctors didn't like a bush nurse showing them up, and the massage association was scared of the competition. Sister Kenny's in her sixties now, and her methods have been recognised in England and America, but there's only one Kenny clinic in Sydney. It's a real disgrace, but you know what they say — you can't be a prophet in your own country!'

Kath had never heard that saying but she nodded. She was angry that no one had ever told her that there was another way of treating this horrible disease.

After Sister Gately had gone, Kath went back to Meggsie's room. He looked miserable.

'Gee, Mum, I don't want to do those horrible exercises or have those hot packs. The exercises hurt and they're boring, and they probably won't even do anything.'

'Listen to me,' she said, in a sharper tone than usual. 'You're going to do them whether you like it or not, because Sister Gately said they're going to help.'

'Like fun they will,' he muttered, and added, 'I don't even like the old bat.'

He turned back to his book, and Kath left the room with a heavy step. What he needed now was courage and confidence, and she didn't know how she was going to get him out of this defeatist mood.

Talking to Verna Browning usually cheered her up, but when she knocked on her neighbour's door half an hour later, she found Verna absorbed in her own troubles.

'I'm worried about Ted,' Verna said. 'He hardly eats a thing, and spends most of his time moping around. At night I can hear him pacing up and down in his room like a caged tiger. I've never seen him like this, but he won't tell me what's going on. And I think he's spending too much time at the Journalists' Club. I'm sure he's pining for that New Australian girl up the street, but he won't talk about it.'

'That's love for you,' Kath said.

She understood how Ted felt. Her parents had done their best to try and stop her from marrying Jack because she was so young, and he was a Protestant, and irresponsible, but she'd been on fire, and she'd known she couldn't live without him. Even now, after all he'd done, the memory of their lovemaking still made her body stir with yearning. Sometimes she wondered whether she would make a different choice if she could turn the clock back. And sometimes it crossed her mind that perhaps the choice she'd made had somehow been responsible for Meggsie's illness.

No one warned you when you had children that you'd never stop worrying about them, Verna thought as she changed from her house dress into the seersucker frock she'd made for Christmas. She'd intended to cook Ted's favourite dinner, to tempt him to eat something, but the power was off again, so she picked up her string bag to do a spot of shopping in the Junction instead.

Closing the gate behind her, she smiled ruefully as an old saying came into her mind. *Little children tug at your apron strings, big children tug at your heartstrings.* When Ted was little, she'd worried about him getting scalded by boiling water or being lost in a department store. Now it was his state of mind she was worried about. She'd tried several times to get him to talk, but he sounded so irritated that she stopped asking. After all, he was entitled to his privacy.

Pop Wilson raised his large-knuckled hand in greeting as she walked past, and she wondered, as she often did, what had become of Nola. Behind their polite and pleasant exterior, it seemed that everyone was locked inside their own cocoon of secrecy, and she wondered how it would be if people spoke honestly about their feelings.

She gave an involuntary shudder. We'd all be swamped by a torrent of self-indulgent waffle, she thought.

It might suit the New Australians, who were excitable and overemotional, but it certainly wouldn't do for Aussies.

Especially not Aussie blokes, who were stoic and reserved to the point of being inarticulate. Ted probably took after his dad. Alf always clammed up whenever something was bothering him. He'd become distant and withdrawn, struggling in silence with his demons, and she'd understood him well enough to leave him alone until he'd solved his problem. They'd lived their life in calm companionship without raised voices or arguments. The only argument she recalled was over his decision to join up.

Now that she thought about it, there was only one aspect of their married life that disappointed her, although she'd never alluded to it. They hadn't been intimate since Ted started high school. Although she had always thought that sex was greatly over-rated, she missed the physical closeness when Alf stopped reaching out for her at night. Like the young women whose letters she often read in the *Women's Weekly*, she was too embarrassed to talk to him about it. Now that it was too late, she wondered whether he too had been too shy to broach the subject. Perhaps Alf too had had a secret he'd been unable to share. Verna sighed. Why did it take a lifetime to gain some understanding?

She'd almost reached the end of the street when she glanced at Mr Emil's place. His white face appeared in the front window and, a moment later, vanished from view. Mr Emil was another of Wattle Street's mysteries, and as Verna continued on her way to Oxford Street, she wondered whether he'd ever admit he'd left the money under Kath's door.

Inside the room where the two coffins lay, Emil lit the candles and paced up and down the room, wondering how to find the words to ask the ghosts of his dead children to absolve him of his promise. It was a sin to break a solemn oath given to a living person, but it seemed even worse to break a covenant made with the dead. Four years had passed since he'd vowed on his children's souls never to perform magic again. Would they understand and forgive him if he broke that vow? Could he forgive himself?

Chapter 48

Anna Vestermanis lived in Coogee on a hilly street that resembled a roller-coaster, and by the time Ted had reached her flat, his heart was thumping in his ears.

She opened the door cautiously and kept the chain across it while he held up his press card and explained why he'd come.

'You never know,' she said as she removed the chain to let him in. 'I live alone, so I have to be careful.'

Mrs Vestermanis was a small, thin woman and her jerky movements reminded Ted of a wary sparrow. Although she looked quite young, the brown hair brushed back from her forehead was speckled with grey.

'Your English is very good,' he said.

She inclined her head at the compliment. 'I was an English teacher in Riga,' she said, ushering him into her lounge room.

A sad atmosphere permeated the room, as though it was in permanent shadow and no sunlight ever warmed its cold walls. From the sparse furniture and lack of any ornaments, it seemed little more than a roof over her head. The only personal item was a small framed photograph on the mantelpiece.

'I've come to see you because of the letter you wrote about a man you recognised from Riga,' Ted said.

She nodded and clasped her hands, which were trembling. 'When I saw him I couldn't believe my eyes. I thought I would vomit in the street. He was in Arajs Kommando. But you Australians don't know about them.'

'I do,' he said, and took the photo of Paulis Olmanis from his pocket. 'This was their uniform, wasn't it?'

She took it from him and the colour drained from her face. In a hoarse voice she said, 'But that's him. That's the man I saw in town that day.'

She stood up and started pacing around the room, clasping and unclasping her hands. She stopped by the window, glanced outside, shook her head several times, mumbled something in a foreign language, and came back to have another look at the photograph.

In an unsteady voice, Ted asked, 'Can you tell me anything about him?'

'This man was in charge of a death squad outside Lipaja at the beginning of 1942,' she said.

Ted sat forward, trying to control his agitation. 'Are you sure? Perhaps the man you saw in town just looks like him.'

She gave a bitter laugh. 'Mr Browning, you are very young, and thank God you have not seen what I have seen. So you do not know that there are faces you can never forget, even when you try.'

She jumped up. 'Before we talk, I make coffee, yes?'

He heard her moving around in the tiny kitchen, opening drawers, clattering dishes and setting something on a stove.

A few moments later the tiny flat was filled with the aroma of brewing coffee.

She set a cup of black coffee in front of him and apologised for not having any milk. He tasted it, but even after stirring in two heaped spoons of sugar it was too bitter for him. Anna Vestermanis drank hers in quick gulps, and gazed into her empty cup as though she could see scenes from her past in the coffee grounds.

After placing the cup aside, she jabbed the photograph of Paulis Olmanis with her index finger and shuddered. 'There were three groups doing the shooting that day. Germans, Latvian police and that bunch of thugs, the Arajs Kommando.'

She was staring into space as she talked. 'They'd told us we were being relocated, but as soon as the lorries stopped in the woods behind the beach and we saw that long pit, we knew why they'd brought us there. I'll never forget the screaming and crying, and the sound of those rifles shooting and shooting, and seeing people crumpling and falling.'

She paused and looked up. 'Did you know that in Lipaja they lined people up so they couldn't see their faces, and shot them from behind?'

He shook his head and swallowed.

'I had my arm around my little sister. Her face was white and she was shivering, but I told her we'd get away. She was such a pretty little thing, only eleven. I thought surely they would let her go. They started pushing us towards the pit and ordered us to take off all our clothes, everything, and we stood there naked in front of all those men. I didn't think I could bear it. But I looked straight into that man's face and I begged him to let us go, at least to let her go. She was only a child. And he looked straight back at me without any expression at all, and he said, "Today Jewish-Bolshevik blood must flow." I still hear those words in my sleep.'

Ted tried to swallow again but there was a rock in his throat and he coughed instead. 'You were actually there?' he asked. 'Then how come …'

'How come I survived? I also ask myself this. I did not want to stay alive in a world like this.'

Her eyes slid to the photograph on the sideboard. 'That's my mother, father and my little sister. See how lovely she was? He killed them all that day.'

She blinked away the tears, straightened her shoulders and continued. 'When I fell into that pit, I thought I was dead. Perhaps I fainted. But that night, some villagers came to the forest to see if they could find any gold or diamonds on the dead bodies. One of them noticed a tear in my eye and told his companion that I was still alive. I heard them arguing whether to leave me there or not, but finally they pulled me out of the pit and took me to their hut. I suppose I became their good deed, their passport to heaven,' she said bitterly. 'Did you ever hear a story like that? One tear was all that stood between me and being buried alive in a grave full of corpses.'

Ted had trouble filling his lungs with air and he took several deep breaths before he could speak. 'But you only saw the man in charge of that squad for a short time. How can you be sure that he's the one you saw in town the other day?'

'I told you already,' Anna Vestermanis whispered. 'Never I will forget that face as long as I live.'

She looked at Ted. 'I will tell you something interesting. Before the war, I did not feel anti-Semitism in Latvia. Jews and Latvians got on well. When the Germans came and started their evil propaganda about Jews being Communists and committing atrocities during the Bolshevik occupation, I did not think anyone would believe their lies. But they did. Suddenly they hated us. I would never have believed how easy it is to turn neighbours into enemies, and decent people into killers.'

She gave Ted a long, penetrating look. 'You are a journalist, you want to understand the world, so I will tell you this: if it could happen there, it could happen anywhere.'

Her words disturbed Ted so much that it took him a while to gather his thoughts. 'If it ever came to it, would you be prepared to testify against him?' he asked.

'And go through all that horror again?' she said. 'You do not know what you are asking. You are asking me if I want to go back to hell.'

'But you might be the only person in Australia who could give evidence against him. Wouldn't you want him to answer for what he did?' he persisted.

She sighed again. 'I thought when I came to Australia I was finished with the war. I wanted to look forward. But the past lives on in us, no? Well, if they need my testimony, I will give it.'

Ted didn't realise he'd been holding his breath until he let it out.

On the doorstep he remembered to ask her about something that had puzzled him ever since he had come across her letter.

'What made you send the letter to the Anti-Fascist Society?'

She shrugged. 'It was fate. When I came out of a tearoom in a small street behind the Hotel Australia and saw that man, I was so shocked that I almost collapsed, and I had to lean against a building. When I moved away, I saw I was leaning on a plaque of the Anti-Fascist Society. I decided it was a sign, so I wrote to them.'

She gave him a crooked smile. 'What do you think about this, Mr Browning? Do you believe in fate?'

She surveyed him expectantly while he struggled with a reply. He knew he owed her an honest answer, but the truth was too complicated to unravel and too painful to contemplate.

'I don't know,' he said finally. He thanked her for the interview and left.

Ted's face had a greenish hue as he walked beside Lilija along the dappled paths of Hyde Park two days later. The sun was about to set on this pleasant evening in late summer, and people walking through the park after work stopped and pointed at the boughs of the acacias and eucalypts glowing in the sunset.

The beauty of the evening was lost on Ted. Holding Lilija's hand more tightly than usual, he led her to his favourite corner of the park, a recessed secret garden, where sprays of violet wisteria spilled from a trellis above the benches and perfumed the air with its delicate fragrance.

He cleared his throat a few times and clasped her hand so tightly that she pulled away from his grip. She had come straight from the hospital, and with her hair pulled back into a knot she looked more beautiful than ever. He was panic-stricken as he looked at her. Perhaps he didn't have to tell her. He could tell Gus his investigation hadn't produced anything concrete and continue seeing Lilija as though nothing had changed. But he couldn't base his life on pretence and lies. There was no way out, and he knew it.

'Ted, something is wrong, I feel so,' she said in her lilting voice. She pressed against him and stroked his arm. 'Tell me. What is it? I did something to make you sad?'

He gazed at her with such intensity that she looked alarmed.

'Lilija, I don't know how to say this. I know it will be a big shock, but there's something I have to tell you.'

She stiffened, and from the anxious way she looked at him he realised that she thought he wanted to break it off, that he didn't want to see her any more.

Putting his arm around her shoulders, he drew her closer. 'It's not about us. It's about your father.'

'He say something bad to you, yes?'

Ted had rehearsed this scene in his head a hundred times but the reality was much worse than he'd imagined. He took a deep breath and squeezed her hand so hard that she cried out.

'Lilija, listen. You know you said your father fought in the Latvian army, that he was a war hero? Well, that isn't true.'

She drew away, frowning. 'I do not understand. What are you talking about?'

He was squeezing her hand again. If only there was some easy way to say this. But that was like wishing you could hurl a brick through a window without shattering the glass.

'Your father wasn't an ordinary soldier fighting the enemy in battle. He was in the Arajs Kommando.'

She looked at him uncomprehendingly and he realised he'd have to tell her the brutal truth.

She sat very still while he spoke, but he could feel that she was simmering with anger.

When he'd finished, her face was white and taut. 'I do not believe you!' she burst out. 'You lie. My father never do that. I will not listen.'

She stood up and he pulled her down again.

'You've got to listen. Your father's the one who's been telling you lies. One day it will all come out — do you want to be the last person to find out? Do you want to go through life believing lies?'

'They are not lies!' she shouted. 'You do not know my father. He is good man. Honest man. I believe him, not you.'

Ted took out the photograph she'd given him and pointed to the armband on her father's sleeve. 'See that? That's the armband of the Arajs Kommando. I checked it out.'

She stared at him. 'You checked? You used my photograph to spy on my father? Why you did this?'

Ted tried to put his arms around her trembling shoulders but she pushed him away.

'I wouldn't lie about something like that. I love you, and I'd give anything for it not to be true, but it is.'

She was glaring at him, and her eyes burned with resentment. 'How you know this? If not you lied, then other peoples lied. Communists hate my father so they made up this story. Why you told me this?' she hissed. 'You hate my father, yes?'

He tried to imagine how he would feel if someone were to tell him that his own father hadn't died a hero at Tobruk but had really been a mass murderer. Like her, he wouldn't believe it, and like her, he'd try to find reasons why someone might have invented such a story. He would recall how kind and gentle his father had been, and how he'd admired his integrity, just as she was doing now. He'd be furious with anyone who tried to smash one of the foundations on which his life was based. Would the identity of the bearer of such news shake his faith in his father? He sighed. Probably not.

Lilija had turned her back to him, clenching her fists, and when he placed his hand gently on her shoulder she shook it off.

'I know it's very hard for you to listen to what I'm telling you. I'd feel exactly the same. But I've met a woman who recognised him. He was in charge of a death squad —'

She didn't let him finish. Eyes flashing with scorn, she said, 'And you believe her lies! Why is so important to you to say terrible things about my father, why?'

He tried to explain that he didn't have a vendetta against her father. 'Please believe me, I wish none of this was true, because the last thing I want in the whole world is to make you unhappy.'

But as he spoke, he had a hollow feeling of defeat in the pit of his stomach. It didn't matter what he said or what evidence he offered, she would refuse to believe it. And she'd hate him for saying it.

In a hoarse whisper, he pleaded, 'What will it take for you to believe me?'

With an angry gesture, she grabbed her bag and started to walk away.

'Lilija, wait!' he shouted.

An elderly couple strolling arm in arm along the path glanced at him sympathetically, and the woman whispered something to her husband as they walked past.

Ted sprinted towards Lilija and caught up with her in three strides. 'Please don't go!' he pleaded.

She turned towards him. 'Leave me alone!' she cried, and he watched as she hurried from the secret garden and disappeared.

With a groan, Ted sank onto the bench and kept slamming his fist into the wooden seat until he could no longer feel the pain.

Chapter 49

Ted was at his desk trying to cobble together a story about the problems that old-age pensioners and young mothers were having with the ever-increasing power cuts. It was part of Gus's current campaign against the striking unions, but he was overwhelmed by his heartache over Lilija and, to make things worse, the other reporters were going hammer and tongs about the situation in the coalfields, and he couldn't concentrate on the problems people had trying to cook their meals and wash their clothes. A child in an iron lung had died in hospital as a result of a sudden power cut, and Gus was pressuring him to find some heart-wrenching story which would outrage the readers, but all he had was a succession of people whingeing about the inconvenience of the gas and electricity rationing. He was fighting the urge to run out of the newsroom and go straight to Lilija. He'd fold his arms around her and press kisses on her face and she'd realise how much she loved him …

The daydream came to a sudden end. Gus was in the newsroom, ranting about one of his pet themes, the delayed construction of a hydro-electric scheme in the Snowy Mountains. 'That bloody premier of ours should stick a pin into his bum, wake himself up and get on with the job,' he was saying. 'He reckons it's gonna take twenty years and cost a hundred and sixty-six million pounds, but I reckon we won't see it in our lifetime.'

Ted looked over what he'd written about the power cuts and groaned. He couldn't infuse any life into his article, which was weak and clichéd, and his head ached from lack of sleep. If only Lilija's father was dead. The intensity of his hatred shocked him, but it was true. He had never wished anyone dead before, had never imagined that he could feel such malevolence. But he couldn't deny it. If Paulis Olmanis died then all his problems would be over and Lilija would come back to him.

Gus had gone out, but an argument was raging about the coal strike. Predictably, Joe Black defended the miners. 'Fair go!' he was shouting. 'Those blokes are fighting for a 35-hour week and better conditions.'

'Listen, mate,' the industrial reporter was jabbing his finger into Joe's chest, 'you're dreaming. This is about union power, not miners' conditions. What will their conditions be like if there's a national strike and they're all out of work? Hundreds of thousands of poor buggers will be out of work before this is over, and they'll all hate the miners, but will those Welsh and Pommie bastards who run the unions give a shit? Not bloody likely.'

Ted was so absorbed in the argument that he didn't pick up the receiver until the telephone on his desk had rung several times. He didn't recognise the gruff voice that barked, 'Is that Ted Browning? Got a message for you from Trixie. Wants you to pull your finger out and get cracking with that article you're supposed to be writing about her. And another thing. That sheila you asked her about. It was Nola Wilson.'

Ted opened his mouth to say something but the line went dead.

The heated voices in the newsroom receded as Ted tried to make sense of what he'd just heard. It couldn't be right. Pop Wilson's daughter was a nurse, she couldn't have anything to do with the callgirl who was shot dead in her Kings Cross apartment. Perhaps there was another girl with the same name. But the more he thought about the nurse who'd vanished and had been erased from her father's life as though she'd never existed, the more plausible it became.

Although he was shocked by the news, he was also intrigued by it. He couldn't understand how a respectable girl like Nola had turned into a prostitute called Scarlett O'Halloran, and he supposed he'd never know, but here under his nose was a true story with all the ingredients of a mystery novel. An attractive, decent girl who for some reason had become a callgirl and been murdered by a client. It sounded like the plot of a Raymond Chandler story, or the script for an RKO movie starring Humphrey Bogart, Edward G Robinson and Lauren Bacall. And here he was, spending his time writing about Kosy kerosene heaters, fuel-powered coppers, cold dinners and unwashed children.

He thought about Pop Wilson. Pop always had a friendly word for everyone, and he'd never given any indication of the pain he must have felt at the rift with his only daughter. Had she ever contacted him? And if so, did he know what she had become, or why?

Suddenly he sat bolt upright. Pop would have to be told. He'd have to identify the body which still lay on a cold slab in the morgue, unclaimed. Ted pushed his typewriter away, reached for the phone, dialled the Darlinghurst Police Station and asked for Detective Sergeant Mitchell.

'Remember the callgirl who was shot in Macleay Street in June last year?' he began. 'Did you ever find out who she was?'

'No, mate. Drew a blank. What's your problem?'

Ted couldn't keep the gloating tone from his voice. 'I thought you'd like to know that I've found out who she was.'

'Oh yeah? Smart guy, eh? Okay, spit it out.'

There was a tight knot in Ted's stomach and a sour taste in his mouth when he hung up a few minutes later. As he sat at his desk, he could visualise the scene at Pop's place when the police knocked on his door.

'Are you Mr Wilson?' the cop would ask. 'Do you have a daughter called Nola?'

Pop would nod, his chest tightening, suspecting that he was about to hear the news he'd been dreading for years.

'I'm afraid I have some bad news,' the detective would say.

Ted could see the smile freeze on Pop's lips and his face blanch as he swayed on his feet and held the doorframe for support. He would ask the cop to come in and offer him a drink, which would be refused, and then with trembling hands he'd uncork the bottle on the sideboard and pour himself a glass of port, sloshing some of it on the carpet. Then he'd sink into the worn armchair in front of the mantelpiece facing the photo of himself as a lifesaver. He'd swallow the port, and in a dull voice he'd ask what had happened.

He'd listen in silence, head bowed, then pour himself another drink, too numb to show any emotion but too distraught to stop the shaking of his hands. Perhaps he'd let out a soft groan and bury his face in his hands.

'Are you all right, Mr Wilson?' the officer would ask, and of course Pop would nod and say he was okay. Next, the officer would ask if he'd accompany him to the morgue. Too polite to refuse or ask for more time, Pop would rise heavily from the armchair, and with a disbelieving shake of his balding head, he'd take a shirt from the bedroom drawer and his old jacket from the hook in the hall, put on his felt hat, shuffle out of his house and get into the police car for the most terrible ride of his life.

The argument about the miners' strike had fizzled out and, as usual, no one had changed their mind.

Joe Black stopped by Ted's desk. 'You look as if you've seen a ghost,' he said. 'We're going to the Journos' Club. Want to come?'

Ted jumped up. A drink was exactly what he needed. But before he could grab his hat, the sickly smell of Gus's cigarette filled the newsroom.

'How's your war crime investigation going? Found lots of Nazis hiding in Sydney closets, have you?'

Ted shrugged and made a noncommittal response. His swollen hand ached, and he didn't feel up to discussing war criminals. But from the expression on his boss's jowly face, it was clear that Gus wasn't going to be fobbed off.

'Come into my office,' he growled.

Gus flung himself into the large black leather armchair on the raised platform and, as usual, Ted felt like a schoolboy about to be hauled over the coals by his headmaster.

'You've been wasting a lot of fucking time on this Nazi investigation of yours,' Gus said. 'I'm the one paying for that time, so I want to know exactly what you've come up with.'

Since his meeting with Anna Vestermanis, Ted had been in turmoil. The scenario that was unfolding before him with chilling inevitability was about to test his personal and professional integrity. After months of investigation, the scoop he'd always dreamed of now lay within his grasp. He sensed he had the power to reveal something of immense national and human importance. He could already see the headline with his by-line. WAR CRIMINALS AMONG US. No reporter worth his salt would bury such a story. But if he wrote an exposé naming Lilija's father, he would bury his dreams for their future together.

Gus knew he was following up a lead about a Latvian migrant who might have committed war crimes, but if Ted told him about his interview with Anna Vestermanis. Gus would insist on running the story immediately, and Ted needed time to reflect on the enormity of what he was contemplating. And he had to contact Lilija and let her know the story would soon appear. As he stammered an evasive reply, Gus cut him short.

'Cut the fucking crap!' he shouted. 'You knew all that months ago. I want to know who these bastards are, where they are, what they did, when they did it, what they're doing now, and what proof you have to back it up. Jesus fucking Christ, do I have to teach you the basic rules of reporting after all this time? I can't figure out if you're plain stupid or bloody incompetent.'

Ted sat in silence. He was tempted to defend himself by telling Gus about the interview with Mrs Vestermanis, but fear held him back. He needed more time.

Gus pulled himself heavily to his feet and leaned over the desk until his red face was only inches away from Ted's. In a less belligerent tone, he said, 'Look, son, we both know that our politicians don't want to expose these Nazi bastards, so your only hope — and it's a small one — is to present as much evidence as possible to back up your claims.'

Ted nodded, and assumed the conversation was over, but Gus said casually, 'I suppose you've already talked to the

Latvian bloke? Because you've got to get a quote from him even if you break into his house to get it.'

Ted fought a rising feeling of nausea. He opened his mouth to say that there was no chance of getting Mr Olmanis to talk to him as he'd refused to have him in the house or anywhere near his daughter, when he remembered that he'd never told Gus about his involvement with Lilija. A small voice in his head told him that now he had a way out which wouldn't compromise his integrity. He wouldn't be able to write the story because the man accused of a war crime would refuse to talk to him.

Chapter 50

Deep in thought, Sala was walking towards Dr Feldman's place, when she saw his elderly neighbour weeding her garden.

Straightening her back with a groan and pushing her big straw sunhat back from her eyes, the woman said, 'Nice day for a stroll.'

Sala stopped by the white picket fence and looked at the floral kaleidoscope of petunias, dahlias and snapdragons. Behind the familiar flowers were bushes she had never seen before. Some of their flowers were shaped like long brushes, with fine crimson filaments, while others resembled furled scraps of apricot-coloured tissue paper with long yellow stamens.

The woman followed Sala's gaze. 'The red ones are Callistemon. "Bottlebrush", we call them, and you can see why,' she said. 'And that bush over there is a hibiscus. Do you have those where you come from?'

A light breeze stirred the leaves and petals, and Sala breathed in a perfume that made her close her eyes with pleasure. 'It's that bush over there.' The woman was pointing to a dense bush covered with violet, blue and white flowerets.

'Bet you've never seen one like that before,' she said. 'Three colours on one bush. Yesterday, today and tomorrow.'

Seeing Sala's puzzled look she added, 'That's its name. Because of the three colours.'

'Yesterday, today and tomorrow,' Sala repeated.

As she looked at the flowers, she felt calmer than she'd felt in a long time. The garden was a haven of tranquillity where no dark thoughts intruded and no words were necessary.

'You are a very good gardener,' she said.

'I do my best, but it's a never-ending race between me, the snails and the weeds, and they usually win,' the woman laughed. 'You do any gardening yourself?'

In the city apartment where Sala had lived as a child there had been no garden, but her mother had kept small pots of scarlet geraniums near the window. In spring their housekeeper often came home with sheaves of lilac or little bunches of lilies-of-the-valley she'd bought from the peasant women at the market. Sala would press her nose against the sprigs of lilac or the tiny white bells of the lily-of-the-valley until she felt dizzy with their perfume. She'd never thought of having a garden, but the idea of growing her own flowers suddenly filled her with joy. Not just the plants she knew, but these strange Australian ones, with their exotic flowers and peculiar names.

'I would like to have a garden like yours one day,' she said.

'Well, when you do, come over and I'll give you some cuttings to get you started,' the woman said.

Sala pushed open the gate to the Feldmans' home and rang the bell, pressing her face against the glass panels of the front door to see if Dr Feldman was coming. Although she hadn't gained any insights or resolved any problems over the past two weeks, she was looking forward to seeing him again. Perhaps Mrs Feldman was right and talking to someone who listened and tried to understand did ease some of the burden.

She pressed the bell again, and a moment later she heard Dr Feldman hurrying down the hall, talking to Felix.

'I was tidying the back garden,' Zenek panted. 'I'm not much of a gardener, but I don't want to let the neighbourhood down.'

Sala nodded. 'I was just talking to your next-door neighbour about gardening.'

They were standing in the hallway, and he seemed about to usher her into the front room when he said, 'It's such a beautiful day, why don't we sit outside?'

The Feldmans' back garden was a rectangle of yellowish grass surrounded by spindly hydrangea bushes whose mauve clusters rose above crinkly brown-edged leaves.

'I think my secateurs are too blunt,' Zenek said ruefully, surveying the result. Pushing aside the heap of woody twigs he'd snapped off, he wiped sticky cobwebs and dead leaves off two wooden chairs and invited her to sit down while he went inside to make tea.

A light breeze ruffled her hair and carried the scent of

yesterday, today and tomorrow from the garden next door. When she had a garden, she decided, she would plant that bush.

Zenek returned with a tray and placed it on a wobbly table. 'No biscuits today,' he said. 'But we do have cake.'

As Sala nibbled Franka's homemade poppyseed cake and laughed as Felix pounced on beetles crawling across the grass, she wished she could prolong this pleasant interlude, but the conversation stopped and she was aware that Dr Feldman was watching her and waiting for her to speak.

She put her plate down. 'I've been thinking about what you asked me last time,' she said slowly. 'About having so much trouble deciding what to do about that letter.'

He nodded.

She looked down at her hands and he watched her twisting her wedding ring around her finger. 'I didn't tell you what happened in the cellar,' she said.

'Would you like to tell me now?'

She took a deep breath, and for the next hour she described her stay in Ernst Hauptmann's cellar.

'Do you think you fell in love with him?' Dr Feldman asked.

She blushed, and he added, 'That would be quite normal, under the circumstances.'

'Nothing that happened to me feels normal,' she said.

'How does it feel?' he asked.

She looked up at the cloudless sky, then down at her hands again. 'It feels as if there's something wrong with me.'

He nodded. 'You're blaming yourself, but anyone in your situation would have done exactly the same. You did it to survive. What happened wasn't your fault.'

His words were comforting but she sensed that he'd sidestepped the issue.

'So what happened to personal responsibility?' she asked, more sharply than she'd intended. 'Is it all right to do whatever we like just because it's not our fault?'

He was studying her. 'What do you want me to say?' he asked at last. 'That it *was* your fault? Will that solve the problem?'

Suddenly she was sobbing. 'I'm the problem,' she whispered hoarsely. 'It's me. I'm no good. A decent man loves me but I only want men who are bad for me. First Ernst, and now ...' She stopped, not wanting to reveal her recent infatuation with Alex.

'Perhaps you fell in love — or thought you were in love — with the man who saved you because it validated your sexual relationship. Perhaps being in love gave you permission to be intimate and to enjoy it.'

She reddened again.

'Don't forget that you were completely at his mercy. He had the power of life and death over you, and that relationship kept you safe. Perhaps you still don't feel safe, so you're falling into another relationship with someone who has more power than you. Love is a very strange phenomenon,' he continued. 'On one hand we want to replicate the delights of a past love affair, but at the same time we don't want to repeat its mistakes.'

She was still silent.

'I want to ask you something,' he said. 'If it hadn't been for the war, and the fact that your life was in danger, would you have had a sexual relationship with this man?'

This time she had no trouble replying. 'Of course not! I was seventeen. And we lived in different worlds. My parents were doctors, and he was a farmer.'

'So the only reason you did it was because you were in his power. Because he forced himself on you.'

'It wasn't like that!' she exclaimed. She wished she hadn't come, that she hadn't started delving into this snake pit of tangled emotions. Dr Feldman could never understand, and she could never explain how it had happened, or how she had felt. It was impossible to re-create those circumstances and the powerful emotions she and Ernst had both felt.

'You're still making excuses for him,' Dr Feldman observed. 'Don't forget that you were all alone, totally isolated from everything and everyone. You were craving human contact, and he took advantage of that.'

'You don't understand,' she said. 'I don't suppose anyone can.'

'I understand one thing,' he said, and his eyes were half closed, whether against the sun or to conceal his thoughts, she couldn't tell. 'You've been struggling with yourself for a long time over that letter. If he was as good as you say, then why haven't you written back to support him?'

'It's Szymon,' she stammered. 'He got so angry ...'

'So Szymon stopped you?'

She looked longingly at the door leading to the house, and he followed her gaze.

Leaning forward, he said, 'I know this is very hard for you. You're very brave to try and deal with it. You can come back and talk about this another time if you prefer.'

He was making it easy for her to leave but she didn't move. 'It wasn't just because of Szymon,' she said slowly.

For a few moments they sat in silence. Then he looked straight into her eyes. 'Sala, you need to face the fact that this man took advantage of you. Maybe he was sorry for what he did, and maybe he won you over, but the fact is, he forced himself on you knowing you couldn't do anything to resist. So in that sense, he is a rapist.'

Tears sprang to her eyes. 'I just can't think about him like that. I can't,' she whispered.

'He obviously had some redeeming qualities and you can choose to forgive him if you want to. But you can only forgive someone after you've confronted what they've done. You need to stop deluding yourself about the nature of your relationship in the cellar, because as long as you do, you won't be free to love anyone who is your equal.'

'I'm still confused about that letter,' she said and she couldn't keep the reproachful tone out of her voice. 'I still don't know what to do about it.'

'When you're ready, you'll know what to do.'

Zenek walked with Sala to the front gate, and as he watched her walk away he felt the familiar pain in his chest. He knew what it was. Although the cardiologist he'd consulted at Franka's insistence had diagnosed angina pectoris, Zenek knew it wasn't a physical problem. It amazed him that so many doctors still resisted the fact that powerful emotions could produce muscle spasm.

He stood at the gate for a long time after Sala had disappeared from view, and thought about guilt, responsibility and forgiveness. With a sigh he turned to go inside. It was far easier to forgive others than to forgive yourself.

Sala walked slowly along Wattle Street, still unsettled by her conversation with Dr Feldman. Her Latvian neighbour was on her verandah holding a metal watering can, and for the first time Sala noticed that she had scarlet geraniums in window boxes.

'Your geraniums are beautiful,' she said.

The woman looked up. 'Geraniums grows good everywhere,' she said. 'In my home, big garden with trees and flowers, but here is not space. So geraniums only.'

As Sala listened, she realised that it wasn't just the window boxes she hadn't noticed before. Although the woman lived only a few doors away, she had never really looked at her, or said anything other than a perfunctory hello while walking past. Her reticence had something to do with the fact that this woman came from a country that had been allied with Germany. But looking at her now, Sala saw a displaced woman like herself who had lost everything and was trying to rebuild her life in a country where she had no roots.

Putting out her hand, Sala introduced herself.

Her neighbour placed her watering can on the ground, wiped her wet hands on her apron and shook her hand.

'Marija Olmanis,' she said. 'You like, I give you geranium.' She snipped off a small piece of stem and handed it to her. 'You put in soil, in pot, in warm place. Will grow.'

Back in her room, Sala looked at the cutting dubiously. Could such a short piece of stalk, severed from its parent plant, put down roots in new soil, and bloom? It didn't seem likely, but she decided to take a chance and plant it anyway.

Chapter 51

Summer had finally ended. Gone was the relentless heat with its steamy days and sultry nights, and by mid-March the mornings were crisp and the air was invigorating. Sala's life had become easier as well. One of the office girls in the Jewish Welfare Society had left to have a baby, and now that Sala's English had improved, Franka Feldman had recommended her for the job, which involved four hours' office work a day. Sala was overjoyed. Not only would she earn more money and have easier and more interesting work, but she'd be able to fit her hours around her lectures. As long as she filed the papers and articles in the correct folders, and typed the letters by the end of the day, it didn't matter whether she did it in the morning or the afternoon.

'You're so good to me,' she said when Franka told her the news. 'You're like a fairy godmother.'

Franka looked at her searchingly. 'Have you decided about your course yet?' she asked. 'You'll have to enrol soon.'

'I have decided,' Sala said.

'So what will you be — doctor or medical technician?'

Sala shook her head. 'I will learn about flowers and plants.'

Franka couldn't conceal her astonishment. 'How come? Where do you do a course like that? What kind of job will you get when you've finished?'

Sala laughed. 'That's just what my mother would have said. With the same look on her face. I've made some inquiries and there's a course in horticulture starting soon at Sydney Technical College. Who knows, when I finish I might get a job designing gardens.'

Franka sat back in her chair and took off her glasses.

'How did this come about?'

'Funnily enough, it was my last visit to your husband that got me thinking about gardens,' Sala said.

She thought back to the day that had led to her decision, starting with the conversation she'd had with the Feldmans' neighbour, and ending with her own neighbour giving her the geranium cutting. She had liked the earthy smell of the soil and its crumbly moist feel as she'd pushed the cutting into it. She'd left the pot on the windowsill to catch the sun, as Mrs Olmanis had suggested, and watched it every day, wondering whether it would take root and thrive or wither and die.

While looking through the newspaper on the tram one morning on her way to work, she had seen a notice about a certificate course in gardening and horticulture at Sydney Technical College. Instead of going home after work, she'd gone straight there. From the moment she'd seen the imposing brick building decorated with stone reliefs of lizards, wombats, echidnas and kangaroos on its rounded arches, and the waratahs, banksias and flannel flowers in the doorways, she knew she'd made the right decision.

The registrar had explained that she didn't need any prior qualifications to enroll in the gardening and horticulture course, which involved a total of four hours a week, but to do garden design she'd have to wait until she'd gained the gardening and horticulture certificate. The lecture fee was one pound five shillings per term or three guineas for the year.

'It's perfect,' she told Franka. 'I can afford the fees, and the hours will fit in with my office work. For the first time since I've been here I've made a decision without struggling. I know this sounds odd, but it feels as if gardening is going to be my anchor.'

Franka blinked several times and wiped her eyes. 'I think you've made a wise decision,' she said. 'It's wonderful to watch things grow. And maybe one day you'll be able to teach Zenek something about gardening.'

That evening, Sala was surprised when she heard Szymon's key turn in the door earlier than usual. Now that she had decided on her course, the anger she had felt towards him had melted away. She was glad he was home early so that she could tell him her news.

She waited while he hung up his hat and flung the newspaper on the table, but before she had time to say anything, he said, 'Sit down, Sala. I want to talk to you.'

There was something about his tone that made her sit on the edge of her chair.

'I've decided to move out, but you can stay here as long as you like,' he said. 'I'll keep paying the rent.'

Her heart was pounding. She must have misheard. He couldn't be leaving her now that she'd started sorting out her life.

'But Szymon,' she said in a tight voice. 'I wanted to tell you about my new job, and the course I've enrolled in.'

He looked at her, but there was no warmth in his glance.

'That's good,' he said. He didn't ask about the course. 'I hope it works out for you. Did you hear what I just said? I'm moving out.'

She sprang from her chair and started pummelling his chest. 'You can't do that to me! I suppose you've met someone. Don't tell me you're leaving for some flirt who's turned your head.'

He held her flailing wrists. 'As it happens, I've met a woman who enjoys my company and doesn't think I'm crass and vulgar. And how come it's all right for you to carry on with a married man, but it's not all right for me to meet someone?'

The blood rushed to her cheeks and she wondered how he knew about Alex.

'No, it's not all right!' she shouted. 'I'm not carrying on with anyone. And you're married to me!'

'But not for much longer,' he said coldly. 'I don't know what's the matter with you, Sala. You've made it very clear that you don't want me, and now you're making a scene because I'm moving out. I thought you'd be relieved so you can be with your boyfriend. You don't know what the bloody hell you want.'

She sank down on the chair, her chin on her chest. It had never occurred to her that it would come to this. Even when he'd said several weeks before that they should separate, she hadn't really believed him. She was panic-stricken, and didn't know why. Although she often criticised his lack of sensitivity, and resented him for not being the suave, polished man of her dreams, she had never seriously contemplated life without him. In some corner of her psyche, she knew she needed him and she had assumed that he needed her too.

'Don't you love me?' she whispered.

He made an impatient gesture. 'We have to face it, Sala, we've both made a mistake.' He was speaking quietly and without rancour. 'But we're still young, and we can make a new life for ourselves. We want different things, you and I, and there's no reason why we shouldn't both have what we want. For one thing, I want to have children, and you don't.'

At the mention of children she felt something rising in her throat, threatening to suffocate her.

'I never said I didn't want children. I just didn't want them before we were settled.'

'Be honest. You didn't want them with me,' he retorted.

She was about to contradict him but didn't know what to say.

'I want you to know one thing,' he said. 'It's not your fault and I'm not blaming you. It's just that I've realised that I deserve better. I want someone who can accept me as I am. I don't want to spend my life being a poor substitute for a peasant in a cellar, or a suave Casanova.'

Shocked, she turned away. When she turned back, he was pulling a suitcase from under the bed. He took his clothes from the wardrobe and folded them with a precision that infuriated her so much she had to restrain herself from hurling them onto the floor. He didn't speak until he'd finished packing.

'I'm going now,' he said quietly. 'I'll pick up the rest of my things tomorrow.'

Night fell and Sala sat there, motionless. She knew she'd reached a crisis in her life, but the enormity of it paralysed her and she didn't know how to react or what to do. As she replayed the scene in her mind she was struck by the dignity with which he'd spoken. It was his comment about deserving better that had stung the most. But she knew he was right. She had been resentful and critical, and she hadn't appreciated him, and now it was too late.

Perhaps she deserved better too. That's what she'd always thought, and she'd made that clear to Szymon in so many ways. She'd married him in haste and desperation. In her mind, she heard Dr Feldman asking, *Would you have married him if it hadn't been for the war?* Of course she wouldn't. She married Szymon because she'd lost everyone and she was alone. When you're drowning, you even cling to a paper raft to save yourself.

'We are the choices that we make,' her father used to say. But marrying Szymon had been the wrong choice, so she was lucky because now she would have the opportunity to have a happier life. But she didn't feel lucky.

Exhausted, she fell asleep. Once again she dreamed she was in a house where everything was ugly and strange and again she saw a trapdoor and rushed towards it. Her heart was pounding as she raised it. Any moment she'd be with Ernst again. When she looked down, she felt that familiar rush of joy, but it wasn't Ernst waiting for her at the bottom of the ladder. It was Szymon.

Before she was fully awake, a thought formed in her mind. *The biggest secrets are the ones we keep from ourselves.*

Chapter 52

Kath was in the kitchen making pikelets for the boys' afternoon tea, taking advantage of the brief time that the gas was on during the day. The doorbell rang. Putting down the bowl of batter, she hurried to the door, wondering who it could be. The milko had already left her two bottles on the doorstep that morning, the agent collected rents on Mondays, the ice cart delivered blocks of ice on Tuesdays, Sister Gately wasn't due until the following day, and Mr Emil came on Saturdays. But this was Wednesday afternoon and she wasn't expecting anyone.

Thinking about the nurse's next visit, she sighed. Meggsie's refusal to cooperate made the exercises a daily battleground, and she wondered how much longer she'd have the strength to persist. No matter how much she bullied, cajoled, threatened and shouted, he wouldn't listen. 'I'm not going to get any better, Mum,' he'd burst out the night before. 'I hate doing those stupid exercises, they hurt. And the hot packs are a waste of time. Why can't you just leave me alone?'

She was still sighing when she opened the door, but what she saw made her forget everything else. The man on her doorstep wore a black satin cape lined with scarlet satin, and a shiny black top hat, and he held a baton in one hand. His dark hair was slicked back and he'd pencilled a thin black moustache on his upper lip and a goatee beard on his chin. His presence was as impressive as his appearance, and she could tell that this was an experienced showman who knew how to hold audiences in the palm of his hand.

He stood there without saying a word until she cried out, 'Mr Emil? Is it really you?'

She was about to ask why he was in fancy dress when he placed a warning finger on his lips and whispered, 'I want to surprise him.'

Meggsie stared open-mouthed at the apparition in his doorway.

'Morris the Magnificent couldn't make it today so the Great Novello is here instead,' Emil said with a bow and a dramatic flourish of his cape.

It took Meggsie a few moments to collect his wits. 'Mr Emil!' he exclaimed. 'Gosh, what a great costume. You really look the part. I thought it was really him.' He sat forward. 'Can you do any tricks?'

Emil placed his top hat at the end of the bed and lit a cigarette.

'Tricks?' he asked. 'What kind of tricks?'

While he was talking, he made a fist of his other hand, put his lit cigarette into it and opened his fist. There was nothing in his palm. Meggsie's eyes were round with amazement. 'Gee, what did you do with that cigarette? Is it back in the other hand? Or in your sleeve?'

Emil showed him both hands, palms up, and shook out both sleeves.

'How did you do that? Will you show me?

'Show you what?' Emil said with a deadpan expression. 'I don't know what you mean.'

Casually he took four lengths of rope from his case and, as Meggsie watched, the four pieces turned into a whole rope. Before his astonished eyes, scarves appeared and disappeared, and coins vanished into the air.

Emil placed a deck of cards on the bed. 'Spread them out and choose one, but don't tell me which one you chose,' he said. He shuffled the cards several times, cut the deck three times, and riffled through them until the jack of spades was on top. 'This is the card you chose, isn't it?' he said.

'That's incredible!' Meggsie spluttered. 'You're like a real magician, Mr Emil,' he said. 'Can you teach me those tricks? Please?'

Emil looked into his eyes. 'There's more to magic than simply doing tricks,' he said. 'Magic is very powerful.'

'You mean like a potion or a spell?'

'Much more powerful than that,' Emil said gravely. 'Magic is the art of making the impossible seem real. It shows that if you believe in something strongly enough, everything is possible.'

'Can it make my polio go away?'

Emil paused. He knew how important his answer would be.

Over the past few weeks he'd noticed that Meggsie had become increasingly dejected and pessimistic. During his last visit he'd found Kath sitting at the kitchen table, her head propped in her hands. For once she didn't have a welcoming smile or a cheerful comment. 'I'm at the end my tether,' she burst out. 'It's a battle to get him to do those exercises. I don't know how long I can go on like this. Sister Gately was my last hope and now all your money's being wasted.'

Emil didn't understand everything she'd said, but he realised that the boy had lost hope. He knew that he could help Meggsie regain confidence but he also knew that this would come at an enormous cost to himself.

It tore him apart to break the vow he'd made on his children's souls, but he had come to the conclusion that his responsibility to a living child was even more compelling than his promise to two dead ones.

Looking deep into Meggsie's eyes, he said, 'The source of magic is deep inside us, so you have to start by believing in yourself. That means believing you'll get better.'

Meggsie nodded, and his eyes were gleaming with excitement. 'And then will you show me how you do those tricks?'

'Magic isn't a game,' Emil said. 'It's entering a secret society which is thousands of years old. Do you know what an oath is?'

Meggsie nodded eagerly.

'Before you can become a member, you have to take an oath never to reveal the secrets, or the magic will lose its mystery and its power. Will you do that?'

'I swear I won't tell anyone, not even my brothers,' Meggsie said. 'Scout's honour. But can anyone be a magician, or do you have to have special powers?'

'Anyone can do magic if they believe in it,' Emil replied. 'And if they practise a lot. It's like your exercises. If you don't do them properly every day, your muscles will stay weak and they won't work properly. To do the tricks, your hands have to be very strong so you can control them and move them in a smooth, flowing way, because misdirection plays a large part in performing magic.'

Meggsie leaned forward. 'What's misdirection?'

'It means distracting the audience. You have to learn to make large flowing movements to take their attention away from the small movements where the magic really happens. You want them to keep their eyes on something flashy, so they don't see the important things. That will come with practice. Lots of practice.'

Meggsie's face seemed to crumple. 'My hands aren't very good,' he said. 'I haven't got much strength in them.'

'That's why you have to practise so they get stronger,' Emil said. 'I've brought you some small balls that you can squeeze, throw up and catch, and every day you have to try and do it longer and faster. And when your hands are strong enough, and you can do some of the tricks, we will give a little magic show together. You can be my assistant.'

Meggsie looked as though he'd jump out of his skin with excitement. 'Can I wear a top hat too?'

'There is one thing more,' Emil said, and his eyes were boring into Meggsie. 'Magicians have to be honest.'

Meggsie looked away. For several weeks now, ever since Mr Emil had started visiting him, he'd been struggling with himself. Should he confess or not? The more they talked, and the closer they became, the worse it seemed to keep the secret from him, but at the same time the harder it was to own up and risk losing Mr Emil's friendship.

The comment about honesty made Meggsie feel sick. He'd already resigned himself to the fact that God had punished him, but perhaps unless he admitted what he'd done, he'd never be able to do magic.

He stole a glance at Mr Emil. He was sitting in the chair, looking at Meggsie as though waiting for him to say something.

'Mr Emil,' Meggsie began in a tremulous voice, 'I have to tell you something.'

He said it in a rush to get it over with, and added, 'I know I should've told you sooner. I'm real sorry for what I did. Honest.'

He looked down at his hands, not wanting to meet Mr Emil's gaze. He tried to steel himself for the telling-off which was sure to follow. Or, even worse, perhaps Mr Emil would just walk out of the room without saying a word and never come back.

'I have waited for a long time to hear you say this,' Mr Emil said quietly. He spoke in a serious voice, but to Meggsie's surprise, he didn't sound angry or upset. 'We all make mistakes, but it takes courage to admit them. So let us shake hands. And no more secrets between magicians.'

As they solemnly shook hands, the burden that had weighed Meggsie down for so long suddenly lightened, and he couldn't stop smiling.

As Emil was leaving, they heard Ethel Merman belting out her hit song, 'There's No Business Like Show Business' on the kitchen radio.

Meggsie gave his visitor a conspiratorial look. 'Can you hear that, Mr Emil? Show business. That's us!'

'You certainly know how to cheer Meggsie up, Mr Emil,' Kath said as she walked with him to the front door. She'd watched Emil performing his tricks and had heard what he'd said to Meggsie. She had always believed there was more to their mysterious neighbour than met the eye, but this surpassed anything she'd ever imagined.

'He hasn't sounded so happy in weeks. And those tricks! You're quite a magician.'

She'd hoped to engage him in conversation, but he just nodded and was gone.

From inside his room, Meggsie was calling her.

'Mum, let's do those exercises now. I've got to hurry up and get my hands stronger.'

Back in his own house, Emil sat in front of the two coffins, his hands clasped in front of him as he watched the flames on the candles flicker.

'I wanted to keep my promise, but I had to help that boy,' he whispered. 'You want me to help him, don't you?'

He sat communing with the souls of his dead children until the candles guttered and their flames burned out. It was time to release their souls and let them rest among the stars.

The light of day had faded and he went out onto his verandah and looked up.

The first evening star was twinkling in the clear southern sky, and beside it, another one glittered just as brightly. They glowed like candlelight. Emil breathed in the cool night air, and for the first time in many years he felt the consoling beauty of the universe.

Chapter 53

'You're bright and early this morning,' the conductor said as he handed Sala her thruppeny ticket. 'Goin' down to the beach for a swim, are you?'

Although she was working in the office now, she still woke early. Ever since Szymon had moved out, she hadn't been able to sleep; after tossing from side to side, she was always relieved to see the first light of dawn ending the darkness of the night.

It was Saturday and, lying in bed that morning, the whole day had stretched ahead of her. Apart from the rye bread and cream cheese she'd planned to buy from the new continental delicatessen in Bronte Road, she had nothing to do. It was a diamond-bright morning, crisp and clear, and on the spur of the moment she had decided to go to the beach.

Sitting on the top of the stairs leading down to the beach, she slipped off her sandals and looked at the beach shimmering in the opalescent light of morning. Swimmers were already diving into the water, and surfboard riders were skimming and weaving through the waves, arms outstretched like tightrope walkers.

Along the water's edge, where the sun-tipped waves rolled onto the shore before being sucked back to sea, a narrow border of wet sand offered a firm foothold for the runners. Young men were jogging; children were running ahead of their parents; and small groups of friends strolled together, laughing and chatting, and every now and again they let out a scream when the waves rushed in and sprayed them.

Sala's feet sank into the soft sand. As she strolled along the water's edge, people smiled or said hello as they passed, and for the first time since Szymon had moved out, she felt a little less alone.

When she'd come back to Łódż after the war and discovered that her parents had not returned from Auschwitz, nor had the aunts, uncles and cousins she loved, she had stood in one spot holding her head, as though turned to stone. For weeks she would stand outside their houses and look up, expecting to see a loved face at the window. She realised now that she had never stopped looking for them.

And now, with Szymon's departure, she was reliving the anguish of that loss all over again. She told herself that she was relieved he'd gone, that what she missed was a familiar presence, someone who shared her space, not the man himself. She reminded herself that Szymon had always irritated her. She was angry that he'd come for his things while she was at work and hadn't contacted her since then, and she tried to convince herself that she didn't care.

Sala sank onto the sand and gazed at the beach with wonder, like a girl who has just realised she has always been in love with the boy next door. She had lived in Sydney for almost a year without really seeing the beauty of this curve of fine, pale sand connecting two rugged headlands.

She didn't know how long she sat there, entranced by the view. There was no past, no future, and no pain, just the warmth of the sun, the softness of the sand, and the dark blue waves rolling in from the far horizon. After an hour or so, she brushed the sand off her feet, fastened her sandals and walked towards the tram stop with a lighter step.

Back in Wattle Street, three boys rattled past her in a billycart, shouting as they careered around the corner. The only other person she saw was Miss McNulty, who was leaning against her picket fence beside her black cat.

Sala was about to cross the road so she wouldn't have to pass the cranky old woman, when Miss McNulty looked up and said, 'Looks like it's going to be a nice day.'

Surprised, Sala nodded. 'It was lovely down at the beach this morning.'

'I used to live near there,' Miss McNulty said. 'A very long time ago.'

'We didn't have a beach in my home town,' Sala said. 'Or a garden.'

'No beaches or gardens?' Miss McNulty said. 'Where was that?'

Sala told her about Łódź, where people lived in apartment blocks and bought their flowers at the market.

Miss McNulty clucked her tongue. 'No wonder you wanted to come out here, then.'

Sala looked down at the cat, which was rubbing against her legs, and bent to stroke it. 'That's Sooty,' Miss McNulty said. 'He's nearly as old as I am. He likes having his chin tickled.'

Inside her room, Sala went straight to the table, took out a writing pad and a bottle of ink, filled her fountain pen and started writing.

In reply to your request for information about Mr Ernst Hauptmann, I'd like to start by saying that this is a personal account of my own experiences. I met Mr Hauptmann before the war, when he used to deliver food from his farm to my home. He was honest and reliable, and my parents had a very high opinion of him. After they were deported to a concentration camp, I was alone, and I would have been deported too, if Mr Hauptmann hadn't offered to hide me. Although I didn't give him any money or valuables, he took me to his farmhouse, and when the SS realised I was Jewish he hid me in the cellar for about eighteen months, against his wife's wishes. He didn't even tell their relatives I was there, in case they reported him for sheltering a Jew. He risked his life for me, because SS men often visited the house, and if they had found me, he would have been shot.

She paused, and chewed the end of her pen, wondering what to write next. Although she would have preferred to leave it at that, for all she knew it might have been Ernst's wife Urszula who had made the allegation about him in revenge for his affair with Sala, which had endangered her as well. Urszula may have told the investigators about their relationship, and if so, they'd dismiss Sala's letter as biased and unreliable. She'd have to tell the whole truth.

I feel I should mention that on one occasion, when he'd been drinking, Mr Hauptmann forced himself on me, but when he was sober, he regretted what he'd done, and I have forgiven him.

As I said at the beginning, this is a personal testimony. I don't know about anything he did during the war, but I do know that, thanks to him, I survived.

Ernst Hauptmann was not a hero, but he was brave enough to risk his life to save mine with no thought of financial gain, at a time when many people denounced Jews and turned them over to the Gestapo.

In conclusion, I'd like to say that war creates extreme situations which often blur the line between good and evil. I believe that few people are wholly good or wholly bad, and that circumstances can affect their actions, but even evil-doers can redeem themselves.

She put down her pen and reread the letter. The last paragraph had taken her by surprise. Until she'd written it she hadn't been aware of her own philosophical attitude. As she read her own words, tears came to her eyes, but whether she was crying for herself, for Ernst, for the victims of war, or for ordinary people struggling to live up to their dreams of themselves, she didn't know.

As she sealed and addressed the envelope, she felt as though she'd finally set down a crushing burden, and she wondered why it had taken her so long to write the letter.

She glanced at the solitary geranium on the windowsill. When Mrs Olmanis had given her the cutting, it had looked as though it was about to wither. In the first two weeks she had watched in distress as the stem dried up and shrank. Although several times she had been about to throw it out, she hadn't given up on it, and now she saw that it must have put down roots because a tightly furled leaf of tender green swelled the top of the stem.

Chapter 54

Kath was on her hands and knees scrubbing the verandah, thinking about the change in Meggsie since Mr Emil's last visit. He'd stopped complaining about Nurse Gately's exercises, and tackled them with a determination that astonished her. As soon as he'd finished the exercises, he'd start squeezing the little rubber balls Mr Emil had left him, grimacing with the effort.

She heard Meggsie calling her and went inside. He was throwing the balls and catching them.

'Look, Mum, that's seven I've caught in a row!' he said. 'Yesterday I only caught six. When Mr Emil and I do our show, will you make me a cape like his?'

She smiled. 'Just keep practising with those balls and doing your exercises, and I'll see about the cape.'

As she was tidying his bedside table, she glanced out of the window and saw Miss McNulty crossing the road. It was unusual to see the old woman out in the street in the evenings, and Kath wondered where the old bat was going. She was taken by surprise when Miss McNulty opened her gate. Probably coming to complain about the boys making too much noise with their billycart and scaring her mangy cat.

Kath braced herself for the inevitable barrage. Instead she heard a scraping sound in the hall. An envelope was lying on the floor. A moment later she heard her front gate open and close again, and she saw the old woman scurrying back across the street.

Now she's leaving me poison pen letters, Kath thought. Hasn't even got the guts to tell me to my face.

Kath picked up the envelope, surprised by how bulky it felt. She opened it and whispered, 'Jesus, Mary and Joseph!'

Inside was a wad of banknotes. She sank to her knees on the floor and started counting. Fifty pounds. 'Jesus, Mary and Joseph,' she said again.

'What is it, Mum?' Meggsie called out. 'What's wrong?'

Without replying, Kath went to the kitchen and took down her jewellery box from the top of the dresser. She took out the first envelope, which still had most of the money inside, and compared it to the one which had just arrived. They were identical.

She sank into a chair, trying to figure out why Miss McNulty had just delivered an envelope with exactly the same amount as Mr Emil had left her several weeks before.

It was like trying to solve a mystery with vital pieces of evidence missing. How come Mr Emil had left the same amount of money in exactly the same envelope as Miss McNulty? As she kept going over all the facts, she realised that she hadn't actually seen Mr Emil leave the money, and he'd said nothing to indicate that he'd put it there. She had assumed he was the secret benefactor because of his mysterious manner and his recent friendship with Meggsie, and she'd taken the fact that he'd said nothing about it as an indication of his shyness.

But now, as she looked at the two identical envelopes, and thought about the secretive manner with which her neighbour had dropped the envelope and crept away, it hit Kath that her secret benefactor wasn't Mr Emil at all. It was the last person on earth she would have suspected.

With trembling fingers, Kath tore off her apron and hurried across the road. When Miss McNulty opened the door and saw who it was, her mouth puckered with dismay.

'I know you don't want to be thanked,' Kath said quickly, 'but I had to come and thank you.'

Miss McNulty made a deprecating gesture with her wrinkled hand. 'I don't like fuss,' she said, and started to close the door, but Kath refused to be cut short.

'I've been having a tough time, and your money has made all the difference. Now I can continue paying the nurse to give Meggsie the exercises that might help him walk again. But apart from that, I can't tell you how much it means to me that you wanted to help us.'

'Well, if you're going to stand there talking, you may as well come in,' Miss McNulty said.

She padded down the corridor in her felt slippers until they were in the darkened lounge room. The windows were closed and the only source of light was a small fringed lamp on a glass table.

'I don't want the light fading the carpet and the upholstery, so I keep the windows closed and the blinds down,' the old woman said, following Kath's gaze. 'Well, I suppose you'd better sit down now you're here,' she added.

Kath sat in an armchair, and as she placed her hand on the white lace-edged antimacassar she reflected that the furniture was in far better shape than its owner, and would outlast her.

If the old biddy could be blunt, so can I, Kath decided.

She leaned forward. 'I'd like to know why you did it. It's not as if there's any love lost between us.'

Miss McNulty didn't reply at first, and her expressionless face made Kath think of a house without windows.

'I know what it's like to be different from everyone else, and how it feels to be ridiculed and treated like a freak through no fault of your own,' she said. 'I heard some of those young larrikins making fun of your boy one afternoon, and it made me hopping mad.' Her voice dropped so low that Kath had to strain to catch what she was saying.

'I know how it feels because everyone looked down on me. My father was the last hangman at Darlinghurst Gaol.'

Kath sat very still while Miss McNulty told her about her unhappy childhood, about being bullied and ostracised, and made the butt of jokes and jibes. No wonder the old woman had become reclusive and spiteful. Life had dealt her a rotten hand and she had passed it on to others.

'That's terrible,' Kath said. 'You couldn't help what your father did for a living.'

'He couldn't help it either,' Miss McNulty snapped. 'He never wanted to be a hangman. He used to drive a horse cab and everyone liked him, but after his accident, his face was so misshapen that people wouldn't get into his cab, and no one would give him a job.'

Kath was pensive. How unfair life was. Injustice reverberated through so many lives, gathering momentum with each generation. Instead of showing compassion, people tormented others in trouble. Perhaps they thought that by distancing themselves from misfortune they'd protect themselves from it.

'It was really generous of you to give me all that money,' Kath went on. 'As soon as I get a job, and get back on my feet, I'll pay you back.'

'I don't want you to pay me back,' Miss McNulty said. 'I'm an old woman, and I don't need much. I've sold a rundown cottage I had up on the cliffs at Bondi, and I'll never use up all the money.'

Kath stared at her, trying to take it all in. She'd heard stories about Nosey the hangman, and Meggsie had told her that Nosey's spooky cottage was haunted, but she had never suspected that Miss McNulty was the hangman's daughter.

The cottage above Ben Buckler had been rotting away for decades, a monument to her useless life and her painful memories, yet Maude had lacked the courage to let it go, to free herself from the misery it represented. It wasn't until Verna Browning had told her that Kath couldn't afford to pay for Meggsie's treatment that the idea had come to her. The cottage was no use to her, in fact it kept her chained to the past, and if she sold it, she'd have more money than she'd ever be able to spend. For the first time in her life, Maude had wanted to do something for someone else. But she had been determined to do it anonymously to avoid the sentimental slush she had no time for.

She had always shunned displays of emotion. There had been too much of that at home. The vitriolic outbursts of her embittered mother, angry that her husband had been robbed of a lucrative, respectable job and been turned into a pariah and a drunkard. The shouts and curses of her father, and then his harsh drunken sobs. And little Maude, running from the room with her hands over her ears so she couldn't hear them fighting.

Kath broke into her reverie. 'I hope you won't take this the wrong way, Miss McNulty, but you're the last person I would have expected to help me. I always felt you looked down on me because I was a barmaid. But it wasn't my fault I became a barmaid, any more than it was your father's fault that he was a hangman, so I would have thought you'd be more understanding.'

Maude was taken aback. She hadn't expected such a forthright comment from anyone, especially a woman to whom she had just given so much money. She was about to make a tart reply when she thought better of it. No one had spoken to her like that because no one cared what she said or did, or whether she lived or died.

'Sorry if I upset you,' Kath was saying, 'but I just had to get it off my chest.'

The old woman made a gesture that could have signified irritation or grudging assent.

Kath stood up. 'I'd better get back to the boys. Why don't you come over and have a cup of tea some time? Meggsie would love to hear all about the old days.'

Maude's throat closed up, and all she could do was nod. She'd lived on this earth for ninety-two years, but no one called her their friend, asked her opinion or wanted her company. They smiled to her face but she knew they made fun of her behind her back. In all the years she'd lived in Wattle Street, no one had ever invited her in for a cup of tea or wanted to hear anything she had to say.

'Thanks,' she mumbled. 'One of these days I might do that.'

Chapter 55

Three weeks had passed since Sister Gately's last visit, and when she came to check on Meggsie again, she noticed the improvement in his muscle tone.

'His hands are much stronger, and there's some improvement in his legs as well,' she said to his mum. Turning to him, she said, 'I can tell you've been doing your exercises, young man.'

Meggsie smiled to himself. Ever since his conversation with Mr Emil he'd felt more energetic, and as he kept on with the exercises he could feel his arms and legs becoming stronger. He often reminded himself that he was going to get better.

'It's Mr Emil,' he blurted out. 'He's given me these little rubber balls, and I've been practising with them. And he said —'

His mum cleared her throat loudly and shot him a warning glance. He wasn't sure why his mother didn't want him to tell Sister Gately about Mr Emil, but he suspected it was something to do with the fact Sister Gately liked to be in charge.

'Well, whatever you've been doing, you're coming along nicely,' Sister Gately said, giving him a pat on the back. 'Keep on with the exercises, four times a day if you can.'

'Don't worry, Sister Gately,' Meggsie said cheerfully. 'I will. And don't be surprised if you get an invitation to a magic show one of these days.'

Joan Gately turned to Kath and shook her head in wonder. 'He's not the same boy.'

'It's magic,' Kath said, and winked at Meggsie.

When Sister Gately had finished examining Meggsie's legs two weeks later, she turned to Kath and said, 'I've been thinking for a while now that it's time to give walking a go. Let's swing his legs over the side of the bed and see how he goes.'

Kath's heart was pounding so fast that she couldn't catch her breath. Excitement mingled with apprehension. How would Meggsie cope with the disappointment if he couldn't do it? She bit her lip and twisted her hands inside the pocket of her apron as she prayed to all the saints to let him walk again, forgetting that she no longer believed in them or their miracles.

Very gently, Sister Gately pulled Meggsie up to a sitting position and turned him towards her so that his legs dangled over the edge of the bed and his feet touched the floor. Then, taking his hands in hers, she gradually pulled him up.

Kath pressed her hands against her mouth. He was standing, but a moment later his legs wobbled, his knees buckled, and he sank back onto the bed, his face crumpling with disappointment.

'Not to worry,' the nurse boomed. 'Rome wasn't built in a day. Let's try again. Up you get. Take your time.'

This time Meggsie's legs wobbled a little less and, gripping Sister Gately's hands like a drowning man clutching his rescuer, he took one tottering step towards her, let go of her and stood for an instant on his own.

The look on his face showed that he could hardly believe what he'd done.

Kath leapt to her feet, screaming, 'You did it! Holy Mother of God, you did it!'

Tears were pouring down her face and she was laughing and crying at the same time. The moment she had dreamed about for so long had finally arrived.

The God she'd stopped believing in, who had rained one misfortune after another upon her, had finally redeemed Himself in her eyes with that one act of grace.

His face taut and white with the effort, Meggsie took another wobbly step, and then another, before collapsing into Sister Gately's outstretched arms.

Tears were shining in her eyes too. 'Good lad. You've done well,' she said, patting his shoulder. 'Now that you know you can do it, I want you to try taking a few steps every day, holding onto your mum's hands at first till you can do it on your own without her. Better have a rest now.'

She said something about getting him crutches, but Kath was too excited to take it in. All she could think of was that she'd just witnessed the miracle she hadn't dared hope for.

When Sister Gately had gone, Meggsie couldn't stop talking. 'I have to tell Mr Emil! And Hanny! I want to tell Hanny.

Now I'll be able to go back to school and play with the other kids, and I'll be able to do that magic show. I want to have another go at walking, Mum. Can you help me?'

'Don't overdo it. You know what Sister Gately said. A bit at a time.'

'Just once more. Come on!'

Her hands shook so much that she could hardly keep them steady enough to support him. Every nerve stretched taut with concentration, he shuffled towards her, as awkward as a newborn giraffe.

'I did it again, Mum! I did it!'

She wiped her streaming eyes and hugged him. 'Thank the Lord,' she kept repeating. 'Thank the Lord.'

Chapter 56

Too excited to keep still, Kath rushed over to Verna Browning's place to tell her the good news. Incoherent with joy, she hugged her friend and danced around the hall with her.

'I still can't believe it,' she kept saying.

'That nurse has certainly done a wonderful job,' Verna said.

'But Mr Emil is the one who got him started. He's the real miracle worker.'

Verna sighed. 'I wish he'd come here and work some magic on Ted,' she said.

That evening, as rain pattered on the roof and the wind rattled the windows, providing an apt soundtrack for her Saturday night serial, *Inner Sanctum*, Verna heard the front door open and close. Putting down the sleeveless vest she'd almost finished knitting, she came out to the hall before Ted could slip into his room.

'Have you had your tea?' she asked. 'I saved some meatloaf for you.'

'Not hungry, thanks, Mum.'

She smelled beer on his breath, and supposed he'd been at the Journalists' Club, the only place that served alcohol after six o'clock.

'Well come and have a cuppa and warm up.'

'Some other time, Mum, it's late.'

Normally she would have given up at this point, but this time she persisted. 'I don't know what's going on, Ted, but whatever you've done, I want you to know I'll always stand by you.'

He almost laughed, but what came out was a harsh grating sound. 'Thanks, but I haven't killed anyone.'

'I wish you'd tell me what the matter is. You've changed so much I hardly know you. I'm worried.'

His face seemed to fold in on itself and a moment later he made a strangled sound she hadn't heard since he was twelve years old and had been scratched from the cricket team.

She waited until the sobbing subsided, led him to the kitchen and put the kettle on the stove.

'Ted, whatever it is, there's got to be a better way of dealing with it, love. You're letting this eat you up. It's no good keeping everything inside.'

He looked away, clearly embarrassed at his show of weakness. 'It's too complicated. And talking about it won't help.'

Verna tightened her lips as she turned the teapot three times and poured the scalding tea into their cups. 'You think

I'm ignorant, but even if I didn't finish high school, I still know a fair bit about life,' she said.

He was staring into the distance and she'd started to wonder whether he'd heard what she said, when he started talking. He talked slowly at first, and then, as he became more upset, the words tumbled out faster and faster until he had told her the whole story.

'So, can you solve my problem?' he said, unable to keep the anger from his voice. 'Can you tell me what to do so I can live with myself and not lose the girl I love? It's like Bob Dyer's *Pick-A-Box* show,' he said bitterly. 'Only instead of choosing between the money or the box, I have to choose between the story and the girl. And whichever one I choose, I'll lose.' He looked up at her. 'You're the one with all the worldly wisdom, you tell me what to do.'

She ignored his sarcasm. 'I don't know the answer, and even if I did, I wouldn't tell you what to do,' she said. 'But your father always used to say that we pay for everything we do in life, and we have to live with the consequences. Whenever he couldn't decide what to do, he knew the right decision was always the hardest one.' She sighed. 'I suppose that's why he joined up.'

'And look where that got him,' Ted said.

She nodded. 'He did what he thought was right.'

'That's what Dad used to say. But what do you say?' Ted asked.

'I think you really know what to do. Maybe you'd like me to talk you out of it. Either this girl loves you or she doesn't. If she doesn't, then you've got nothing to lose. But if she loves you enough, she'll find a way to come back to you one day.'

He uttered an exasperated grunt and pushed his chair from the table. A moment later she heard him close his door.

Chapter 57

Ted spent the next few days racking his brains for some way of getting in touch with Lilija. The letter he'd written and slipped under her door the week before had gone unanswered, and he supposed that her father had intercepted it. Increasingly desperate, he'd tried to call her at the hospital, but a disapproving voice had told him that Nurse Olmanis was on duty and couldn't take personal calls. Once, he had caught sight of her turning into Wattle Street, and he'd run after her, calling her name, but without looking back she had hurried into her house, slamming the door behind her.

With every passing day the conviction that he had to confront Paulis Olmanis about his past grew stronger. No matter how desperately he tried to convince himself that he could let the matter drop, he knew he had to see it through to the end. But first he had to talk to Lilija again. Even if he couldn't change her mind, he might be able to convince her of his love.

A few days later Ted was called into the morning conference to give Gus, his deputy and the news editor an update on his investigation. He was proud to see that they looked impressed, especially when he described his conversation with Anna Vestermanis.

Gus leaned forward, spraying ash over his polished mahogany desk.

'Got a quote from the Latvian bloke yet?' he asked.

While Ted gave an evasive reply, Gus lit another cigarette, leaned back in his black armchair and surveyed him with his reptilian gaze. 'Even if the bastard talks to you, and we run this exposé of yours, no one's going to do a bloody thing about it. Immigration will keep defending its screening process, the new spy service will keep using former Nazi collaborators and deny it, and if the Latvian government asks for his extradition, our government will refuse to deport him on humanitarian and political grounds. They'll claim that the Communists will kill him as soon as he sets foot there. And on top of that, they'll say you're a Commie or a fellow traveller. So don't kid yourself that you're about to change the world.'

Ted found it hard to sit still through this barrage. His lunch was rising into his throat, and in a strangled voice he said, 'Does that mean you're not going to run the story?'

Gus gave a sardonic laugh. 'Well, if I don't, you can always offer it to the *Tribune*. Those Commies will lap it up.'

For several moments Ted heard only the loud ticking of the wall clock and the thumping of his heart. When Gus finally spoke, Ted jumped as though a gun had suddenly gone off.

'It's a bloody good story, son, and when it's finished I'll run it just to show those bastards in Canberra that we know what's going on.' Gus had a combative gleam in his eyes.

'We'll make the buggers squirm when they have to answer questions in parliament.'

Ted was in a daze when he left Gus's office. Praise from his boss was as rare as a heatwave in Antarctica. But how on earth could he get Paulis Olmanis to talk to him?

The following Monday morning, instead of going to the office, Ted stayed home. He was standing at the window, waiting for the rent-collector to appear. When he saw the familiar figure with the leather satchel turning into Wattle Street and opening the gate of the Olmanis house, Ted slipped out and hurried towards him.

The rent-collector pressed the bell, the door opened, and at that moment Ted squeezed past him and came face to face with Mrs Olmanis in the doorway. Before the startled woman had time to speak, Ted called out, 'Mr Olmanis, can I see you for a minute, please?'

Paulis Olmanis strode into the hall, and as soon as he saw Ted he stiffened and raised his fists. His face contorted with rage, he grabbed Ted by the collar and shouted, 'Get out or I'll call the police!'

As he was being shoved out of the hall, Ted turned and shouted, 'Were you a member of the Arajs Kommando in Latvia? Were you in charge of a unit that shot civilians outside Riga in 1942?'

Paulis Olmanis's eyes were flints. 'I never heard of that unit. I don't know what you're talking about,' he hissed, and with one powerful thrust he flung Ted onto the verandah and slammed the door behind him.

'Strewth,' the rent-collector said, and without waiting for the rent, he hurried next door.

Ted picked himself up, brushed himself off and rubbed his bruised knees. He limped away, despondent over his disastrous encounter. At least he'd managed to confront the man, whose violent response spoke for itself. Then the significance of Paulis Olmanis's denial struck him. He'd denied knowing about a group whose uniform he was wearing in the photograph taken in Riga in 1942.

Half an hour later, Ted was leaving for the office, elated at the prospect of telling Gus that he'd caught Paulis Olmanis out in a lie. He was at the gate when he heard an ambulance siren. The ambulance stopped outside the Olmanis house, and he watched with dread as the ambulance officers went inside. A few moments later he saw them carrying someone out on a stretcher, and saw Mrs Olmanis running beside it. Her face was white and crumpled, and in her broken English she kept repeating, 'Quick, go quick. My husband very sick.'

A small crowd had gathered on the footpath outside their house, and as the ambulance sped away Ted hurried towards them.

'I reckon the old boy had a heart attack,' Pop Wilson was saying. 'I just come out on the verandah when Mrs Whatshername came running out of their place, gabbling and carrying on, and it took me a while to sort out what she was on about. Said something about him getting bad news and then clutching his chest and collapsing on the floor. Said his face was grey and he was sweating and couldn't catch his breath, so I ran to the phone box and called the ambulance.'

As the neighbours speculated what the bad news could have been, Ted edged away. He felt sick. He knew what had caused Paulis Olmanis's heart attack.

Several weeks went by and Ted's efforts to contact Lilija proved fruitless. Neither she nor her mother were ever at home, and he never came across her on the tram.

One evening when he came home, his mother sat him down, and from the look on her face he steeled himself for bad news.

'That girl up the road — I can never pronounce her name — Lily, is it? I saw her and her mother getting into a taxi this morning, and they had their suitcases with them. In the afternoon a truck came for their furniture.'

He stared at her uncomprehendingly.

'They've moved out,' she said.

'Just like that?' He couldn't keep the desperation from his voice. 'Do you know where they went? Did they tell anyone where they were going?'

Verna shook her head. 'It doesn't look like it. They got into the cab and drove off without saying a word to anyone or giving the street a second glance. Sorry, love,' she added as he covered his face with his hands. 'I know you're upset.'

The following day, unable to stand the uncertainty any longer, he rushed out of the newsroom at lunchtime. He had to see Lilija. He'd look for her at the hospital. If she saw how distraught he was, how he couldn't live without her, she might relent. He couldn't live with this anguish.

He ran into the courtyard of the hospital, scanned the names of the wards, and dashed in and out of several entrances, knowing that he probably looked like a madman. Two nurses in white caps and navy capes were crossing the courtyard, but when he asked if they knew where Nurse Olmanis worked, they stared at him and edged away, nudging each other and whispering. He knew that his erratic behaviour was attracting attention, but he didn't care. All that mattered was finding Lilija.

Claiming to be Lilija's cousin, he asked the sister behind the reception desk if he could see her for a moment to tell her something important. She gave him a curious look and said, 'Nurse Olmanis doesn't work here any more.'

He pleaded with her to tell him where she'd gone but the sister shook her head. 'I'm sorry but we can't give out that information. I think you should leave now,' she added in a stern tone.

He was walking blindly towards the exit when a young nurse ran up to him. 'I heard you asking for Lily,' she whispered. 'You must be Ted. She told me about you.'

He spun towards her, overjoyed.

'Did you know her father died?' she said.

He stared at her, too shocked to speak. Many times he had wished that Paulis Olmanis was dead, but the knowledge that his wish had come true, and that he'd been partly responsible for the heart attack that had caused his death, made his knees buckle. He couldn't pretend to grieve but he felt guilty. Although he knew he wasn't thinking rationally, he wondered whether he'd underestimated the lethal power of malevolence. With an effort he turned his attention back to the young nurse who was saying something.

'Lily and her mum decided to move away when he died. She said she didn't want to stay in that horrible street any more.'

His tongue seemed stuck to the roof of his mouth. 'Where did she go?' he rasped. Without realising it, he'd grasped the nurse's arm and raised his voice. 'You've got to tell me where she is. At least tell me where she's working.'

The nurse pulled away, and from the way she looked at him, he sensed that she was weighing up how to say something unpleasant. 'She left the hospital because she didn't want you to find her.'

Ted stumbled from the grounds of the hospital feeling like a hollow shell. Passers-by turned to look at him as he walked along Macquarie Street with his head down, muttering to himself as his mind churned with recriminations. Near Bridge Street someone grabbed his arm to stop him falling under a bus. Suddenly he gave a bitter laugh. By granting his wish, fate had turned the perpetrator into a victim. Now Paulis Olmanis would never have to answer for his crime.

Chapter 58

Empire Day had come round again, and most of the reporters were hurrying to the Journalists' Club, but Ted was sitting at his desk, staring at his by-line in the morning paper. His story, headlined THE WAR CRIMINALS AMONG US, was accompanied by a photo of an accusing Anna Vestermanis holding the photograph of her murdered family. The caption read, *I'll never forget his face as long as I live.*

Passing his desk, Joe Black noticed Ted's dejected face. 'You should be chuffed,' he said. 'What's up?'

Ted shrugged. He couldn't bring himself to rejoice at his hollow victory.

Joe gave him a shrewd look. 'Here's a tip straight from Caesar's mouth. Once you've crossed the Rubicon, don't look back. Just keep going.' He looked at his watch. 'Come on, mate, it's lunchtime. Let's go and drink a toast to our glorious empire, because if Gus is right, we won't be celebrating it much longer.'

Gus's editorial that morning had poured cold water over the fervent patriotism of many readers.

What on earth has happened to the British Empire? he wrote, sounding like an exasperated preacher railing at his wayward congregation. *One by one, its members are breaking away. Eire, India and Burma have gone. Ceylon and Malaya will go soon; South Africa calls itself a republic, and Canada is closer to America than to Britain. Only Australia and New Zealand remain, but we're paying a heavy economic price for our loyalty. Perhaps it's time to think of our own future. Today Australia is being enriched by an influx of migrants from all over Europe, and their allegiance is to this country, not to England. Instead of celebrating Empire Day, perhaps we should consider celebrating our own nationhood with Australia Day.*

Staunch monarchists like Maude McNulty were appalled by what they regarded as Gus's disloyalty to the King, and conservative readers compared his salvo to the Boston Tea Party, but some Australians, old as well as new, regarded his editorial as visionary.

But there was no mention of any subversive ideas about the end of the empire at the Bondi Junction Primary School that day as the children gathered for assembly in the yard in front of the flag, and recited the pledge in singsong voices: 'I honour my God, I serve my king, I salute my flag.'

While the headmaster gave a patriotic speech about the significance of Australia's bond with Britain, which had brought civilisation, progress and justice to people all over the world, the boys fidgeted and pulled faces at the girls who smothered their giggles in their floral handkerchiefs. When the headmaster's speech was over, they all stood up straight and sang 'God Save The King' in solemn voices.

Then the school captain, a girl in Hania's class, came to the front and recited all the verses of Dorothea MacKellar's 'My Country' without stumbling or making a single mistake, and murmurs of envy and admiration ran through the gathering.

When it was time for the choir to sing 'Land of Hope and Glory,' Miss Finlay, the pretty, young music teacher, came out in front of the assembled schoolchildren, held up her baton and waited until all eyes were on her before she brought it down. Standing in the front row of the choir, between Beverley and Tina, Hania looked around for her mother, who caught her eye and waved.

As she sang, Hania felt little jabs of electricity prickling her spine. The singing was a silver thread which drew their voices together and united them all until religion and race, past and present, no longer mattered. Her own voice blended in with all the others, connected and indistinguishable from the whole. Beverley glanced at her friend's glowing face, reached out and took her hand, and Hania squeezed back.

After school had broken up for the day, the children ran home to prepare for Cracker Night. They took out the fireworks they'd been buying with their pocket money for the past few weeks, collected wood for the bonfire and heaped it in the middle of Wattle Street just as they'd done the year before.

By the time the first star appeared, the bonfire was crackling and spitting sparks into the sky. As rockets sizzled, Catherine wheels twirled, and tom thumbs exploded, the street resounded with children's excited voices.

Kath's boys were shouting and jumping aside as they hurled double bungers onto the ground. Mr Emil was outside, talking to Kath, and they were both watching Meggsie, who was on the other side of the street, talking to Miss McNulty. A few minutes later he hobbled back on his crutches, dragging his legs but grinning as though he'd just won a race.

'Gee, Mum, Miss McNulty was just telling me about Empire Day when she was at school. Did you know she was once Britannia in the procession?'

Verna Browning, who was standing nearby, smiled to herself. Maude McNulty now had a new audience for her stories.

Ted wasn't in the mood for celebrating Empire Day, but the shouting and whooping of the children, and the snapping of twigs in the flames, lured him outside, and he stood on the verandah, watching the scene around the bonfire.

Pop Wilson was out there as usual, bantering with the kids and chatting with the adults as he checked that there was enough wood to keep the fire going, and that the children didn't let their crackers off too close to the flames. Ted wondered if anyone beside himself had noticed that behind his jovial façade, Pop wasn't his usual light-hearted self. He promised himself that one of these days he'd definitely drop in to Pop's place for a chat.

He looked out of his front gate in the direction of the house where Lilija used to live. Was it only one year since he had been bewitched? It seemed like a lifetime ago. Now he'd never feel Lilija's warm body or her soft lips, and he'd never hear her lilting voice whisper that she loved him. The memory of the times they'd spent together made his eyes water, and he took out his handkerchief as though to wipe away a smut that had flown into his eye. His father had been right. Every decision carried a price, but the price of integrity had been too high, and in the end it had all been in vain.

Hearing the commotion in the street, Eda Kotowicz came outside. As she stood leaning against her fence, Sala Wajs came over to talk to her, and they stood together in the glow of the bonfire, entranced by the magic of the fireworks.

'It's strange how different everything looks now,' Eda said.

'Everything *is* different,' Sala replied.

Eda glanced at her friend and realised she wasn't just talking about the street.

A shriek of girlish laughter made them turn around. Hania and Beverley had just released their rockets, which fizzed as they soared to the sky at the same time. They fell at the feet of Ilona, a shy Hungarian girl who had just moved into the Olmanis's house with her parents. As the newcomer stood alone outside her place watching the fireworks, Hania ran towards her, holding out a lighted sparkler.

'Don't be scared,' she said. 'Come and join in.'

And taking the girl's hand, she led her towards the warmth of the blazing bonfire.

When all that was left of the bonfire was a pall of smoke rising from dying embers, and the street was quiet again, Ted leaned on the gate, looked up at the indifferent stars, and felt an aching emptiness.

It seemed as though, in his search for answers, he'd drawn apart a succession of curtains. Each one had let in a tiny chink of light, but now the light had faded.

He was only twenty-three and he was wondering how he'd manage to get through the rest of his life. Looking outside, he saw Pop Wilson, a lone figure in the deserted street, sweeping up the ashes of the bonfire. Despite his heartache, Pop still made sure the children enjoyed their Cracker Night.

Ted's thoughts wandered to his other neighbours. They were all suffering their own despair. Each of them had secrets, heartaches and disappointments, yet in some mysterious way they'd found the strength to endure and transcend them. It took so much strength to get through even an ordinary life. But perhaps there were no ordinary lives.

He thought about his own disillusionment. But perhaps it hadn't all been in vain. Perhaps one day, thanks to his investigation, other war criminals who had found sanctuary in

Australia would be brought to justice. Perhaps this had been his first step towards finding the width and depth of his life that his father had talked about so long ago.

It was past midnight when he went back inside, but his mind was seething with ideas. Too churned up to sleep, he took out his fountain pen and began to write. Several hours later, when the first rays of light appeared in the night sky, he put down his pen. He'd just written the first chapter of his novel. *Wattle Street.*

Acknowledgements

I'm indebted to many people who so generously shared their expertise and experience with me. I'm very grateful to Professor Mary Westbrook for sharing her vast knowledge of polio, and for providing me with valuable information. Naomi Penny was kind enough to share her childhood experiences with me.

Peter Kahn of the Tramways Museum refreshed my memory of Sydney's tram system and supplied valuable details about timetables, routes and fares. Detective-Sergeant Bill Harris filled me in on police work in the 1940s, magicians James Karp and Michael Giblin gave me fascinating demonstrations and explanations of their craft, and Dr Paul Valent has given me some valuable insight into the effects of traumatic experiences.

I'd also like to thank Maggie White, Reference Librarian at the State Library of NSW, and Kimberley O'Sullivan Steward, Archivist at Waverley Library. Thanks also to Gillian Thomas, Bridget Griffen-Foley, Rod Kirkpatrick, Kate Evans, Jolyon Sykes, Liz Pidgeon, Katherine Howell, Kay Whitty, and Malcolm Voyzey, all of whom have helped me to increase my understanding of some aspect of life in Australia during the late 1940s.

I am extremely fortunate in having such a professional team at HarperCollins and I'm grateful to Sue Brockhoff, Jo Butler, and Amanda O'Connell for their patience, understanding and support. A big thank you to my editor, Julia Stiles, for her skill and sensitivity. Linda Funnell encouraged me to write *Empire Day* after hearing some of my recollections about life in Sydney in the late 1940s. I can't thank my agent, Selwa Anthony, enough for her remarkable professional acumen, warm friendship, and unfailing support.

Finally my heartfelt gratitude to my late husband, Michael, who sadly passed away before *Empire Day* was published. He was, as always, my first reader, and his fine literary judgement and perceptive comments have enhanced the novel, just as his sense of humour, generosity of spirit, and belief in me lit up my life.